Man o' War

Man o' War

BY CORY McCARTHY

DUTTON BOOKS

DUTTON BOOKS
An imprint of Penguin Random House LLC, New York

First published in the United States of America by Dutton Books,
an imprint of Penguin Random House LLC, 2022

Visit us online at penguinrandomhouse.com.

LIBRARY OF CONGRESS CATALOGING-IN-PUBLICATION DATA IS AVAILABLE.

Manufactured in Canada

ISBN 9780593353707

10 9 8 7 6 5 4 3 2 1

FRI
Design by Anna Booth
Text set in Sabon LT Pro

For August,

who wouldn't let the sharks keep me

CONTENT ADVISORY

This book contains depictions of gender dysphoria, internalized homophobia, self-harm, cissexism, and racism. Take care of yourself but also know that this war is won with joy.

I began in Ohio
in this town where everyone carries
wavery memory: home,

the sun flatlining the horizon, the wind
to what surely must be another world.

Why does the field begin to ripple
blondes and blondes and blondes?
Perspective can do its thing anywhere.

—Maggie Smith, "Ohio Cento" from *Goldenrod*

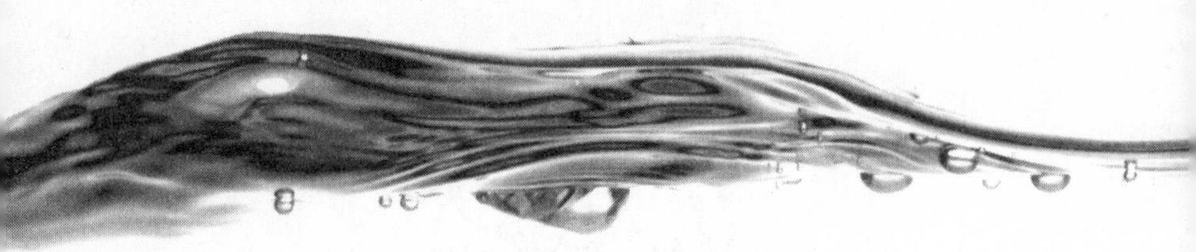

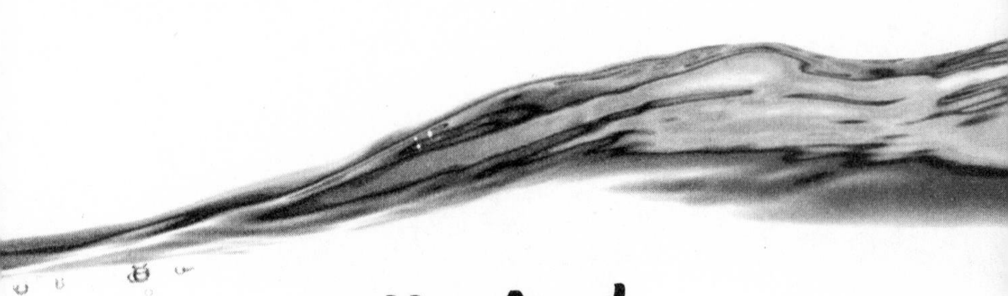

jellyfish

Jellyfish have no brains or hearts. Maybe that's why there's no difference in lifespan or behavior from those in the wild to those in captivity. Mating is done in a crowd. The males gather up, turning the sea cloudy with their . . . sperm packets. Then the females swim over and eat it.

And that's as romantic as it gets.

— 1 —

WE WERE ALWAYS CHANGING. We were never naked.

I shouldered into the locker room minutes after the final bell. My lungs stung from the bleach in the air, my eyes from the glare off the white, sterile tile. Half the team was already undressing, but I would be first in the pool. The water was calling.

Locker room etiquette was all about getting suited up without giving too much away, a competition in cleverness with varying techniques. First up, the line of bathroom-stall changers waited. They had all the privacy, sure, but also the greatest risk of dropping clothes in the toilet. Deeper in, the craftier engineer types were busy turning their towels into makeshift curtains. Again, a decent amount of concealment, but setup and takedown meant they were often late to warm-up. The ones I called *potato sackers* were in the middle of the action, pantless and giggling per usual. These swimmers retracted their arms and wiggle-dressed inside of their shirts, flashing beaver along with their above-average self-confidence.

I had long since gamed the system; I was already in my suit. By the time I reached my locker I was half out of my jeans, tugging them off with my boots. My hoodie went next. The locker slammed shut, and I was headed onto the pool deck before the rest of the team arrived, the water calling.

Catherine stooped outside the door, her schoolbooks in three tote bags hanging off her buff shoulders. She was correcting the locker room sign from *girls'* to *women's* with an oversized Sharpie, and I almost didn't ask because Catherine was an avocado. You couldn't tell from her shell if she was green on the inside or that rotten horror show of a color.

"Adding graffiti artist to your college application?"

She didn't look up. "The men's reads *men's*, and the women's reads *girls'*? That's some patriarchal fuckery." Ah, an overripe day.

"Nah, Dweiller drew a dick on the boys' sign, and Scanlon had to replace it. That's why they don't match."

"The principal could have ordered two signs. He doesn't think this is important. He is wrong."

"How you have the energy for civil disobedience is beyond me." I braided my hair back and squinted at her work. "You could have written *vaginas* and really messed him up."

She exhaled heatedly. "Go break the seal before Joss beats you to it."

Walking around the pool, I resisted dipping my goggles, priming my lenses to the cold. They'd fog as soon as I dove in, and yet I needed to preserve that stillness. Twenty-five meters and not even a breathing wave to the surface. That kind of perfection ate at me.

I climbed the diving block, my least favorite part of this whole place. Diving blocks were all jerks, but the one in my lane was a particular asshole with mildly loose bolts. The two-foot-high platform angled toward the water steeply, and I felt like I was falling even when I turned my feet sideways and gripped with my toes.

I stuffed my braid inside my cap as the boys' team filed out of their locker room. While the girls'-room occupants always trickled to the pool, delayed by their changing styles, the boys dumped out as one. Did they dress like that too? In a pod of penises?

Joss shouted my name so loudly it wasn't my name, echoing off the cedar rafters and glass walls that dripped gorily with condensation. I ignored him and returned to the pool.

The water was still as a mirror. I broke it with my body.

Hands, head, chest.

Gravity kept a strict line between air and water, and I sailed across it.

Within minutes, other bodies crashed in, the team shredding the surface. I was half done with my warm-up by the time I felt the other six swimmers in my lane start their sluggish five hundred meters. The seven of us fitted into an uneasy mechanism, keeping distance but never too much. I lost count of my laps, driving my arms, legs straight and slicing. I had to hold back in practice otherwise I'd lap my lane mates until they hated me. Time-wise, I should have been practicing in the penis-pod lanes, but Coach had heart failure the one time I'd asked to be moved.

Still, swimming was swimming. I wasn't a boxed-up torso in the water; I was streamline. No one tapped my foot to lap me, and yet I finished last. My teammates were in a neat line, one hand on the wall, while they licked goggles, adjusted suits, and fought caps.

Coach Kerrig kicked off practice her favorite way—by singling me out. "You lost count again, McIntyre? I didn't. Thirty-eight laps. How many were you supposed to swim?"

"Twenty laps," Gia said with the breathy enthusiasm that made me ache to drag her under by the ankle. "Standard warm-up."

My mind sloshed as I treaded water and shook out my ears. Joss was on the far side. He winked, and then winked again, probably because he thought I'd missed the first one. I smiled to avoid a third. Last year Kerrig had figured out that we were grabbing each other under the surface, and we'd been separated by sex ever since. That mostly took care of it.

Kerrig bellowed the first exercise. "One hundred free, *get out*, twenty sit-ups, one hundred free, *get out*, twenty push-ups. Rinse, repeat."

We briefly became a choir, harmonizing a groan. No one liked deck work.

Coach kicked off the rinse and repeat with a tight whistle blow, and I scrambled to find my stroke rhythm without pushing off the wall. The fastest swimmer in each lane had to go first, and I was the fastest. That was half of the reason Kerrig hated me.

After four laps, I got out and started my twenty sit-ups. Catherine's feet clamped down on mine every time they started to rise, and I tried to hold hers down at the same time. It sort of worked. The deck was crowded, the team on top of one another, streaming as we crunched and counted and grunted.

Somewhere around my twelfth sit-up, Joss's long, hairy leg snaked around my chest, pinning me. My abs seized. Catherine shot up, savoring an opportunity to punish men for their "physical hubris." She latched her considerable weight to my ankles, creating a perfect person-v.-person balance with my body as the scale. I obediently roared into action, rising inch by inch, straining everywhere but managing a full sit-up despite the weight of another human holding me down.

The cheers were short-lived. Joss slid into the water fast, and the rest of the team splashed out too. I fell backward on the sandpapery tile.

Coach Kerrig stood over me, her nose holes black pits. "Take it seriously."

She took those words seriously enough for the both of us. I slid back in like a seal. The water calmed and hated me in equal parts. Some days I felt docile, gliding. Today I punched the surface with each stroke, shouting curses no one could hear. I swam to make my body do something on command; I didn't swim to beat the person beside me. That was the other reason Kerrig hated me.

When it was time for our twenty push-ups, Joss was waiting to race, brown skin streaming. I wiped the floor with him again. He loved it; he was going to be all over me when we got out of here. "My girlfriend is a sexy beast!" he crowed before diving into the shallow end, invoking Kerrig's knee-jerk tirade about broken necks.

Gia was doing push-ups from her knees next to me, grunting through her words. "I think I'm turned on by how much he wants you. Is that weird?"

"Yes."

"Can I have your boyfriend?"

"Yes."

More laps. Exhaustion turned my mind to lava, thoughts rolling downhill, destroying small realities. Gia was a better fit for Joss. It would be easy to set up, and it'd mean a calmer winter break. No obligatory texts or social appearances. No back-seat grope fests. Breaking up with Joss would be a hassle, but honestly, what else was today good for?

It was the second-to-last day before winter break of sophomore year. No tests or monstrous zits. Another day branded forgettable. I swam over Gia on accident, and she really was a wily cuss, picking a fight that echoed off the cedar rafters. Coach hollered too, and I sank, sank, sank from every single sound.

Have you ever rested on the bottom of a twenty-foot pool and looked up? It's not easy; you have to let all the air out of your lungs. But there's a moment past breathlessness that's peaceful, no matter what day it is or isn't.

— 2 —

FRIDAYS TENDED TO BE MORE PROMISING. This particular Friday was the last day before winter break and an all-day field trip for the sophomore class, our annual voyage to SeaPlanet.

The day had potential; I could almost smell it. Pre-school-vacation day was always drama ripe, the perfect time to drop a mic if you were holding on to one. In a matter of hours, we'd split up, tapping out of each other's lives for entire weeks. To get haircuts we weren't sure of. Date people we *really* weren't sure of. Some would revert to a state of childlike dependency on toys and video games. My brother was a compelling case of this last sort. As I poured my Mini-Wheats, he plucked the plastic prize out of my cereal bowl.

"Hopping frog," Everett diagnosed. "Knew it." He unwrapped it with interest. He'd been growing out his hair, and the curls weren't giving in to gravity. When he caught me studying him, he studied me back. "You always look too tired during swim season. Have you thought about coffee?"

"Tried some last week. Still gross, but I'm wearing my taste buds down."

"Of course, you're probably just massively depressed." He positioned the frog on the table, pressed the butt down, and let go. The green frog rebounded off my face. "Were you on the phone with Joss all night?"

"Only until two. He nearly cried. I thought I owed it to him to hear it through." This time the frog shot over my hunched frame.

"Fake." My brother wasn't capable of using my name, but any

rhyming variation was fair game. "You're a disillusioned heartbreaker. How many does he make?"

I loaded a bite on my spoon and pointed it at him. "Joss tried to pull that crap too, but I helped him see the actual pattern. I'm the third person to dump him this year, and he's starting to think he's never going to have the upper hand in a relationship again."

"Maybe it's because he's gay."

I didn't hit my brother, but in my mind my fist flattened his nose. "Maybe it's because everyone at school is a damn racist who yells at him to enroll in every sport just because he's Black and tall. He's under a lot of pressure."

"Someday you're going to stop drinking chlorine and realize you're wasted on physical games. Debate could use you."

"Vote of confidence noted." I drank the remains of my bowl milk. "He's half interested in Gia Silver already, so it should be a peaceful school break."

"Peaceful as in you don't leave your bedroom apart from swimming at obscene hours all by yourself at the empty pool?"

"Peaceful," I agreed.

Dad wasn't home, but Mom was coming from the other side of the house. I tracked her movements like Ms. Pac-Man had been released, mouth chomping. She left her bathroom, obsessively turning off lights. Our split-level ranch was one of three house styles in our suburban neighborhood, all built during a residential boom in the sixties. We'd moved to Haley when I was in third grade, and I still hadn't gotten the Big Mac feeling out of my mouth when I looked around.

Everett started to eat faster, head down.

Mom descended the stairs, crossing the foyer as I reached for the cereal to pour a second bowl. She entered the kitchen, heels clicking on the tile, and stole the box from my hand. "These cereals have too much iron for multiple servings."

Everett shot me a look, and I nodded.

"How so?" I asked.

"Liver cancer, cirrhosis, and heart disease have all been linked to high iron levels from children and teenagers abusing cereal servings." She poured coffee and drank it black. Mom wasn't too skinny, but she kept herself half starved. Her deep summer tan was finally fading, and she was closer to Everett's light brown shade. She never got as white as me.

"What about the high sugar levels?" my brother asked. "Haven't you always said those could be a problem?"

"A *direct* correlation from sugar abuse to diabetes!"

Everett pumped a fist out of her line of sight. We played bingo with Mom's hot zones, and he'd definitely needed sugar = diabetes. If memory served, he might've just won this week's round.

"Why are you both smiling?" she asked. Everett had dubbed her Negativity Sherlock a few years back. She could diagnose catastrophe in anything, at any time. It truly was unparalleled. "Fine, make jokes about me," she said. "I don't have feelings. I'm just a mom. Daughter, eat something else if you can't stop yourself from overeating." She held the cereal box by two fingers as if carbs were deer ticks and slid it into the cupboard.

I shoved my cereal bowl in the dishwasher.

"There's a Lunchable for your SeaPlanet day." Mom was smiling that white flag of a smile, but I was too tired from talking Joss off the ledge. Sometime during kindergarten, Mom had started buying Lunchables whenever we had a field trip; I think she saw it on a commercial. A dozen years later the marketing campaign lived on.

"You care about my iron intake and then you buy me Sodiumables?" I picked out a green banana from the fruit bowl. "You're an enigma, Mother."

"Your grandfather calls his wife *Mother*." She stole my banana, swapping it for a mushy one. "I'm your mom."

"I'm still waiting on the DNA results." I put it back. She knew I only liked the green ones, and yet she rejected my taste as stubbornness, even after I did a report for chemistry on the increased levels of sugar in overripe fruit.

Bananas aside, the battle was on, and it wasn't even seven in the morning. Mom pulled a comb out of thin air and dragged my hair into a neater ponytail. Even from behind I could feel her inspection begin.

Everett collected his things, frog included, trying to escape our impending fight. He jangled his car keys. "'Tis time, O learned scholar."

Mom held me down by the ponytail, fastening the elastic tight enough to survive one of those dance rehearsals from my gruesome past. She turned the stool to look me over, as if she were deciding whether to continue to clean me up or let me go, a calculated loss like the sticky quarters at the bottom of her purse. Everett had secured himself in the bank account of her heart at birth, by the more traditional Arab American means: a penis.

There were years when I'd tried to pass these female quality inspections. There were years when I managed it. I don't remember when I gave up.

Her eyes bored into my shoulder, and I was too late to stop her from yanking the neck of my hoodie to the side to spy on my underwear. Or lack thereof. "You aren't wearing your suit all day again! You know what nylon does to your vagina chemistry."

"LEAVING WE ARE," Yoda Everett yelled from the foyer. "ESCAPE BEFORE VAGINA TALK WE MUST."

I pulled away while she gripped at my shoulder, my elbow, my wrist, finally fastening a death hold on my pinky. A near getaway.

"You'll get another infection."

My face went hot, and she'd won. Well, she'd gotten to me, but like hell was I changing for her. "It's the split tank. I'm wearing the top. Regular bottoms." She knew I was lying, but I was already leaving, Lunchable forgotten even though it would bizarrely hurt her feelings. I told myself it didn't matter. Everett would make the evidence disappear long before I got home from swim practice and shut myself back in my room.

When the sweltering bus started to reek of chlorine, my peers threw me under it.

"Seriously, McIntyre?" Gia yelled. "Do you always forget to shower?"

"I swim twice as much as you do!" My middle fingers danced above her seat. "And I shower twice as much." I craned my head over the seat back and growled softly, "And Joss is free and clear now, *as requested*."

Her annoyance transitioned to intrigue; she was too easy to play. To be honest, I high schooled fairly well. Call it the allure of the masculine female or whatever, but I'd dated my bullies from sixth grade, mildly destroying them. My predatory success positioned me at the teetering top of the social food chain. I handed my peers sarcasm, intelligence, attitude. They ate it up. They hadn't bitten my fingers in years, so yeah, I was due.

I grumbled as I slid back against the last seat. The short one. *My* seat.

Catherine sat folded up beside me in the other prized back-row spot. "Take your hoodie off." Her knees were tucked against the seat back, her AP chem book on top. "You're just too hot. This whole bus is a damn sauna."

"Can't."

Catherine threw me one of those looks like she was storing information. Taylor Woods issued a few artistic gags from three rows forward, and Catherine stood up to yell over the masses. "Hey. The smell could be coming from me."

We all knew this was a false confession; she believed in essential-oil-rich lotions. I was the one who'd made the bus smell like a cloudy hotel pool. My eyes were red from it.

Taylor pinched the clasps and tugged down the squat window. The bus driver yelled, *Hey, why do you think I can't see you this is winter in the greater Cleveland area put it back up*, and Taylor put it back up. I gave her the sorriest smile, and she puffed out her cheeks as if she were attempting to hold down vomit. It was cute.

I looked out the window. Catherine vacillated between AP Chem and spying on seven different conversations at once. "Joss has resecured his masculinity," she reported minutes later. "He's taking out Gia. They're going to see that horny vampire movie. Rated R. Multiple sex scenes."

"Oh no, he didn't really love me," I deadpanned just as SeaPlanet came into view.

There was nothing in Haley, our Midwestern suburban hamlet, apart from one infamous marine life theme park. Every year, each grade got a free-for-all day at the park. When we were younger, we came in the spring to watch the interactive events practice for the upcoming season. Oceanography majors ran about in wetsuits and headset mics, commanding seals who'd become coke fiends for icy dead fish. Those poor animals always had names like Sweetie Peetie or Tuna Man.

The upper grades got to experience the less-stimulating winter season at SeaPlanet, which meant all the outdoor animals were double-stuffed in the Orlando location. No doubt we were about to be funneled into the aquarium, the only year-round exhibit, all day. Time to commune with the other confined creatures.

The bus roared by general admission, taking us to the employee entrance at the back of the park. Many of us crowded the windows on one side, ignoring the bus driver's droning in order to peer through the privacy fence at the abandoned orca tank. What happened there? Let's just say SeaPlanet called them orcas, never *killer whales*, learning the hard way that domestication is not as simple as a rebrand.

The bus did that miner's-cough stop with the door pop, and we groaned to our feet. We were the last to arrive, most of our class already lined up by the door of the aquarium in the icy rain, a gray tableau for sure. Someone had spray-painted vampire fangs on the dolphin logo over the door. I wondered if they hadn't gotten around to cleaning it off, or if it was part of the employee entrance. An inside joke about how the park sucked teenagers dry by way of minimum wage and teal polos.

The door bottlenecked with sophomores, and Catherine and I jostled forward down the aisle a few feet at a time. Shouts rang out about coats and bags and lunches.

"Take them, leave them, I'm not your parent," Mr. Monte hollered, flashing those unfortunately stereotypical jazz hands. That's literally what I thought every time I saw them: *how unfortunately stereotypical.*

When we hadn't moved in minutes, Catherine gnashed her teeth.

"Find your partner. Stay together." Monte fanned himself with a magazine. "I've got my *Vanity Fair* and so help me if any of you interrupts my salty field-trip vibes. This place ought to be burned to the ground, but no one is asking me."

"I've got a query," I muttered, out of earshot of our queen of a theater teacher. "If you knew something about you was a cliché, a stereotype, would you—"

"A cliché isn't a stereotype," Catherine shot back. "Which one do you mean?"

"Both, but also neither."

Catherine applied lip gloss. "I don't accept that. A cliché denotes a loss of meaning, death by overuse. A stereotype is a distillation of truth, often to the point of falsehood."

"I mean stereotype, then. If something about you was a stereotype, would you subvert it? Out of self-preservation?"

"McIntyre, is this because Joss is circulating a list of your butch attributes?"

"Excuse me?" I laughed with the force of a stubbed toe. "I'm not butch. I'm a tomboy. There's a difference." Tomboy was the best word anyone had ever given me. My brain had gift wrapped the memory, a bow around the afternoon I was sprawled *unladylike* on my situ's living-room floor, and my mom glanced down from the kitchen table with that I-give-up look. Situ had said, *I was a tomboy too. It's okay.*

While I'd sputtered, Catherine had come to one of her patented smart-ass conclusions. "Yes, those words are different. They're also adjacent to the rainbow family."

"Tomboy is *not* rainbow." I was so instantly upset I scowled at Catherine's back. She could handle anything in the world but physical scrutiny. I went for it, bull-to-red-cape. "There's a stain on your right butt cheek. You must've sat in something. It's brown."

Catherine tucked her coat around her ass and bowled down the aisle, our peers parting for her as easily as the water in the lane.

Off the bus, I hunted for Joss through the crowd. He stood next to Gia, laughing at a joke that had one hundred percent been about my chemical smell or oversized clothes or Hulk shoulders. I pulled out my phone and texted, *Do I get to see your list.* He stared at his phone for a long minute before a new text came through and I regretted asking for it.

McIntyre's butchiness: legs, shoulders, clothes, name, jokes, orgasm

Okay, fine, but WTF was that last one?

I typed back fast: *all true,* and headed into the familiar dark ceilings and glowing glass of the aquarium. Now he knew it hadn't worked; I wasn't as upset as he'd been last night. That would make for a flat finale to their little group puke on me.

Tell me how an orgasm could be butch.

They were fucking with me. They were fucking with me, and I was too tired from swimming hours every day to destroy them all, but a few low-hanging fruit in my class? Yeah, maybe. I hated how easy it would be. I had a lot of hate. I don't know where it came from, but when I sank into it, it proved bottomless. My own personal Mariana Trench full of gays, gynecologists, Mike Dweiller, God, and all the other killer whales.

— 3 —

CATHERINE FOUND ME seated on the floor against the enormous central shark tank, the showstopper in the aquarium. Our class was loud and obnoxious, unimpressed by the ocean's greatest hits. Even I was bored. High above, the metal ceiling creaked as the aquarium employees crossed the catwalks to access the tops of the tanks.

"There wasn't anything on my ass. You're a vulva." Catherine sat beside me and unpacked a textbook. "I don't need your tantrums today. I'm already on the rag."

"Jesus. Stop."

"Hey. You're meant to commiserate with me, not provoke insecurities."

"Sue me if I don't see how commiserating about bodily fluids bonds anyone. You want to talk about what I hacked up in the sink this morning? Would that make us closer?"

"Tell me one of your useless facts about this place." She was placating me, engaging my obsession with facts about marine life in captivity; it worked.

"You know why we never see great white sharks at aquariums?"

"Because sales for *Jaws* merchandise would suffer if it lost its monster mystery?"

"They can't survive being pulled out of the water. No bones. Their organs collapse under the weight of their own body. They're also sort of allergic to electromagnetic fields."

Catherine hooked an eyebrow over her book. "You mean the

electromagnetic fields that every person, cell phone, light, heater, and filter in this place is emitting right now?"

We rolled our heads up and back to look through the thick glass. Poor fucking sharks. Joss and Gia walked by holding hands. The pointed affection I could take, but why lash out at me with that stupid list?

I took my head out of my hood. My face felt swollen with sweat. "I got Joss's list. I take umbrage with my jokes and sex stylings being overly masculine."

"*Butch* isn't an insult, you know. Especially in the rainbow community." I somehow managed to point out that that wasn't applicable in this situation, and would she please stop lobbing rainbow crap at me. "I didn't think you'd slept with Joss," she added into my hostile silence.

"We rounded a few bases. He was perfectly adequate."

"You're furious." Catherine looked out at our obnoxious class. "Who's for the guillotine? Joss, Gia, or Mike Dweiller?"

"Always Mike." I cracked a vicious smile. "Although I'm sure he's busy at the Penguin Encounter trying to get the emperors to look at his dick through the armhole of his T-shirt."

"*Ergh*. Your specificity is disturbing."

Catherine lost herself in her endless homework, and I grew angrier as the morning wore on, sinking further into my trench. SeaPlanet was only a good time because my class knew it so well. We'd mapped the shadiest corners, softest couches, and snack machines. We knew exactly how little the eels did during the day and that the soft red octopus named Sally would never let us see more than two tentacles.

We shared mutual respect for the enormous pillar of a shark tank and its seven sharks from three smaller species. We'd walked endless circles around it, hands trailing the glass, our classmates growing distorted on the far side in hilarious ways. This was home base. Where we'd connected beyond class, gender, race, ability, and every other kind of tank. In kindergarten, we'd all been terrified together by the rows of serrated teeth. By third, we'd become fascinated with predators, trying to solve the equation of strength and security. In sixth, we craved all the blood and feedings, and by eighth, we were trying to fall in love with each other by the light of the blue-green six-inch-thick glass.

And tenth? Well, I couldn't tell what we were doing anymore.

"We only have two more of these field trips left," I thought aloud.

"The school is putting an end to trips for fifth and up. It was an item on the student council agenda last month. Apparently, we don't *appreciate* this experience." Her gaze pointed to the spot where Mike Dweiller had appeared, dry-humping Sally's tank. Mr. Monte shot over, swatting Dweiller with his magazine. When Mike fled past us, he stuck his tongue through the fork of his fingers.

"You'd think he'd come up with some new material."

"It's his signature move." I turned to Catherine. "If this is our last time here, we should do something special. Something worth remembering."

"SeaPlanet tattoos?" Catherine shut her book, sitting tall, called into the moment as if a camera had blinked on. "No, wait, let's get jobs here this summer. Come on, you guys!" She sounded straight out of a Disney Channel show. "It'll be nonstop fun!"

"You laugh, but I'm right." I got to my feet. "We'll all miss this place someday."

"Where are you going?" Catherine asked. "Don't *encounter* without me."

"I gotta get stung. See you in ten."

My path took me by the new lovebirds. Unlike my other exes, Joss already felt like a lost ally. It's not like there were a lot of minorities in our grade. Joss was biracial, Black and Scandinavian, Shaun was Korean American, and I was white-ish. Depending on who you asked and if my mom was around to assure you that Arab Americans were just white people. Nothing to see here. Which might feel true if it didn't need to be repeated so often in such awkward ways. For years, Joss had been someone I *could* have had a real conversation with about these crappy just-pretend-you're-white feelings. I should've thought of that before I turned him into a temporary escape.

Deleting people was a perfectly acceptable self-soothing habit. As I trudged across the dark hallways of the aquarium, I dragged every memory of Joss into my mental trash. And then I hit empty. Twice.

In the far corner of the aquarium, a dark, curtained section bore a crooked sign for JELLYFISH HAVEN. I pushed the heavy velvet aside, unsurprised to find the moody love grotto deserted. The place smelled musty, and thanks to the black lights, too many of us knew what had been done in here over the years.

The neon glass pillars brimmed with blooms of jellyfish. Some were translucent, barely visible. Others glowed with flat-screen-worthy hues. Unlike the other marine life in the park who stared bleakly from their tanks or hid outright, the jellyfish gave zero fucks if anyone was looking at them. Must have been the perk of evolving without eyes.

Also, I'd been wrong; the place wasn't deserted. As I circled the pillars, I became aware of a person seated in the farthest corner, their teal polo giving away their role. A spy meant to keep Dweiller from Dweillering. I spied on them myself, misreading a shaved head through the glass for a bald one. What I imagined to be a retiree from the local nursing home in need of cash was someone about my age with Cleopatra eyeliner and a plaster cast from shoulder to palm. The name tag read INDY, with SHE/HER written beneath it in caps-lock Sharpie. She was reading Bradbury, *The October Country*, and as far as I could tell, hadn't looked up since I'd entered.

The more I stood there, alone but for this random—okay, *very* pretty—girl, the more I itched to acknowledge her, an odd impulse in my body. It rattled about inside until I blurted, "No hearts or brains. Just look how happy these assholes are in their tiny prisons."

Indy looked up. She had brown eyes and white skin that glowed by way of the black lights. She sniffed. "I'm here to thwart troublemakers. The literal jerk-offs and graffiti gifted. My shift manager didn't say anything about poisoners."

"Excuse me?"

"Are you smuggling chlorine in your hoodie? The tops of the pillar tanks are padlocked. You'll have a hell of a time dumping it in."

She thought I was a jellyfish assassin. Fascinating.

"I only poison myself, thanks. Swimmer."

"Obviously." Indy went back to her book, turning a page. "I'm messing with you."

The jellyfish in the pillar beside me bloomed and shrank, causing the glow to shift elsewhere. I wondered how she could read in the dark, and if I'd wronged her in another life. I'd lived so many at this point. Lost count, honestly.

I retreated to the far end of the so-called haven and stared into a boxy, empty tank. Something new. It felt completely out of place, a narrow, tall space with vented filters on each side. "I think whatever was in here has gotten loose."

She closed her book and came over. When she stood beside me, she was short with a flat chest and strong shoulders. A fellow athlete, maybe. "This is the Portuguese man-of-war tank. A designer murder box."

I smiled like maybe she was joking; SeaPlanet was amoral, but they didn't outright kill their creatures; there was no entertainment value in that. They claimed to use their facilities to rehabilitate injured marine life, keeping only the ones that couldn't be re-released. The ones who were worn down by captivity, a process I imagined to be akin to algebra homework and wearing an underwire.

Indy tapped the plaque beside the tank. "Man o' wars can only survive in the open ocean. They require the tides to feed, to exist. I've been working here for three months, and they've already had four die.

Apparently, there's great scientific value in watching them expire while these filters approximate lunar tides."

"But it's not even a jellyfish." I read on the plaque's description, snagging on the first line. "What the hell is it doing in here if it isn't a jellyfish? Just because it *looks* like a jellyfish, they toss it in here. To die. Right. Fucking sociopaths."

Indy barked a surprise laugh. "Wow, calm down, Justice League. The man o' war isn't here, is it? This is just an empty, abysmally expensive tank. Give me your number, and the next time they drop one in, we can *Free Willy* the misunderstood venomous jerk." She talked in a swift rhythm; it felt warm.

"But where are we going to release it? Lake Er—"

"Them. Man o' wars aren't an 'it.' They're a whole colony of organisms living together. Symbiotic as a whole." She grinned ever so slightly. "A polygender."

"God, is *everything* queer now? Even the damn sea creatures?" I laughed. She blinked, gauging my sincerity no doubt. I couldn't help her there; I had no idea what to do with my own roaring, unpredictable intensity. "I'm just saying, we can't very well *Free Willy* the colony into Lake Erie. No tides apart from the trash rolling ashore."

Indy scowled; she didn't like me. I'd never picked up on a person's vibes so hard, and it stung. "Lakes don't let things go, do they?"

Well, shit. "That's a crack at me. Do we know each other?"

"You don't remember me. Unbelievable. We went to school together until the end of fourth." She cocked her head. "I don't know why I'm surprised. You haven't changed. That might be the same hoodie. And I bet you haven't cut your hair."

Oof. She had a stunning verbal right hook. My hand traveled to the long, damp ponytail at the back of my skull. I'd cut my hair at least twice since fourth, but that detail didn't prove her wrong. I think it proved her right, but it wasn't my fault hairdressers were nearly as bad as gynecologists. I tried one more time to vent the tension. "I assure you my oversized sportswear is replaced every few seasons. But I don't know who you are. I don't remember an *Indy* in our class. Ever."

"I had a different name. I'm homeschooled now." She bit into her words. Maybe debating on saying something else.

"Look, I'm sorry if—"

"*Don't* say you're sorry if you don't even remember!"

The heavy curtains of the Jellyfish Haven parted, letting in Joss and Gia. Even Dweiller would have been easier to deal with than these two pesky fish. Joss looked confused, but Gia had those big eyes, taking in how close Indy stood, raised voices hanging in the air. I had to admit we looked like we were in the middle of something heated, bathed in the effervescent glow of a few hundred black-lit jellyfish.

"What's going on here?" Gia grinned. Indy ducked out, turning her face away from Gia. "Wow, now you're fighting with SeaPlanet employees. Downward spiral much?"

Joss laughed. I punched him right in the damn shoulder. Then I snapped my fingers in Gia's face. "Girl who left our grade in fourth. Name?"

Gia thought for a moment. "There were, like, four." She rattled off names of people who moved and whose parents got divorced, and finally she said the right one.

"Her," I barked, needing to put a stop to the stale stream of gossip. "Story?"

"Total baby dyke." Gia paused. "I hear she got hot because she's a state-ranked gymnast. Wait, was that her?" She dropped her voice. "How the mighty have fallen. Jellyfish Haven duty. Poor, pretty lesbian."

I pushed past them and out. The air was less close and humid, but that didn't mean I could breathe any better. Our class moved in waves, and I was going against the tide, everyone coming back to the shark tank for the live feeding. I spotted the edges of an artfully shaved head turning toward the Penguin Encounter, and I followed.

A long ramp dropped down a cool hallway with carpeted walls, opening up on another darkened room. Here the only light came from the life-sized shadow box full of stoic penguins behind a moving walkway. During the summers, the Penguin Encounter was the only air-conditioned building in the park, thus the exhibit required mandatory motion from its spectators. Get them in, get them out, before anyone locates the token dead penguin.

Indy was leaning against the moving handrail, texting awkwardly with one hand while the other was pretty useless in the huge cast.

"What happened?" I pointed to her arm. "Shark attack?"

"I'm on break. Go away."

I tried to remember her. She'd left because her middle school bullying came early, but the rest was MIA. There were rainbows involved, maybe. As established, that sort of thing had a short shelf life in my mind.

"I'm sorry."

"And what are you sorry for?"

"For whatever our class did. Was this one of Dweiller's doings? I swear I'll eat his heart in the marketplace before long."

Indy's eyes were locked on her phone. "You need me to like you. Interesting."

It was a minor torture, standing there, staring at someone who wasn't looking back. My brain was full-on having a tug-of-war. I thought she was pretty. I wanted to be like her. No, I thought she was pretty because she was pretty. No, I wanted to be like her and that's why I thought she was pretty. No, she was right: I wanted her to like me.

Yes, I wanted those things.

"I like your aesthetic." This was a Catherine word; it felt odd in my mouth.

She didn't look up. "Ah yes, what's that terrible saying? I don't dress to impress the opposite sex."

Her words turned me sideways. I stared at the penguins, but I didn't see the married pairs, swimming, standing. Instead, I found the penguin who'd turned the mirrored wall into a soul mate. Beak to glass-pane beak, I'd never felt so ashamed of this park. This me.

I looked at Indy again, and I didn't look away. The moving walkway took one minute and forty-three seconds to encounter all of SeaPlanet's penguins. One minute and forty-three seconds of staring at Indy's perfectly round head and natural pink lips and sound shoulders to realize that maybe I wasn't organically homophobic like everyone else.

Maybe it was more of a survival instinct.

The ground stuttered as the walkway came to an end. The cool voice warned me over and over. When Indy took a step off the sliding floor, she made it look easy. I tripped.

She put her phone away and looked at me with legit kindness, as if she sort of knew what I was going through. "Time to feed the sharks. If we don't do it like clockwork, they eat each other."

I trailed Indy back to the shark tank, and we ran into Catherine. Unlike me, she took one look at Indy and sighed. "What a day to be assigned to work at this salty hell. You shouldn't have to see us assholes ever again."

"Appreciated." Indy's cheeks were instantly red. "How are you, Catherine?"

"Still here." Catherine turned at me. "You encountered without me. How dare you."

"You remember her?" I asked, still trying to regain any sense of ground.

Catherine whacked me in the shoulder. "Your *flags*, idiot. God, I think you've started drinking the chlorine."

Indy winced and shot away, joining the other teal shirts.

Flags.

Oh, okay. I did remember.

Shit.

My class gathered around the massive tank. There were over a hundred of us, and yet I knew almost everyone. A family of sorts. I couldn't remember how many of them had worn my handmade flags on their shoulders—a lot of them, too many—on that day in fourth when we learned about *hate crimes* and that our parents said things in private that we weren't supposed to admit in public.

"Who's ready for feeding time?" A real cheese-ster millennial was working a remote mic. My class hollered their approval. "And who'd like to help Indy feed the sharks?"

Indy stood on the bottom of the winding stair to the catwalk. She seemed half as confident and radiant as she did beside the glare of the Penguin Encounter. And that was my fault—granted it was because of something I did six years ago, but wounds were wounds. And guilt was guilt. My hand shot in the air as if it had a well-thought-out plan that didn't include me. Other hands shot up too. Good. *Don't pick me*, I chanted.

Cheese-ster bellowed, "The lovely lady gets to pick!"

Indy scratched her ear with her middle finger, and Cheese-ster turned green. After an excruciating beat, Indy pointed at me, and I swore in a stream under my breath, hustling to follow her up the clanking stairs, out of earshot of everyone else.

What could I even say? *Sorry I traumatized you with my feral insecurity. No hard feelings?*

Christ. I was sweating again, filling my hoodie with the stench of the pool, my suit sticking to me. My mom was right. I shouldn't be wearing it for this long, even though I used to do it all the time. Hormonal gifts that kept on giving.

The catwalk wasn't as epic as I'd always imagined from the floor. You couldn't see the people below, and the top of the tank looked like a hot tub. Plexiglass panels had been flipped open on hinges, the surface bubbling from the filtration system.

Indy fussed with buttons on a console, and I definitely remembered now. She'd worn a rainbow flag to school for #lesbianvisibilityday. Her boldness revved up our parents, causing way too many but-how-do-you-know-about-lesbians? accusations. Apparently, we were too young, which felt naïve even then since we'd grown up watching Ellen DeGeneres dance up the stairs in those tiny, perfect suits.

"I'm sorry for the flags."

"We were ten," she countered. "Your window to apologize has expired."

"Would it help if I told you we haven't done anything like that in years?"

Not since they did it to me.

"Your class hasn't ganged up on a marginalized student to traumatize them to the point of social aversion in years? I don't know why that doesn't make me feel better."

"Karma has already taken a crack. They branded me *dyke* in sixth for months. Dweiller—" *Held my head under the water of that one until I stopped thrashing.* "I didn't even know what a dyke was. Just that it was bad."

She winced; I winced.

Indy hit a button and all the filters shut down with a groan. "Look, I only brought you up here to say that I'm not interested in opening up old wounds. Your life and my life have zero future overlap. In all dimensions."

Oh, wow.

I was *her* Dweiller.

Without the filtration system churning, the surface settled. I stared into it, entranced. "All the parents were upset. I felt . . . sick. I asked my mom what the opposite of gay was, and she said *normal*. So, I thought why not #normalvisibilityday, and I drew the flags." So many people had worn them, spinning my upside-down gag into something that felt so wrong I started shaking just thinking about it. "It was supposed to be a joke. To get all the parents to stop acting like we'd been poisoned."

Indy looked as if she were envisioning pushing me into the tank. I wanted her to do it; I deserved it. She moved toward a huge bucket full of icy blood and chunks of hacked-up fish. "I knew it would be weird to come to work today and see my old grade, but I thought maybe some of you grew up okay. I'm not exactly happy to be wrong."

"Yeah, I'm not okay." The words were small, heavy. They dropped into the saltwater tank below and sank past the circling sharks, all the way to where our class shouted and pounded at the glass, longing to eat me alive.

The surface grew flat, impossibly calm, and my breath tightened, the water calling. And here's the real truth about changing: No one beats swimmers. We race. We time each other. I could get out of my tracksuit in less than three seconds before a race. I had a feeling this time it took less than two.

The water was still as a mirror. I broke it with my body.

Hands, head, sharks.

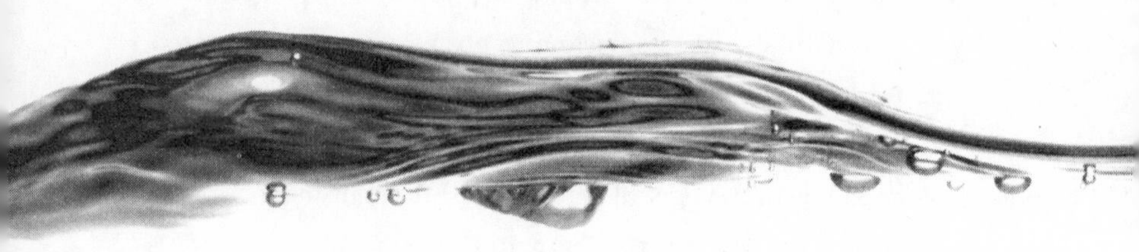

sharks

As apex predators who live in every part of the ocean, even beneath the Arctic ice, sharks deserve the fearsome reputation and dedicated, weeklong TV programming. One might say they're going extinct *in style.* Natural loners, when they do have to mate, the male bites onto the female the entire time.

Smaller shark species can briefly survive in an aquarium before developing anorexia. But hey, that's okay because as fellow apex predators, we don't mind that captivity axes their life expectancy from several decades to one starving year. It's not so much eat or be eaten.

More like, be entertained or be entertainment.

— 4 —

"THAT THING about diving into the shark tank? That was mostly an accident."

The SeaPlanet hiring manager, a Mr. Sims, scrolled through my application. I could tell when he'd gotten to the interesting part because his finger came to an abrupt halt on the tablet screen. The air-conditioning unit, which must have been left over from the Civil War, filled the tin human-resources trailer with a battle hum. "I heard about the kid in the shark tank, although I was at the Orlando park then. Was that last season?"

"Year and a half ago. There was a five-hundred-day ban on my presence here. And that was up . . . yesterday. Which I took as a good sign."

His face did not betray his thoughts. "A good sign to apply to work here?"

"I live three miles away. Where else should I work?"

Sims leaned back and his chair gave a tiny scream. He seemed tired like an old white man, but I guessed his age was somewhere greater than undergrad and less than adult. He'd probably been interviewing high school kids every twenty minutes for the last three weeks straight. I could picture his fridge: Bud Light Lime and oxidized sriracha. "That's not the answer we hope for at SeaPlanet," he concluded.

"Oh, right. I want to become an oceanographer," I amended with all the vocal enthusiasm of Siri. "The ocean speaks to me, and I must follow its call."

"How many times have you been to the ocean?"

Low blow. Ohio was landlocked states deep. Unless you count Lake Erie, and if you've ever seen Lake Erie, you wouldn't.

"The locals here are always so insulated." Sims shook his head. *A local at SeaPlanet of Ohio is better than a franchise bitch.* My counselor would be so proud that I'd held that one in. Something about coming out this past year had left me saltier than ever. Sims clicked a box on the screen, and it made a *netch* sound. " 'Aspires to biology or related career' works just fine. I have a feeling your classmates have helped you game the system."

"You don't have to ask the same questions every single year."

"As if I write the questions." He was nearly smiling, which was weird. He couldn't actually be considering hiring me. I'd told Taylor this was a complete waste of time—why would SeaPlanet hire someone who was behind the park's "second-worst insurance nightmare"?—but she'd insisted we apply. And what the girlfriend wants, the girlfriend gets. "So, how does one accidentally fall into a shark tank?"

"*Mostly* an accident. I didn't plan on diving in. And I know how suspicious it seems because I was wearing my suit, but I always did that back then." And lesson learned in antibiotics and Diflucan. "I was going through something, but I'm done there."

Which was true. Now instead of frequenting the gyno, I saw a licensed mental health counselor for my bimonthly dose of *why me*.

"The sharks didn't bite. Not even a nibble," I told him, remembering the burn of the frigid water loaded with salinization chemicals. Sims was right; I'd never been to the ocean, but I was pretty sure the sea didn't scald like that. "Everyone wants to know if the sharks bit me, but you've seen the tank, those are low-level sharks. Under four feet. I was a big, crashing predator. Also, I found out afterward that sharks in captivity turn anorexic and pretty much always die of starvation within a year." I could tell that this was new intel to Sims, but not a deal breaker. One needed flexible morals to work here.

"Everyone overreacted, if you ask me."

Sims stared like I'd been talking for a long time. I wrapped it up. "It's not like SeaPlanet took out a permanent restraining order. I wrote an apology to the owner of the park, and he wrote me back." I pointed to the tablet. "I attached the pdf in references."

"Would you do it again?"

He was asking if I had plans to drop myself into another tank, but it felt like he was asking if I'd come out again. Hold my breath through the shark-week-turned-entire-season, answering every intrusive question from family, friends, and foes like a robot who could only say *lesbian.*

"No."

He looked at his tablet and returned to the mandatory questions, his own programming kicking in. "If you were babysitting, and there was a knock on the door and the baby started crying and you were cooking something on the stove, what would you do?"

"Question my life choices."

"You have to answer if you want me to consider your application. Sarcastic charisma isn't on this checklist, River."

"River?" I repeated.

"Rain?" His finger poised to scroll all the way back up my application to my name but his expression begged for me to just tell him. Finally he found it on the screen. "Knew it was a water name. So I was pretty close." He squinted at the tablet. "Your answer?"

"I'd check on the baby, turn off the stove, and answer the door." Nailed it. Taylor had drilled me on this ridiculous question at lunch. Apparently how swiftly you answered mattered a lot more than what you said. They hired quick thinkers and multitaskers at SeaPlanet; like I said, morality was optional.

Sims clicked a box, and the tablet made that satisfying *netch* sound. Was I actually doing well?

"Are you hiring me? I thought this would be a long shot."

"In my experience—and all I do is run interviews for SeaPlanet parks—the only essential quality a person needs to work here is the ability to put up with nonstop BS. You seem skilled at that. But let me ask you one more question. Do you *want* to work here?"

"My girlfriend wants us to. More quality time, plus minimum wage. Cue the summer of love or whatever."

"*Girlfriend. Girl*friend."

"We're lesbians, Frank."

"Ted."

"So I was pretty close."

Sims barked a laugh. "I'll have to run this through the higher-ups, but technically you answered the questions correctly." He looked down at my application. "And you've applied for pearl diver, so your odds aren't bad. We've only got two qualified applicants for the team so far. You can really hold your breath for over a minute?"

"An active minute. Not just a submerged minute. There's a difference. Exertion requires more oxygen. I should be headed to states in the one-hundred-meter freestyle by senior year." He had no idea what I meant. "Also, if you want to know, my peers never apply for pearl diver because of those Hooters cleavage suits. We take bets on if you hire on breast circumference alone."

"Holding your breath is more important." Oh, his white neck had turned a glorious shade of fresh sriracha. "We're done here, and believe it or not, your candor is appreciated. You'll get an email either way, probably soon. This is the last day of interviews."

I shimmied out of the narrow hallway of an office, trying not to notice how Sims stole a look at my chest with a hairy eyeball. Christ. The tablet made its token *netch* sound, and I couldn't help wondering if he'd clicked the DD box.

"Did you flirt with him?" Taylor sat cross-legged on the top of the picnic table beside the SeaPlanet's employee pickup circle. She didn't look up from whomever she was texting, probably her mom. Taylor was tight with her mom. Even got a bob to mimic her mom's high school graduation photo on the mantel. "My odds are good. I flirted with him."

"I chose a different kind of manipulation. Naked truth."

She kept texting. "If men are stupid enough to be manipulated by a woman's smile, why sheath that weapon?" This wasn't a question I was meant to answer; Taylor's default setting was rhetoric professor. Over the years, Catherine had found Taylor's feminism to be askew at best, but it had been nearly a year since Catherine had spoken to me, so maybe Catherine was askew. Askew and homophobic.

I glanced out at the quiet two-hundred-and-fifty-acre theme park. It wouldn't open until Memorial Day weekend; the next few weeks purely for hiring and training. Soon my junior year would wrap up like a *meh* daydream, and this underwater Disneyland might actually become my everyday normal. Weird.

"Sure you don't need a ride?" I stubbed my Doc Marten into the dirt. Ever since Taylor came into my life, I'd gotten flashier in the fashion department. Snug jeans and a smothering amount of fitted flannel. "We could park at the tracks."

"Mom is nearly here. We're going to raid Kohl's khaki department before everyone gets their you're-hired! emails, so I don't have to spend the entire summer in one pair of beige shorts. I'll get you some."

"No need for khaki. I applied for pearl diver. If they hire me, I'll be walking cleavage."

Taylor put her phone down and smiled straight at me, which warmed even after a year of dating. She liked me. When she looked at me, she got turned on, and that turned me on. "You said you were settling for concessions!"

"Changed my mind. First time I came to SeaPlanet, I thought the pearl divers were actual mermaids. When I realized they were swimmers, it was just as cool. If I've got to be here, I might as well honor my younger self's daydreams."

"That's romantic." Taylor beckoned for me to come closer. I checked the mostly empty employee parking lot before stepping into the net of her arms. "You realize you weren't heart-eyes over the divers because they're swimmers. You liked hot girls, even then."

"I do like hot girls." This was, at least, a fact I could get behind.

She cocked her head and played with my ponytail. "You'll get tips in that position."

"Not a bad incentive. *If* I get hired."

"You will. So, Saturday . . ."

Liquid heat spread through me, settling in my legs. Saturday was storied, and it hadn't even happened yet. I rifled off the data I'd been sent to collect. "My parents are leaving at eight a.m. It's a two-hour drive to Miami University, add a few hours to pack up the car and eat lunch, plus the trip back."

"We could have fifty orgasms in that window. We should keep a tally."

"Fifty each?"

"We won't know until we try." She'd gotten her hand wrapped up in my long hair. At least she wasn't trying to braid it again. "I'm going to kiss you, and there's no one here, so you don't have to act like your boot is suddenly and dangerously untied."

"I haven't done that in months."

Taylor kissed me, soft and slow. I kept my eyes open, until I caught her checking and sealed them shut. I tried to make up for it in wandering hands, and she made the right sounds, so I was doing a good job.

"McIntyre."

Taylor pulled away sharply to face the intruder into our ill-timed make-out. I didn't. I froze looking in the opposite direction. Because I was back in the shark tank, shocked to the point of forgetting how to tread water in that burning cold. Indy'd hauled me out with one furious and fearful hand. Once I was back on the platform, she'd cursed fluently and given me a slap I could still feel on my left cheek.

That was the last time I'd seen her.

I turned slowly. Indy looked different. The labret piercing, Cleopatra makeup, and plaster cast were gone. Now an asymmetrical cut with dyed black hair framed those soft brown eyes. Same teal polo, but now paired with the kind of baggy jeans that cling daringly to hips. More masculine, but just as much aesthetic poetry.

There was something about looking at this person that made me want to swear.

Indy cocked her head. "Ah, you remember me this time."

I opened my mouth but words had gone the way of the dinosaurs.

"Who are you?" Taylor asked. "I'm Taylor Woods, *her girlfriend*."

Oh, great. That's just what we needed to top off this fuckety reunion: fork-tongued jealousy. Taylor, at least, hadn't been at our school when Indy had been driven out like a Monty Python sketch gone horribly wrong, me galloping in the lead, waving hate flags.

I did my best. "This is Indy. Indy is . . . was in our grade. In elementary school."

"Aw, is that all I mean to you? After what we've been through together, I'm almost hurt." *And* Indy had picked up the jealous snake in our midst and was charming it. So she was still mad. That was fair. I'd always assumed that my stunt had gotten Indy fired, but I'd been afraid to ask. Wow, I was a coward.

I reported to Taylor's glare. "Indy is the lesbian who saved my life in the shark tank sophomore year. They would have eaten me for sure if it weren't for her quick thinking." Okay, that was a stretch, but this conversation was already out of control.

"*Not* a lesbian." Indy's head shook once, a succinct rejection. "But

I definitely saved your ass. I'm the one who convinced them you were experiencing a mild psychotic break and not protesting animal cruelty. God, they loathe PETA around here."

Indy was talking, but what was she even saying?

Not a lesbian.

Not?

Taylor snuggled into my shoulder, relief palpable. "Okay, that's weird, but makes way more sense. If you had a secret ex, I'd kill you."

My insides twisted, wringing out dark feelings. Congenial laughter came from someplace, maybe even my mouth. Taylor secured my hand on her waist.

Indy looked at the humming tin box of the human resources trailer. "You aren't interviewing, are you? There's no way they'd hire you. You're a walking liability."

Taylor's phone dinged, the universe announcing one of those inopportune moments of bizarre synchronicity. She scrambled to check her email. "Well, *I'm* hired! Assistant shift manager at the Dolphin Cove!" she yelled. "Check yours."

I felt scrutinized as I pulled my phone from my back pocket and scrolled through the newly arrived emails. When I saw *Congratulations from SeaPlanet!* in the subject line, I nearly threw up in my mouth. I handed the phone over, and Taylor started texting her mom and butt-dancing on the top of the picnic table.

Indy swore so exquisitely that I worked very hard not to smile, not to stare, not to even look. When she walked off, her voice reached back for me. "Stay away from the predators, McIntyre. And the tide pool. That's my section this season."

"Will do!" I called out, which must have sounded accidentally flirty because Taylor dug an elbow across my side before continuing to text announcements. I sat beside my girlfriend and watched Indy drive off too fast in a silver-purplish car that had hit its peak a decade ago. Somehow, she even made that look hot.

"I don't get it." I couldn't hold back a second longer. "Indy left school because she is . . . was . . . a lesbian. So, Indy is a *former* lesbian?"

"She's clearly bi or pan. Met a cute guy and expanded her repertoire. It happens to the best of us. Not me. I'm not losing my gold star for any penis."

It wasn't the first time I'd heard this from her; it wouldn't be the last. Times like this I wished I could dash her entire speech at my feet and examine the pieces with Catherine, or Everett. But the latter was at college until Saturday and the former was dead to me. Though it felt odd, the year I'd spent with a steady girlfriend had also been the loneliest of my life.

Taylor's mom pulled up, and I kissed Taylor goodbye. Her mom waved—her mannerisms always too excited as if someone off-camera had a gun to her back—and I pretended to read the lacquered park map. The pearl divers worked at the Seaport Village. North end, out of the way, badly attended. Dolphin Cove would be teeming with kids at all hours on the west side by the main stadium. The tide pool was as far from where I'd be working as possible, two hundred acres standing between Indy and me all summer.

That would be enough. I didn't need to know how she'd become *not* a lesbian.

— 5 —

THERE WERE A LOT OF RED FLAGS AT THERAPY.

The largest one was that my licensed mental health counselor—whom I'd dubbed Henrietta Churchiness—was in some way acquainted with my mother. Alums from the same sorority or graduate school, maybe. They were mum about it. All I knew for sure was that, after a brief waiting period, things I disclosed to Henrietta made their way back to me, regurgitated in Mom's forcefully relaxed questions.

There were also too many cross-stitched plaques with Bible verses sans the attribution. As if taking off "Psalms" made a quote secular. The last flag was that Henrietta was going through menopause and couldn't help but tell me about every hot flash that overtook her petite physique—which was often when I talked about having sex with girls.

Considering the first flag, I spent most of my time tormenting Henrietta for her unprofessional nature. Nothing major. I moved her chair a few inches to the left when she stepped out of the room. Turned up the thermometer. Described Taylor's cervix.

The usual.

But two days after my latest surprise encounter with Indy, I wasn't on my game. Henrietta was doing her patented prolonged stare. She was about to start one of those what-if sentences, and I beat her to it.

"What if I'm not in the mood today."

"I could talk about menopause. I know that's one of your favorite topics."

I looked out the window. I had to go straight from this appointment to pearl-diving training at SeaPlanet. Meet the rest of the "team." Which made me miss swimming even if the season had ended months ago on a pointedly bitter note.

"What if you told me what you were thinking about right now."

"*Turn from evil and do good,*" I said robotically, reciting the plaque that lived just to the left of her never-in-fashion coif. And then, because I did actually want to talk about it, I said, "Swim team. I miss it. A lot."

Henrietta uncrossed her legs and recrossed them. Another flag: She always got too excited when I started talking. That look-at-me-living-dangerously-on-the-edge-of-my-conservative-comfort-zone enthusiasm. "People who experience depression often need vigorous exercise. Without it, you're likely to feel unmoored."

"You've told me that. Do you know what unmoored actually means?"

"I do. Do you know how many times you say *actually* to me in each session?" She made a quick note in her journal that couldn't have been more than a tally. "I repeat myself because, most of the time, you're not listening. It's funny that you think you're the only cynical youth I've ever met. What if you didn't invent disillusionment?"

"Have to work on being more original." I looped my fingers around my ponytail and pulled. "Well, Karen, I was thinking about the last meet of the season. Districts. I started off the four-hundred-meter relay, did my four laps, but when I hit the wall, no one dove in after me. Because we were already disqualified. Because it was the two-hundred-meter relay. I was only supposed to swim two laps. Coach went Vesuvius in front of six schools' worth of people."

Henrietta had never written so fast. I tried to ignore her scratching pen. "What did that feel like?"

"Funny. I couldn't stop laughing at Coach's anger. That bright red, round face, trying to make *me* feel bad for accidentally screwing up. She was only embarrassing herself."

And if that were true, I wouldn't have spent the last two months thinking about her words every day. Every single day. *Get your head in the game.* How cliché. Stupid. Did she have a handbook called *Coach Phrases for Bad Screenwriters*?

You're not even here.

That one was harder to shrug off. At least I hadn't repeated it out loud. Henrietta would combust at such rich psychological fuel.

"What if your coach was here right now? What would you say to her?"

You're right. I'm not here.

But I couldn't say that, and now I had to find some way out of this.

"How does someone become *not* a lesbian? Because they're . . . bi or pan?" Talk about eruption; that one vomited out. To me, those labels were identical tanks at the SeaPlanet aquarium. Side by side, same artificial salt water, stale lighting, and concrete coral in slightly varying designs. "What's the difference between those terms anyway?"

I loathed asking this, but I couldn't type a single word into a search engine without my mom finding out, and I already knew too much about Taylor's feelings on anything not-lesbian.

Henrietta wrinkled her nose, the telltale sign that she was about to cross her fingers behind her back. "I attended a gender and sexuality seminar a few months ago. Those words mainly differ in that they describe *how* someone is attracted, not necessarily to whom. *Bisexual* people can experience different kinds of attraction to different genders. *Pansexual* people can experience a similar kind of attraction, no matter the gender identity."

I was impressed she knew this much, could be this eloquent about something she definitely didn't even believe in. "But that's all manure to your god, is it?"

"You're forgetting our deal. I don't bring up God and neither do you."

"Fine. So if someone was *formerly* a lesbian, that's because they've grown in a new direction, or maybe were . . ." I wouldn't say *confused*.

Fuck that word and every person who used it against a queer person. "Mistaken? Can you be mistaken about your sexuality?"

Cue the most wrinkled nose in Ohio. "Gender and sexuality are fluid . . . for some. They start in one place and transition when they're ready." She continued with the smallest smile. "Are you thinking you were rash in coming out? Are you once again having feelings for the opposite sex? It's not too late to alter your path, to see if there's a man whose presence in your life makes your future so much easier."

"*Please*. I've held enough pork swords to have a good understanding of what they can and *can't* do for me."

Henrietta's face became a furnace, her journal a fan. Within a minute she'd stripped off her cardigan and sat in a tank top, her white, sun-spotted shoulders hunched and red. "*Pork swords* is not a euphemism I'm familiar with."

"Heard it in a movie." I stared at my hands. They looked like my dad's, which was a constant comfort. "I've got to get going early. I have a new job. Mom says I'm supposed to tell you about it. I'm going to be—wait for it—a pearl diver at SeaPlanet this summer."

"SeaPlanet hired you? Even after what happened?"

"Shock to me too, but apparently I have two much-desired characteristics. Big lungs and bigger breasts." She didn't laugh. Maybe that was her real job, to reveal that my humor was nothing more than sleight of hand.

"What does a pearl diver do?"

"Serious? You've never been to that corner of the park? It is out of the way, I get it." I became animated, moving to the end of my seat. "Pearl divers have this large, deep pool where they dive like merpeople, filling buckets with oysters for the watching guests."

"Oysters?"

"Then the guests whack the poor suckers open with hammers, hoping to find pearls."

Henrietta looked like she couldn't tell if I was messing with her. "Are the pearls artificial? The oysters?"

Good question. "I'll find out soon enough. Yesterday I picked up my 'uniform.' Looks like a little girl's bathing suit got stuck in that neon taffy-puller beside the walruses. I even had to pledge to shave my legs and armpits before each shift. That can't be legal."

My mind drifted back to where we started, drawn as if by a strong current. "It's funny cuz on swim team, we don't shave on purpose, to build up drag all over our bodies." She looked confused, and I clarified. "Drag is what makes you slower in the water. We use body hair and extra suits and stuff to slow us down when we train."

"So you shave for meets?"

"Only for the last one. The night before the last big meet, districts, we have a shaving party. We eat too much pasta and shave all the hair on our bodies. Together."

Henrietta experienced another hot flash. "Does it work?"

"Work? Well, yeah, the shaving slims a few milliseconds, but mostly it's for bonding. The guys always shave their heads. Mom won't let me. We had a huge blowout about it."

I started to slip back, down into the icy water of that memory. I'd come home from the shaving party with the most brilliant idea to shave my own head. It would be a surprise to the whole team at districts. Mom ripped the clippers out of my hand and told me I was acting manic. She slammed the door, and I stared in the mirror at no less than four years of stringy, chlorine-damaged hair. I held my face under the steaming hot water in the sink, and when that wasn't enough, I hit my head against the drywall until it cracked.

Funny, Mom hadn't said anything about the property damage.

You're not even here.

Henrietta's voice came from a distance. "You fought with your mom about your hair?"

"Sounds silly when you say it like that." I probably had a concussion at districts. Maybe that's why I blew the last race for the whole team. Or it was just a good excuse. I stood up. "Personally, I think Mom might've dropped me a few times when I was a baby and doesn't want the evidence on proud display." I snapped my fingers, smiled. "But if she admits to that much, perhaps she can write off my sexuality as collateral damage."

"Always so funny when the truth smarts," Henrietta said, clucking her tongue.

"I'll find out about those pearls for you and make you a necklace. Something to remember me by." I left, trailing red flags in my wake.

The pearl-diving pool at Seaport Village was in two levels. The upper level was a wooden platform beneath a "Japanese House" that wouldn't hold up in any culture outside of Hollywood. From here, the divers had a bird's-eye view of the park and a slight break from the fluorescent-teal madness of the rest of the place. The Muzak twanged dulcet, foreign sounds that were not attempting to be music so much as mildly interesting white noise.

The guests who climbed the stairs could lean on a balcony, looking into the depths of the pool and down the divers' swimsuits. The bottom level of the pool was on the pedestrian path through the koi ponds. A great glass wall gave everyone a view directly into the tank.

It was through that glass that I made direct eye contact once again with Catherine Guernsey. She was floating cross-legged at the bottom of the pool decorated by a fake seafloor and brightly colored practice oysters. The pearl divers all had black Swedish goggles, which honed Catherine's current beady-eyed glare. So she was going to be a diver too. Of course. She was the only one on swim team with bigger lungs than me.

Was I supposed to wave? Give her the middle finger for ignoring me this past year? Honestly, ever since the shark tank, she'd been weird. And we hadn't spoken one word during junior-year swim team, which meant things were *wildly* awkward for everyone else. Looked like the pearl-diving team was about to get a dose of our standoff.

The other three girls were struggling to fill their buckets, shooting back to the surface and gasping like amateurs. Catherine was still just chilling at the bottom, judging. I climbed the steps, ducking under the balcony to cross the wooden platform. Not wood. Plastic made to look like wood. Well, at least I wouldn't have to worry about splinters.

The top of the pool looked like a hot tub. No, shark tank. Hot tub. Honestly, how much difference is there? It's all temperature and teeth.

An older, thin Asian woman approached in a pearl-diving uniform. Her body was twenty, her face forty. This was a storied person in our community. "Mrs. Cheng?"

"You must be my late diver. McIntyre?"

"My parents did put that on my birth certificate."

"Another mouth. Great. I'll pair you with the other one, Catherine Guernsey." She pulled up a mini clipboard, hooked to an actual scuba belt.

"Ah, that won't work because—"

Mrs. Cheng looked at me with such paused intensity that I stopped talking. "Where'd you get changed? Don't answer. You're not going to do that again. You're to arrive five minutes before your shift, wearing your suit beneath the SeaPlanet tracksuit. You'll take that off behind here." She placed one finger on a paper screen. "You'll be in the water within the first minute of your shift. You'll never be late again."

"Sorry. I was at therapy."

She stared; I stared.

"I'm one of those queer-os." There was something about Cheng that undid my cool, made me feel like a seventeen-year-old who was, against all evidence, not a second older than seventeen. I bumped my fists, *still* trying to talk my way out of this corner. "Need to get a . . . lot of help with that. For obvious reasons."

Mrs. Cheng cocked her head to the side and beckoned me closer. Like maybe she wanted to give me a hug or a smack. "Dive. Fill the buckets. Smile at the guests. That's the whole job." She held up a warning finger. "Don't flirt with the cute boys." She wrinkled her nose, but unlike Henrietta Churchiness, this scrunch was pure amusement. "Or girls. Same rules apply. As well as the enbies and agenders and demi-everythings. *No* flirting."

Mrs. Cheng went back to her clipboard, and I shimmied to the edge of the pool, dropping my legs in. I wouldn't dive this first time. Swimmer law: Treat each new body of water like a strange dog. I tested the temp and found it wasn't nearly as icy as the shark tank but not warm either. And it had that same artificial salt water aura. What would that smell like coming out of my sweat all summer? Poor Taylor.

Catherine surfaced, placing a bucket of plastic oysters on the edge of the platform.

Mrs. Cheng whistled. "Catherine Guernsey, your partner is the queer-o."

Catherine's head snapped toward me and then to our supervisor and back again.

"She's teasing me." I slipped into the lukewarm water. "I called myself that."

"So you've started cannibalizing your self-esteem. I knew it would come to this."

"How's Yale? Or was it *Harvard*?" I dropped the *r*'s in the last word like a total tool, wincing through the aftermath of her glare.

"I'm going to apply to Princeton early decision, thank you. I know you don't have the grades to get in. It's a relief to know that no matter how fast you manage to swim next season, no Ivy League recruiter is knocking on your door."

I grabbed my chest, recoiling. "Buckshot to the heart, Catherine. Suppose I'll just end up at a shitty in-state college like *everyone else we've ever met.*"

"Please. Buckshot? Guns are only for the tiny brains of frightened, cis, white men."

Mrs. Cheng barked a laugh so loud and hard that Catherine and I both jumped. And something wild happened. We smiled together. It was begrudging, but it happened.

"She can hear everything we say, I guess," I added, pressing the rimless Swedish goggles around my eyes. These babies were tops at keeping water out, but they also dug straight in and left raccoon rings for hours. A few people on the team wore them, but I preferred the ones with suction and a stiff nose bridge.

"Fill the buckets!" Cheng hollered.

Catherine dumped her bucket back into the pool. We tipped our faces into the surface to watch them sink and accidentally fall on the other three divers.

"What are they like?" I asked.

"Madisons."

"That's not nice."

"Kindness is a virtue. Nicety is a waste of breath. All three of them are named Madison. I'm not making that up." Her voice was so familiar in its severity, its impeccable seriousness. I'd missed her so much that the feeling rattled through me like thunder.

The three girls surfaced to introduce themselves, and I could tell that my pal Mr. Sims had a type. Brunettes with orthodontist-perfect smiles and heart-shaped faces.

"Holy Trinity, get out of the water and learn about oyster shucking. The other two can *actually start diving now.*"

The three girls clamored out, not one of them aware that you're supposed to use your legs to get out of water. Propel yourself, the arms just guide. I watched Mrs. Cheng head down the stairs with the Madisons before I spoke to Catherine under my breath. "I cannot believe you wanted to be a pearl diver. This is a feminist nightmare."

"This is feminist nightmare *gold*. I'm going to take down this entire 'Japanese House' in an exposé by the end of the summer. This is research."

"No, this is SeaPlanet. They keep one hundred penguins in an oversized freezer. They're not going to care about cultural appropriation." I knew we were supposed to practice diving, gracefully scooping oysters, legs in full butterfly kick because it was the closest to some mermaid tail action, but Catherine was talking to me, and I didn't hate it.

"I miss the team," I admitted, watching the down-shot of my long legs and her stout, strong ones treading beneath us, such a familiar sight. Waiting for Coach to give orders. Fooling around before practice. Floating comatose afterward.

"I miss when you actually swam and didn't get us disqualified," she shot back.

"Yeah." We were still staring down. "That was bad."

"I also cannot believe they let you work here."

I scowled, kicking harder, lifting higher out of the water for this one. "I cannot believe you're as smart as you are and yet you're still a raging homophobe."

Catherine's head jerked toward me, and she splashed water hard in my face. "Don't even. You're the reason we don't talk."

"Me? What did I do other than come out to you?"

"You sent me a text that read: *I'm coming out as a lesbian.* And if you remember, I wrote back—"

"*Are you sure?* Which is just about the worst response you can have when someone comes out to you. Of course I was sure. I was so brainwashed by everyone badmouthing queers all the time that I had no idea I was queer. I tried to choose sharks over humans, but it turns out I have to live in this shitty tank, not that shitty one." I splashed her back.

"Are you sure you want to come out as a *lesbian*. That's what I was asking."

"But if you only . . . What?"

"Are you sure about being a lesbian? From what you've disclosed in our conversations you're more likely pansexual. And gender nonconforming."

"Ha." I shivered. "That sounds bonkers complicated." My stomach became a heavy knot, and I let it sink me to the bottom, where I waited as long as I could, grabbing some damn oysters for good measure. Taylor liked to rage about gender nonconforming people; I liked to avoid the entire subject.

I should have known that Catherine wasn't going to let this go. The second I resurfaced, she launched back into it. "But you didn't bother to find out what I meant. You stopped talking to me."

"*You* stopped talking to me," I pleaded.

Catherine pulled her goggles off and rested them on her forehead. "I could be wrong about your identity, but I'm never going to be wrong about something like this. I don't forget. I map every social encounter. I wish I could forget. You hurt my feelings when you ignored me all swim season. I don't have backup fake friends like you do to pass the time."

"Why would I ignore you?" I regretted the question instantly. Faster than instantly.

"Because you know I'd call you out on any bullshit, and whatever you're in with Taylor Woods is some real bullshit."

6

I LEFT DIVING PRACTICE walking fast in the other direction than the pearl divers, as if I had somewhere urgent to go. Really, I had to work through my storming feelings before I went home and ran between the raindrops of Mom's negativity. Dad wasn't home. His job kept him traveling and us in this town with a braggably high educational ranking.

The idea that I'd been the one to avoid Catherine was absurd.

It was also probably true.

But Taylor and I had just barely gotten back together after the Great Prom Debacle, which was why I'd agreed to apply to SeaPlanet in the first place. Needless to say, I wasn't up for detailing my messy relationship with the likes of Catherine, who wouldn't budge on facts. And I couldn't avoid the truth that only one week after my districts disqualification, I had a semi-public mental health meltdown in the parking lot.

Which doubly stung because everyone had acted like it made sense that I was losing my mind. As if being in the LGBTQ+ community was like joining a cancer survivor group. Then again, coming out was probably as much fun as chemo. I shouldn't make light of that. A lot of us don't make it. That's what Henrietta Churchiness told me during our first session. That it was important to get help because queer kids who don't feel supported are at high risk. She went on to point out how important it would be for me to feel seen, heard, accepted. Otherwise I might check out early. That's how she said it. Check out early.

Why did people say those things to me? Were they hoping I'd go full high school musical to let them know I did indeed feel seen and heard?

Or were they just singing, once more into the chorus, that they'd accept my identity as long as I accepted their condolences?

My eyes teared, and I wiped at them with the backs of both hands. I growled as the artificial salt water dried on my skin, burning, making more tears leak out. I'd been heading toward Taylor's station at the Dolphin Cove, but that's not where my feet had taken me.

Turning into the cul-de-sac of the south corner of the park, I hunched as I walked. Taylor blamed my layered sports bras. She'd been trying to get me to stop wearing them lately. Things were going downhill fast.

When I finally looked up and found Indy upside down, walking on her hands along the railing of the tide pool, I started grinning like a fool.

She was right there. What a relief.

I couldn't stop from yelling, "You call me a walking liability!"

Indy's legs tucked, and she landed as light as a feather inside the wooden booth of the announcer's pavilion. She was still pretty far away; I wasn't entering her turf without permission. Indy squinted and picked up her mic, her job basically a never-ending Q and A. "Welcome to the tidal zone, gather up folks and meet the gang." Indy's voice issued through the rock speakers camouflaged in the landscaping. "All except you, McIntyre. That's close enough. These poor creatures don't need you testing out their swimming hole."

"I come to apologize," I yelled, glancing around to see if any other employees were watching. The park was odd when it was this empty. The crew at the nearby fudge shop were certainly listening. Also, the sky was clouding over in a hurry, bruising itself up.

"Apologize for what?" Indy said into the mic. "This time." I took a step closer but her showy, announcer-voice stopped me. "Not so fast! Tell me from there."

"Serious?"

"Good and loud so the people in the back can hear."

"The shark tank!" I yelled, the words bursting.

The mic crackled. "What did you do with the shark tank?"

"I jumped into it. Like a deranged idiot!"

She put her mic away, sitting on a high stool and kicking her legs up on the booth. I took this as an invitation. By the time I'd gotten close enough to take in the perfect musculature of her legs in those khaki shorts, she was saying, "I don't feel like forgiving you, but how about this, I'll let go of your latest stunt if you answer a burning question."

"Deal." I leaned on the balcony, pulling my hat to the side, arms crossed. The SeaPlanet tracksuit wasn't helping my look, but why was I thinking about my clothes?

"You have a girlfriend."

"That's not a question." Her expression told me I was wrong. "Taylor and I have been together for over a year. She was my come-out excuse."

Indy cocked her head. "You used your girlfriend as an excuse to come out?"

"That's not what I said."

"Pretty much is, though." Indy was staring, and I tried not to blush but ended up remembering that I'd been tearing up two minutes ago and felt even redder. "I want to hate you, but every time I see you, I feel like maybe you just need a hug. Hard to hate that." She dropped her legs down and smacked her own forehead. "Ugh, this must be what it's like when dinosaurs go all heart eyes for jerks."

"Dinosaurs?"

"Allocishetosaurus rex." She nodded as if she'd come to an unfortunate conclusion. "That's it, McIntyre. Your shtick is irresistible bad boy, and I'm too queer for it."

I was absolutely speechless, my entire body humming. She'd just said she hated me, but also maybe that I was irresistible. And I wouldn't mind being her bad boy, *Jesus*.

She smiled as if she could tell how much I enjoyed the compliment and wasn't done messing with me. "Pearl diver, huh?" Indy flicked the goggles around my neck. "They're always trying to get me to get in the string suit. They think I'll do some gymnastic moves with the dives, but you know, I have dignity."

"I do not have any of that. Thankfully." I leaned over the edge of the tidal zone enclosure, shocked. The pit was still empty. A hose was filling up the water trenches on one end. "So, you're practicing with an empty tank? What's the point of that?"

Indy quirked one eyebrow, picked up the mic, and launched into a speech as fluid and faux-jovial as anything at the park. "Welcome to the Tidal Zone, friends! Let's learn about this exciting place between the binary that is sometimes water, sometimes land. 'Tidal Zone' comes from the science-friendly phrase *intertidal zones*, which sum up the four zones affected by low and high tide. Let's talk about those zones right now, shall we?" Indy lowered the mic. "Amused yet?"

I slow clapped.

She turned toward me, and I read the latest name tag. INDY, just like last time, but stuck on afterward as if Mr. Sims had printed it off in an antique label maker were the pronouns SHE/THEY.

I was staring; she noticed.

"*She* is okay today. None of them actually fit."

I was still staring. "Is this why you're not a lesbian anymore?" Indy looked wildly surprised. "Last week when we saw you, you said you're *not* a lesbian now."

"Pretty sure I never said I was a lesbian. Also, lesbians can use they/them pronouns, you know that, right?" I blinked. She held out a hand, stopping me from trying to respond. "The flag I wore to school in fourth was misleading. My mom is a lesbian. I was supporting her. I was ten. It was all mom-hero adoration. I had zero idea I was about to become a target for kid, parent, and administrator alike."

"But you're queer, right?"

Indy almost laughed as if she couldn't tell if I were joking. "Please tell me I'm not the first nonbinary person you've met. That poor, intolerant school you go to."

"Isn't being nonbinary a joke."

Her expression crashed with anger and hurt. It happened so terribly fast, and I wanted to stuff the words back in my mouth. "I'm sorry. That's a fucked-up thing to say."

"Whatever." She looked away, growled, "I know your type. You've got a backpack full of ugly things people have said to you, and you shove them on others like those coupon pushers at the front gate. You should work on that."

I felt the slap she'd given me after pulling me out of the shark tank. My cheeks flamed, remembering how hard and succinct her hand had been. She'd been trying to shut me up then too. A host of SeaPlanet employees were descending upon us, and I had been saying something over and over. Couldn't stop.

Couldn't remember it now, either.

Heat lightning whispered on the horizon. The air thickened with humidity, the leaves turning over.

"Calling it a day here at SeaPlanet training!" a voice boomed through the hundreds of camouflaged speakers in the park. "Employees, don't forget to clock out and return any borrowed items to their original location. Remember, only eleven days to opening day!"

Indy tucked everything away at the tiny pavilion, locking the mic away. I waited for her, not knowing if I could do this. Knowing I had to. It's why I'd made myself shuffle over here in the beginning. We fell into step on our way out of the park. It felt like a miracle that she let me walk beside her.

"Indy, do you remember what I was saying when you pulled me out of the water?"

She whipped her head to face me. "You *don't*?"

I shrugged.

"I don't think I want to tell you."

I shrugged again.

"There you go, acting like the puppy no one wanted."

I stared straight up. The Midwest was good at summer storms. At least once a week, the sky ripped open and let itself fall out. "Want to hear something sad? I think I came out as a lesbian because I thought you were one. When I look at you, I feel like, maybe I'm not the only one of my species. But if you're not even a lesbian, what the hell am I?"

Indy's voice softened. "I don't know a literal thing about you, guy."

"That's probably why it's easy to talk to you." I was lonely sort of permanently, and I hadn't realized it until I was in her presence. Now I couldn't *not* see it. It was all over me. We passed around the empty orca tank. A huge privacy fence blocked the view with a big wooden NEW ATTRACTION COMING SOON! sign. It had been there for five years.

"I kind of hate everyone right now. I'm in therapy for it. It's not working."

"Yeah." She looked sorry for me. "That stage sucks, I'm not going to lie."

"What stage?"

"When you realize the only thing about being queer that sucks is not-queer people."

The sky started spitting at us. Tiny drops that hit the skin too hard. I let it prick at my arms, face, neck. My lips wetted, and I bit at the air with frustration. "You mean straight people?" She frowned, and I course-corrected. "Dinosaurs?"

"Yes. Well, the shitty ones. And their agendas. Without them, we'd just be . . . us."

That felt like an ultimately crushing fantasy to indulge in, but I managed not to point it out. Taylor was running up the path to the employee lot, calling my name over and over.

"God, I hate that word," I muttered, catching Indy's side-eye intrigue before summoning a fake, innocent smile for my girlfriend.

Taylor jogged over in her teal polo, her hair knotted on the top of her head like little goat horns. Her arms shielded her from the rain, but her voice carried. "Dolphins are total assholes!"

Indy and I laughed hard and low, very similarly, which made us glance at each other with amused surprise.

Taylor unzipped my tracksuit the moment she reached my side and pulled half the jacket over her head like an umbrella. My cleavage was a hundred miles long. I ached to cover my chest but had learned that the action called more attention than letting it hang out. "I've seen things, I tell you!" Taylor said, too shocked to even be jealous this time. "I've *seen* things."

"Dolphins really are assholes," Indy confirmed. "I was assigned to the cove last summer for two weeks before I had to get out of there. Plus, there's a lot of people with dolphin kink you've got to watch out for. I did pull a four-year-old out of the tank when their parents balanced them on the railing for a photo op. But it's hard to feel like a hero when you only have to be one because people are idiots."

"Where'd you go from there?" I asked, enjoying her storytelling voice.

"Tour guide. I could walk backward for the rest of my life."

"I'd go on an Indy tour. I imagine you have a refreshing take on things."

"*Hey.*" Taylor looked like she might be angry if she wasn't so tired. "Take me home." She pulled me down the walkway, and I turned back, unable to stop myself from leaving. I hadn't even said goodbye, which, considering the personal stuff I'd just dumped on Indy, felt wrong.

But Indy was getting in her silver-purplish car, so I guess we were done.

Taylor and I ran through the rain to my car at the far end of the employee lot. While most of my peers had cars within a year or two of their manufacturing date, my stick shift, low-slung two-door was ten years old—but she was the best color blue. Dad's travel-happy employment meant we got to live in this town where the city taxes were high enough "to keep out the riffraff," but all our clothes and accessories came secondhand and mocked.

I slammed the door, popping my seat back. I'd gotten drenched talking to Indy and hadn't even noticed. Taylor was dripping too, which must have been a turn-on because she peeled off her work polo and straddled me in the driver's seat. "How was training?"

"Interesting. I like my boss. Catherine is a diver too."

"Catherine can go to hell for how she's ignored us." Taylor's mouth connected with mine, and my head swam. I couldn't deny that kissing her was better than kissing anyone else I'd been with. Maybe *better* wasn't the right word. It was . . . more.

What would it be like to kiss someone like Indy?

"I can't wait for tomorrow," Taylor whispered against my lips.

"What's tomorrow?"

She leaned back, honking the horn. I remembered that we weren't alone but very much in public. Indy could drive by any second. "Tomorrow is *our* Saturday. Alone?"

Ah, how could I forget.

Taylor had written our names on a blank page in my retired biology notebook, tucking it half under my pillow with the pen clipped to the top. She was being quite literal about wanting an orgasm tally. Shit.

My room was relatively organized after my panic cleanup this morning when my parents left to pick up Everett from college. Dad had come home from his business trip so late I hadn't even seen him yet, but that was normal. I switched on my speaker, linked my phone, and started scrolling. I'd been assigned to make the playlist for this . . . event.

I sat on my bed, hoping Taylor would take her time coming out of the bathroom. Hoping she wasn't in there putting on lingerie or something else that felt straight out of a, well, straight story. What had Indy called them? Allocisa-something. *Dinosaurs*. That was easy enough to remember, and it was nice to have a name for them when they so pointedly had a name for us. Then again, it did highlight the weird feelings I had about my girlfriend's behavior. Taylor liked me, liked girls, but she *loved* the dinosaur games of attraction. She made me watch *Sweet Home Alabama* and *Downton Abbey* and so many other romantic-y nightmares. I wanted to ask if she noticed that the queers in those stories were nothing more than dramatic fodder, that we should suffer in silence—until the hero notices.

What did Indy watch at home with her lesbian mom? Were there entire channels for people like us?

I clicked shuffle and Florence + the Machine started up. Good old Florence and her cosmic love. That had to be correct mood music, right? I fussed with the fading black curtains I'd made out of a sheet—because Mom refused to buy actual black curtains—closing them tight. I switched on the string lights over my desk, hoping that would be enough illumination. I couldn't do this in the light, which bothered Taylor *a lot*. Then again, I was starting to think everything I did bothered her. How had I ended up here?

Oh yeah, she was right *there*.

After the shark tank, after I'd gotten dragged home to explain what happened, I realized fast that Mom was not going to accept me as queer on concept. I'd need a living, breathing girl on my arm to make this viable. I'd asked Gia if she knew any secret lesbians and found my way to Taylor's locker. I'm charismatic as hell when I want to be, and we tangled fast. We made plans to come out, got it done and over with. I'd dated guys for less, and we were supposed to have someone lined up all the time. It was the near-surefire way to avoid scrutiny.

My heart was starting to pound against my temples. This was not the time for an anxiety attack. I paced, trying to feel sexy, Indy's face in my mind. Those shoulders. Indy smiling. Indy being the one about to enter my room . . . and me.

"Seriously?" Taylor shot in wearing a matching lace bra and underwear. She looked like an ad in *Cosmo*, much less like a person I wanted to kiss. She wrestled my phone out of my hand and turned the screen at my face until it unlocked. Florence stopped singing, my room too quiet.

"I gave you one job. *Find romantic music*, and you chose the saddest song about love being literally blown about the universe."

You hate me.

She caught my panicked expression and calmed down. "No sad songs. That was the one thing I asked. Florence's last name might as well be 'misery loves stabbing people.' "

"Every single song is sad, if you're listening."

Taylor snuggled against my headboard, pulling her phone out of her bag. "I'll take that challenge. I have the *perfect* song to make love to. Link my phone to your speaker."

She handed over her phone, and I winced at the home screen image: the two of us in prom dresses before her mom's living room mantel. Taylor had been a strapless princess in purple with a full skirt. She put me in black satin, which was supposed to make me happy. Only, the person wearing my face was a hooker. An angry one. And that person was having the worst night of their life, shark tank included.

Taylor seemed to understand that this was not the memory I needed right now. She swiped the image away, and I linked her phone. She immediately began a song, and I sat on the edge of the bed with my back to her. "This one is so happy, love. It's literal rainbows."

"Somewhere Over the Rainbow" started playing, the cover by Hawaiian singer Israel Kamakawiwo'ole. She put her arms around my hunched shoulders, holding me from behind while the song detailed dreams that were so far away they might as well be over the rainbow, in an imaginary place. Where was this elusive happiness? She could feel it in the same words that filled me with nothing but isolation.

Taylor sang along sweetly in my ear. I could feel her smiling, and it made my breath tighten, my heart hammering each beat. She pressed her hands under my shirt, caressing upward. My arms locked down, my back set to her. Finally, *finally*, she felt me rejecting this.

"What's wrong now?"

"I'm not going to take my shirt off."

"I wasn't asking you to, was I?" Her voice spiked fast. "I know the rules. You get all of me, but I get half of you."

I swung to face her. "It hurts. As in *pain, not pleasure.*"

"And that's because you've got a bunch of cysts from wearing too-tight sports bras. My mom told me all about it. You did this to yourself! Probably on purpose, knowing your self-flagellating ways."

I was speechless.

"Is this about that girl Indy? I didn't say *anything* when I found you with her yesterday. I wasn't jealous. I trusted you and—"

"Stop. She's not a girl." I stumbled to say it like Indy. "She . . . *they* are nonbinary."

Taylor made a disgusted sound. "You're kidding. We're not doing the nonbinary fads. My mom said people tried to do that midway gender crap when she was a teen too. If you've got a vagina, you're a girl. Penis? Boy. If your vagina wants to dress up like a man—like *you* do all the time—you're not less of a woman. Women can be anything. Including manlike, but they're still women." Her voice shook. "Women can be *anything.*"

My body crackled between anxiety and anger. I couldn't look at her. "What about intersex people?" She gave me a questioning look. "Remember? We learned about them in sixth-grade biology. They're all around us. Millions of them."

"They always have a dominant sex trait, and there are surgeries to help them fit in. Please, this world is full of enough bullshit. We don't need to go reinventing gender."

"This stupid song is on repeat!" I yelled, crossing the room, my back to the corner. "Turn it off. And it's *not* happy. Listen to the fucking words, Taylor. It's about being so miserable that you have to imagine a world that's happy."

She gathered her things, tugging on clothes. "I cannot believe I thought we were going to have a day for *us*. My mom was right. You can't help sabotaging good things. This is prom all over again." She glared, daring a response, but she couldn't see me because I wasn't even here.

Taylor left, and I followed her out with my mind. Down the hallway, the stairs, across the foyer, and through the front door. Which slammed. She slammed her car door too and then drove off too fast. I had to disagree with Indy; there were two things about being queer that sucked. The dinosaurs, sure, but also their world. The one they weren't willing to share with people who were different. People like me.

Damn it, maybe I *was* gender nonconforming or nonbinary or something else. Why didn't I have Indy's phone number? Everett would be home soon, and he'd see how I'd come out and somehow gotten worse. Catherine could tell without even talking to me.

Anxiety attacks never just happened. They pulled, built, crested. The worst kind of riptide. This one dragged me under as I reached for the notebook, the blank page with Taylor underlined on one side. My name on the other. Who the hell were these people? I squeezed the pen and scribbled out the names. When that wasn't enough, I stabbed it into the back of my hand. The blood didn't flow until I pulled it out. The pain came much later.

— 7 —

WHEN I'M OLD, I won't make my family sit around a table to eat dinner. There's enough societal pressure in this world without staring down the barrel of generational divergences with our evening meal. Dad ate like someone still getting over having too many siblings, head down, food in. Mom believed we didn't notice how she pushed portioned bites to the edge of her plate with a fork that seldom went to her mouth.

I'd imagined that having Everett back would rebalance things, but something had happened to my family during their sojourn to Miami University—so much so that they hadn't noticed my hand. My brother had shaved the sides of his head, and it made him seem narrower, streamlined. Beside me, he ate fried rice like a zombie.

"Taylor and I broke up." I showed them my hand. "Lost my temper. I've already emailed my therapist about it. No one needs to freak out."

My dad looked up from his Chinese food. "I broke my parents' windshield when my high school girlfriend dumped me."

"Really?" This made me feel so much better. Which was surprising.

"Don't tell them that," my mom said.

Dad put food in his mouth. Chewed, swallowed. "Anger happens."

Awkward silence, awkward chewing.

"So." I couldn't stop myself. "Anyone want to tell me why you're acting like Everett knocked someone up?"

Everett snorted hard before shooting our mom a look.

She scowled. "Please. Don't let me stop you. If you have something to tell us, now is as good a time as any." Mom was downright radioactive. Now they all had my attention.

Everett shot me a look from the side. "Mom was pawing through my boxes and found my pride flag."

I turned to our matriarch, ready to clash our genetically matched tempers. "At some point you're going to have stop malfunctioning when you see rainbows. Everett is supporting me."

"It's not a rainbow flag," my brother said. "It's the asexual flag."

"Oh," I said before I actually understood. "*Oh.*"

Mom put down her fork. The older I got, the smaller she became. Not in size, but in feeling. These days she seemed to be about as big as an eight-year-old. I bet that felt pretty shitty on her end. "I'm not upset with you, Everett. I'm trying to understand."

"I choose not to be sexually active, and Mom has decided I must have a hormonal imbalance. She wants me to get my blood drawn. She's made an appointment."

Dad ate more food. Mom stared us down. I had to admit that I was outside my element here. I experienced far too much sexual attraction these days. Well, not *today*. I surprised myself with a laugh, and everyone glared.

"Well, we've got five days to June. Happy pride, brother. We should hang up that flag and see how long it takes for someone to cherry bomb our mailbox."

Mom burst into ugly tears. Her shoulders shook, her head struck down, shaking while Dad rubbed her back. Her sudden, poignant grief felt like someone had flipped off the safety on my anger. Aimed it.

"Oh no, poor Mom. You have *two* queer kids."

"*Don't* use that word," she snapped. "You know that word means something else to my generation. It's an insult. A slur."

I kept firing. "Can't you see that maybe *your* generation is the problem?"

Taylor's mom clawed into my mind, shouting about *midway gender crap*, and I felt sick.

I closed my wounded fist, flashing to Mrs. Cheng of all people, who must have been in high school with my mom but who had no problem nicknaming me *queer-o*. Mrs. Cheng, who'd instantly noticed my stabbed hand at pearl-diving practice this afternoon. Mrs. Cheng, who'd grown oddly protective as she cleaned and wrapped it with a SeaPlanet first aid kit. She didn't ask me how it happened, and that left me feeling like she didn't have to.

Mom needed a few beats to gather her comeback. "Yes, blame generations, daughter. That's what I did. It was all my parents' fault."

"The whole town will wonder what you did so wrong in raising us," I muttered.

"To your room." I'd engaged the dad growl. Oops.

Mom shook her head. "No, you're right. I must have done *something* wrong. And now I'll never have grandchildren."

Everett and I started laughing so hard we couldn't stop, even if it was a desperate kind of humor. Team-based. I glanced at my brother and knew that this was really bad, actually. All Mom cared about was grandbabies. She'd been talking about the nonexistent progeny since I was too young to understand that she meant *my* hypothetical kids.

"Mom, Mom." I reached across the table, and she recoiled from my hand, which stung despite everything. "Mom, I'll give you tons of grandkids." I surprised myself by being serious; I totally would raise kids. If I had some queer, joy-filled person like Indy at my side, I could raise a million sticky-handed and tooth-gap-grinning kiddos. They'd have rainbow capes and scream through the neighborhood on bikes. It was by far the sweetest future my imagination had ever painted.

A surprise firework.

Was it even possible? Not here in the hard-hearted heartland, that's for sure, but maybe somewhere else. Were there places where queer people just walked down the street holding hands? Pushing strollers, walking dogs, growing beards?

"It's cruel to make promises you won't keep." Mom's voice snapped me back to reality. She stood and left the kitchen. I tracked her journey out of habit. She veered into the foyer to pick up her phone from her purse and headed to her bedroom. Time to call Mrs. Winooski and complain about her lot in a voice way too loud for our discount drywall.

Dad blinked one eye at a time. "I missed something. Why does she think people like you can't have children?"

I pushed my remaining food from the center of my bowl to the outside. There, all done. "Mom knows we *can*. But there's a difference between having grandkids and having grandkids you can brag about." The words were easy enough to say, but they turned that firework of joy into a smoky imprint. If I did find the person of my dreams and made a family, she wouldn't go to her church group with pictures and proud stories. My happily-ever-after was her shame.

"You're both too harsh on her." Dad ate. Everett's head bobbed as if he were listening to hip-hop that only he could hear. "She's stronger than you give her credit for. She's experienced a lot of hate. She only wants to save you from the same trauma."

"True," I managed. She wanted to save us from our truths by teaching us to live the lies. Just like Taylor's mom. And Taylor. And the rest of this tiny, cloudy tank of a town.

Everett knocked on my door after ten. Our parents' light was already off. They'd been quiet in their room together since dinner. The silence itched through the house like the start of a bad swimsuit rash.

"Got a present for us," my brother said. "Come on."

I followed him out, and we went to Dad's car. In the trunk, he hauled out the set of crappy dishes that had kept him fed in his dorm all year. "Let's go to the lake."

Ohio is a land of boxes. Boxed acres upon boxed acres, as my geography teacher had proven with pictures taken from a plane window. We lived within the box of our state, county, suburb, but Haley was further divided into walled neighborhoods. They were named, themed. Park View was on the lower end of the upper-middle-class scale of this affluent place. Instead of a pristine community pool, we had a man-made lake surrounded by broken playground equipment and the permanent scent of burned hot dogs.

For all its faults, I'd loved this little park in the middle of our neighborhood. As a seven-year-old swimming on the summer team alongside burly seventeen-year-olds, it had been my first taste of freedom. Of strength and pride. Now it was a muddy memorial to my first broken heart.

Even though Everett had been silent along the walk, he noticed my switch in energy. "Forgot you hate coming here."

"Me too. Every time. Until I get here." Because the feeling was sealed up in another kind of box. My therapist referred to my malfunctioning memory as a self-defense mechanism. The sealed containers of things I couldn't face. My internal storage unit was full these days, and I could already feel myself packing up Taylor, shoving the bad memories out of sight along with the good ones. After all, our time together hadn't been entirely left of happy. We'd had dozens of better moments, but those—like the races I'd won and friends I'd made on the lake's team—proved to be more painful to remember than the bad.

"Does happiness hurt you more than sadness?" I asked my brother.

He looked over with one crazily arched eyebrow. "Uh, no."

So it was another broken piece of me. How many did that make?

"Wonderful," I muttered.

The dark water glistened. I itched beneath my doubled-up sports bras. Lake rash, everyone called it. Over many summers, I grew allergic to the cocktail of algae and algae-killer. I swam faster to get out of the water, changed faster to get out of my suit, but the misery of permanent itching was too much. I dropped out, and every single one of my friends dropped me. Being eleven blows.

"It was the worst drive home." Everett turned from the lake, taking the trail down to the abandoned basketball court and its rimless backstops. "Mom insisted on driving with me, googling 'low testosterone,' and asking questions about my *condition*. She's really good at making you feel bad about something you're proud of, you know?"

"Do *I* know? She crawled inside my sense of joy years ago, interrogating every giggle." That felt cold. "She wants to know what might hurt us before we do, a sort of soothsaying maternal instinct. But you're not used to her disapproval, are you?"

"No." I'd never heard my brother sound so low. "She's very good at it."

We slid down the last little slope, probably coating ourselves in poison ivy. Everett unpacked the box of ceramic plates and cups, setting a picnic at center court. "I'm really happy. That's the part Mom *really* didn't want to hear."

I kicked my big brother's foot. "Tell me everything right now."

"Her name is Karina, from Dayton. History major, sophomore. Epic nerd. We're talking Tolkien tattoos. Miami has an ace spec group, and we sort of hit it off all at once."

"Am I going to meet her?"

Everett didn't answer; he didn't want to bring her here. Of course he didn't.

"I'm surprised Miami has an ace spec group."

Everett looked around the dark center of our neighborhood. Nature-made lakes. When man made them, they came out all shallow muck and dead turtles. "Not everywhere is like this, Bake. Insulated. Petrified.

Some places let people be different. Some places celebrate people for it. One more year, and you'll be out."

Yeah, I'd be out of Haley and funneled into a nearby state school, on scholarship for a women's swim team, if I was lucky. I'd be navigating closed-minded people like Gia, Dweiller, and Taylor, or maybe just those exact same humans. Four years of that. And then what? Where?

Why?

"You're not going to tell me it gets better, are you?" My throat thickened. "I'm sure hindsight is delightful but current-sight is killing me."

"What happened with Taylor?"

"She's Taylor. And I'm me. That's what happened."

"You break the drywall in the bathroom?"

"Months ago." I rubbed Mrs. Cheng's bandage on my aching hand. It was starting to amaze me how much you could hurt yourself without anyone noticing. "I'm fine."

"Oh, *fine*. That's a great word."

"It's the best I got." For one second, I thought about telling him about Indy, but what would I even say? There's a person I run into sometimes who makes me feel better than fine? "I'm okay." Somehow this sounded even worse.

"I'm home now."

I put an arm around my brother's back, and he put one across my shoulders. We looked over his handiwork: a twenty-piece set of ceramic dishes perfectly placed. An imaginary feast poised for a family dinner under the night sky; our mom had taught us well. The moon watched us smash every last one.

— 8 —

MEMORIAL DAY LIT UP OUR CITY like New Orleans at Mardi Gras. There were parades and fireworks and candy. Mom and I got showered by Tootsie Rolls as the marching band made their way down Main Street, playing a Twenty One Pilots medley.

"Get the green ones!" she hollered, and I scrambled to gather the paper-wrapped candies in the bottom of my shirt. We ate together, watching the parade funnel through downtown. Everett wouldn't get up, and Dad was already knee-deep in yard projects, so it was the just the two of us.

Mom folded each wrapper into a tiny, perfect triangle before reaching for another. "When does your shift start?" she called over Billy Joel, who was crooning from the radio in the orthodontist's convertible. His wife/administrative assistant sat on the top of the back seat, wearing a prom dress and smiling like the winner of some hellish pageant.

"One," I said. "I should miss the early-bird frenzy of opening day."

"But you'll have to be there for the first evening. That will be crowded."

"Free firework show."

"But you'll be working. You won't be able to enjoy it."

"Okay, Mom." I ate candy, ignoring the constant ache of my hand. It'd grown stiff and I was a little worried about having to dive all day in that fake salt water. We kept our backs to the gazebo, having gravitated toward a pocket of families with young children. This was ideal for me because I didn't want to see a single person from school. No doubt Taylor had started talking about how I broke up with her . . . over text. This placement also worked for Mom, who loved watching toddlers collect candy and show their parents.

"When Everett and you were that age, I could make your whole week perfect just by taking you to the ice cream shop as a surprise. Your happiness was so infectious." My teeth were welded together by sugar and preservatives, otherwise I might have responded. "Now everyone in our house is miserable all the time."

I stopped chewing. "I'm not miserable all the time."

"Yes, you are. Which is also infectious, you know."

I started to arm myself for battle, but a large part of me just wanted parade candy and zero fights for once. "What if I'm happy right now? Think about it. No more lake-effect snow or bitter spring. I've got a job. Everett's home."

Not to mention, junior year was pretty much over. We'd showed up every day for tests this past week, and the last days before summer break were lame duck. I was going to cut this year and pick up some extra shifts. Now that I'd broken up with Taylor—this time it would stick, damn it—I needed my eyes on a different horizon. So, money. I should make money, and then I wouldn't need to work during swim season. More time to practice and attract a recruiter. I might even patch things up with Catherine. "I could be happy."

"You're not happy. You're a string of calls for help. One after another, like Christmas lights going out." She glanced down at my bandaged hand. "But I'm not feeding that immature attention-grabbing. If you have a problem, come talk to me or Karen about it."

"So you can make everything about you?"

"You're projecting."

"Do you *talk* to Karen about me? You do, don't you? That's against their therapeutic code of whatever."

"You're underage and a danger to yourself. I can talk to her about anything I want."

My mom thought I was a danger to myself. Which meant this was how she treated someone who was a danger to themself: dismissal and disappointment. Then again, this was probably how she was treated, growing up the only child and daughter of man who was still shouting to the heavens for a son decades later. A man who leaned so hard into his stereotype that it hurt to look at directly. The patriarchal Arab. I loved my jidu, but the way he crowed at every little thing Everett did made me seize up inside.

Wonder what it did to Mom.

I picked at the grass. Pluck and throw. Pluck and throw. "I don't blame you. Neither does Everett. People in Gen Z are different. We want to be allowed to be different."

"Tell me what it is about man-of-wars." I knew her tones. This one was the *I've been overthinking this request.*

"What do you mean?"

"You know I'm talking about your search history. The marine life, well, you've been looking up that stuff for years, but you look up pictures of Portuguese man-of-wars almost every day, so I have to ask. Or you can talk to Karen about it, and she can let me know what's . . . going on there."

Oh my god, I had to get this conversation back under control before she found some horribly awkward way to ask if I was jerking off to them. "They're a misunderstood creature, that's all. We vibe. They're beautiful too, in their own way."

"They're poisonous."

"No, they're venomous. There's a difference."

"Are you getting bullied at school again? Is that what this is about?"

"No more than reason. Not great, but not bottoming out either." She really didn't believe me. Maybe because if she was my peer, she would not have been kind to me.

"Kids are mean. Teens are worse. Adults are the true monsters."

Her sunglasses hid the lines around her eyes. My mom had considerable anxiety, and I couldn't always see it. It filtered through her negativity so seamlessly that when it stopped, it was even more alarming. Did this make her catastrophic thinking more like catastrophic worrying? Maybe it was the only way she knew to protect herself, her own corrupted survival instinct.

"Mom, how are *you* doing?"

She waved at someone across the street. Her smile didn't crack but this tone was no-nonsense. "I don't want this conversation with you right now. I want Tootsie Rolls and sun." She shrugged off her jacket, letting her light brown shoulders out. They'd get browner and browner all summer. Everett had that skin too. I didn't; I burned like Dad. Irish-lobster red. That's how they all joked about it.

The parade kept going and going. It seemed every convertible in town was wearing balloons and crepe paper. Every softball and baseball team had their own pickup. I watched the lake's swim team float go by and hid my face. A few of my former neighborhood friends were waving in their team suits. Six years later and they all still acted like I walked away on a whim. Then again, I didn't tell them about the horrific rashes. Who would?

SeaPlanet's float came by next, bearing the arching teal logo. The trainers wore their wetsuit uniforms, tossing taffy from the life-sized-walrus candy dispenser. Keemee, the SeaPlanet emperor penguin mascot, waddled by, and I darted into the street to rescue candy—accidentally making eye contact with Keemee's enormous, hollow glass eyes.

The mascot came toward me at a speed I didn't think possible with those zipped-up legs. I tried to run, rebounding off the gazebo and the wall of people. I turned back, face-to-beak with the oversized, padded suit. The mascot held out its penguin arms—are they still wings if it can't fly?—for a hug.

"Hell no," I said, despite the sudden community outpouring of *aww*s.

"You won't even hug a stuffed penguin," a raspy voice teased from inside the suit. "Are you that hopeless, McIntyre?"

It was Indy. Indy was in that suit.

I grabbed Keemee and spun the penguin around as if we were newlyweds taking photos. At first, I could only feel the suit, but it folded in until I found Indy, their body solid against mine for the briefest of milliseconds. I put them down, and they were gone, waddling to rejoin the float, passing balloons to the screaming children in its wake.

My face ached with a smile.

Mom found it suspicious. "Do you know the person in that costume?"

"Not really."

"That was weird. Those suits are covered in little kid germs, you know. We should go home now so you can wash up."

"Sure." My gods, this smile was permanent. I was going to suffer nerve damage.

"Elena!" Mrs. Winooski came weaving through the crowds at the edge of Main Street. The woman was my mom's partner in all crime. Mass. School board. Yoga. "Elena!"

The dialogue entered a stream of fluent Midwest-mother-speak that I couldn't possibly comprehend. I spent most of the time looking for a last glimpse of Indy in that ridiculous Keemee costume. *Wait.* I was single now. Indy was . . . possibly single. We were going to work less than two hundred acres apart. Thanks to Everett's dare years ago, I knew I could run the distance of the entire park on one filled chest. Indy would be one breath away. We only got fifteen-minute breaks, but I'd be making the dash whenever possible.

I snagged a flying Snickers from the air and made a noise that caught both women's attention. They turned to stare at me.

Mom squinted. "What was that?"

"Would you buy 'surprised joy'?"

"Not from you." Mrs. Winooski laughed. She gave me an unwelcome side hug as if this cushioned things. That was the disorienting thing about moms like Mrs. Winooski. She seemed to genuinely care about me, and her genuine care came through small acts of casual terrorism. "Isn't 'bad mood' your aesthetic?"

"No," I said in a foul tone that bronzed her point.

"Loving these updates on Nicole!" Mom said, shifting back to their scheduled brag-exchange. She pulled the ultimate move and tucked my arm around hers, fixing me to her side. Mom hadn't done this for years, not since we attended mass together. I felt like a damn purse. "Everett has also had a phenomenal year. Four-point-O is still his default setting, even in college! He did get a"—she whispered behind her hand—"*tattoo*. But he's one of the backups to the quiz bowl team, which went to nationals last year."

Mrs. Winooski was no fool. "No challenges?"

"Oh, the laundry! I had to send him so many packs of underwear. He kept ruining whole batches with bleach. One time his clean whites got stolen straight out of the dryer."

I'd heard this monologue so many times over the last few months that I nearly had it memorized. The stolen whites were always the clincher.

And yet, Mrs. Winooski was too cunning, too practiced in this high-stakes game of brag competition. "What about a girlfriend? Did he get one of those too?"

Mom went rigid.

"Yes," I said.

"Yes," Mom agreed.

"Karina," I said, "from Dayton."

"Karina," Mom concluded. "We're looking forward to meeting her."

The parade ended, the cop car rolling up Main Street, blue lights circling. I was about to say something crass and immature to break up their gossip ring, but I heard shouting. A last, straggling float was working its way up the street, flying a rainbow flag. Taylor had a megaphone, calling for attention. I recognized nine people from school with her, all of them walking with signs, all with the same message: WE DESERVE A GSA.

Mrs. Winooski did us the great service of reading it aloud. "Is that the Gay-Straight Alliance?"

My mother looked to me, and I answered, "I think they've sort of updated it to Gender-Sexuality Alliance, which is all about getting together to talk gay agenda stuff." My mother squeezed my arm so hard I mouthed a silent *yowl*, which should have been enough, but then Taylor passed, eyes turning red and furious at the sight of me.

I mouthed, *I'm sorry,* before feeling sorry. Or even agreeing to the words. Her head whipped forward, and she started a love-wins chant in the megaphone. Her middle finger reached back toward me, which seemed a logical addition. The only ones who returned the shout were the nine souls behind her. The parade onlookers watched them but didn't cheer or boo. They had no opinion on the subject. That is what they wished to convey, and that is what they conveyed. I hated them all so much.

"Shouldn't you be with them?" Mrs. Winooksi asked. She had daring shaved sides for a dinosaur, with a frizzly mop on top.

"Taylor and I broke up."

"But you were so sweet together. What happened?"

"Our periods kept syncing up, which of course started World War III. Couldn't stop fighting. Perhaps God was onto something after all." Okay, now I was just begging for bad karma. Mom shook me, and I answered flatly, "I'm not part of the queer clique at school. Even if the principal would let them have their group, they wouldn't want me in it."

It wasn't the kind of thing you wanted to admit to yourself, let alone to the "town fixer," as Everett called her. Mrs. Winooski's main goal in life was to sniff out other people's problems and then enact solutions. I can't tell you how many of my peers ended up with prom dates because of her matchmaking. Or jobs because she put in a good word. Even my relationship with Taylor had gotten her stamp of approval, and I can't say we hadn't benefitted from her insistence that we'd been personally sanctioned.

Mom had been so relieved.

"This one needs friends, Elena. I've been telling you this since you moved here and started swim team. You remember how that was my idea? Now there might be college sports, I hear." She turned at me. "*If* you keep your head in the meets, you'll get recruited by a good school." Christ, of course Mrs. Winooski knew I'd blown it at districts, but her sympathetic look surprised me. "I'll make a few calls!"

"Our best to Nicole!" I shouted, tugging my mom away. "Lord, she's got a terrifying amount of influence in this town." I was still linked around my mom's arm. She actually laughed. I loved it when she laughed. "You know, we've got to freshen up Everett's brag sheet. What do you tell people about me? Do I have a stolen-whites clincher?"

"Swim team, mostly. But that's been rocky. You used to have a long-term relationship, but I'll have to toss that line. You could give me more to work with in the grades department."

"I'll study when they give me something interesting enough to study."

When we reached the parked car at the library, she let go of my arm, and I said *ow*, and then she asked me four hundred times why I'd said *ow* until I showed her the spot on my side that ached like a broken rib.

"Do you know what it's from?" she asked.

"My pearl-diving suit has no support. My chest keeps getting smashed."

"You're probably standing with your shoulders too far forward. You have the worst posture I've ever seen in someone so young."

"Wonderful, thanks," I snapped. "Why are you being so weird about Everett's new girlfriend?" I flared. She always dismissed elements of my life, but she'd never done it to my brother before. I didn't like it. I wouldn't stand for it. "It's making him feel bad."

"You've talked to him! It's not a real relationship. It's just . . . they're friends."

"You can totally have a relationship without sex, you know that, right?"

"Yes, and it's called *friendship*. I swear your generation won't be happy until you've broken all the words that we need to make sense of things."

"Maybe your generation isn't entitled to understand everything."

"I don't like your tone."

"Surprise, surprise."

We drove home in silence, all two miles. Between downtown and our house, there were seven bright red yard signs remaining from the psychotic election half a year ago, and I knew how to look out different windows to miss them. This worked well enough, but avoidance could do nothing about the great oak in our neighbor's yard, forever ruined by the blue sign they'd strung up from a branch by a noose. Mrs. Winooski had been the one to get it down, but she could do nothing about the swinging, ghostly memory of what our neighbors thought about those who disagreed with them.

I felt sick by the time we'd made it home, but that wasn't unusual. Mom parked in the driveway, and I dumped the green Tootsie Rolls in her cupholders before getting out. Dad was mowing something fierce, his entire face dripping. "I should get him some water."

Mom said my name curtly. "I'm tired of being on my guard with you. Could you please revert to the little girl who put on dresses and wanted all the American Girl dolls? Just for one night. We can watch *Princess Diaries*."

I stared. She smiled kindly; she had no idea.

That girl didn't exist. And now I regretted being so good at faking it. Mom was nostalgic for a time when I'd been playing a part to please her. She'd been so determined to make her daughter feel wanted the way she'd never felt truly wanted. I was supposed to right the wrongs of her childhood. I knew this was my job, and I knew I'd failed. One night being pretty in pink wouldn't change that.

Dad cut the lawn mower and waved. The distant skyline fizzled and popped, drawing our attention. Rockets zigged up the blue, popping and leaving smoking scars on the clouds. Daytime fireworks could only mean one thing: SeaPlanet was open for the season. Soon we'd be able to tell time by the citywide echoing of the stadium cheers at the noon, three, and seven o'clock shows. This was summer in Haley.

—9—

UNLIKE THE SPITTING STORM and empty bleachers of my last training session, the park was alive. I'd been to enough opening weekends at SeaPlanet to know this was indeed going to be a long shift.

Community discount brought in more people from our county than imaginable. The marine shows filled the air with shouts as I parked in the employee lot, now decorated with teal balloons and navy streamers. Clocking in and passing through the antechamber of the employee lounge, I took in boisterous cliques of summer unions. The concession peeps. The trainer cohort. The crowd control crowd. Ticket boothers. Special-event coordinators. And last, but not least, the half-costumed walkaround entertainers. I tripped on a foam shark tail and got a mouthful from the person carrying the head under their arm.

I nearly ran bodily into Mr. Sims. He smiled at me for a prolonged moment until he placed me. "You interviewed me."

"I hired you, River!" He put an incredibly unwelcome hand on my shoulder. "Can I give you some opening-day advice?"

"No, please."

"You'll know it was a successful first shift at SeaPlanet if your smile is stuck and your legs feel like they've been beaten by a souvenir baseball bat." I think Sims had a few of those Bud Light Limes for breakfast. Yikes.

"You're wasted on hiring, Frank. You should look into giving your own TED Talks."

"Which is funny because my name is actually Ted."

"And the winning point on your CV," I muttered, leaving Sims in the employee lounge, entering the park proper, wondering if I should have asked why he thought my name was *River*—and maybe also why I didn't mind it so much.

SeaPlanet was nearing capacity as I wound my way to the north end of the park. Children were screaming, families moving in packs. Teal rent-a-strollers ferried eleven-year-olds about, their oversized limbs jutting at odd angles like battle-wounded. Park security had the only SeaPlanet uniform that wasn't teal. They were gray with hard lines, nicknamed the Confederates until SeaPlanet headquarters found out and threatened to fire anyone on the spot for using the word (or so the urban legend goes). They certainly stood out in a summer crowd of bare arms, burnt shoulders, and large-brimmed hats.

Anyone in a uniform made me turn sideways. Ever since I'd come out, I was more on edge in crowds, and for some reason I hadn't remembered that when I agreed to work here. Then again, maybe it wasn't because I came out. Maybe it was because I was older now, not a cute androgynous kid but a teenager with mixed-gender signals laser-projecting out of me, inspiring those what-are-you boomer glares. I'd gotten good at giving the look right back, but it didn't make me feel better.

At the pearl-diving house, I climbed the stairs and ducked under the balcony, crossing the pool deck to change behind the paper screen.

"I have something for you, queer-o," Mrs. Cheng said, bringing out a diver's vest and looping my arms through it. She let me zip up the front and my chest deflated by solid inches. I moved things around until it felt more comfortable, wincing at my sore rib spot. "Your binder doesn't fit right," she diagnosed.

"What?"

"Your binder. It's probably too small."

"What's a binder?"

"Oh, baby." She closed her eyes and seemed to count. Had I said something wrong? "We'll get to that. For now, this should help your confidence in the tank. How's the hand?"

I clenched it and opened it. The water-tight bandage was shiny.

Mrs. Cheng went to help the Madisons with their diving belts, and I stepped around the paper screen. Catherine had been on for a few hours already and was lounging on one of the chaises we used for breaks. I walked over, stretching my arms behind my head. It still felt odd to be walking over to talk with Catherine after we'd ignored each other all swim season.

"You got a vest," Catherine pointed out. Her own cleavage was a thousand miles long, but she seemed into it. She was texting, probably to her long-term, military-schooled boyfriend, Anders.

"Mrs. Cheng took pity on me."

"She's the best supervisor I've ever had. Hey." Catherine motioned for me to stretch my lower half. "It's more leg work. A complete inverse of our training. It might give us an advantage on the team for senior swim. Also, yes, Mrs. Cheng is the shit. I saw her wife drop her off this morning. They hugged goodbye as if they actually appreciate each other. Maybe love wasn't invented by greeting card companies."

My imagination locked on Catherine's words. I could see every frame of that story. And now I needed to know what a binder was and how the stable queers kept finding me. "So that's why she loves calling me queer-o. She is a queer-o."

Catherine went into a zenlike state, her phone balanced on her knee.

"Can I borrow your phone?" I asked. Forgotten relief trickled through me as she handed it over. Catherine had let me borrow her phone—and therefore her unmonitored search engine—countless times in our day. I'd missed this minor freedom a lot. Although a quick search for "binder" brought up too much about the three-ring variety and something about transgender people, which couldn't be right. Perhaps this was just another queer shorthand I'd been walled off from.

While licking my goggles to keep them from fogging, I watched families gather around the glass wall of the pool below. This was a quiet spot in the park. No rides or games or decadent fast food. Here were benches for nursing parents and space to let the two-year-old out of the stroller for a spell. I made eye contact with a kid in shorts and a T-shirt, no gender signifiers whatsoever. They waved at me. I waved back.

I was jealous of their ease and happiness. Clearly no one had told them they had to pick a side yet. Maybe they'd get lucky and no one ever would.

By the first official minute of my one o'clock shift, I used the newly empty pool to do a small, showy salute and a pike, coming up to cheers.

Mrs. Cheng squatted at the edge of the pool, and I swam over. "Was that *flirting*? That looked like flirting."

"Yeah, but I was flirting with all of them. That's got to be the right move."

She patted my head, and I felt good. Real good. Every time I saw Mrs. Cheng, I liked her more. When she talked, she seemed to be telling the truth. Or maybe I just believed what she said. I couldn't say for sure; it was such a new feeling.

I had that warm hum again. This summer might be better than the previous ones. That's what I imagined while I dove for oysters and waved at families through the glass and beat my legs like a tail until my abs turned to putty. I'd heard that at the end of the first day, the employees closed the park and ran around mad before they left. I was going to the tide pool so Indy couldn't miss me. Which means, I was seeing her . . . tonight.

"What's that smile?" Catherine asked. "It's creepy."

I clung to one of the floating buckets, hearing Coach Kerrig scream, *Get off the lane lines,* in the back of my head. "Catherine, what does it say about me that when I smile, I make people suspicious?"

Catherine scowled. "I'll have to think on it. The answer isn't immediate."

"I look forward to the full report."

We'd been at it for hours, and we were all getting groany. The Madisons had been diving like sleepy frogs since dinner break, but almost all the visitors had gone home or to one of the evening shows.

Mrs. Cheng bopped the small bell that signified there were people down below, waiting for a diver. "One of the Madisons, your turn!"

The Holy Trinity debated among themselves, and the oldest one, who was starting at OSU in the fall, stood up on the edge and dove in. She had been mother-henning the other two, who were both sophomores, and in my opinion too young to be working their cleavage for tips.

Catherine floated on her back. "Hey, if you're not with Taylor anymore, can we hang out again?"

"You want to hang out with me even though I dropped you for my girlfriend?"

"Not really, but I don't have many other options. Also, we have like six years as friends, and you only dated her for over a year. I win. It's just math."

"You do. But what . . ." My question disappeared as the elder Madison shot out of the water, climbing the edge with record speed to duck behind the paper screen. "What the f—"

Mrs. Cheng zipped over, and Catherine and I made eye contact at the sound of sudden tears. Big, ugly tears.

"I'm going to go look." I flipped around in the water and kicked hard to get deep. At first, I saw nothing but the dark blue tank through the black, beady goggles. I moved toward the wall until I saw someone on the other side, pressed to the glass. Dark outlines of clothes . . . and a pale squashed dick.

And the worst part was that I somehow knew this exact dick.

I shot up as fast as Madison, scrambling on the edge, while Catherine called out, "What is it?"

"Fucking Dweiller! Well, we're not at school for once, and I'm kicking his ass."

I reached the balcony, but Mrs. Cheng caught my arm. "You'll get fired. No matter what he did, if you hit him, you will be fired. And he'll probably get off clean. I called security. They'll be here in a few minutes."

Madison cried harder behind the paper screen.

"In a few minutes, he'll be in the ball pit with all the little kids." I yanked away and struck down the stairs, wet and furious. Dweiller had seen me coming and was trying to taunt me while he ran. But he wasn't faster than me. Not even barefoot.

I took him down by the back of the shirt before one of the pop-up souvenir shops. I threw him into a bin full of stuffed jellyfish as big as five-year-olds. He hollered, but I pressed him down, beneath the stingers and incandescent streamers. My own personal swarm.

I pinned him with my knee. "Seems like me and your dick are coming full circle. Wasn't this the problem that started all the problems? You show me your dick against my will. I'm eleven, so I throw up. And you tell everyone I'm a dyke. You beat me with the word until I can't hear my own name. Sound familiar?"

"You're crazy!" he yelped. "You're a psycho! HELP!" He sounded like a small child being torn open. *"Help me, someone!"*

I let him go and backed away. He stood up on the mountain of stuffed jellyfish and sneered. "Those're actually nice tits when they're all smashed on me."

I hit him like a linebacker, took him straight to the pavement. He howled like I'd hurt him, but it was all part of his show. Mike Dweiller was only good at two things: being a sociopathic pervert and getting away with it. Right now he was trying to win the gathering crowd, and it was most likely working. I'd watched him do it for years at school. On sports teams. Not to mention the collective trauma of sixth-grade camp.

I flipped him on his front and twisted his arm behind his back. "Say you're a predator. Admit it." When he refused, I pressed his arm higher, twisted. "Say it!"

"I'm a predator."

"Louder."

"I'm a predator!" he screamed. I let him go, and I wasn't prepared to feel sorry. He cowered, not a boy, but a creature of slime and white male privilege, unchecked for so long he might as well be Gollum. So many people were watching. Dozens. Maybe a hundred. And I was still dripping wet. Security streamed toward me from every direction, gray uniforms closing in, and I ran.

In my defense, I didn't go straight to Indy. I didn't go to Indy at all.

My brain, drunk on adrenaline, drove me to the employee parking lot. I squatted between the cars to keep from being seen, my bare legs sticking together. When I reached the row where my car was parked, I remembered that my keys were back in my tracksuit by the pearl-diving pool. The doors were locked, and I swore feverishly, looking around for anyone, finding no one. A balloon popped nearby, and I scurried to Indy's silver-purplish car. I lifted the handle, surprised and relieved to find it open, and crawled inside with a thankful groan. My teeth wouldn't unclench, and I pinned the tight balls of my fists against my eye sockets. What came out of me next wasn't language but pure feral agony.

And then I screamed for real because the driver's-side door whipped open. "Oh, thank god it's you."

Indy leaned in, looked around. "And who else did you think would be getting in my car? Besides you, apparently."

"Security guards," I muttered. "I got in a fight. I'm hiding out. Sorry—"

"I heard it all on my radio. Word is you pounded the notorious Sea-Planet pervert." Indy whistled and slung butt into the driver's seat. She popped the chair back with ease and looked over at me from the side. "Fights means fired around here. No matter who you hit."

"Yeah."

"Do you need your overly dramatic fix before you go? The shark tank is on the other side of the park, but I bet you could make a real splash in the walrus pit."

I started to laugh, and then I was hyperventilating. Indy helped me unzip the vest, exposing most of me to all of her. "Don't look."

"I wouldn't."

A hiccup broke free, and I stuffed it down so hard I sounded like I was choking. I tried to speak, but the swell of my chest got in the way, and now I couldn't see anything. "Do you have a shirt or something?"

Indy reached into the back seat and tossed forward a hoodie. It was mammothly oversized and velvety soft. I marveled at it before stuttering out a few words. "Tell me this isn't your boyfriend's."

"It isn't my boyfriend's. Sometimes I'm masc. This seems to be a hard concept for you . . . which is odd. But then I bet you still think about me with locked she/her pronouns."

My face answered for me, and Indy's expression countered with disappointment. How could I be daydreaming of being with someone like this? We didn't know each other. Was that the thrill of it? Because she . . . they . . . were a stranger? My chest distracted me, refusing to be kept down by my arms.

"Bad dysphoria?" Indy asked, a cooler tone this time.

"I don't know what that is."

"Body dysphoria. When your body makes you feel the opposite of euphoria." Indy nodded encouragingly, and I squinted. "It's like a painful disappearing inside your skin."

Huh.

"My therapist said it's depression from feeling ostracized as a lesb . . . queer person."

"Dysphoria and depression are cousins, for sure. But they're also different."

"Are you saying I've been getting therapy in the wrong direction? Awesome. Great. Love it." I covered my face with my hands. "I don't have energy for this. My mom is going to kill me when she hears I got fired."

Indy reached for my shoulder but stopped a few inches away. I looked at the place where we were not quite touching.

"You can touch me." But I sounded unsure, even to myself.

Indy withdrew. "I don't really want to."

I sank so much deeper at those words. That was the piece of Indy I couldn't seem to hold on to. I could imagine being with her, kissing her, having kids with her (?), but I couldn't seem to remember that I was her bully once upon a time. *Their* bully.

"Because I'm your Dweiller."

"I wouldn't say that. You're just . . . at war with the entire world. You have been ever since I met you." Indy gave me an apologetic smile. "I think there's something enormous going on inside, but my experience was different. There were no closets for me. I never came out because no one ever put me in. I don't have internalized homophobia."

"You're saying I do?" I didn't know what that was either, but this one I didn't want to know. "Just add it to the pile. I'm anxious and depressed, and apparently, I disappear inside my own skin like some kind of homophobic homo. Yeah, right. I'm afraid of myself."

Something cracked so hard in my chest that it reached my face. If I moved, I would start crying. I didn't move.

Indy tried a smile. "Who taught you how to talk queer? I'm over here mentally preparing myself for the moment you refer to 'the Gays.'"

I laughed with surprise, tipping the balance from tears. I started to catch up to my breath, cleaning my face with my knuckles. "I don't know anything. Taylor swore lesbians are women who love women and flannel and Docs and Indigo Girls."

Indy blinked hard, exhaled harder. "Those are stereotypes, not *laws*. And they're way dated. Like nineties dated. You don't even need to be a woman to identify as a lesbian anymore, not that a person ever should have had to. Gods, I loathe identity policing."

"Yeah, well, it *felt* wrong, but how am I supposed to know any differently?" I could hear the desperation in my voice. The raw, lonely begging.

"There's this thing called the internet, and—"

"And my mom guards my browser history like a dragon." Now Indy looked really sorry for me. "What's a binder?" I blurted.

Indy reached in the back, rummaging through a clothes pile to pull out a thick elastic tube top fastened by industrial Velcro. "This is a binder. It flattens your chest."

"That's for trans people. I'm not trans."

My voice was very loud in the small car.

Indy held out a hand as if needing to calm me down before continuing. "It's for humans. Trans people, sure, but also nonbinary folk of all sorts. I mean, a lot of cis people wear them too. Athletes. Actors. Literally any human who needs it."

So I could get one and tell people it was about sports when they inevitably required an explanation about it. Well, shit. That could work.

"Where do you get one?"

"In Ohio? Only online. I got this in San Francisco. My grandparents live there. They have these amazing queer shops that . . ." Indy trailed off, staring at my face. I wondered what she saw there, but I didn't want to know. "Honestly I'd give you this one if I thought it would fit. If it's too small, it can mess you up."

Of course it wouldn't fit. Indy was nearly as muscular as me, but completely flat chested. Or maybe that was because she . . . they . . . were wearing one of these contraptions. I couldn't even tell. Could it be that easy to feel better?

I held the aching spot on my side where my rib felt like a stress fracture. "Can wearing too many sports bras hurt you too?"

"How many do you wear?"

As many as I need.

My eye caught movement in the sideview mirror. Sims and a security guard walked through the parking lot, hunting me. No doubt they'd used the cameras. I thought about asking Indy to drive away, but SeaPlanet knew where I lived.

Sims and his companion turned down our row of cars, beckoning me to get out.

"Time to spend hours in the park manager's office. Again. Wish I had pants."

Indy tossed me a pair of basketball shorts. "You said, 'Let me out.' "

I pulled on the soft mesh nylon, grateful. "What?"

"That's what you said after the shark tank. *'Let me out, let me out, let me out.'* I've never heard anything so sad in my life. Every time I hear 'Under Pressure' I think of you."

The security guard tapped the glass next to my face with the butt of a flashlight.

"Any advice on how to get out?" My heart pounded. "I fucked it up the first time."

"Sure." Indy sighed, and I'd never wanted to feel so close to someone before. To lean in, and not just with my body but the stormy soul that came with it. "My mom says, 'Don't fight the dinosaurs. Not one piece of who you are is about them.' "

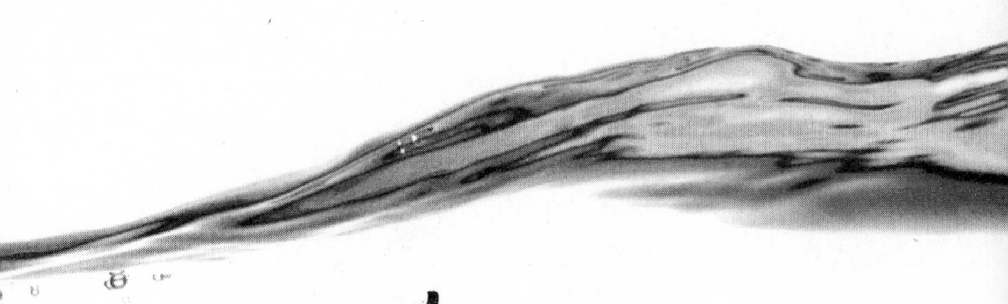

seahorses

Seahorses have the adaptive superpowers of a chameleon. They often live near intertidal zones or other shallow habitats. In captivity, seahorses survive about a fourth of their expected lifespan, dying from the distress of loneliness—and that's because they're a deeply monogamous species.

In the wild, mated-for-life couples dance together every morning, tails entwined, changing colors. After the female impregnates the male, daddy seahorses give birth a few weeks later to nearly two thousand babies.

About ten will survive to find their own forever mates.

— 10 —

OCTOBER BROUGHT OUT THE BEST AND WORST in Haley. Orange and black suited Ohio. Hay bales and scarecrows and skeletons seemed at home among the burnt foliage.

I kicked at a pile of yellow leaves, waiting for Everett at the end of the driveway. Like all the seventeen-year-olds who'd come before me, I was about to go on one of those patented life-changing weekends where a high schooler tastes undergrad-flavored freedom. (It's mostly Natty Light and Sonic Tots.)

Or at least, that's how Everett had advertised it when he called and invited me on his road trip to Ohio University for Halloween. Senior swim started the next week, so it was good timing. There would be no underage drinking once I began training; this was the season that mattered. Senior year marked a solid decade of competitive swimming, and I would care about each race, I swore it. I'd care so much Kerrig would have to be nice to me.

One of the neighbor kids rode by on a bike. He took one look at me and drew a plastic, Sharpied-black gun from the holster on his boot. I drew the blaster at my hip and returned fire. Always fun to pretend to shoot at someone for no reason.

Told you: the best *and* worst.

I sat on one of the decorative rocks by the end of the driveway, hoping for a mom-free getaway but knowing that wasn't likely.

Where are you? I texted Everett.

Here, he replied just as a silver SUV turned down our street. I gathered my backpack, but I wasn't quick enough. I heard the front door open and shut. Mom's fast feet pattered down the walkway while Karina parked in the drive.

Kylo Everett jumped out of the passenger seat, his cape billowing. He snapped open his red, cross-handled lightsaber and whirled about, ending in a fearsome pose. I slow-clapped.

Mom seemed determined to find the right words before responding. "Well, it looks . . . official. Was it expensive? Disney items are always so ridiculously priced."

Kylo took off his helmet. "Karina made it for me." My brother looked down at his costume as if she'd given him the gift of a lifetime. "She's a skilled cosplayer."

Our mother looked confused, so I supplied, "That's a person who makes an art form out of dressing up like—"

"I know how to use a search engine, thank you," she said, highlighting the other reason I needed to get away for the weekend. Mom was very much done with me; the feeling was mutual.

Everett pushed ahead. "She's made the best Rey costume I've ever seen. We're going to Comic-Con next summer. Karina has an in."

Mom took this as her cue to scurry around the SUV and talk to Karina. I watched the poor girl valiantly try to shake my mom's hand before getting half tugged out the rolled down window for a forced embrace.

"You'd think she'd get the hint," I muttered. "If she doesn't get out of the car, she doesn't want a hug."

Everett tossed my bag in the trunk and squinted at my silver-fox wig. "What is this? You're supposed to be my Han Solo."

"I am. You didn't specify which Han Solo."

"Everyone always means *New Hope* Han, Bake. Also. *Force Awakens* Han is not as recognizable, you know."

I gave him my best look of mock horror, opening up my brown

leather jacket to reveal the hole I'd burnt through the chest of my shirt, setting off the smoke alarm in the process. "But I'm ghost Han."

"You're *dead* Han," my brother deadpanned. His face suddenly lit up, and he mock thrust his lightsaber through my chest, which I could barely feel because my binder was basically a bulletproof vest. "Yes, that's going to be the perfect joke."

Mom came around the SUV and gave me a hug, kissing both of my cheeks. And both of Everett's too. I never doubted that she loved me. She was so good at that, but I rarely felt like she liked me. Rarely? Never was possibly more accurate.

High above our family scene, the oak tree dropped red leaves while the twinkling, disembodied melody of "It's a Small World" drifted down as if on cue.

"No way," Everett said, tilting his head to look straight up, to search for the stuffed orca.

After our first trip to SeaPlanet—when I was seven and Everett was ten—we'd come home with stuffed sea creatures that played said song when squeezed. Everett had tossed his high into the oak, wedging it in the fork of two branches.

Ten years later, the killer whale still crooned in the right wind.

"That's so creepy!" Mom shouted, covering her ears. "Be safe. *No* drinking!" She shot inside, and I watched Everett look at the house. Dad wasn't home. I knew that look. To go in, or not? I had that look on my face every single day I came home from school.

A young, pale brown person stuck their head out the SUV back door.

"Is that tree singing 'It's a Small World'?" he asked. No, *they* did. I was getting better at not assuming gender. Sort of. I was trying anyway.

"It's not the tree. It's a small stuffed orca Everett threw into the tree a decade ago."

"Whales in trees," the newcomer pondered. "That sounds like the Midwest in a nutshell."

"Harvey spent his first year at Miami gathering intel on Ohio life. His blog series is taking off! *Hashtag: Behind the White Curtain.*" Everett climbed in the passenger seat, and I hauled butt in the back, officially meeting my seat partner for the three-hour drive.

"Not that I'm judging Ohio. I'm from Jersey." Harvey was dressed as C-3PO in that he wore a T-shirt that looked like the protocol droid's chest.

I cocked my head. "Doesn't everyone hate where they're from?"

"I don't hate Jersey. I just love its many, many faults."

"Huh," I said. "I definitely don't love Ohio's faults." We pulled away, and Mom waved goodbye from the front window. She'd be alone all weekend, and I wondered if it would be a welcome aloneness. My mom did have a tree-falling-in-the-woods type energy. If no one was around to hear it, was she still detailing the world's potential pitfalls?

Harvey looked from me to my brother. "You're more white-passing than Everett."

I'd heard sentences like this before, but normally the way the person said it was . . . gross. Like a compliment. Harvey didn't say it like that, at least, but I still didn't know how to reply.

"I'm . . . white. Everett isn't."

He laughed, then paused. "Oh, you believe that. Sorry."

I couldn't tell if he was apologizing for saying what he said or that I believed what I did. Maybe both.

"Go easy, Harv," my brother tried. "We weren't raised to talk about skin, remember?"

Harvey had a professorial air that wasn't threatening and yet still pushed at me. "Sounds like an ideal breeding ground for colorism." He stared at me until I shrugged. It was true; I didn't know how to talk about this, and I was not allowed to practice.

We left Park View, and my shoulders let go a little. Everett turned the music down and rolled his head back toward me. His hair was even shorter than last time I'd seen it, and I wondered if I'd look like him if I had less than six years' worth of bleached hair piled under my Han wig. "You can de-costume for the drive."

I looked down at my killer leather jacket, men's pants, and boots. "I'm perfectly comfortable."

"Even with the wig?" Karina, who really was a tremendous Rey due to her naturally slim build, straight brown hair, and white skin, added, "I can't stand a wig. I cosplay around them."

"You know I need you to be my Moira Rose someday," my brother pleaded. "As soon as I get Johnny's blue suit."

"Yes, well, *Schitt's Creek* is an obvious exception."

"God, I love you." He swung back to face me. Possibly because my brother had just dropped the first L-bomb I'd ever heard out of him. "I still can't believe Mom let you come."

I could explain that one. "She thinks you two are kindergarteners because you don't have sex, and that we're going to eat candy and wander around campus in costume like huge nerds."

"We are going to do that," Karina said.

"Just with *a lot* of booze," Everett added. C-3PO Harvey toasted with a flip flask that bore the symbol of the Rebel Alliance. "Did she make you promise not to drink? She always did that to me back in high school."

"She did. I swore I wouldn't."

My brother whistled. "How do you lie to her so well?"

"Easy. She's always lying to me." I turned toward the window. The trees were in perfect citrus flux, all blood orange and tangerine. Haley looked nice for once, probably because I was leaving it behind.

We stopped at the eternally long light beside the entrance to Sea-Planet, which was covered with spiderwebs, ghostly projections, and ghoulish jack-o'-lanterns. The autumn festival was in full swing, the very last weekend of the season. No doubt Indy was working there now, teaching all the little kids about how the tide comes in as well as out. I put a hand flat on my heart, on the binder that had appeared in my hands, a gift from Indy couriered through Catherine.

"Wait! This is the SeaPlanet town? You didn't tell me that!" Harvey's enthusiasm hummed. "Can we just . . . Could we swing through?"

No, please.

"Some other time. Maybe." Everett played with the stereo. "Jake, tell Harvey about your hot day in SeaPlanet's employ." I was honestly surprised he hadn't asked me to recount my dive into the shark tank, but maybe that was officially old news. That was almost two years ago.

"Who's Jake?" Harvey asked.

"He means me. When he was little, he would only say versions of my name to drive Mom mad. Bake, Make, Jake . . . Drake. Fake when he's mad."

"My favorite is Cake, but it's not for every occasion."

"Everyone at school calls me McIntyre," I volunteered, a rumor I was perpetuating myself with startling success.

"Should I call you McIntyre?" Karina made eye contact with me in the rearview mirror. She could see me. It wasn't such an impossible feeling once you knew how to look for it, and I'd been searching it out since that day in Indy's car, a season that was also a lifetime ago.

"McIntyre's good. Thanks."

"But tonight you're Han," Everett cut in, rather seriously.

"That's Dad to you, Ben."

Everett bounced his hands off the dashboard and legit howled. "This is everything I ever wanted! Halloween at OU with a pack of fanboys."

"Try fanbies. More gender inclusive," Karina said.

We were still at the light, and I tried not to stare down the wooded drive. I hadn't been back since my fight with Dweiller. I might never go back; I didn't know how I felt about that.

"Did someone really get eaten in the orca tank?"

"Yes," I said while Everett said, "Urban legend. No one knows what really happened."

The light finally turned green, and Karina hit the gas. Harvey nearly twisted himself into a pretzel to catch every view of SeaPlanet from the road, which wasn't much beyond a delicate landscape of greenery meant to camouflage the high, electric fences. I turned too, wondering if I could see anything, catching a glimpse of the top of the "Japanese House."

"You worked at SeaPlanet for only one day?" he asked. "What happened?"

I leaned back and thought for a moment; Everett couldn't wait. "Beat the pulp out of the town pervert in front of like a hundred people. Fired on the spot." It was a pretty good summary even if I'd only punched Dweiller once. Mostly I'd screamed at him, but those shouts had felt as good as punches because I knew he'd keep them longer than bruises.

Fired on the spot. That was more of a stretch. After Indy's car, I'd found myself in three days straight of meetings with park officials to determine what happened, who was to blame, and if my actions were justified. In the end, Dweiller had gotten barred from SeaPlanet for life, and I was dismissed. The park refused to contact the city police out of fear of bad publicity, so Dweiller had taken his show elsewhere. That had been the hardest part to accept. This place was always going to come down on people like me with the force of a hammer, whereas people like Dweiller only got sighed at.

After the incident wrapped, I'd returned the clothes I'd borrowed from Indy via Catherine, my phone number curled up in the pocket of the basketball shorts. Which was a dead end. Maybe Indy washed them and never found the note. Maybe Indy found the note and threw it away. I had to admit I'd spent a lot of time searching for Indy on social media and found nothing. They either had a veiled screen name or didn't spend their time online.

Or they'd blocked me.

The binder seemed to be the only thing they were willing to give me. Which was fair.

At least it hadn't been a lonely summer. I got a surprise phone call from Mrs. Cheng the day after SeaPlanet let me go. She asked if I wanted to join the landscaping crew for her homeowner's association. And that's how I'd gotten some new muscles and my first touch of my family's brown skin by spending every day sweating, mowing, and weeding. Between that and the binder, I'd regrown some of the confidence that had evaporated when I'd come out.

Even though my summer glow had faded, I still went to the Chengs' once a week to watch TV on their exceedingly comfy sofa and eat snacks and not hold my breath through my mom's negativity waterboarding. The fight and firing had been bad, but a few weeks ago, I'd declared that I wouldn't see the biased therapist anymore. That did not go over well, not even when I mentioned that Henrietta Churchiness had definitely misdiagnosed me.

Unlike the first time I'd run headlong into Indy, that second round left me calmer. Or maybe just spending time with the Chengs changed things. With Catherine's assistance (and search engine), I'd looked up those terms Indy had spoken in their car, and the right words did that thing right words always do: create a sense of communion. Body dysphoria had to be where all my anxiety came from, my disconnect. And internalized homophobia . . . pretty sure that was the well of my endless depression. And anger. Odd how naming the madness eased it.

And yet, I wished for one more run-in with Indy. To say *thank you* for once instead of *I'm sorry*. To prove that I was more than chaos and misery.

All Hallows' Eve was hopping when we reached our destination, the right butt cheek of Ohio, tucked in the armpit of West Virginia. Brilliant foliage had lined our entire journey, ending with the grand finale of a redbrick campus covered in drunken, costumed college students.

Karina had filled us all in on the drive. She'd been enrolled at OU for half a year, before transferring to Miami U, to be closer to her mother's "multiplying nerves." The so-called haunted city called Athens housed Ohio University, as well as five cemeteries that created a pentagram around the campus, a crumbling Victorian asylum . . . and a few million ghost stories from tripping undergrads.

Karina paid to park in someone's driveway, which was shockingly necessary as every side street and parking lot was stuffed with cars. Harvey took note of the costumes and the fall air and the sounds of drunken mistakes rushing through it all.

"Harvey's a filmmaker." Everett adjusted his Kylo helmet. "He notices everything."

"Where's this asylum?" Harvey asked. "I need to experience it."

"The Ridges is across the river, up on the hill. We are *not* going there tonight." Karina shook her head at Harvey. "Too many cops."

"The Ridges?" I asked. Even the name prickled through me. "How very Stephen King."

Harvey pointed at me. "See? Those are the kind of faults you fall for, kid."

"Kid? You're, like, two years older than me."

Harvey pulled on some gold pants over his shorts, which I recognized as Everett's novelty droid sweatpants. "We get older faster in Jersey. After two months in Ohio, my chief observation is that you all mature incredibly late. I think it's because you're not allowed to fail around here." He looked down with disgust. "And you still wear sweatpants. You all have heard of joggers, right?"

"They itch my ankles." Everett plopped on his Kylo helmet and did a few warm-ups, lightsaber nearly taking out a group of slutty drag nurses on the street corner.

"Everett should not be any part of your study. He's special," I said, laughing at my big brother. "He's going to be this way forever."

At least, I hoped so.

We walked down the main street, passing restaurants, bars, and more bars. In front of each and every one was a line thirty people long, drunk people hollering. I'd come for Everett and to get away from home. I had not come to turn into a fall-down seventeen-year-old. When Harvey's flask came around, I sipped from it.

"I'm starting to see why this place is the party school." I played with my blaster.

"This is nothing." Karina took in the scene. "Tonight will be *bonkers*. This whole street will shut down, filled with thousands of dancing, dressed-up people."

"Can someone explain what's so great about Halloween at Ohio University?" Harvey asked. "Ever since I got to Miami, people have been like 'Fuck OU . . . unless it's Halloween.' "

Karina was ready. "Okay, so there are three ranking parties in this country: New Year's Eve at Times Square, Mardi Gras in New Orleans . . . and Halloween at Ohio University."

"You're kidding."

"Nope. They shut down with the influx of people. It's also one of the top party schools in the nation. Number one in 2015, according to *Playboy*."

"I hear the drunk people get put in the city's empty swimming pool. Imagine getting arrested for public intoxication and waking up at the bottom of an empty pool." Everett narrowed his Lebanese-green eyes on me. "Don't end up in the literal drunk tank, Bake."

"And why am I specifically getting this warning?"

"You know why."

That was probably fair. I did make horrible decisions when push came to shove.

Karina looped an arm through Everett's. "Come on. Britta's house is down this block."

"Who's Britta?" I asked.

Everett, who had de-helmeted and *not* simply pretended to sip from the flask, spoke loudly. "Britta is Karina's ex. In the spirit of full disclosure, I'm not jealous. Or worried about this arrangement."

"That's right, Kylo," Harvey said. "Keep shoving down those feelings. We're going to find you in the bathroom smashing your helmet and scaring the stormtroopers."

I put a hand on my brother's shoulder. "He's fine. Because he *loves* Karina."

Everett whistled. "Three hours, Fake! It took three whole hours for you to tease me about that. That's a record for you."

"What can I say? I'm maturing." Something pounded happily in my chest as my brother's girlfriend tugged him closer and nudged his cheek with her nose.

Harvey took a picture of them with his phone. "There really is nothing better than two nerds in love."

Britta's house looked like Greek life housing on the outside, but it held some secrets. Like, it was big enough for twenty people to live in, each with their own rooms, and the place was only rented to LGBTQ+ folks. The glittered, oversized letters in the living room proclaimed the place to be RAINBOW HAVEN, which reminded me of jellyfish. And Indy.

Britta, who had her own girlfriend and didn't appear remotely interested in Karina or threatened by Everett, was dressed as Dr. Jillian Holtzmann from *Ghostbusters*. She beckoned us into the party and gave us the necessary pointers about drinks and bathrooms. Introductions happened while I took in the cavernous living room, where dozens of rainbow flags had been hung—so many different pride flags that I felt blinded and awkward.

The feeling was magnified by the room bursting full of queer, confident people.

A bowl of buttons went around our small circle, and I wasn't paying attention, so Everett plucked out one and handed it to me. A pronoun button. *She/her*. I stared at it so hard that it felt hot in my palm.

"You don't have to wear it, if it makes you uncomfortable." Britta smiled at me. "Also, who the hell are you?"

What a complicated question. I looked down at my costume. "Who am I dressed as or who am I in general?"

"Obviously, this is dead Han Solo, my estranged father." Everett was drunk already. When did that happen? "But also this is Cake."

"*McIntyre*," Karina said, stepping in, making it all better until she abruptly stopped making it better. "Senior in high school. So we have some underage energy here, if you know what I'm saying."

Britta nodded, her tall Holtzmann hair flopping. "My little brother is here with his on-again, off-again partner. Indigo is your age . . . which must explain your *very odd* similarities."

"Indigo. Sweet name," Karina said, bustling her hips to the house music, the theme song to *The X-Files*.

Britta looked over the crowd and yelled in the tenor of mead, "Hey, Chauncey! Where's Indy?"

My head snapped away from the flags, the buttons, my pulse triggered. I saw Chauncey first: a tall, skinny, effeminate blond. He sat on the overstuffed couch, licking his own thumb as if he'd just eaten something gooey but delicious. Also, he was dressed as Harley Quinn, and it was very much working for him.

Deep down, I knew this Indy couldn't be my Indy. That would be too coincidental. Not even when a short, buff person materialized from beneath the arm of the willowy pretty boy. Oh, right. *Indy*. A miniature

Indiana Jones came toward me, dressed in full khaki with the whip and wide-brimmed hat. The hat was tipped down, covering their face while they did the dance of stepping over a million legs shoved around one coffee table. This person hadn't stopped at just Indy but added a silver fox wig nearly identical to mine, and also crow's feet. Huh, I should've thought about drawing the wrinkles on.

The person finally entered our tight circle in the foyer. They looked up. Why did everything have to be so shoulder to shoulder at these parties? It was too hot in here. The room might explode. And *my* Indy was looking at me like they did not recognize me.

They turned to Britta, a fleeting relief because Britta pointed at me, and yelled, "We have to get a pic of the two old-ass Harrison Fords!"

Indy was looking at my costume, not my face. But then they did look at me. "So, you're *dead* Han Solo. I like it, but wow. Dark."

And then—there. Right there. They scowled at me, jerked their head to the side.

"Fucking McIntyre?"

I wasn't ready for the hug that enveloped me. Indy was holding on to me, and now the entire room was taking pictures of the two old-ass Harrison Fords hugging on each other, particularly Chauncey, who started giving directions as if we were staging a photo shoot. But forget him, because two things. Two real, true things:

One, Indy was happy to see me.

Two, Indy was not remotely sober.

They let go and grabbed my lapels, giving me a shake.

I was laughing, I think. "Hey to you too."

"Chauncey, this is my shark tank." Indy shook their head and squeezed their eyes tight. "Ah, that stuff is so strong!" They turned to me, their face inches from mine. "I wanted to see you again. I told the stars we should meet up, but *not* at SeaPlanet. Hell no." Indy spoke slowly and curiously like a very stoned person.

I couldn't help being amused. "I'm your shark tank?"

"Oh, you know what you are." Their exceedingly flirty smile turned toward their partner. "This one knows exactly what they are. Watch out."

I had no choice. I did the Han Solo shrug. Blaster and all.

Everett burst out laughing. Karina and Britta looked amused but also stumped.

"Why aren't you at SeaPlanet?" I asked. "It's closing weekend."

"Believe it or not, I exist in places that aren't saturated in toxic teal."

I stepped forward, a little, and let myself imprint on how it felt when Indy looked at me. Like I was exactly myself. "Tell me, are you *Kingdom of the Crystal Skull* Indy? That's . . . bold."

Indy drew their whip and pointed it at my blaster. "I am Dr. Jones, retired archaeologist who is spending my last years making reparations and returning items to the cultures I've been stealing from."

Harvey bellowed a laugh that stopped all of us. He pulled out a tiny notepad and took notes at a furious pace. "This is gold! Pure white gold. Keep talking."

Indy looked confused all the sudden. They swayed on the spot.

Harley "Chauncey" Quinn draped an arm across Indy's chest like a seat belt. He was a thousand stories taller than both of us. "We're walking Court Street, Gogo. Ready?"

"Yeah." Indy turned all the way around and pushed between Everett and Karina, and out the front door. *Fast.* As if they were trying to get away from me.

Gogo?

Chauncey skated off next, and Britta followed, leaving me with Everett and Karina.

"Cakes, who *was* that?"

I wanted an excuse to follow them, but I had nothing. "That was the person who pulled me out of the closet. I mean, the shark tank. Jesus! I'm not even drinking yet."

Karina swooped an arm around me. "Let's fix that."

I couldn't say much about the next few hours. The house party raged. I waited for Indy to come back. I'm sure I did other things. Crossed rooms, climbed stairs, met humans, drank beers. The Halloween playlist looped, and I was listening to "Thriller" for the fifth time when I found Everett waging intense D&D in the living room before a wide audience. That's when Chauncey came sprinting in on socked feet, carrying his skates, running straight at me.

— 11 —

"INDY?" I peered under the dent in the branches. Beside the library, a line of boxy bushes created an alcove against the brick. I didn't want to think of how many people had ducked behind there to get busy. Of course, that was definitely not why Indy had crawled back there. "Indy? Chauncey said you asked for me . . . or should I call you Gogo?"

"I'll end you if you do." Indy's voice was shaky. They were hunched over themself, curled in a tight ball beneath the branches. I came closer, and they held up a hand to stop me. "I've puked. Don't breathe."

"It's a good thing I can hold my breath for over a minute."

"Flirting? Right now? Really?" Indy asked, the questions turning their voice solid again.

"Is Chauncey still out there?"

"Yep." Chauncey's existence in Indy's life turned me into a *yep* person. I wasn't proud.

"Tell him I'm done. I hate his terrible friends, and he's never to call me again. Or text me." They paused. "Tell him you're taking care of me for the rest of the night. I know I'm asking a lot, a fuck-ton, but you do owe me."

"Are you serious right now?"

Indy gave me a serious look. I ducked out of the bushes to where Harley Quinn was still gripping his skates to his chest. I recited the words I'd been given. His shoulders dropped, the heart on his cheek all smeared.

"I didn't know how strong they were!" he called into the bushes.

Indy didn't respond. "I have to drive them back to Haley tomorrow," he added to me.

"I'll get Indy home," I volunteered out of nowhere. "Promise."

"Sure. Have a great time. Just don't get too attached because Indy is always on their way out!" he shouted into the bushes. I didn't know what he meant, but it didn't seem like a throwaway line. He swore and crossed the street, slamming his skates in a wire trash bin.

The city was quieting down now that the bars were closed, but there were still enough drunk creeps around to keep my guard way up. Shouts cropped up from various blocks, echoing through the city. The streets were absolutely trashed. The night was beyond the reach of the moon, but the morning was going to come late.

I helped Indy crawl out. "We should find a place to eat. Sit down. Check your vitals."

"Oh gods, it was the dankest pumpkin bread. I'm going to be buzzing for days. He knows I can't stand strong edibles, and he *swore* it wasn't strong." This was not the Indy I knew. This was a complicated person in a complicated relationship that I had never once imagined when I daydreamed about my Indy. I liked them even more.

"Where are you sleeping?" they asked. "Hotel? Please say hotel. I'll be so nice if you find me some place to sleep that's soft."

I shook my head. "We couldn't book a room. Apparently, Halloween here means you have to plan your trip a year in advance. We're sleeping on the couches at Britta's house, if anyone ever vacates them. I should warn you, Everett can wage D&D for *days*."

"I was supposed to sleep in Chauncey's dorm." Their voice had a hollow quality that stirred up my protective instincts.

I glanced at the street vendor that had appeared when the crowds left the bars. "Look at that, the Burrito Buggy is still open. Let's get you something to eat that isn't radioactive. Afterward I might be able to get Karina's car keys." I bought Indy a bean burrito while they sat on the curb, holding their legs. I'd assumed they were a vegetarian—which caused me to get scolded and then made us both laugh. The kind of desperate laughter that comes with the revving down of alcohol and dank edibles in your veins.

"Wait, no. Explain." I wiped a tear from the corner of my eye. "How can assuming someone is a vegetarian be a microaggression?"

"Assuming lesbians are vegetarians is totally a microaggression."

"But you're no lesbian. As previously established and then confirmed with that"—I exhaled loudly—"incredibly attractive androgynous model of a boyfriend you've got."

"Partner. Ex-partner. He's a demiboy. And we are only good at sex and breaking up. But yeah, Chauncey is *beautiful.* And he's extremely aware of it at all times."

We walked back toward Britta's queer house slowly. I waited too long and my sentence came out of nowhere.

"I'm *also* not a lesbian." It was still a relief to say this aloud, not because I had anything against the identity, but because it was a relief not to falsely label myself.

"Last time I saw you, you were a mess about that one word." The same straightforward Indy came through, but their tone was more anxious as they rode their unfortunate high. "The words aren't supposed to fuck you up, you know. They're supposed to help."

"I'm learning." I hadn't said this aloud before, but I was ready. "I'm pan."

Indy smiled. "Pronouns?"

I let the answer to that be silence.

Indy didn't push. They offered a bite of their burrito, and I ate some. It was good, but it probably would have been amazing if I'd still been tipsy. "It would be better with meat," Indy said. "Because I like meat."

"Noted for next time."

And then there was an odd moment because *next time* implied that we weren't running into each other anymore; we were going to know each other. Starting now. My heart stumbled on that, and I wondered if Indy had any of the same feelings, but when I looked at them, they were intent upon their burrito.

We reached the queer campus house, and I could tell that not only was the party still going, but Chauncey and the rest of them were visible from the front window. I climbed the steps to the wraparound porch, peering about. "There's an old couch out here."

"*Couch,*" Indy crooned. They shot by me with a sudden burst of speed and threw themself across it. I sat on the balcony, my back to a support beam. "The sun will be up in a few hours. Karina has a spot in her back seat. We'll take you back to Haley, if you want."

Indy's eyes were closed, voice deadpan. "Oh no, then you'll know where I live."

"Yes. And I'm going to give you my phone number."

"I already have your number." Indy pulled out their phone, and moments later, my pocket hummed. I checked my phone and found many smiley faces wearing sunglasses, punctuated by a dozen rainbow flags.

I laughed, but then it sort of hit me that they had found my number, bothered to put it in their phone, but never messaged me. Not all summer. Also they'd sent me *flags*, which still meant something between us. "Indy, do you want to punch me? Right in the face?"

"Do I want to punch you?"

"For what happened in fourth. What I did."

They looked out across the dying night. "I don't want to hit you. I'm mostly sad for little you. I think you backassedly saved me from your fate of being so entrenched in anti-difference that you can hardly breathe."

That hurt more than a punch.

I shrugged off my dead Han Solo jacket. "If you change your mind. I've got a nose you're welcome to break."

"So weird." Indy cocked their head on the arm of the couch, taking me in more openly than they ever had before. "You know, you're going to be a hot old guy someday."

"Is this you being nice to me?" I asked.

"Maybe. You did find me a Chauncey-free place to sleep."

I smiled. "You give the oddest compliments. One time you told me I was the token bad boy. Now I'm your silver fox?"

"Flirting again. Always flirting. I don't date people I don't know, McIntyre. Chauncey and I were friends for half a year before I kissed him." Six months? I'd die. "Come here."

I crossed the porch to where they were sprawled across the deflated, old couch. Apart from lying down on top of them—an urge that rolled through me like a tsunami—I wasn't sure what to do or what they wanted.

Indy sat up and started pulling off their costume. Hat, whip, button-down khaki shirt. It was unseasonably warm this Halloween, and I was thankful for the tank top underneath. Chauncey's Harley Quinn costume was meant to show off his assets, but Indy's costume had buried their strong body.

"I've never seen you without the teal polo. Nice shoulders."

They looked down at their arms as if they'd forgotten about them. "They're getting smaller. I quit my gym right after my arm fractured in three places. Mom was so confused. She thought I loved it. I thought she loved that I did it."

"So, you're not a gymnast anymore?" I sat beside them.

They danced their arms and wrists, a move accompanied by joint pops. "Figured I should stop before every part of me made those sounds, but you want to know the most fucked-up part? I finished my coursework to graduate last spring, but I've still got to get a sports credit from my stupid elite homeschool program. Can you believe that? Ten years competing in gymnastics and somehow none of that counts toward my high school diploma." Indy turned their face into my shoulder, surprising me with the sudden affection. "I swear I'm going to go play forty hours at the indoor mini golf course, just to give the program the middle finger."

They tugged off the silver wig, revealing a completely shaved head, which I hadn't seen since the shark tank. Indy's head was perfectly round up close. I longed to run my hands over it. They caught me ogling and laughed. "You're really attracted to me. It's nice."

"Nice for you? It's nice for me," I managed. I took off my costume a piece at a time. My hair came down like an avalanche of straw when I removed the wig, twisting past my shoulders, dry and yellow. Indy picked up a piece of my hair and inspected it. "Death by pool chemicals," I explained. "Swim team starts next week. How about you join the team for your credit?"

"Can't swim. I can only tread water." Indy wrinkled their nose at me. "Did you know that *blond* is one of the only gendered adjectives in the English language? Blonde with an *e*? Feminine. Blond without an *e*? Hunky man. Complete bullshit!"

A drunk abruptly ran across the street at the sound of Indy's shout. "You better run!" they added. "I'm coming for your gender binary!"

"My hair is black," I admitted. "I was light-haired as a kid. My mom prefers I dye it." I tied it back in a messy knot. "Light hair is currency in her world."

"Ew."

I cringed. My mom's views on things were racist, and yet my family let it happen. I felt as guilty for letting her dye my hair as for letting her believe that light hair and skin were coinage. That being a heterosexual, cisgendered person was normal, and that everything else was . . . not. Then again, she lived in that world; she didn't create it. My voice came out gruff. "So, are you calling me blond with an *e* or without?"

"The word shouldn't be gendered at all. But then if we change it, if we adopt the word without the *e*, we're leaning into the patriarchy, painting with a masculine brush. And if we adopt the word with it, we risk feminizing being fair-haired. Both of which are unacceptable." Holy shit, Indy's brain was fast. Even on dank pumpkin bread. "If you make me choose, you clearly have no *e*. But Chauncey? Definitely an *e*. And if *I* bleached my hair? The word wouldn't work, no matter my daily presentation."

"Because you're nonbinary."

"Which you think is a joke."

"I don't." My words were cautious but still unsure of themselves. Indy seemed to be doing the same mental math. Were we about to hit an insurmountable wall? "I don't think it's a joke. I never did. I said that because I'd just spent an entire year in a relationship with someone who insisted a gender spectrum was unnecessarily . . . newfangled."

Indy crossed the porch in a leap. They stood up on the railing with surprising ease. "Sumeria, Babylon, Assyria. Those are some of the oldest human civilizations. The kalû, the gala, the assinnu. Those are different, documented nonbinary genders from those civilizations, literal thousands of years ago. Oh, not to forget the deity Ishtar, who was all about gender ambiguity and transformation. A whole-ass ancient god of not fitting into the system."

They did a cartwheel on the railing and landed softly at my feet. "Still sound newfangled? Or is being nonbinary older than the binary gender roles we're now forced to dismantle with our bare, bleeding hands? Singular they/them pronouns date back to the fourteenth century and were used by Chaucer, Shakespeare, Dickinson, and Jane Austen. But people don't like to hear that. Historical facts are so annoying when they ruin your contemporary bias."

I couldn't help squirming. Agreeing with everything they said was easy. Facing it, living it, was exquisitely hard. They noticed. They always noticed.

"But . . . you know who you are a bit more than last time, don't you? Is that your binder I spy under your Harrison aesthetic?" Their fingers prodded my shoulder, and I stood up, putting some distance between us. "Sorry," they said. "I didn't mean to—"

"I'm just trying to get my bearings. On where we are. Earlier today I was daydreaming of seeing you again, and now we're sitting around, and I don't know what's happening." I sat back down and muttered, *I'm okay,* and they acted like it hadn't happened. A tiny gift. "Thank you. For getting the binder for me." This was not remotely the gratitude I wanted to convey for the best present I had ever received.

"Fits okay? I had to really guess on size."

I nodded; it was all I had.

"Can I use your leg for a pillow? I can't put my face on that headrest. Gods know what has been done on this couch."

"I think so." I meant it, which was weird. I hadn't been able to sleep within a foot of Taylor those handfuls of nights we managed to arrange secret sleepovers. Then again, I didn't need to sleep tonight. I could just sit here and forgive God.

Indy spun on the sofa, always with that practiced body awareness. Their head rested on my thigh. "Hey, McIntyre, I think we're becoming friends."

"Yep."

— 12 —

"HOME," I hollered, shutting the door behind me. Mom came scurrying from the kitchen, which was issuing strong scents of browned lamb, cinnamon, and allspice. She nearly knocked me over pulling the front door back open. She looked out for my brother in time to watch Karina's SUV drive off. I shut the door again.

"*Hi, Mom.*"

"Please don't do that right now. I see you. You're here. You're always here. My son is the one who keeps swinging by without coming in the house."

For once I had to agree with her. "Okay."

She blinked at me, startled. "Okay, what?"

"Okay, you're right. He's avoiding you. That sucks."

"Why?"

This was a serious question. Which meant I had to dig around and find a tone inside my body that could possibly give a serious-type answer. Sarcasm rose in me like bubbles from the depths. "He's probably just . . . upset. Or embarrassed."

"Upset about what embarrassed about what?" she asked without pause. "I didn't handle it well when he"—she pulled out some actual finger quotes—"'came out' to me. It was so sudden, and I didn't even know about this new asexual business. It was so much easier when you came out. At least I was prepared. I'd had some years to get used to the concept."

I dropped my bag on my foot. "Are you implying you knew I was queer before I did?"

"When you were tiny, you had these . . . signs."

"And you ignored them?"

She started to speak and stopped herself. "There were years that I convinced myself you might actually like the boys you were hooking up with. I really hoped you did. If you didn't, that would be too sad." I touched the wall, thoughts spinning. "No matter what I say right now you're going to take it wrong," she added, almost as if to beat me to the punch.

"I had the best weekend," I said. "Thank you for asking."

"Oh, I'm sorry. I'm sorry!" Mom hugged onto me. "Watch a movie with me. *Sound of Music*? I got us each our own tub of hummus, and I made hushwee."

"You make that for me or to get Everett to come inside?"

She shot away and stopped in the kitchen doorway, wrestling with a look that might have been shame. "Everett doesn't want Karina to get to know me because he doesn't like her, and he's breaking up with her. *Or* because he loves her, and he doesn't want me to know about it."

I didn't have to answer; my silence proved something.

Her eyes welled. "You two should bring me your joys once in a while. Not just your miseries. I could use some joy too." Mom left, and most people would think we'd just got in a fight, but this was called Sunday at home. I went upstairs and closed the door to my bedroom.

Ordinarily I changed the second I entered. My space, my comfort. But I sat on the edge of my bed and thought about the filthy pants I'd worn two days straight. The ones Indy'd slept on. The Indy who'd spent the entire next day with me, apart from a two-hour exit interview with Chauncey. Ohio University had grown on me in that short span. For once we talked about lighter things. We had a lot of favorite music in common, and almost no movies.

I checked my phone. No messages. Which one of us would break first? The suspense was already killing me.

My phone rang with an unlisted number, and my nerves assumed it was Indy, even though they were now saved in my phone. My heart jolted while I hit answer.

"McIntyre," a familiar growl boomed. "What do you think of the plan?"

"Catherine? Why is your number locked?"

"I'm encrypting my calls, obviously. I meant Coach Kerrig's email. Did you read the email?" She was always so impatient. "Check it now. I'll wait."

I had a silent punchy tantrum at being sucked into the swim team's weird drama when I only wanted to sit here in my Indy-printed clothes. (Oh, shit, I was in trouble.) I opened my email, skimming it. What I found was . . . interesting. "Coach wants to start a dive team?"

"Every meet we miss out on those points because the other team has divers. I'm sick of it. Did you see the points Chagrin was able to score on us last season by having those clumsy divers? They don't have to be good; they just have to get up there and not get disqualified. It's automatic points. Who should we ask? Joss is a no-brainer. He can already dive so well. Gia?"

"Decidedly ungraceful," I said, mind whirring. "I could dive."

"You act like the block is a tilting iceberg in the middle of the Pacific circle. And that's *every* time you step on it. I can't imagine what you'd do on the high dive."

"Fine, but not George. He always false starts. Catherine?"

She did not enjoy the poise in my voice. "What? Just say it."

"Do you think homeschoolers could pad the team? Like how there's those two in marching band? And our quarterback. He is totally a homeschool ringer. He finished his coursework like three years ago and just trains nonstop with his nine siblings."

"You know a homeschool diver?"

"I know a homeschool former gymnast who could possibly be an excellent diver."

Catherine sighed hard. It nearly knocked me over. "But then I'll have to train Indigo. We can't afford a coach, so I already told Kerrig I'd shore up on the basics. I suppose she's a possibility. Get her to tryouts. This is your charge."

"How did you know I was talking about Indy? I never said anything about them."

"Apart from when you saw her and fell out of the closet, literally into a shark tank?"

"I really shouldn't have dove in the damn tank," I muttered.

"Apart from when she gave me a present for you? How about the time I returned an outfit of hers with no questions asked *and* your phone number in the pocket?"

"You sneak."

"You didn't tell me not to look. And what about when you were all over her Instagram, which was yesterday. Yes, apart from all those times, you've never said anything about her."

"They, Catherine. Indy uses they/them."

"*Actually,* Indy uses she/they most of the time. Right now her Instagram profile says she/her. I'm looking at it right now"—a pause to gather emphasis—"how did you spend the weekend with someone without knowing their pronouns?"

I'd been thinking about her with the wrong pronouns. Again. No wonder our endless flirting was scheduled for nowhere fast. "What's her handle on Instagram?"

"If you don't know it, it's because she doesn't want you to. Get her to tryouts. I'm already looking up dive tutorials." She hung up.

"Damn it, Catherine!"

I crossed the room, locked the door, and called Indy. It rang four times before she answered.

"You're calling me. That's so not playing it cool. I like it."

"You've got me blocked on Instagram," I countered.

"Shit, I do. But that's old. I signed up for it in sixth, and I blocked all the accounts I didn't want to see popping up in my suggested feed."

"Can you unblock me?" I said just as Mom knocked on my door. "Hang on, Mom."

Indy's voice sounded exhausted. Like maybe she was lying down. "Why the sudden urge to be my cyber friend? I thought we were going to be real life friends."

"I heard . . . Catherine told me your pronouns are on there, and you keep them updated, and I want to know so I'm thinking about you the way you think about you."

Indy was quiet. "That's sweet. You know you can always ask for my pronouns. Honestly, my IG isn't going to help. Right now it says she/her because my profile is public facing, and I'm trying to get a job at the library. They check your social media, and like your delightful ex-girlfriend, the Boomer Friends of the Library don't want to learn how to use gender inclusive language. They're 'too old.'" Their voice changed. It slid sideways, into hurt. "I had some really awkward interviews before I figured that one out. Ugh, this feels shallow."

Indy had kept talking because I didn't say anything. Couldn't say anything. I'd gone and gotten angry on their behalf. Mom knocked again, and I opened the door to stop the noise. She danced in tubs of hummus and swung a bag of Syrian bread under my nose. I waved her back, motioning to the phone. Mom beckoned for me to follow the dancing hummus.

"Sometimes you have to be someone else just to exist in this place," Indy said. "Does that make sense?"

"Yeah." Of course it made sense; I was being raised by someone who'd been actively erasing her cultural heritage her entire life in the name of ease. I doubted my mom even knew she was doing it. And like hell did I want to be the one to point it out.

Was that any different from when she suspected I was queer and said nothing?

"Did I lose you?"

I came up for air. "No, no. Just something you said made a lot of sense. So, they/them?"

"From you, yes."

From me? I'd have to unpack that later. "Indigo, I've gotta go eat an entire tub of hummus and watch *Sound of Music*."

"You don't like that movie."

"I don't like it. *I love it.*" I enjoyed every beat of Indy's laugh and hung up before I realized that I hadn't even told Indy about dive tryouts, but then, Indy loved intrigue. A challenge. I couldn't just ask. I screenshot Coach's email about tryouts and texted it. No comment, which signaled its own little dare.

I went down to the den where Mom had set up a small feast on the coffee table. The opening credits were rolling, and I could feel her relief ripple through the room when I sat beside her and started ripping up Syrian bread. The hushwee was steaming, and I plucked out a hunk of lamb. It was perfect. She'd really gone all out for my brother, not that I was surprised.

"Mom, what if I give you updates on Everett until he gets his act together? For example, he joined the Arab American group at Miami."

"He shouldn't have done that. He's barely Lebanese."

I flinched. When she said shit like this, it always sounded like, *You're barely family.*

"If something goes wrong, any kind of terrorism here or back there, he'll get dragged into it." For once this wasn't my mom's negativity superpower in action. Her early twenties were stampeded by 9/11. That's when she took passing to an entirely new level. The old pictures and Dad's grumbled warnings proved it.

Mom artfully dabbed her hummus and added a scoop of tabbouleh, pinching it in the fold of her Syrian bread. "He won't get jobs if they have any kind of security clearance. There go his chances of working for the government. I wish you two would *listen* to me. It's not safe."

I wanted to tell her that nothing was safe. Not for me. Not in this place. I wanted, suddenly, to point out that all I truly knew about myself were the things that weren't true. I wasn't her daughter, or a lesbian, not a real Arab, but also not white enough for Haley. It was an impossible way to exist. But her eyes were on Julie Andrews, and I couldn't ruin this movie for her. Not to mention, if she actually asked who I was, I didn't have an answer, did I?

"Mom, I want to cut my hair. Short as my chin. Before swim team starts this week."

"You won't be able to put it in a ponytail. You'll hate it."

"Please listen to me."

She looked at me, gauging my sincerity. "No home haircuts. I'll make an appointment for after school tomorrow."

"I want to dye it back to my real color. Black."

"Your hair is light brown." I showed her my roots, and she changed her mind. "My situ had that same hair color." I somehow refrained from telling her that she also had that hair color, hiding under a hundred thousand Midwestern blond highlights. "Senior swim, new you?"

"You're going to let me? But you've always said you love my hair light."

"I don't tell you what to do with your hair. I only stopped you that one time from shaving your head when you were clearly hormonal and waving your father's clippers around."

I spent the rest of the seventeen-hour movie picking through my own brain. I'd dyed my hair over the years, mostly out of boredom, always with the same bleach-blond boxes that lived under the bathroom sink. She hadn't made me; that was the lie I'd told myself. But she'd been happy. So happy when I put on dresses. Happy when I watched her movies. Happy when I blow-dried my long hair and showed her the bright color.

Other people's happiness was the worst kind of mind control.

— 13 —

THE FIRST DAY OF SENIOR SWIM TEAM was a Wednesday. I didn't know how to feel about things starting midweek. Was it more memorable? Less? Someday I'd stop interrogating time for its usefulness.

Not today.

Today was scheduled to be unforgettable. I showed up at swim practice like usual, changing as the Flash. Not only did I have new chopped black hair, but this year I was practicing in a shorty wetsuit. It'd create amazing drag, and I'd be a burning muscle mess for weeks while I got used to it, but then I'd be faster. Growth by fire, the water way.

Not to mention it held everything in tight like the vest Mrs. Cheng had given me my one shift as a pearl diver.

I padded out to the pool deck with a sense of premature euphoric recall. Someday I would miss this place. The aqua pool simmered under the beams of white light. Everyone else was still changing in their personalized ways, and the water was calling, the stillness impeccable.

Coach had given orders to meet on dry deck before the first practice. Probably because the first time we jumped in the water for the season we acted like six-year-olds at a pool party for a solid half hour.

I walked around the lanes to the far end. I rarely came back to the two ignored low dives sandwiching the high dive over the deep end. Standing beneath the high dive, looking up, I felt my legs waver. Vertigo from the bottom up. Over the last few days I'd spent an inordinate amount of energy trying not to think about this moment in this exact place. Would Indy show up? We hadn't spoken since the weekend, although I had walked backward in time through their Instagram feed. All the way to the first picture, a selfie of an eleven-year-old titled "Indigo Waits's First Shaved Head." I won't begin to attempt to describe the pure joy on Indy's rounder, smaller face.

Honestly, I felt untethered when all that hair slid over the black cape at the hairdresser, too damaged by chlorine to donate. The dark color was harder to get used to. I'd had a few too many people ask me if I'd joined a band, and no one believed that I dyed it to match my roots.

"So. You're going through a mid-teenage crisis."

"Hello, Catherine." I met her on the team benches and closed up my shorty with the tether on the back zipper. "You look exhausted."

Catherine had bags under her eyes, but her posture was spectacular. She wore three layers of bathing suits, the outer one saggy and full of holes, her own drag medley. Her cap and goggles dangled from her hip where she'd tucked them into the elastic hem of her suit. "I've been diving nonstop since Sunday. I'm going to take captain of the dive team for my applications as well."

"Get it," I said.

Catherine started flexing, twisting. Her large frame called for a lot of space in a hurry. I sat on the bench and started tugging my cap on. "Don't you have any goals? Coach was talking to recruiters about you last year. Not the big ones, mind you. But a few semirespectable ones. Division 2 schools."

"You help me keep a good handle on my ego, you know that?" I was having a hell of a time getting my hair into my cap. Ordinarily, I could just coil my ponytail and shove it on in less than a second. Now my hair was too short and stuffing it up under the silicone a few fingers at a time was going to kill me. "I've been thinking about OU. I had a good weekend there."

"Division 1? Not possible." Catherine watched me struggle with detailed concern. "You're going to have to put your cap on in the water now, after your hair is slicked back. You shouldn't have gone that short. Or you should have gone boy short and gotten your crown."

"I feel attacked."

"Good." Catherine and I smiled together because this was how she made me feel seen.

"Think Coach is still mad about districts?" I asked.

"Yes."

The rest of the team filtered out. Joss made his way over, the one hundred feet of his torso and the two inches of his Speedo making declarations. The boys never did drag. I might need to change that this year. I'd bring it up with Captain Catherine soon enough.

He slung an arm over my shoulder. "Can we make up this year?"

I detangled him from my skin. "I'll think about it."

Keeping us dry on deck didn't exactly work as Coach Kerrig imagined. After all, we were thirty practically naked teenagers, shoved within a few feet of wet tile and metal benches, nerves rebounding. Elbows and jokes and collisions welcomed Coach's entrance instead of a more traditional greeting.

The most important thing to know about Kerrig was that she reeked of an Olympic chance gotten away. The one-hundred-meter butterfly had crafted her round shoulders dozens of years ago. She was much smaller than Catherine—my height—her swimmer's frame immovable. On land she was an ancient turtle. The few times she jumped into the water with us, her flip turns had tsunamic tendencies.

"Welcome to swim team," Coach Kerrig started, concluding my ability to listen.

Catherine and I were tucked at the back of the pack, and she leaned over to ask, "Do you think Indigo Waits will show? It'd be a coup."

I acted cool. "Probably."

"You're like just an absolute mess on that score, aren't you?"

"All signs point to it." I stuffed some spare strings of hair up under my cap. There were dangling stray hairs everywhere; I might go insane.

"You're not terribly good at relationships. You should take some pointers from me and Anders." Catherine and her boyfriend were married at sixth-grade camp, the one year our school's week overlapped with the all-boys military school an hour away. As far as I could tell, Anders and Catherine were set for the rest of their lives, their relationship having more in common with nuclear fusion than puppy love.

"I'm not bad at relationships," I tried. "I've just never been used by one. I've used them on a few others, sure. Now I'm the mark. Indy could dismantle my entire being with a few well-aimed words." Which I knew to be fact because Indy already had. Twice.

Catherine stared at me outright, even though Coach was bound to bust us for not paying attention. "Interesting. I never realized it before."

"What?"

"You're a romantic. I suppose that was hiding beneath all that dead hair and ruthless revenge relationships. Do me a favor and don't lose your mind. This is an important season."

Side chatter was gaining ground and Coach's voice rose. "We'll end practice ten minutes early to clear the lanes and hold tryouts for the new dive team. Some of you will be trying something new. Good for you. The rest of you are going to watch from the bench, supporting this important addition to our season. We've put a call out to the school at large and might have a few additional members to our swim family."

The team clapped obediently.

"Potent speech," I grumbled, smacking my goggles between my hands.

"Seniors!" Coach boomed. "Come forward."

There were only seven of us, including Gia, Joss, and Catherine. Seniors didn't always stick around for that last year. We were the few, the proud, the seniors. I stared at the underclassmen anew. I hadn't pressed myself to get to know them, and now they looked like small strangers. Each year, the seniors drew extra attention from the team, and I hadn't anticipated I would dislike it so much until the moment they were cheering for us . . . because we'd made it four years? Surely, we could hold on to our enthusiasm for something more substantial.

Catherine, on the other hand, had entered her element. "As your captain, my initial mission is to team up Bigs and Littles. If you're a frosh or new, you'll get assigned a big fish. If you're an upper classman, you'll get a Little. Remember that the pairing is a secret until the halfway mark of the season, so Bigs, plan your presents with an air of secrecy. And keep the snacks healthy-ish."

Oh, shit, I'd forgotten I have to be a Big this year, but who would my Little be? I took in my fellow teammates, realizing something even more paralyzing. If Indy showed up, this bizarre cohort was going to have a front-row seat to my . . . let's just say *affection*. With Taylor, it had been such an escape. No one saw us together until we were kissing outright in the hall. Mostly, we made a home on her bed and tangled in a way we couldn't have possibly enjoyed at school without taunts. The point being, if Indy was here . . . right here every day . . . there was a near guarantee that I was going to fall all over myself. I needed to start making friends fast, or at least allies. And that was when I noticed that everyone—and I mean everyone—was staring at me.

Kerrig's temper broke with record speed. "McIntyre, if you can't pay attention while you're being introduced, I'm going to kick you off this team. I don't care how fast you are."

What a welcome. I saluted and muttered to Catherine, "You're right. She's still mad."

"The shorty is too much drag," Coach fired at me. "You'll pull something."

"I'll start at the back of the heats until I regain my speed."

"You'll start slow. You'll keep it steady." Coach was interested now.

If I could manage to swim with the wetsuit, I would grow much faster. "Sure you can handle it?"

"Yes."

Catherine dug her elbow in my side. "Introduce yourself to the Littles."

"I'm McIntyre." I was supposed to give more information but having daydreamed straight through the other seniors introducing themselves, I was at a loss.

"Don't mind this one," Catherine announced. "In love."

I tackled Catherine into the water. It happened so fast I had no time to assess the fallout. Which was considerable. Coach taught all the Littles about her temper, her raised voice bouncing off the cedar rafters while Catherine thrashed me in the water. In the end Joss saved the moment by throwing Gia in, and then we were all six-year-olds at a pool party until Kerrig's whistle nearly exploded from all that trilling.

I swam my laps that first hour with a great grin on my face, filling my mouth with more pool water than usual. I knew Indy would come. I knew that more with each passing minute. It felt like the giant timer over the lane of my life had been engaged. The race was on. Excitement turned the water bluer, cooler, friendlier. Same old chlorine, whole new world.

Indy wore a man's suit.

The scandal had hit full pitch by the time I'd finished warm-down, crawling out of the water in my shorty, breathing so hard I rolled over right there on the gritty tile to pant.

Gia got in my face, my line of sight straight up her camel toe. "There's someone here to try out for the dive team, and she *cross-dressed*. Coach is losing her damn mind."

That's all it took. One fucking sentence from Gia to wring my daydreams and drip out the cold truth. This was a bad idea. I hustle-walked around the pool deck to where most of the team was lined up on the bleachers, less like first graders now due to sheer exhaustion. They huddled in their towels, cheeks red and eyes rimmed by goggle lines. Joss was unhooking the lane lines on the deep end, clearing the area beneath the diving boards.

Indy stood before Coach and Catherine, holding conference, and I invited myself straight into it. "What's going on?"

"She can't try out in that," Kerrig said.

I fired up. "*They* can—"

Indy stopped me with a hand on my wrist, which had a sort of power over me. The pause left me looking over their attire. Boy's trunks and a nylon tank, a flat chest and muscles everywhere. "This is my bathing suit. I didn't have time to buy a *woman's suit.*" They spoke the words as if they were poisoned. Coach liked reverence from her swimmers, and she wasn't going to get this from Indy. Which had already landed them on the shit list. Alongside me.

"You're going to want to see Indigo dive. State-ranked gymnast," Catherine stated.

"That was years ago." Indy punctuated those lines by stretching twice as far as any of us could in several directions.

Coach finally exhaled, although it did nothing for the puff in her shoulders. "Have you ever been on a diving board before?"

"I trained on springboard."

Coach waved Indy toward the boards where the other divers were waiting to try out, including Catherine, who went first. I started toward the team, and then I decided against it. I'd invited them here. I had a duty to protect them from whatever was about to happen.

"Thanks for the warm welcome," Indy whispered. "I swore I'd never step foot in this school. Suppose the pool doesn't count exactly. This is how much I like you. Take note."

"Noted." Concern doused the electricity I might've picked up in those words.

"Do I need a cap or goggles for this?"

"Just a team suit. It's uniform." Why was I so goddamn nervous? My heart pummeled my chest so hard that old rib spot ached. Or maybe Coach was right, and I had pulled something. Catherine finished the three standard dives. Her form was acceptable on all three, although far from perfect. Joss tried out next.

Indy watched him perform a decent front flip, an impeccable pencil dive, and just about the worst backward dive imaginable. "He's going to need more arc—" Joss's back hit the surface at the perfect belly-flop angle. The *crack* of his skin was quickly followed by a chorus of sympathetic *owwws* from the team. "So, this sport is minimum physical effort, maximum embarrassment factor," Indy muttered. "I'm so glad you tagged me in."

"Why do you think we didn't have a dive team to start with?" I admitted.

Joss got out of the pool sheepishly, grabbed a towel, and joined the rest of the team. Two lowerclassmen got up next, and I could already tell by the way they climbed the stairs on the low dive that this wasn't going to end well.

I turned my back and played with the strap on my goggles. "The chlorine is high," I warned. "Shock treatment still settling down. Try not to open your eyes."

"Come try out, they said. It'll be fun, they said."

"I said none of those things. I sent you the tryouts info. That's all." I flipped my goggles for possibly the one-too-many-eth time.

Indy grabbed them, inspected them. "Why are they so stiff?"

"They're plaster cast. Mom had them specially made for my bumpy Arab nose."

"You're Arab?"

"No," I said, which was faster than explaining and what I had been raised to say. Indy was up next. "Ask me about it some other time when there aren't people listening."

"Your anxiety is ridiculous right now." Indy grabbed my forearms, massaging them. "All I did—for years and years—was compete. Trust me. The only one who's nervous right now is you. And it's really cute. Stop it, I have to concentrate."

Coach called, "Indigo Waits."

Indy walked toward the high dive. They climbed all the way to the top. Before anyone had a chance to be worried or ask questions, they'd completed a low-splash pencil dive.

The team actually stood to cheer. Coach looked like a guard dog on sudden high alert. I clapped too, watching Indy return to the surface. I expected some kind of triumphant grin, but I found their brow furrowed, concentration folding up their expression. Their face cleared the surface, but only just. They doggy-paddled with fierceness toward the side of the pool. I hurried to the edge.

From where the team was watching, I assumed they'd all think I was flirting with Indy. I was actually surprised that Coach hadn't ordered me over to the benches yet. I pretended to sit on the edge and congratulate Indy on the dive when, in actuality, I used my foot like a hook beneath their arm and dragged them to the side. They clung to the edge.

"Hey, you can dive. And you *really* can't swim."

"Slander!" they called, spitting water, lips wet. I wasn't ready to find out if Indy knew how to get out of a pool correctly, so I offered my hand, clasping palms around thumbs, and deadlifted them on deck, their body knocking into mine briefly.

"I am impressed," Indy said, streaming beside me in a way that steamed through me.

They succinctly completed the front flip and a back dive, surfacing each time like a Labrador paddling to a dock. I hauled them in for the third time, grinning. "I'm teaching you how to swim. Soon as possible. Like, tomorrow."

"Deal."

When Coach announced they'd made the roster, I wasn't ready for the soul buzz of being proud of Indigo Waits. The team seemed to have a new, shiny focal point, and I found myself secured on their left. Now this spotlight? This one I could stand beside.

Coach called the first practice, and I entered the locker room with them. We trailed in, nearly twenty girl-assigneds, seeking out lockers and hollering, joking, and jockeying. Indy followed straight behind me, and by some stroke of luck or fate, the lockers we'd chosen were side by side. We dug for our clothes, and I sort of hoped they were about to duck in a stall and change like Catherine. How they changed was going to mean something, and I didn't know what that meant to me.

I tugged my shirt over my head before I remembered I was still wearing the shorty. While tugging the shirt back off, Indy took it upon themself to unzip my back. I peeled out of it and wrapped a towel under my arms in a hurry. When I finally tugged off my blasted cap, my hair pulled in all the wrong directions. The silicone had kept it half dry, half wet, standing up everywhere.

Indy smirked, nodded at the new style and color. "That's a move."

I shrugged. "I think I blew it. The comments I've been getting range from existential crisis to 'are you a drummer now?' "

They laughed. "Aw, you wanted to look sexy for me."

"Um, did it work?" I dragged both hands through my hair and gave them my best smile. Indy's cheeks pinked, and I had that heart-cannon confirmation that they *did* like me.

Which was suddenly terrifying.

Gia glanced over, definitely eavesdropping. Okay, that was enough exposure. I moved swifter than ever into my clothes, underwear added before the suit even came off. I was only barely, slightly, ever so minutely aware that Indigo's style of changing was to become naked and then get dressed. As if no one had taught them to self-shame correctly.

When my suit fell out the bottom of my basketball shorts, Indy looked up at me, impressed. "That was some Jedi-mind-trick changing."

"Right back at you."

— 14 —

"I TAUGHT INDY HOW TO SWIM."

Over-practiced in my mind, the words came out with accidental fervor. Mrs. Cheng's wife, Freya, was washing a stockpot beside me. I waited to dry. The carved wooden sign over the breakfast bar read, HERE THERE BE SAUCY, OLD BROADS, and that pretty much described their cozy ranch.

Freya hummed with approval. "Swim lessons? That's terribly romantic."

"Terribly!" Mrs. Cheng disagreed by way of a shout. She was the retired chef of the evening, drinking her wine, feet kicked up on the sofa while Freya and I cleaned. It was always this way at their house. Someone delightfully cooked. The other person cleaned. No one growled or threatened while slamming ovens. No one did the dishes while yelling into the stagnant air of the house. It was a nice change.

"Don't listen to Bea." Freya squinted back at her wife. "She's thinks *Orange Is the New Black* is date-night-worthy. Tell me about these 'swim lessons.'" Her eyes widened in surprise. "Wow. Why did that sound so dirty? Apologies."

I nearly snorted into my drying towel. "Well, it was innocent. Sort of. There was some 'accidental' skin brushing. But we weren't alone. Catherine, the dive and swim captain, oversaw every single move. She would only let me teach Indy the three-stroke move that the divers have to perfect lest they be disqualified. I'd like to have shown Indy how to do backstroke. Breaststroke at least."

Freya dropped the stockpot in the soapy water, exploding suds onto both of us. "I'm sorry!" She could barely talk she was laughing so hard. "That's . . . too much."

Mrs. Cheng came over, taking Freya out of the way with a spin of the shoulder. I'd turned the color of the center of the earth as my imagination flickered with the imagery that had sent Freya cackling like a middle schooler—although I was laughing pretty hard myself.

"Are you talking about *my* Catherine Guernsey? She's captain twice over, is she?" Mrs. Cheng took over the good work of the chili that had burned to the bottom of the pot. "The same Catherine Guernsey who got me early retirement benefits from SeaP? My *favorite* pearl diver?"

I'd forgotten they'd spent all summer together. After I'd gotten fired, Mrs. Cheng didn't talk about what was happening at SeaPlanet. I'd been pretty proud of Catherine for writing the promised exposé a few weeks back. The *Plain Dealer* printed it and everything. It didn't go viral, unfortunately, and SeaPlanet's response was to say that the pearl-diving exhibit was going to be renovated for the next two seasons, which was their answer to anything that came under fire.

Except the killer whales.

"Have I told you, queer-o, that no diver has ever gone free of a nickname from me? Not one, not in nineteen years. Apart from Catherine Guernsey."

"You've told me. She does seem to require a full name." I tried not to be jealous. I wanted to tell them that I had a new name, maybe. I hadn't said it aloud, and yet it was there, already on me. In me? Whatever it is that names are supposed to do, I felt it with this one. But like hell was I going to try and explain that.

Freya filled the Brita pitcher. "I'm still not hearing enough about the swim lessons."

I was handed the pot to dry and the equally impossible task of describing what it was like to swim with Indy. "I told you. There was a lot of near-innocent bumping around, and at one point they put their arms around my shoulders, and I gave them a short orca ride about the pool."

"That's how you get eaten," Mrs. Cheng said, and Freya elbowed her hard. "What? It's a top-tier predator, and SeaP was, like, 'Let's put it in a bathtub and give it treats!' "

The Chengs' sixteen-year-old Jack Russell terrier named Hugo came trundling in.

"Bea. You said the word," Freya admonished, rather seriously.

"What word?" Mrs. Cheng asked.

"The t-word. Now he thinks he's getting one, but he's already had his *t-word redacted* for the day."

Mrs. Cheng dried her hands, got a dog treat, and fed it to the grizzled, ancient cutie. "When I'm a hundred and twelve years old, I really hope you give me extra treats, Frey."

The three of us retired to the couch. It was nearly time to go home, already dark out. Swim team practice made me late to my weekly dinner, and I was exhausted. I wanted to stay on the Chengs' velvety sofa forever. It was a blissful place. They never called me daughter. They made good food. They liked their home. It was everything I wanted. Almost.

"Can I bring Indy with me next week?"

Freya looked concerned, but Mrs. Cheng spoke. "How fast are you moving there?"

"Slow. Turtles. Tortoises. Whatever's slowest. We haven't even kissed yet." Something dawned on me. "We haven't even held hands yet."

"That's not what I mean. How slow are you going toward making Indy the entire world when you close your entranced green eyes there?"

I threw a pillow at my elder as if she were no older than Everett. She caught it and tossed it right back, knocking me in the head. "No one wants to be deemed perfect," Freya added.

Both of the responses made me nervous.

"I am not inflating Indigo Waits to planet-sized proportions." Which was easy to promise since I was pretty sure I'd done that ages ago. "We're getting to know each other."

"Tell me about their family," Freya said. "Siblings?"

"Um, their mom's a lesbian. Oh, do you know her? Charlotte Waits?"

"We know all lesbians," Mrs. Cheng said seriously. "Every single one in the state of Ohio. There's a conference, you know."

"Really?" A second pillow nailed my head. "Okay, fine, Indy's mom is a lesbian and . . ." I tried to imagine Indy's father, but I couldn't remember if he'd ever been brought up or didn't exist. Come to think of it, Indy had very high walls. Wonder what that was about.

"Have they always lived in Haley?" Freya tried.

"I think so." I didn't know. I didn't know anything about Indy.

Mrs. Cheng got up, took my elbow, led me to the front door. She always knew when I couldn't make myself leave, and she always kicked me out in bizarrely warm ways. "Go find out about this person you adore. You'll be knocked out by how much more you have to love."

My house was quiet and dark, and I closed the door behind me with relief. Then my dad came down the stairs, and we scared the living death out of each other. Afterward, he clutched his chest, and I swore the lesser evils of the four-letters. My dad was lenient up to a hard line.

I headed into the kitchen for water, always thirsty during swim season. "Are we alone?"

"In the universe? Not likely." My weird came straight from him.

"In the house."

"Mom's at a yoga-with-cats class. Apparently, she does yoga and cats swat at her. Or climb on her. I'm not sure how that would be relaxing, especially at forty dollars a lesson."

"Mom found a workout for the exact hour I'm over at the Chengs'. She hates it when I go over there. She thinks they're trying to replace her as my moms." I'd never said that aloud before. It sounded bad; it felt true.

"Or your mom found a workout at the exact hour you're gone so that she has more time for you when you're here."

"Because I'm so delightful?"

"Swim season is hard on her. She's alone a lot." He had me there, and he knew it.

I filled a glass from the tap, drank it in one gulp. "There are several sides to every story. What's your story, Dad?"

"It's a snoozer. We'll skip it." My dad took out a tub of ice cream, and we sat in the dark kitchen, digging in spoons. "How's the team looking this season?"

"Not too bad. Catherine, Joss, and I are bound to garner some attention at some of the larger meets." I felt particularly self-aware. "I'm not looking forward to talking to recruiters. They're hard to get a feel for."

"I can see that. I was nearly recruited to the Coast Guard Academy. At the end of the day, I didn't believe a word they said, and I walked away. I wish they gave undergrad degrees in gaslighting. That'd actually help you survive this world. Speaking of, where are you hoping to go? Maybe there's a sibling discount to Miami U."

"Maybe OU," I said. "Although I doubt I'm fast enough. Did I tell you we're starting a dive team? Catherine and Joss are diving. As well as . . ." An old friend? Was that at all accurate? "My friend Indigo Waits, a former gymnast."

"Well, that is quite a name." My dad's name was Trey, but he went by Micks. This was incredibly confusing to me when I was a child. "Is this . . . a special person?"

"Indy is amazing." Ah, my tone was so telling. I could picture the Mrs. Chengs sitting on the sectional, asking for caution. "But we're just getting to know each other. We hardly know if this is a—"

"Love story?"

I grabbed my face with my hand. "Sure, yeah."

"I think you can know most things about a person from their name. Indigo Waits. He sounds like a self-propelled artistic type. Watch out for those artists."

He. What an odd assumption. We ate ice cream, silence wedging between us in the dark.

"Hey, can I ask you something? Do you like your name? Trey?"

"No. No, it never seemed to fit me. Never sounded right."

Huh, I hadn't suspected such a succinct answer. "Is that why you go by Micks?"

He shrugged. "It's a little better. My favorite is Dad."

I was very tired, and somehow that lowered shields inside. "If I picked out a different name, would you and Mom use it for me?"

My dad's thoughtful quiet told a hard story. "I think I could, given time to adjust."

"That's what I thought." Both the way he might respond and the pointed lack of response about Mom. "Well, if I never ask her to call me something else, then I'll never have to deal with how terrible it feels when she won't."

That stung more than I wanted it to.

"Do you want me to call you something else?" he asked. "I could try."

"I don't have anything picked out. I was only thinking," I lied, got up, stretched. "Must bed." I became immediately and exceedingly sleepy. Another fallout of swim team season was dropping dead asleep by eight o'clock. Making it to my bed wasn't always a given. I stumbled up the stairs and tucked into my room. I hit the mattress face-first. When I closed my eyes, I saw Indy treading water in the deep end with me.

"Firm legs keep you afloat," I'd said—and current me hooted a laugh. Freya was right; this was way too much innuendo.

My legs had slid against Indy's a few times, and when Catherine took a break from spying on us to practice underwater butterfly kicks across the length of the lane, I felt bold. "You picked this up too fast. I wanted more one-on-one time. Tell me, are you on the rebound?"

They squinted, water collecting on the fuzz of their wet, shaved head. "Rebound rules are for dinosaurs. I just sort of feel things through when I'm interested in someone."

"I would like to go out with you."

"Oh, that's way too dinosaur for me." Indy turned on their back, floating impressively for someone who couldn't swim. Back floats took a lot of trust, and Indy had the upper hand now. I could feel how much I wanted them to like me. It was all I could think about.

"Is that a no?"

"We can hang out."

Catherine had returned then, ending our chat. And I'd spent an awful lot of time since that moment facing the truth that I didn't know how to be in a real relationship, dinosaur or otherwise. I'd never bothered to be present before.

But I was here now. And it was already hard.

Near dead on cold sheets, I thought about reaching for my phone in my pocket, but I couldn't move a finger, let alone my whole arm. *Hang out* seemed to be what the Chengs were talking about, right? They were saying I should get to know Indy more, and that's what Indy had offered. Okay, I could follow this lead. I rolled over and texted Indy, still so tired I could barely move, and yet motivated. *Let me drive you home from practice tomorrow.*

Indy wrote back right away. *Sounds kinky. I'm in.*

— 15 —

WHEN PRACTICE ENDED, I got out like a sea lion, beaching myself across the tile and sliding all the way against Indy's legs in my ridiculously heavy wetsuit. It let go of the water it kept pressed against my skin, creating a small lake around me.

"I feel like I should drop a frozen fish in your mouth." Indy looked down at me. "Do you always practice so hard you nearly pass out? Sergei, my Ukrainian gymnastics coach, would say you're promising yourself a stress injury."

I bounced to my feet to prove that I could, but I'd misjudged the angle, and we were nose to nose for a hot second. I smiled. When I got too close to Indy, I felt invincible. That outcome was a little addictive.

"McIntyre, stay. Waits, go," Coach hollered, trekking toward me in that plastic-looking jogging suit.

"She's a Neanderthal," Indy muttered.

"Yep."

Indy left and I started to peel out of my shorty, just to prove that I hadn't swum my own arms off, which I very nearly had. Everyone else was changing in the locker rooms, and I wondered which school Coach would bend me toward this year. Last year she'd been scheming to turn me into a Buckeye, but I could not see myself living in Columbus for four years.

"What's up?" I offered a smile; I should have known better.

"You're not to go in the locker room when the other girls are in there."

That was not what I was expecting. Plus Coach wasn't looking at me. She stared at her clipboard, which didn't have any paper on it. "This isn't because you're gay. There were complaints from the other girls about you flirting in there. We can't have that in the locker rooms."

Like all serious things with Coach, I could not quite take this seriously. "Complaints? Beyond Gia being a god-awful gossip, who else was complaining?"

"The number of complaints isn't important. Remember, McIntyre, I don't get paid enough to explain to you why you can't act like this around regular people. Get it?" She breathed out hard; it gusted at me. "You have to get it? Understand? *You can't be like this.*"

Oh, I understood.

I suddenly understood how deeply closeted Kerrig was. I'd never noticed it before. She stood there glaring and seething like some Dickensian warning of how miserable and mean I'd become if I kept my identity shut down and locked up.

If I'd never met Indy.

"Can I use the guys' locker room?" I asked quietly.

"The handicap bathroom. Or wait for the team to come out before you go in."

The handicap bathroom was overrun by everyone in school who was too nervous to poop in the communal stalls. There wasn't enough air freshener in the galaxy. And I'd never be first in the water again. "I'll wait."

"This isn't because you're gay," she said again. "You've been gay for years, and I didn't ban you. This is because of your behavior."

"I'm not going to sue you."

I turned and dove in the water, misjudging the shallow end. My palms scraped the tile, belly dragging on the bottom. I swam away, down the steep slope to the deep end. At the very bottom I let out the kind of scream that could kill a person. The water kept the secret.

When I drove Indy home, I couldn't tell them what happened. It was less about hiding the truth and more about being worried they'd quit. Instead, I pretended like Coach and I had been arguing over schools she believed I should swim for next year. But I was shit at pretending.

"And you missed my street." Indy pointed. "I tried to get your attention. Are you asleep at the wheel?"

"Sorry." I pulled into a driveway to turn around. The truth that Indy had been living two miles away in a neighboring housing hamlet this whole time ate at me.

"I'm there." Indy pointed to a small, dark purple house on the corner. They still had Halloween decorations up, which meant their neighbors probably loved them. Mom would have a field day criticizing that alone. I wish I didn't hear her words in my head so much, especially the ones she hadn't even said.

"How have we never crossed paths?" I asked. "I'm only next door in Park View."

"Oh, yours is the neighborhood with the brown man-made lake."

"Truth." I had the scars to prove it. "But that's where I learned how to swim, so I try not to knock it." Harvey had been right; you could love a place for its flaws, but it was a lot of work. Like treading water with your hands on the top of your head, which Kerrig had made us do for twenty minutes this afternoon. I was so tired. So tired.

I pulled in the driveway, resigned to go home and go to sleep. Anything to stop reliving that conversation with Coach.

Indy got out and stooped to look through the open door at me. "I wasn't going to invite you in because I'm pretty sure that's what you were hoping for all along, but now you seem so . . . out of it." It was kind of them not to say *dysphoric*. "Do you need to come in?"

No.

No, I didn't.

Say it.

I killed the engine and got out. Ordinarily when someone said something that sunk me, I went home and shut my bedroom door. I didn't tell anyone. I overthought the event to death, but I also didn't let on to anyone that it had happened. For a long time, that felt like the only way I could come out of it with my head up.

I followed Indy inside. The place was blasting with music and delicious smells. Indy's mom had friends over, and they were hanging out in the kitchen, eating and talking loudly. They cheered hello to Indy, but we shot by them, and I found myself in Indigo Waits's bedroom, the door pressed shut behind me.

"I should have warned you. It's queer divorcée night." My eyebrows raised, and they added, "Mom runs a club for all the other moms who got married and pregnant after college, per dinosaur formula, only to realize that a straight-passing life wasn't going to be enough. I swear they never stop celebrating each other, which is sweet. But I'm glad our generation doesn't live in the closet for appearance's sake."

I hadn't even looked around their room; I was so stuck in my own head. "It's weird you think I'm part of your generation. I still put the dresses on when I have to. I wear the nice bras and lipstick when deemed necessary." The trick wasn't to avoid the mirror but to look straight at it with my head erased. That person in the mirror was pretty, classically hot. They just weren't me. "It's good to know there's a club for me on the other side, if I have to choose the path of least resistance."

Indy hugged me rather hard and suddenly. It took me a few seconds, but I hugged them back. When I held them, hands clasped at their lower back, I felt better. Grounded. Indy smelled like the pool, so warm and solid. They let go after a minute. "Sit. Talk."

I sat on the edge of Indy's desk chair. "Coach won't let me in the locker room anymore unless it's empty. Someone said we were flirting."

"We *were* flirting."

This wasn't the reaction I anticipated. "I feel really . . . off about it, which is stupid because I've always felt awkward and horrible being in there with all the actual girls."

"*Actual girls*," Indy repeated contemplatively. "Well, you're right to be upset. It's definitely some homophobic nonsense, but I'm not surprised. I heard your school wouldn't even let the students have a GSA."

"Mrs. Winooski sorted it all out. They have one at the local library now, since the principal wouldn't go for it," I explained. "I'd take you but I'm persona non grata."

"I'm sensing a good story."

"Not necessarily. You remember Taylor?" Indy nodded. "Head of the group. She has decided that I am her evil ex for the sake of her compelling life story, and I'm obliged to let her imagine that kind of drama. A parting gift."

Indy started stretching on the rainbow area rug in the center of their floor. "She sounds like a very small person. That's sad."

Maybe all of this was too sad. I tried to shake it off. To look around. Indigo Waits's room was a treasure trove of stuff. Eclectic, odd collections were piled everywhere. There was a shelf full of rocks from every place they'd been. There were records. Lots of books. They had a small couch in addition to their full-sized bed, which I spent as little time looking at as possible because my mind steamed. Dozens of holiday lights crisscrossed the ceiling, although they weren't on.

You could tell a lot about a person by their room. The first category was the presence of parents. Indy's messy room looked like it was founded, organized, and run by Indy, no adults consulted. My mom cleaned my room once a season—without telling me—which kept it specifically less me-oriented. The second category was comfort. Indy's room had a TV and sofa, a hangout area in addition to more traditional sleeping and changing needs. So they spent a lot of time in here, maybe.

"Are you close with your mom?" I asked.

"Some years are better than others. She's super supportive apart from the times when she's imagined a different future for me. She wasn't stoked when I quit gymnastics, or when I told her I was moving to San Francisco after graduation."

My pulse didn't like this answer, but my mind reassured me that graduation was a thousand light-years away and Indy was only a few feet from where I sat. Anything could happen between now and then.

Indy smiled up at me from the floor. "I was born there. It's where both sets of my grandparents live. We should have moved back years ago, but Mom wanted me to keep close to Dad, and the rest is rather boring."

"So you do have a dad."

Indy scowled. "My parents divorced when I was five. Dad lives in Cleveland with my stepmom and two half brothers, who are turning into tiny, privileged monsters. The whole cis boy, blond hair, blue eyes, glow-in-the-dark white skin. When I walk around with them, people act like I'm the misfit babysitter escorting Aryan emperors. It's not their fault, but they're starting to act like people *should* act that way, which is hard to be around."

They glowered more with each sentence. Perhaps I didn't know the answer to Freya's questions because Indy didn't want to talk about it. The facts were all just facts, anyway. I wanted to hear Indy talk about how they saw the world. What they felt. How they inhaled and exhaled so deeply when I felt like I was always, always, always holding my breath.

Indy studied me. "You look like you're waging some kind of battle."

"It's nothing. Coach and I have been at war for years. And long before that I threw on armor whenever my mom came in the room. It's a reflex."

"Yeah, I think I'd like to meet her."

"That sounds like my own personal hell." I smiled; Indy didn't. "She's complicated. Try being Arab in the whitest suburb in Ohio. She's constantly going the extra distance to get people to accept her. The court of public opinion shapes every single thing she does."

They bit their lip. "That explains a lot. Being raised by someone who is afraid of who they are is—"

"She's not afraid. She's traumatized. Terrorized into pretending to be white by people who label all Arabs terrorists." I'd never stood up for my mother before. It made my heart pound.

Indy sat up. "Did I overstep?"

I shook my head. "I don't think I've ever trusted anyone enough to tell them the truth."

"Tell me more about your family." I didn't know if they wanted heritage info or what, but there wasn't much to say anyway. We kissed each other in greeting, Mom made some Lebanese dishes, we had a few Arabic words kicking around, but mostly it was the same old boring American legacy of *pretend like your culture doesn't mean anything until it doesn't.*

The keen loss I felt over the things I'd never get to know about myself felt like too much.

Indy could tell that we'd slid downhill. "Okay. How about a classic? What do you want to be when you grow up?"

"Free?" I joked.

They didn't laugh.

My shoulders were sinking, my whole body turning dark and silent. I didn't want this. I wanted to be with Indy. Flirting. Talking. Whatever felt better and lighter than all this. "What does that mean?" I pointed at a shirt pinned to the wall. It read, BE GAY DO CRIME. "Apart from looking aces on you in that Instagram pic you posted. Wow, I just admitted a lot."

"You always do." Indy said my name, and it sunk my mood to new depths. "You're flinching again. I said your name, and you actually flinched. You don't deserve to flinch so much, you know."

I closed my eyes. "I don't want to talk about that either."

"I'm not going to make you, but if you don't want me to say your name, you can tell me. If you have a name you prefer—"

"Would you call me River but not make me explain why?" I said it fast, before I could rethink every word, including the name, which didn't have a poignant origin story. Someone had called me River by mistake, and it had just felt *right*. "Also, you don't have to tell me if you like it or if it suits me. I just need to avoid . . . all of that. For the sake of my anxiety."

Indy didn't even pause. "*Be gay do crime* means you should be gay however you want to be. You should be called whatever you want to be called. We don't have to bend ourselves to an antiquated society that doesn't bend at all to us."

"I know that." But I was pretty sure I didn't, or maybe I was in the process of learning it. I'd also just said my name aloud for the first time, and Indy was going to say it back to me, probably soon. I both needed and did not want to have that moment.

"I couldn't imagine myself happy," I blurted. "Even when I was little, thinking about who I wanted to grow up to be or do or marry . . . there was *nothing*. Just nothing." Why was I telling them this? "And you want to know the weirdest part? I was okay with it. I thought maybe I was going to die in a freak accident. Me, nine years old, imagining one of those horrible drunk-driver commercials. Totally fine with it." I stood, started pacing. "Then you came into my life. You . . . were the first person I ever imagined having an actual happy life with. I could see our kids' faces. Their bikes. It was wild."

Indy rolled on their side, looking straight at me. "When did this happen? After OU?"

I shook my head. "After the shark tank, before Dweiller. Right about when I waltzed with you in that Keemee costume during the parade."

"You barely knew me."

We were making a lot of eye contact; I was on fire from it. "I knew that. Didn't stop the daydream." They'd pulled in their smile during my bleak monologue, and now I needed to tease it back out. "This is all pretty romantic, if you think about it."

"I'm thinking about it. It mostly makes me upset on your behalf. I'm the only happiness you've ever imagined for yourself? Why are you okay with only having one spark of happiness in your whole life?"

"Because it's a beautiful spark. I think it's us from the future, slipping back into my sense of self at this moment. Giving me something to swim toward."

They grinned. "As your existential spouse, I require that you want more for yourself."

"I know a lot more about who I'm not than who I am. Hey, but I'm . . . trying." I sat hard on the couch, arms thrown wide, head tossed back. "I think I'm trying?"

"Hey, no crucifixions in my room."

"It's a very minor crucifixion."

"Oh, okay, those are fine." Indy walked on their knees across the room and put a strong hand on the top of each of my legs. I stared down into their brown eyes, feeling a million years old. I'd never looked at them without that roaring hunger before. Indy glowed with kindness.

"There are no actual rules. For being queer or dinosaur. There's only your life, your choices." They beckoned me closer and kissed me on the corner of my lips, more tenderly than I'd ever been touched before. "Nice to finally meet you, River."

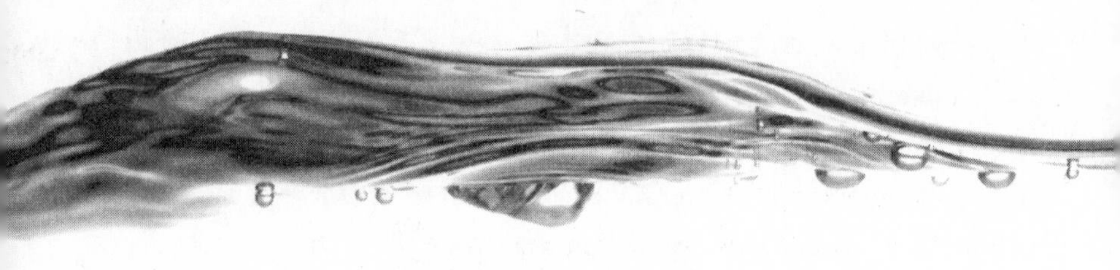

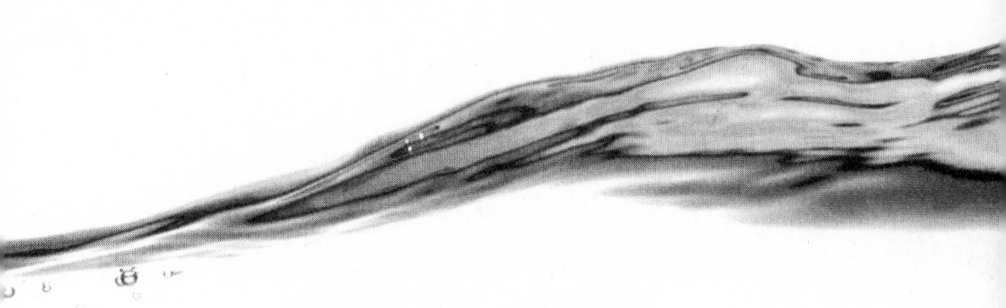

penguins

Penguins are not flightless birds. Penguins fly *underwater*. While their airborne brethren have hollow bones, penguins have solid bones to reduce buoyancy. No one streamline glides like these guys, which is why it's very hard to keep penguins happy and healthy in captivity.

Most penguins mate for life, one of the animal kingdom's famous monogamous—but *not* compulsively heterosexual—species. When they find their soul mate, they give presents and hold flippers.

They also kiss with their eyes closed.

— 16 —

THE FIRST SWIM MEET WAS AWAY, in an affluent city perched on the edge of Lake Erie. Perris was infamous for their nuclear power plant—and the school wealth related to such an extreme endeavor. As the bus took the roundabout to drop us off, I had an epic view of the early-winter sunset, the horizon choked by the steam from those bulbous twin towers.

We cleared the bus without our usual team chatter, entering the glass-walled building that housed the swimming facilities. The entire team paused in the doorway to scowl at the Olympic-sized pristine pool with its stainless-steel drains. They also had a sauna, two hot tubs, and a separate diving pool. Perris was our top tier nemesis, if for no other reason than we understood the undeniable connection between economic privilege and skill.

"Show-offs," Joss muttered loudly.

"They kill us every year," I translated to Indy.

Indy glanced down the fifty-meter pool. "Is it just me or is this twice as long as the pool we practice in?"

"Olympic-sized. Same distance for each race, but you swim half the number of laps. This is how they send all their swimmers to Division 1 schools. It's a massive advantage."

Gia, who had been trying to get back on my good side ever since she'd ratted me out to Coach, shoved in beside us. "But you're faster than their best freestyler. Remember how pissed they were last year when you beat them by a full stroke?"

"My times are better in Olympic-sized," I admitted. "Also, fuck off, Gia."

"It's only proof that McIntyre's flip turns are sluggish." Catherine led the charge inside the intimidating pool, letting that one cutting note be her intro to and exit from the conversation. I hung back with Indy, who was looking at me from the side.

"Are you good?" Indy's smile crinkled their nose. "I mean, I hadn't actually wondered about this before, but you're good?"

"At swimming?" I looked around. The truest answer was that I wasn't the best because I wasn't reliably fast. I wasn't going to the Olympics. Even a Division 1 school like OU was pretty much out of my reach unless I buckled down in some huge way, but that would mean giving in to Kerrig's abusive coaching, and I wouldn't give her the satisfaction. "It's more like I love the water. The water calls to me, calms me. Melts me, sometimes. The rest is okay."

"You going to do something water related for a career?"

I stared at them. "What? Become like Kerrig?" We laughed; I looked for a way out. "I'm not as good as you were at gymnastics, I hear."

"That was a hundred Indys ago." They nudged my elbow with theirs playfully, and the sensation zipped along my arm and lit up my smile. Coach hollered for us to get into the locker rooms, and I hung back, waiting for everyone else to be done. I wasn't surprised when Indy hung back with me, looking at the dive pool with a mildly nervous expression. "Think I'm actually intimidated. Doesn't happen often."

"They're all amazing. We're going to get spanked. Sorry this is your first experience."

Coach hustled toward us, and I stepped back, my pulse stormed like I was standing on the block already. "I wasn't flirting. I'm only standing here."

"There's a gender-neutral bathroom for you. Waits, head to the girls' room."

"I'm not a girl. Let me go in the . . . Did you say 'gender neutral'? How could a bathroom be gender neutral? Do you mean gender inclusive? Granted assigning genders to bathrooms makes about as much sense as throwing a party to celebrate the ultrasound photo of your poor kid's genitals."

Coach balked. Like a chicken. It was beautiful. "I don't care what you are in your head. Go change with the other girls."

"Wow!" Indy crowed, unaffected by Coach's bullshit. It's like they had an invisible umbrella to keep all this shit from raining down on them. I felt it all over me.

I found the much smaller locker room in a daze; it was actually labeled GENDER NEUTRAL. When I stepped inside, I nearly backed straight out. There was a boy in there. A boy with long hair. Who must not have been a boy, and *when* would I stop assuming people's genders based on their body parts? Indy would be so disappointed. I picked a locker as far from the Perris swimmer as possible, changing even faster than usual.

"Never had anyone in here with me before," the swimmer said after a minute.

I pulled on the shorty for warm-up because it was best to trick your mind about drag until the exact moment of the race. "I'm not allowed to change with the girls because I'm attracted to one of them, who isn't even a girl, by the way, but here we are."

The swimmer laughed. And then so did I. Which was as surprising as it was nice.

"They're closed-minded sad fucks." The swimmer crossed the distance between us, gripping a folded towel over their chest. They eyed my shorty, their eyes sharp, crystal blue. "That's smart. I might steal that idea."

"It's heavy," I admitted. "But it helps with dysphoria." I'd never used the word aloud in a sentence before. I was suddenly proud of myself and terrified that I'd done it completely wrong.

"I hear that." The swimmer paused, wanting to say something. "You're from the SeaPlanet town, right?" Oh yeah. I guess we had our own nuclear power plant. Ours just pumped money into the local economy via the capitalistic coup of captivity. Maybe we shouldn't judge. "Is it true it's closing down this year?"

I shook my head. "SeaP will live forever. Like one of those immortal jellyfish."

They laughed again, their voice musical. "Or a pit full of spent fuel rods. Good meet."

"You too."

By the time I left the no-man's-land locker room, my team was warming up in our assigned lanes. Checking for Indy came naturally. Knowing where they were comforted and centered me. When I found them by the diving boards, practicing with the other divers, I finally exhaled and began warm-up.

Acclimating to a new pool meant memorizing the lines on the bottom and the flags on the ceiling. It meant counting strokes to the wall from the point where the lane lines changed colors. The shorty tugged, pulled me backward, and I looked forward to diving in without it, sliding through the water unencumbered.

All pools were different, all water different. This one didn't taste like chlorine. One of those fancy peroxide pools. I should have enjoyed a break from marinating in my least-favorite chemical, but all I could think about was the chugging towers behind the school. Did people here get used to it? Or did it feel like swimming for Kerrig? The pros of being on a team as big as the threat of sudden annihilation?

Warm-ups wrapped, and we got out, making a base camp on the benches out of our tracksuits and shammies and other accoutrement. I spread out my towel wide enough for Indy to sit with me once the divers finished warm-up.

The stands were lofted like at our pool. Parents filled up the bleachers that were both above and behind us. I glanced back only once to find where my parents were sitting on the left side, halfway up. Memorizing their location meant I wouldn't make accidental eye contact; this was important. The stands were nearly full. At least a hundred parents from both sides. This was going to be a very loud meet.

Gia sat hard on the far end of the bench, staring straight ahead. "I didn't mean to get you kicked out of the locker room. You don't have to keep treating me like I'm a dirty spy."

I ignored her. Hard.

Indy padded over, dripping, and sat beside me on my towel. It was the first time I'd seen them in their navy team suit. They seemed perfectly comfortable in a way that ate at me. Maybe my dysphoria wasn't because of my gender-whatever. Indy's gender was a mystery, one they seemed to fully enjoy. What was that dark magic?

"At least our school color isn't SeaP teal," I joked flatly.

Indy craned their head up toward the bleachers. "My mom is here. I did not invite my dad. He's the worst when I'm competing. His face gets red from yelling. Are your parents here?"

"Yeah."

But like hell was I pointing them out.

Catherine strode by, stopping abruptly. "Joss is bringing the karaoke. You're on candy, but there will be no Twizzler fights. Last year we looked like we'd been whipped at districts. Literally." She walked on, giving instructions, and Indy motioned for a translation.

"Swim-team sleepover tonight at Catherine's house. To celebrate our first meet."

"Coed sleepovers? That is more credit than I would have given this group. I'm intrigued; however, I will not be whipped by candy."

"It's nonsense all night long. You'd come?" I asked, surprised.

"Are you going to be there?"

"Yeah."

"Then I'm coming."

My heart found this stimulating, pumping with breakneck enthusiasm. My mouth dried out, and I wondered if the peroxide filter was getting to me. Of course, I'd hoped Indy would be interested in the more ridiculous social aspects of the team, but somehow the idea of spending the entire night with them didn't soothe me so much as utterly freak me out.

Coach walked by and snapped her fingers. "Out of the shorty." She glanced over the rest of the team. "Check each other! A disqualification comes with a five hundred fly." The comment earned its many groans. For most, a five hundred butterfly was a death sentence.

I looked over Indy, pointing to the hoop they wore on their ear cartilage. "That'll get you disqualified."

Indy twisted the earring out. "Don't know why I'm surprised. There are similar rules for gymnastics competition. What am I looking for on you?"

"Anything. Everything. I once got disqualified because I had a hair tie on my wrist. I'm allowed goggles, cap, team suit. That's it." I peeled out of the shorty, unprepared to feel nearly naked before them. I'd spent most of my life in a suit, even opted for suits instead of underwear for years, but it was different now. My body was different.

Hang on, let me rephrase.

People acted very differently when they saw my body.

To reduce drag, the team suits were extra tight, low cut at the neck, high cut on the legs. My hip bones were on display, but when Indy's eyes danced across my chest in an innocent way, my entire soul clenched. I thought of the Perris swimmer holding that towel over their chest, and I needed to cry.

Instead, I slid out of existence. The meet was beginning, the ref giving the opening monologue beside the coaches. I was on deck for the first relay, and yet I wasn't here anymore. I was somewhere in the Pacific.

Riding the tides like a damn man o' war. The surface meant little more than air because my body ran deep and long and unknowable. I didn't realize that my eyes were squeezed shut until Indy's hand slid over where mine gripped the bench. I looked down for a long moment, then I let go of the cold metal and held on to them. Our fingers wove.

Indy leaned their face into my neck, their nose soft on my skin. "You're here, River."

And I believed them, which was its own miracle.

The 200 medley kicked things off, and I swam anchor. My lane was half a length behind by the time Gia butterflied her way to the touch pad, and I dove in, breaking the water like a sleek dolphin, powerful and slippery without the shorty. I swam like I'd been born for it, taking one breath the entire length.

As soon as I slammed the touch pad, I ripped my goggles free to check the fancy electronic scoreboard overhead. My lane number flicked to the top of the list. We won.

I shot out the of the water, breathing hard, water spitting off my smile. Coach held up her hand for a high five, which wasn't as shocking as me actually meeting it with my own. Even though I did not love competition—or really the nerves it pumped through me—I had to admit that I did not hate winning.

At the midpoint of the meet, all the screaming, cheering, echoing, crashing water stopped. The entire pool deck fell deadly silent for the divers. We weren't supposed to make a sound, or even move for fear of disqualification or, you know, massive personal injury. Had I seen a diver hit the board and end a meet instantly with all their blood in the water?

Of course I had.

And now my imagination decided to relive that particular moment, replacing that unknown diver with Indy. All of a sudden I felt sick.

The judges settled at the table on the far side of the pool, and Catherine gave Joss, Indy, and our other two divers one of her patented pep talks. I'd had enough of those in my day to know she was saying a lot of painfully true things in a frank, unfeeling way, but that did not mean she didn't care.

Indy seemed to lapse into a different mode, shaking out their left arm, the one that had been fully casted that fateful day with the shark tank. Could they still feel the fractures that had ended their years on the beam? Like I couldn't get rid of that lake rash inside my suit?

The divers from both teams cycled through, all doing easy, safe, perfectly executed, low-splash dives. Indy nailed two. For their third, they went to the high dive instead of the low. They climbed and climbed, walked to the edge of the long, wavering board, and turned around. *Wait.* Indy shouldn't be doing an inward dive. They hadn't practiced it enough, and it was extra dangerous. My ears crashed with my pulse, my hands clenching and unclenching. Why did I drag them into this? How could I be so stupid?

Indy bounded, getting excellent height, their body flying up, tucking in, their head and body turning toward the board, clearing it by inches before they dropped straight into the water. They resurfaced, swimming to the side like I taught them, getting out with a grin sent my way.

I exhaled.

"She better have cancer to explain that bald head," one of the Perris swimmers heckled loud enough for both teams to hear. My nerves flicked from fear to anger. Catherine gave me a wild-eyed don't-do-any-of-your-crazy-shit look. I didn't care. I stood to destroy the heckler, seeing absolute red, but an arm clamped around my shoulders and kept me from moving.

"Shut your radioactive faces!" Gia snapped loudly, and I forgave her. A little.

Coach growled a warning, and the ref glanced over. My muscles let go one at a time.

I touched the arm still around my upper chest. Joss. I looked over my shoulder at him. I'd been a real dick to him the last two years. I'd hurt him as much as he'd hurt me. Made sure of it. I couldn't not see it when we were this close, which is why I stayed so far away.

"You're welcome." He let go, returning us to our important distance.

I sat in a daze.

The meet returned to its normal volume and fervor, and Indy sat back down next to me. "You okay? Was watching me dive *that* stressful?"

I shook my head, not wanting to tell them about the heckling or my mind holding me hostage since the moment they left my side. Or my ex looking at me like I was the actual devil. When Indy reached for my hand again, I got up and walked away.

By the last event, the 400 freestyle, I stood at the back of my relay as if my body had been filled with cement. Catherine started us out, getting half a length ahead of the other lanes. Gia shot in next, losing a bit of the lead, but not too much. Our freakishly tall, skinny freshman jumped in next, long arms and low weight doing more in this sport than buff muscle ever could. She kept us in the running. I climbed onto the block, Coach tucking in right next to me.

Kerrig didn't say a word; she didn't have to. Her presence was the threat.

Even the blocks at Perris's pool were superior. I found my footing, took my mark, and blasted off as soon as the freshman slammed the touch pad. The first length was gone before I knew it, fifty meters careening by. I couldn't stop thinking about Indy, who'd left competition behind only for me to drag them back into it. They'd left this school behind too. Our grade and people like that heckler who couldn't wait to torment them for being different *and* happy. After all, we were only allowed to be one, weren't we?

It was selfish to pull Indy back into this place they'd found their way out of. Maybe that's what Freya and Bea had been getting at. Indy was good for me, made me feel so much better, but maybe I was no fucking good for Indy. Speeding into my flip turn, I missed the color change on the lane lines, my count thrown off. I flipped, misjudging the distance, folded up wrong against the wall ever so briefly.

"Ever so briefly" in competitive swimming is everything.

The bus ride home was quiet, the team exhausted after our loss. I didn't particularly have the energy for a sleepover. I didn't have the energy for anything.

Getting screamed at in public will do that.

I sat in the back, the short seat, *my* seat. Everyone gave me distance. Indy had gone home with their mom, and not having them around after what happened was a kind of relief. I didn't want them to know how far away I could go inside. And I really didn't want to think about how Indy's mom had seen all that. Well, everyone had. Coach took public shaming seriously.

Indy had looked so different when they went in the other direction, avoiding the bus and Coach . . . and me.

Catherine sat in the other back seat, reading her textbook in the dark. "I did the math. If you hadn't blown that flip turn, we would have won," she said after a solid half hour of silence.

Our first victory against Perris in living memory—blown by me.

"Are you trying to make me feel worse?"

Catherine snapped her book shut. "I won't dignify that question with a platitude. I'm telling you because everyone acts like Perris always spanks us, but we only lost by a few points. We're getting better. And also to explain why Coach was more of an asshole to you than usual."

"She just hates me. It's fine. I deserve it." I paused. "Catherine, if Kerrig goes after Indy the way she goes after me, I'm not going to take it well." Not even Joss could hold me back from losing it then.

"Indy can take care of themself. Do you know anything about the person you're dating?"

"We're not dating."

"Why not?"

"Because I'm mildly venomous, if you haven't noticed."

She snorted. "Why do you think we're friends?" Catherine *was* my friend. I should've been able to say to her that my life and heart seemed to be swimming in different directions, and I felt ripped in half most days. "What did you get your Little for her first meet?"

I winced. "Shit. Forgot."

"You forget a lot of things."

"I do." At this point I knew that forgetting things, losing reality, was part and parcel of gender dysphoria. I knew this, and yet I couldn't say it. "Feels like everyone hates me."

"Maybe you just hate you." Catherine exhaled. "Still. Kerrig is after you more than the rest of us." Her admission surprised me. "It's like we all bother her *a lot*, but you? You make her see red like a cartoon villain. I'm thinking she might be a homophobe."

"Odds are good." Another one of those queer homophobes that were so prevalent around here. Once I'd started seeing them, I couldn't stop finding evidence of their identity rot. It felt like the muck at the bottom of my neighborhood lake: distractingly squishy between your toes while it silently stained your most sensitive skin an oily green. "Helps to know it's not in my head."

Some other dimension of me added, *Hey, Catherine, I was born in captivity, and this tank is killing me*. But this dimension was still stacked against me. The details—the contours and colors of Coach's screaming face in front of all those people—hit my mental trash can. In some far room called my memories, a prisoner tallied up one more point against me, and right then and there I began to stop loving the water.

"I'm going to propose to Anders at graduation," she said randomly. "Thoughts?"

"Sounds good."

"I'm being serious!"

"Of course you are. You're always serious, and you're always correct. But you're not always *right.*"

A few minutes went by. Catherine cleared her throat. "But I am right about proposing to Anders. You agree?"

"Why would you ask me? I've never had a real relationship."

Hey, look, something else I didn't want to be true.

"I'm asking because you've known us as a couple from the beginning. You were part of that first game of truth or dare at sixth-grade camp."

"Wasn't I." I pressed myself to think about her question, and all signs pointed to an answer: Catherine was doubting herself for one of the first times since I'd met her, and that meant she was accessing new emotional muscles. I was weirdly proud of her. But that didn't make it any easier to stay around. I kept slipping below the surface of the conversation. Catherine could have told me she was pregnant with triplets, and I doubt I would have been able to access a reaction.

The bus chugged down the highway. We zoomed passed a sign for the SeaPlanet/Haley exit. The CLOSED FOR THE SEASON patch was stuck on at an imperfect angle, reflective strips blinding from the oncoming headlights. My mind floated to that swimmer from Perris—were they trans? I surprised myself by being able to think the word without a flooding, emergency detachment drowning every semblance of thought. And then I wondered if I was some kind of trans, and the tide came in at once, swaddling me in nothingness for a long time.

The night was hours into its blackness, the air newly wintry. Soon there'd be lake-effect snow, and icicles in our wet hair after practice, and that *cracking* in all the frozen bus windows. I reached for the cold window and used it to gasp back into this galaxy and water planet. This broken country and red state. This small city where people paid money to watch sea animals die in cages made of glass. How could we get out? Where would we even go? Man o' wars couldn't survive in captivity; captive animals couldn't survive in the wild.

"Catherine, have you heard anything about SeaPlanet closing?"

"Yes."

"Really?"

"But they've been saying it for years. It's probably a false alarm."

"Oh, good." Considering how I felt about the infamous place, I had no idea why I was relieved. Maybe because I didn't want to be alone. I thought about Sally the octopus, hiding from everyone for eternity, the penguins in love with their mirror selves, and the killer whale who ate a drunk man in the middle of the night.

Not to forget all those murdered man o' wars.

And I vowed to get out alive.

— 17 —

FIRST OFF, Kerrig could go straight to hell.

The only way to come back from being publicly shamed for having a trauma response to severe, untreated gender dysphoria—what I had started calling man o' war syndrome—was to have the night of my life. She hadn't won, because I didn't hate myself.

So, there.

Only *part* of this pledge was meant to distract me from the weirdness stretched between Indy and me from earlier. They'd said they were going to come to the sleepover, but that was before I'd gone catatonic. Where were we now?

Joss used my distraction against me. He got an arm under my knees, folded my body in half with a roar, and ripped off one of my socks.

Catherine's plush, finished basement went wild with cheers. Her house was perfect for these kinds of group shenanigans, a McMansion with a rec area the size of my entire upstairs. Her parents had barricaded themselves in their suite with instructions for everyone to have fun, not break anything, and clean up. This was lenient, but in truth, we hardly ever did anything beyond eat dangerous levels of carbs and sugar . . . and sock wrestle.

Some unknown person had made up the game years ago, handing it down through the varying incarnations of the swim team. The rules were simple: stay on your knees; the first person to wrestle the other person's socks off won. Sounds simple, doesn't it? But you try getting someone's socks off while also endeavoring to keep your own on.

Joss and I were both down to one sock. His height was a terrible advantage because he could hold his feet farther away than I could. He grabbed at the edge of my calf-high socks, and I clamped down on the cotton with my other foot. We didn't hold back, and then there was a moment when we were tangled in a way that used to mean something very different to both of us. How long ago was that? A thousand years?

I gave Joss a good kidney shock, which reduced him to thrashing laughter, and I ripped his other sock off. I held it high while the team cheered, and this particular round of sock wrestling was over. At this point there were torn, empty bags of candy and sleeping bags everywhere. Past midnight; Indy definitely wasn't coming. *The Ring* was playing on the lofted flat-screen, but no one was buying into its formulaic fear.

I dropped back down to the rug, pinning Joss under my victorious butt.

He gave me an exhausted shove, and we both flopped on our backs, side by side and still panting. One of the obnoxious Littles threw an afghan over us, and up close with Joss's smells and sounds was surprisingly not horrible. I marveled at how much I'd liked him once upon a time. Enough to really close my eyes around him, you know? But as soon as we had broken up, I'd forgotten about all of that. On purpose.

"Thank you. For earlier. I would've gotten kicked out of the meet."

He frowned at me, but it was mostly flirtatious. We wrestled until I pinned all four of his limbs. He gave up with a barking laugh, holding on to me. "Let me say something. I'm sorry about that stupid list sophomore year. It was Gia's idea. She's an evil genius."

"It was a direct hit to the Speedo," I admitted.

"Hey, you broke up with me and then sort of handed me off to her!"

"You went along with it."

"Well, I shouldn't've." I already knew all this about Gia, but it was news that Joss had felt bad about it in the first place. "Is that list why you dove in the shark tank?" The worry in his voice was aged; it had been with him for a long while.

"No." He seemed to be waiting for more, so I added, "I just felt like I was in the wrong tank, so I jumped in a different one. Turns out the tank might be the problem, not the contents." I'd never thought of it like this before. It sort of made sense.

"That was Indy, wasn't it? The SeaP employee who pulled you out? And now you're dating. Wow."

"Who is starting these rumors? We're not dating. We're friends?" Why was that a question? Oh yeah, because Coach had done a number on me during the meet. "Joss, do you think I'm . . ." There really wasn't a better word for this. "Venomous?"

"Yes." I elbowed him, and he laughed. "But you can be sweet too. Understanding. You helped me with that stuff." His voice was low under the stuffy afghan. What had I helped with? Joss reviewed my blank expression with exasperation. My banished memories resurfaced. He'd been turned on by an attitude I'd honed; Indy called it *bad boy mode*, which was a compliment but also invoked the trans conversation I couldn't seem to have, not even with myself. And that's when I remembered that when we were dating and Joss got drunk, he said hooking up with me made him feel gay. Which had made me feel *really* good. It's how we'd gone from pawing at each other's parts to actually test driving them.

"Okay, now I remember."

"And there's your sting."

"Sorry, I just have . . . limited internal memory, so to speak. It's a trauma response."

"Trauma from what?"

I'd just said that aloud. What now? "Personal stuff. Drowning in straight-white-people feelings. You getting any of that?"

He belly laughed good and loud. "Yeah, I mean, I tried to join

Taylor's GSA, but it was way puritanical. Bi judgy. Anyone not wholly lesbian or gay is a person 'in progress' to her."

"She's fucking terrible," I growled.

"Well, she definitely feels the same way about you." We laughed.

"Glad to hear it." I gave him one more kidney shock for good measure.

"Oh my god!" one of the Littles screamed—definitely the one who hadn't hit puberty yet. "Micks is under there with Joss and Indy just walked in!"

I thrashed free in record speed, coming out to an absolute chorus of laughter. My hair was completely sexed up, searching the basement for Indy. But I'd been played.

Catherine pulled off a slow clap. "Ridiculous, Micks, and yet we all want you to know that we're pulling for you and Indigo. Now just to piss off Kerrig."

"Kerrig is a homophobe!" one of them yelled.

I blinked. The entire room—the two-thirds of the team who talked their parents into coed sleepovers—was in on this Kerrig overthrow. It felt worse to know that they could tell Coach was against Indy and me on principle—and better to know that they didn't feel the same way. After Gia's tattle session, I'd been assuming they were all assholes. But then, according to my research on gender dysphoria and internalized homophobia, feeling like everyone hates you is easy.

And believing that they don't is very, very hard.

"Indy and I are friends." They laughed at my red cheeks, and I chuckled. "I swear, we're *friends*." Popcorn flew at me. I found my way through the mess of bodies in sleeping bags and pulled Catherine into a one-on-one. "What's with calling me *Micks*? That's my dad."

"Suits you, and since you won't respond to your name, I had to come up with something far less boy band than *McIntyre*. Half the Littles were starting to crush on you as if you're the swim team's token bad boy."

Like every time this came up, I enjoyed it too much. "Yeah, I might be leaning in there."

Here it was, a gift-wrapped moment from the cosmos, the perfect opportunity to tell Catherine my name.

And there it went.

"Hey, the support is great, but I don't want you all putting noses into my relationship. I'm working on it, I swear. Indy doesn't rush things."

"But there's something special there," Catherine said matter-of-factly. "The team is excited. It's been a long time since Anders and I rocked everyone's world."

"It's true. You imprinted on each other like werewolves." My confidence took a short nap. "Catherine, I don't even know if Indy is into me the same way I'm into them."

Dear cruel gods of existence, don't let that be true.

A person came down the basement stairs to the rec room balancing a large garbage bag bursting with bright, rainbow taffeta. An out-of-breath Indy dropped it on the floor and hollered, "Who wants to play dress-up?"

The bag was shredded. Indy jumped back as the team descended upon tiaras, tights, leotards, platform boots, and other glamour paraphernalia. Indy hopped across the room and its many reclining bodies to reach me.

"Wow," I managed. "That's a lot of . . . stuff."

"I went through a *long* dress-up phase. Honestly, for the right event, I still love it."

"I've seen your old-ass Indiana Jones. What other cosplay is hidden up your sleeve?"

"*Retired* Dr. Jones." Their hand scrunched up my T-shirt at the neck, a flirty warning that yanked our bodies closer and honestly surprised the hell out of me. "And wouldn't you like to know what else I've got."

Catherine studied us in that academically intense Guernsey way.

Indy asked *What the hell* with their expression, and I mouthed *Later.* Catherine clapped a hand on my shoulder. "Your concerns are not valid. Wink."

Indy wore a torn-up sweatshirt over the most adorable flannel pajama pants I'd ever seen. And I experienced the most intense urge I'd ever had to hold on to someone. Forever. Or maybe I was just maddeningly tired.

"Are they ever going to fall asleep?" they whispered to me, marveling at the insanity. The recently near-slumbering cohort had woken back up. There were shouts for more sock-wrestling duels. I thought about challenging Indy but twisting up our bodies like that might actually kill me. Could you die from wanting someone so bad? It seemed possible at this point.

Arguments broke out in a thousand corners, and I leaned toward Indy's ear. "It's two a.m. at the sugar crash party. Come with me." I led Indy out to the basement patio. Houses like this always had several cement patios. It was cold, and I started to box the night to stay warm.

"You're in a good mood . . . but also hyper." They pulled their hoodie tighter. "Should I exploit this?"

"Feeling wildly honest." I sent a left hook toward the Little Dipper. "I want to tell you I've never been in a real relationship. I've dated . . . a lot of people, and it was always for some reason. Boredom, revenge, or—"

"To come out," Indy slid in, a little too ready. "You used your last girlfriend as a come-out excuse. That's what you told me once."

I stopped fighting the air. "We used each other. It felt bad the whole time. You know how we came out? Making out in the hallway during class change traffic, middle fingers raised. We were in some movie in her head, but it was exactly like every formulaic dinosaur rom-com. She wanted the adorably rebellious young-adult romance, not the queer, dark love story I offer." Indy looked like they might need to comment on that, and I rushed on. "That's nothing. I dated all my bullies from sixth grade. Destroyed them. Except for Dweiller. Although he's locked up now. They tried him as an adult, so maybe there is a god."

Indy sat down on a patio chair that should have been put away weeks ago. "Have you been drinking? Should *I* be drinking?"

"These sleepovers are always dry." I shrugged. "We don't need it. Inhibitions lower when fighting exhaustion. You want to know the worst part about my revenge relationships? I actually liked one of them. That was confusing. Why did you give up gymnastics?"

Indy leaned back, surprised by my question or just concerned by how fast my brain toggled in the dark o'clock hours. "I didn't want to give up, but my arm put me on the bench for months. The competition attitudes started to get to me. I wanted to go back to the challenge of the floor, the beam, the bars. Back to doing it for fun, and it was made clear I wasn't allowed to do that. My gym 'needed the spot for serious athletes.'"

I sat down across from Indy, my sugar rush and bleariness starting to mellow. "Did you feel that today at the meet?"

Did I push you back in it?

"A little. But I'm not doing this for glory. I'm doing this because you asked me to."

"And you'll be able to finish your homeschool program with the sports credit."

"And because you asked me to." Indy pulled their hoodie tighter. "Are you sure you're not freezing?"

"Still cooling off. It's so hot in there."

"Sorry I was late. I was arguing with Queen Charlotte, also known as my mother. She saw us holding hands at the meet and thinks I'm doing it again."

The cold bit at the back of my neck. "Doing what again?"

"Shepherding queers out of the closet . . . and mixing that up with romance."

What?

"Good thing I'm not closeted. Came out years ago." The words stuck in my own mouth.

"*Are* you out, River?"

"Yeah, I did the thing and people know, and I don't want to talk about it."

The sound of glass-pane farts chorused through the flat backyard. Behind us, at least ten underclassmen swimmers danced in Indy's finest drag, making out with the sliding door. Without a word, we pretended to laugh at them. And when they went away, we stopped.

"You ever wonder why they bother calling it Stockholm syndrome?" I asked. "Why go all the way to Sweden? They should call it hometown syndrome. I love all of them in there, but also they're holding me hostage."

Indy stood and beckoned for me to follow. We went to their car parked on the street and got inside. They ran the heat until my fingers came back to life. The radio played acoustic folk.

I flashed back months and months to hiding from park security in this car, naked and wet and furious like a newborn who'd come out fighting. "Ah, memories. I haven't been in here since my sole distinguished day of being a pearl diver."

"Also known as the day you finished Dweiller." They pulled the release and pushed the driver's seat all the way back, reclining. "You look just like you did then. Except you have shorter hair and less desperate rage about your person."

Little did Indy know that I'd nearly gone quite ragey on that heckler only hours ago. I leaned backward, head tilted up. My voice dropped all on its own, a growly flirting depth. "I hoped to be further along by now."

Indy blushed, and I'd made that happen. Which left me feeling invincible until they moved forward with careful words. "So, you had a full dysphoric zombie moment at the meet. I haven't had one in years, but I knew what I was looking at."

I smiled at them, but it felt so damn sad. "Tell me about one, if you can."

Indy looked all around the car as if they had to find the right one and there were plenty to choose from. "Well, you know how queer circles aren't always accepting? A few years ago, right before you jumped in my shark tank, I went to a cosplay party with the Cleveland All Out group. 'Dress as your gender identity.' I came as Wednesday Addams because, in my mind, gender is dead. I wore all my pronouns pins, and no one would talk to me. *All genders welcome* . . . yeah right. Until someone agender shows up." They shrugged. "You can talk to me about your gender stuff, you know. I'm ready. I've been ready for it for a while."

I picked at a hole in my pajama pants, making it bigger. "Pretty sure that'd make me your sheep."

"Fuck, I shouldn't have said that. Mom is wrong. I don't always fall for closeted queers. I find people like me, and I want to help them. Also, *you* came after me. Now I care about you, and I don't let many in, so feel lucky and let me help you." They paused. "*If* you want."

I was going to be sick. Or very happy. The difference was minimal. "I don't know how."

"With questions," they said. "Are you trans? A trans man?"

"Can't be," I said fast. "Pretty sure you have to be a man to be a trans man."

Indy looked like they had some clarification to offer, but settled on "Okay . . . I didn't actually think we'd get far with the binary selection. Not to fear, there are many more options and not a single one of them is permanent. Think of this conversation as a starting place. A lot of people don't know their gender beyond their assigned sex. They weren't raised to question it. They weren't taught *how* to think about it. So it's no wonder it makes you malfunction."

"I can't tell if you're joking."

"Of course I'm not." Indy turned down the thermostat, and the hot air eased in the vents.

We were supposed to be talking about me, but I was already regretting the serious gender turn this had taken. Where had all my plans to romance Indy gone? I pulled a thread, and my entire knee was exposed. "What was it like to grow up without people telling you who you are?"

"Honestly? Uneventful. My mom asked me every day at breakfast what pronoun I wanted to use. I tried them all out. She never told me or assumed I was straight or queer, that I'd just sort of figure it out. It's funny, but our community spends so much time talking about coming out that it feels like you *must* have a dramatic story. What a hellish price for admission."

They said "our community" like I was a part of something big and strong. I didn't believe it, though. I'd also never thought about this particular angle. Indy had once told me that they didn't have to come out of a closet because no one had put them in one, and I'd spent so much time dissecting the why and how of coming out that I hadn't thought about the inverse. About how we get in there in the first place. About how the people who claim to love us put us in there as little babies and shut the door. There are no windows in closets. No vents. No escape.

Plus Indy was right; I was not out.

"Nonbinary seems like a better starting point here. River, what about trans masc?"

I was too far in my own head. My voice came from far away. "Trans is too political." Indy's response was stiff, raised eyebrows. "I don't want to go anywhere near that word. It makes boomers' minds melt. And politicians go all Thanos, and *I don't want to.*" I added *please* a little late, hoping to take the sting out of the words that'd crashed out of me.

Indy softened, and I had to admit that I did like this game, but only because of the way they played it. Easy, flexible, as fluid as people claimed gender to be. "How about demigender? A masc kaleidoscope of your own design?"

"But that's just it. I don't want to pick a new word. Sending myself the wrong way down the lesbian highway messed me up. Gender should be more like tides. And I'm a man o' war."

Indy grinned. "You do remind me of a brilliantly multicolored colony of polyps. And like the man o' war, do you use they/them pronouns?" I shook my head once, and Indy understood. That was too much to think about. Even if it felt obviously true.

"Okay." Their seriousness was a gift. "You're my man o' war."

"Interestingly enough, I don't mind being a man o' war. It might be the best gender identity out there. What eats me is that I was ever lumped in with those jellyfish to begin with."

"Assigned jellyfish at birth, the River story?"

"Think about it. I came out looking like a jellyfish, so they threw me in there with them. Didn't matter if I wasn't one. A Midwestern American bloom, bred in captivity. Then they have the nerve to get mad at me for being . . ."

"Different?"

"I was going to say venomous."

"This poor metaphor." Indy smiled. "Yet I have a feeling that someday I'm going to be looking over a sheet of gender options and find man o' war on there. You have dangerous levels of charisma, River McIntyre."

It was the first time I'd heard my full name aloud.

It felt like my name.

They unveiled a new smile. "Do you feel better?"

"Maybe. Yes." I looked down. "The charisma is a smoke bomb. People act like I'm some sort of model who is holding out on them when they see my body. I was afraid at the meet . . . that you were going to look at me and see whatever sexy Barbie shit that other people see."

"I know." Indy took my hand and pressed a surprise kiss to the center of my palm. "But that's not what I see. And there are other things to think about than the people who shut you in that closet. The fantastic side of things. Otherwise known as the rest of your life."

"Like us dating?" I dared.

"Like that." They were staring at me in such a new way. I was used to their questions and analyses. But now they looked at me like what they wanted was . . . me.

The car had gotten toasty, and our sweat smelled of chlorine. We didn't need our outer shirts. I peeled mine off. Indy tossed away their holey hoodie, revealing a tank top with nothing under it. Years of gymnastics had left them so toned. My binder felt extra tight, extra thick under my shirt. We kept to our assigned seating, and yet our bodies squared off in a brand-new way.

"So. Burning question. Why did Catherine say *wink*?"

"I might have told her I like you and was worried you didn't feel the same."

"Someday you're going to just ask *me* and start living." They ran a hand over their shaved head. "Time to break down all that dinosaur socialization. This isn't a game of cat and mouse. It's two humans attracted to each other."

Okay. I could play the honesty game. "I might not know exactly what queer species I am, but I am—yeah, definitely—in love with you."

Indy laughed quietly, staring at my hand held in both of theirs, resting on their knee. "Twenty seconds to take it back."

More than a minute flowed by.

"I don't know the words for how I feel about you." Indy examined my hand with both of theirs, each finger and the lines of my palm. Easily the best touch I'd ever experienced. "But the feeling is strong and all over me. And I want more of it. How do we do this without our usual baggage?"

"I don't know," I admitted. "Slowly?"

— 18 —

WEEKS RUSHED US INTO THE HOLIDAYS, and we wooed each other in a euphoric kind of standoff.

Indy's gender expression went through a chrysalis before my eyes. She slid into she/her, and it was a wild joy to watch her line her eyes in charcoal, busting out a new wardrobe of knit beanies, Doc Martens, and enough flannel to outfit the cast of *Lumberjanes*. Flannel goth but make it sexy. That was the other thing she gave me: things to read and watch and think about.

Her binder disappeared, and she wore nothing under soft button-downs, which drove me absolutely insane. We nearly kissed all the time, cheek to cheek, nose to nose. Anything to get closer. To stake small claims on each other everywhere we went. I spent a lot of time in the shower one knuckle in my mouth, the other hand extra busy. We listened to music, collapsed after swim practice in a heap of sore muscles, our bodies pressed together lengthwise on the couch in her room. I was her big spoon; she was my warmth.

And still, the stalemate continued.

Even at home, away from Indy, I felt full from our laughter, from her attention. Everett came home for the holiday break, and Mom set up her Christmas camels everywhere. My brother had been dodging out on our family for so long that I worried he'd return changed, but when he altered the nativities to include his *Star Wars* figures, I knew he was still in there. Obi-Wan made an excellent wise man, after all, and if Jesus's cradle wasn't meant for Yoda, then why did they swap out so perfectly?

When Indy found out that I didn't particularly enjoy Christmas—a punishable offense apparently—she took swift action. Her mother drove us for hours one Saturday to a park that had been taken over by millions of holiday light creations. Santa and the Bible's iconography had their prominent places, but there were also dinosaurs, sea creatures, and an entire solar system of ringed planets. It was the nerdiest holiday joy I'd ever seen, and it brought out a childlike side to Indy. We sat cross-legged in the back, under the open SUV trunk, looking out, up, and I thought about Everett's roommate Harvey's quirky details that made you love a place. Did anywhere else have a life-sized kraken made out of twinkling lights being harpooned by a pirate ship captained by Santa? If not, well, they were missing out.

I picked up Indy at her SeaPlanet shift one day, utilizing my mad skills of dressing in Everett's clothes and using his season pass to slip by the ticket booth. I found my way to the aquarium. Even though it was off-season and the outdoor exhibits were dry, the aquarium was dead in a way that seemed like a bad sign. Not a low attendance day or month, but year and possibly decade. Perhaps people were starting to prefer life in the ocean rather than crowding together in a musty building full of cold glass, black lights, and dead-eyed fish.

I looked for Indy in the Jellyfish Haven, hoping for a synchronistic revival, and at the Penguin Encounter, where I first realized what that overwhelming feeling meant when I looked at a queer person. The Portuguese man-of-war tank was gone, nothing but a square impression on the carpet to prove that this place had once housed a designer murder box.

The central shark tank drew me in for the first time since that fateful day, and I finally dared to wonder what it had looked like to see me come diving into the enormous pillar tank. Had I looked scared? Determined? Deranged? Joss had asked *why* weeks ago under that afghan.

Why?

Because I didn't have any other choice.

I dragged my hand along the short, boxy paragraphs encapsulating each captured creature in a few sentences. I'd accidentally memorized most of them over the years, and on my harder days, I rewrote them in my mind to include, you know, basic honesty:

Lemon sharks prefer the bottom of the tank, along with the nurse sharks. Also, they're allergic to that phone you're using to take 150 pictures, trying to capture the perfect moment with your buddy on the other side of the glass, his head positioned like it's inside the shark's open mouth.

Indy came up from behind me and held me at the waist. " 'Memories,' " she sang, and I laughed. "Are you thinking about it? Of course you're thinking about it."

"Of course I'm thinking about it. It's easy to think about it now."

"Easy why?"

"Because I'm not there anymore." I pointed up to the place barely visible through the glass: the bubbling surface. "I'm here." I squeezed her arms holding me. "And I don't even know where 'here' is, but for the first time, I'm not fighting it."

"You're really peaceful when you're not at war, you know that?"

I turned over my shoulder, her nose nudging my cheek. Right there, right then, I could have kissed her, but I didn't. And not because I was scared of someone seeing for once; I was scared it wouldn't be absolutely perfect. "I want to kiss you—"

"I want to kiss you too."

Wow, she was ready. Was I the one holding us back now? "*But* Sea-Planet isn't giving me the most romantic vibes."

"Your penance." She kissed my neck at the corner of my jaw, and I shivered in rather delicious agony. "Come with me to clock out."

We walked through the aquarium, toward the employee spaces. I made sure my hand brushed the side of hers in the way that meant *I want to hold on to you*, and she wove our fingers. "River, I want to tell you something, but I have no clue how you're going to take it."

"You better not be dumping me for California." That came out violent, Christ. "Sorry."

She let it go, what a hero. "SeaPlanet is closing."

"Oh, they always say that. It's going to be here forever. A monument to some of the worst choices humans can make, like all those racist Confederate general statues."

"Hey, good people are doing a lot of work to pull those down. And I mean SeaPlanet is really closing. I just sat through the saddest employee meeting." She squeezed my hand. "We might have to move on from all these monumental mishaps."

I couldn't hold back the smile that poured through me. "Sounds like a lot of work. Sure I can't just stay miserable and righteously angry forever?"

"Not if you want to be with me."

And I did. I would do anything for her love to be my truth. "So, this is the last season?"

"They won't open come Memorial Day. They'll spend the summer taking down the reusable gear and tanks to ship to the other parks."

"You're kidding." But of course she wasn't. "But I've still never gotten the Indy tour of this place."

"And you never will, I guess."

We left the aquarium together, and I forced the idea that this might be my last time here into a locked corner inside. I'd parked in the employee lot, and we made our way to my car while the first earnest snowfall began with heavy, wet flakes.

"Got your Christmas present." I opened my trunk.

"Christmas is still twenty-one days away."

"Exactly." I hauled out the box and dropped it in her arms. "You were so upset your mom didn't get an Advent calendar fast enough, so I made you one. There's a present for every day."

She peered in the box of tiny wrapped packages. "How long did this take you?"

I laughed. "Now you can be excited about all the days. Not just the big one."

"That's . . . I can't believe you." She put the box in her back seat and hugged me tight. Her head rested on my collarbone, and I wished I could feel the rest of her against my chest, but my binder was only good at holding things in. Letting things in would have to wait.

Indy and I sat on the hood of my car, watching the snow collect on the arsenic-teal signage. "It's weird. I think I'm going to miss this place. What have you done to me, River?"

For a moment, I thought she was talking about going to California again, a sore subject that took every opportunity to rear its jealous head. No matter what was happening between us, she still planned to take off. For now. But that would change.

"SeaPlanet is all over us. Example?" I pointed to the tin trailer of the human resources office. "I was interviewing for the pearl-diving job, and the dude called me River. I know that's probably not how a person should pick their name, but it felt right."

"Have I taught you nothing?" Indy looked up at me, such brown eyes, hard jaw, soft lips. I'd started wearing boots with an extra inch in order to have this perfect angle on her face. "There's no right or wrong way. When I was little, I used to sing the words of the rainbow. You know, Roy G. Biv? Every time I got to indigo, I sang it like the five golden rings line in 'Twelve Days of Christmas.' It became my nickname, and then, my name." She let go of my chest, and I felt the cold. "Don't you have to go? It's your night with the Chengs."

"You want to come?"

"Oh, taking me home to meet the parents. Are we there already?"

"Please, save your fear for when I actually introduce you to my parents."

Which was exactly how a person should never tempt fate.

I took Indy to her house, the snow collecting fast. She ducked in to change, and I received a 911 text from Everett. At first, I tried to ignore it. I knew what was going on. Karina had finally come to visit, and Mom was no doubt grilling her. How could I help with that? Indy slid back into the passenger seat, looking spectacular in a goldenrod flannel-and-wool jacket, and I started driving toward the Chengs'.

We stopped at the light in the center of town. Not a single other car in sight. The red could last forever here. Sometimes it felt like I'd been stopped at this light since I'd gotten my license. "I have to go home real quick," I muttered.

"Everything okay?" she asked.

"Karina is visiting. Mom *insisted.* Dad took off for a last-minute business trip. Everett's freaking out." I busted the light, driving home a little faster than usual with the snow.

When I pulled in my driveway, Indy craned her neck to look through the dashboard at the house. I hadn't even showed her which house was mine yet, and she'd been chill about it. I took my seat belt off. "Be right back."

"You're going to leave me in the car?" Indy asked, tone neutral.

"No?" I killed the engine. Well, this was bound to occur at some point. I just preferred it to happen after we'd made love a million times or at least kissed so that this bubble of affection didn't have to pop prematurely due to my mom's scorching intolerance.

We entered my house, and no one was yelling. I found what felt like a somber conference on power and privilege at the kitchen table. They were eating Chinese takeout.

Everett called out, “Bakes!”

Mom looked relieved to see me too, until she saw the person behind me. She stood fast, her welcome staged. “Hello! Who are you?”

“Hey, Indy,” Karina said, also relieved.

My brother saluted with his chopsticks. While Mom made her way over to inspect Indy, Everett mouthed, *Get us out of here.*

I’ll try, I mouthed back, desperately thinking of some way to break them free of whatever had occurred before I walked through the door.

“Indigo Waits,” I heard Indy say, offering her hand to my mom.

Mom shook it. “And how does my daughter know you?”

And that’s why I didn’t want any of this. Indy pinked, hardened. She knew that word hit me like a sledgehammer. “Swim team. I’m a diver.”

“That’s good.” My mom’s relief was palpable. She turned to me. “What are you doing here? Isn’t this your *night away*?”

“I was headed to the Chengs’, but I need to bring Ev and Karina with me. They are”—oh hell, why was it so hard to think of an excuse on the spot?—“moving furniture around. They asked if I could bring some extra muscle.”

Mom sat back down, examining her plate. “I imagine it’s hard not to have a man around to move things when you need things moved.” I don’t know who bristled more, Karina or Indy. Everett shepherded them out of the kitchen, and I hung back, checking Mom out. She wanted us to go. That was new; I didn’t like it.

“You okay?”

“If you go now, I can make my yoga class.” She wouldn’t look at me. “You and your brother have such lives before you. Such happiness.” Only my mom could say that without meaning it as a compliment. I realized she was full-on othering us. Her team, after all, was misery, and we weren’t currently on her team, were we?

The ride to the Chengs’ was crowded with Everett and Karina cooling down in the back seat. I learned that what I’d worried would be some kind of roaring insensitivity on my mom's part had been plain awkwardness. Dear old Mom had been sulking.

"I couldn't say a single thing she didn't find fault in," Karina said. "It was bizarre!"

"That's Mom," Everett said. "I did warn you."

"It's sad." Indy spoke only loud enough for me to hear. "She's *so* sad, River."

"Been that way my whole life," I admitted in the smallest voice.

I'd texted ahead to the Chengs, and we opened the door to find Mrs. Cheng excitedly hefting the extension leaf into their dining room table. We told them everything, and Freya agreed that she did have a bookcase to bring downstairs, so the lie could be aligned with truth.

After dinner, I scrubbed dishes with Bea while the rest of them argued about board games. "Indy and my mom have now officially met. I guess it went fine, although now Indy knows I don't talk about her at home."

"We're on *she/her*?" Mrs. Cheng asked.

I nodded.

"And you two have started making out like the stars are falling from the sky, yes?"

I laughed. "Not yet. There's this . . . standoff. It's not bad. It's more like we don't want to rush, but I also don't know what we're waiting for. How long did it take you to kiss Freya?"

"A day." Mrs. Cheng smirked. "But I'm impatient."

I scrubbed at the pan, imagining the Chengs as young, wild lovers. "How old were you when you met?" I needed her to say high school; she didn't.

"Twenty-eight. Freya was twenty-five." She loaded forks into the dishwasher and then smiled at me. "Frey didn't tell you yet? She thinks it's scandalous. I was her scuba instructor, back when I worked at the Orlando park and taught open-water diving in the off-season."

"Tell them how you asked me out!" Freya called from the other room. She could have meant *them* as in all of us. Or she could have meant me. I was as confused as I was hopeful.

"Underwater, with my dive slate." Bea nudged my elbow. "Romantic as all hell."

I'd finished the dishes, but I wasn't done with the conversation. "Maybe this is weird, but I wish we were older. Old enough to have our own places, be our own people." I left out the reality that if we were older, Indy would be on the West Coast, and I'd be . . . where exactly? "You can go ahead and tell me that I'll be old soon enough, and I shouldn't wish away my youth."

"Why would I say something stupid like that?" Bea put an arm around my shoulder, squeezing me. "Being a teenager is one really long night. It's epic until it gets old, and then you sleep it off like a tequila hangover."

"This feels like the antidote to the it-gets-better campaign. The Mrs. Cheng version. *It gets old, and you get over it.*"

"Oh, queer-o." She kissed my temple. "Hang on."

"They're closing SeaPlanet. Did you hear?"

She nodded. "Change comes for everything. Even the sharks."

Unlike Christmas, Indy and I both hated New Year's Eve.

"You're not winning this fight." Indy's voice was testy on the phone.

"We're not fighting. We're arguing." I paced my bedroom, looking for my other sock. One of the perks of having spent weeks flirting and teasing each other was that we'd somehow moved on to bantering at heightened intensity levels. Everything was turned up to eleven. Even event planning. "You've been to Catherine's house. The party will be low-key compared to OU."

"And I'm sure every person I flicked off in fourth grade will be ecstatic to see me again."

"They won't recognize you. Besides, everyone on swim loves you."

"Well, Gia has been texting me. She's such a gossip. Apparently, some of them have been taking bets on when we're going to come out as a couple. Little do they know you're done coming out." It was a gentle ribbing, and I appreciated it. "Also, I still think you're trying to get me to this party so you can kiss me at midnight, and I'm not doing that dinosaur crap, no matter how much you like *When Harry Met Sally*."

Oh, she was on fire, and I loved it. "If you want to kiss me, come kiss me," she said. "We don't need the excuse of Western civilization's calendar randomly wrapping up."

I laughed, found my other sock under the sole of my boot. I pulled it on. "Good thing I didn't give you mistletoe in one of your presents."

"Good thing you gave me twenty-one presents and not one of them was your lips."

I felt the pull of a strong tide, and I went with it. My head swirled, keys in my hand. Out the door. Words were going to need to come back to me. I got in my car and started the engine.

"Are you driving somewhere?"

"Store. Mom needs milk," I lied. "Tell me about all your New Year's." I drove with my phone projecting through my Bluetooth, the entire car warm with Indy's voice. Indy told the story of one year ago that led to the year before it, and before, up to the first one Indy could remember, staying up by herself all alone, a babysitter for her tiny brothers. And I told her about going to the movies by myself last year, and all the years before when I went with Everett, our annual sibling bonding. College had changed that part of us. I wondered what it would change for Indy and me.

All in all, it was three minutes to get to my Indy when I hit the lights just right. Pulling up in the driveway, I marveled at how her mom was throwing a queer-divorcée New Year's party. The house was alive with people drinking and listening to music.

I didn't even know where we were in the conversation when she said, "Everyone on swim team *loves* you. They approve of me, but it's different."

"They all want to be even half as self-confident as you." I climbed her front steps. "My little fish wants to dress *exactly* like you. She's been digging for info about where you shop. And just thinking forward here to future presents, where do you shop?"

Indy began listing small online stores, and I muted the phone, entering the house and heading straight to Indy's room. I waved at her mom and knocked. "Hang on a second. My mom wants something." Indy answered her bedroom door, ear still pressed to the phone. She stared at me for a solid second, and I pushed in. Indy grinned fiendishly, wearing TomboyX briefs and a pajama top with the neck so big one entire shoulder was showing.

The door clapped shut behind me, cutting off the voices and music from the grown-up queer party in the living room. The lamps weren't on, but the many holiday strings were ablaze. I glanced up at them before looking back down at my Indigo in my arms.

"Hey, River." Indy looked impressed. "Something on your mind?"

"I need to check on something." I felt hungry, starving. "Did you say, 'come kiss me'?"

"Yes." Indy nearly laughed, quirking an eyebrow. I took her face in both hands, let the air and her skin and my body *know* that this was happening. My thumb tugged one lip of her smile. She kissed my fingers, and I kissed Indy.

We were soft but certain. My body heated, hummed. I held back, lips parting from hers soon but not fast.

Indy had one palm pressed to my chest, a finger and thumb stroking my collarbones. "Oh, *nice* move."

"We're in love." But that was what insecure guys said when they didn't want to overcommit. "I love you."

"Yeah, you do." She kissed me, and I felt bashful because my insides were downright reveling. Indy's skin was so warm, and my hands around her waist filled me with a firework show. I was happy, excited, terrified. I wanted to do this forever, and also maybe run and hide.

She never did say she loved me back.

I opened my mouth to comment, and she shook her head, pressing me down onto her bed, her knees straddling my lap. She kissed me this time, and it was long and hard, and soul-deep. I left humanity and this planet without losing sensation in one centimeter of my own skin.

Euphoria.

And that's why dysphoria was so aptly named. They were similar experiences, both a flight to a different realm of being, one to endless light, the other? Absolute nothingness. Indigo Waits made me feel euphoric. Like catching the wind, sailing.

Our kissing lapsed into a kind of madness, and I tried to reel it back in before we turned irrevocably naked. "Should we stop?" I asked, eyes searching for hers until I found them and looked away. Too much. Sometimes the way Indy looked at me felt like *way too much.*

Indy was quick to take hold of my shoulders. "Do you want to stop, or do you think we should because yielding is deemed socially respectful decorum?"

I blinked hard, unable to see past the hormones that left me extra aware of my hands and Indy's extraordinary ass. "The second one."

"River, I want . . . you. *Very* badly." Indy's voice had changed, her tone closer, less guarded. When her voice dropped like that, I knew she loved me. Maybe it wasn't simple or straightforward, but that didn't mean it wasn't real. Indy was still straddling my lap, and I held the tops of her hips, thoughts whirlpooling. "I can wait, but if you're waiting for me, I'm ready."

"Right now?" I'd worked myself up to kiss Indy. Now she was asking for a lot more. I could do this; I certainly wanted to. I squeezed her legs, fingers edging toward the feverish center of her body. Indy threw her head back and groaned, and I was nearly undone.

I looped off her baggy pajama top, revealing those sound shoulders, hard nipples, and the excruciatingly soft skin of her chest. Her kisses moved to my neck, and I lost my shirt, my binder pulled as tightly as possible, limiting each breath. Nuzzling the nook between her shoulder and neck, I asked, "Chest? Yes or no?"

"*Yes, please.*"

My hands brushed every inch of her, palms open on her nipples that were so sensitive her sounds grew wild and her knees clamped on my hips. We switched positions, and I sank between her legs. Indy tossed herself backward on the bed, and I tugged away her unders, kissed her wide-open until her body rippled and arched, and she nearly pulled my hair out. She came just like she changed her clothes: unabashed and unbound. Intimidating and proud.

Afterward, she reached for me with the same kind of hunger that had driven me here in the first place, only I was having trouble breathing. Relaxing. Feeling. Her hands went after my belt, and I couldn't help begging my dysphoria, *Not now. Please don't do this to me right now.*

My three-pound binder was holding in a million pounds of flesh. I tried to find the best way to explain how taking it off would kill things for me. Not easy because, as hooking up with Taylor had revealed, having *that* conversation could also kill things for me. I reached to unstrap the massive Velcro side, sure my face was giving me away, and she stopped me.

"Keep it on. It's okay."

I tackled her, flipping us with my weight, lifting my hips to kick off my pants. My skin loved the warm angles of her body. Indy's neck and arms, her shaking legs. We pressed into each other at the same moment, and when I found her eyes wide, searching out mine, I didn't know what was wrong. I nearly asked, nearly stopped us. But there was nothing wrong with Indy staring into me while touching me so tenderly I wanted to cry.

Something was very wrong with all the times before.

Intrusive thoughts rose from my depths. Joss calling my orgasms too masculine. Taylor scolding me to come like a woman, to surrender to it or some shit. I'd long since pretended to finish before I had. I didn't want to do that now, but what the hell were my choices?

I started to cry, an instant scattershot of embarrassment.

Indy stopped, held on to me. I'd never been held this tight. I'd never been this visible. I turned on my stomach, face in the sheets. She drew circles on my back, roughed a hand through my hair, and the pain started to leave one exhale at a time. Indy put on soft music, kissed my fingers while I tried to catch my breath after a few thousand years of holding it. When she brought me a glass of water, I realized we weren't in a fight. She wasn't disappointed. I hadn't ruined this. Indy was waiting, and not for explanations or apologies.

I crawled to her on the bed, those brown eyes a beacon. We kissed madly, came so many times. Our bodies shook into pieces, each one was more satisfying than smashing dinnerware on cement. We stayed in that bed for days, literal years following the countdown of midnight. I left feeling strong and new and irretrievably attached.

— 19 —

I EXPLODED OFF THE BLOCK as Catherine hit the touch pad. Without the shorty, I felt as fast as a damn missile in the lane, shooting through my four laps and nailing all three flip turns. On the last leg, I began to pass the other team's anchor, abandoning my lungs in favor of drastic, strong strokes.

I hit the wall hard; it worked. We'd won our relay.

Afterward, I collapsed on the bench beside Catherine, too tired to shammy myself dry. "Are we winning?" I asked, spitting water off my lips. The intricacies of the point system in swimming had never been my forte.

"We're up ten." Catherine could keep score in her head. Then again, I'm sure she could build entire space stations in there.

The boys' heat of the last event, the 400 freestyle, was racing. It was one of the things I would miss about high school swimming. The gendered teams swam together, not coed racing, but a coed team. That would change in college, where the men's team was an entirely different creature from *the women's team*. Nausea rolled through me, and I held my stomach.

"You okay?"

"Hungry," I lied.

Joss was poised on the diving block to take off after Micah. Joss could get so much spring on those long legs. I'd always been jealous of that. I'd always been jealous of a lot of things about Joss. He had the perfect swimmer's V body, his brown skin notable in this sea of white. I'd never asked him how he navigated the difference. As a basically-white-person, I hadn't felt like I had the right, so I'd just ignored his race. Like everyone else. That must have felt pretty terrible.

Joss had already been tapped by Miami and accepted a place on their team. Catherine was moving to Great Britain two days after graduation, newly determined that the only way to succeed in her life was to find a new country ASAP. Gia was going to OSU. I'd gotten in at a few places, including OU, but I hadn't made any decisions. I was waiting for districts and the dwindling hope that I could catch the OU recruiter's eye. I'd been offered a place on the Akron team, but like hell was I staying so close to home.

Joss charged through his laps, and Gia cheered so loudly her face turned tomato. And it struck me: Soon, after far too many years in forced proximity, we wouldn't know one another. Senior year seemed to keep taking things away. Not only did I feel the impending shutdown of Sea-Planet, but this was my last high school swim meet. Possibly my last ever if I didn't find a way onto a college team.

"Will you miss all this?" I asked Catherine.

"Maybe. Many years from now, but I doubt it," she said. We still had two weeks of practice followed by the notorious shaving party and districts at the end of the month, and yet as my lane mates cheered on the last race, I choked up. Indy and the rest of the divers were at the far end of the pool. I stared at Indy until they looked over, and I waved. "Appears you two can sense each other's thoughts," Catherine observed dryly. "Still not exclusive? Official? Titled?"

"We're official in our own way." I'd had this conversation too many times over the last week. "Exclusivity is not where we begin and end. It's more like we're holding on to each other."

Catherine used her mirrored goggles to check her reflection. "You know how Anders and I are still playing the game of truth or dare we started when we met at sixth-grade camp?"

"No, I did not know that was still going on. I would definitely remember."

"Well, we are. Anders' latest dare is to work on my small talk." Catherine wrung out her shammy, drenching my foot. "You say you are not exclusive with Indigo, and yet if anyone else went near her, you'd take them out." That was possibly true, but I didn't have to agree to it. I didn't have to like it either. Was I supposed to be so requited that jealousy didn't exist? Or was that another one of those dinosaur truths? "Tell me, Micks, are you scared shitless?"

"What?"

"Do you love her so much it's terrifying? That's how I felt about Anders for the first few years. Love is a mutually beneficial vulnerability. A rather large vulnerability. Like having a beautiful, long seacoast but no navy."

I loved that while my internal metaphor was set on man o' wars, Catherine's had her at the head of an island nation. "None of this counts as small talk, by the way, but yes, I do love them. With more pieces of me than I know what to do with."

And yeah, sure, it was terrifying. I stared at Indy by the diving boards. Now that I'd found them, I'd never have to suffer a day without them in my life again. The relief was everything. It felt like sailing.

"You sort of glow when you're happy, did you know?" Catherine was studying me. "You once asked me what it meant for people to be concerned when you smiled. It's probably because your depth of potent misery is only equaled by your ability to exude joy. It shines out of you."

I laughed. "Not sure that's how emotions work. We should ask Indy. No one understands joy like them."

"Them?" she asked. "But I just got used to she/her again."

"Then get unused to it. Stay fluid, Catherine." I popped her shoulder, and she glared at the spot. "This is progress in action."

"The current psychology of progress is flawed. Revolutions dissolve into *Lord of the Flies* far more often than they affect permanent change. There were ancient civilizations on Malta that had toilets. Then they 'lost' the technology, rediscovering it in the Victorian age, four thousand years later. If we could culturally lose the concept of indoor plumbing, who's to say we won't return to a sex-based binary with gender roles in commercial lockdown."

I wasn't Indy, so I couldn't jump on the bench and talk about dead civilizations, but I knew Catherine. Everything in her universe was a concept, an experiment with controlled variables. Her Achilles' heel was individual humans and their tendency to trounce known rules. "I'm nonbinary. And no matter what hat progress is wearing for the day, I'll still be nonbinary."

Catherine looked over my entire being, toes to head. "You make more sense now."

I laughed. Catherine smiled begrudgingly. I had to admit that coming out to someone wasn't so hard as long as there wasn't a scheduled song-and-dance number with it.

The boys finished their relay, now streaming and slap-hugging. The meet was over, but we had a few minutes to collect our selves and things before the winning team was announced. I didn't seem to need to explain to Catherine that I wasn't going to talk further about what I'd just shared. She left it alone, and I loved her for that space.

Catherine carefully wrapped her towel around her torso. "Since we're being so open, help me win an argument with Anders. Consider the baseball diamond of hooking up. Is third base considered sex for people like you? If so, what is a home run?"

I dumped my mouthful of water from my bottle on the tile at my feet. "You want me to explain the difference between fingering and sex?" She nodded; I thought for a moment. "Well, it's . . . intention."

"So, it comes down to nuance. This was my understanding. Not to mention there are lots of sex-based options that are sex no matter what combination of pieces."

"Always so romantic, Catherine."

Indy approached, and I must have had some kind of look on my face. "What's happening here?" I opened my mouth to explain, but Catherine beat me to it, reissuing her original question.

"Queers don't have bases." Indy waved their hand. "And it isn't because of anatomy. I've had plenty of what is traditionally considered sex that hardly felt like sex."

I raised one finger. "I said it comes down to intention."

Indy liked this answer. They moved closer, and my pulse rushed louder than my teammates had been screaming. I clasped my arms around their waist and kissed them.

A last-meet embrace for the ages.

The reaction that rippled through our team left me deeply uncomfortable; Indy too. I think, maybe, someone being cruel wouldn't have shocked me as much as the truth. The other team, Coach, parents in the stands stared like we'd become a livestream porno. Half of them were smiling so slimily that I had an idea to shout something back. No idea what.

"If you had a penis and I had hair, they'd think that was adorable." Indy squeezed my hand before stepping away. I glanced up into the stands at where I knew my mom was sitting. She was looking at the wall.

Kerrig called for everyone to circle up, her eyes boring into mine. The referee announced the winner, and our team had won after all. We did our hands-in, shouting cheer, and told the other side, "Good meet."

And it was over.

I waited for the rest of the team to get changed, hoping that enough parents would grab Kerrig that she'd leave me alone for once. She didn't.

Coach hustled over on muscular legs that had long since turned squat. "McIntyre, about districts. I'm changing the order of the relay. You did well as anchor today. And we aren't going to have a repeat of last year, are we?" I sighed hard, and she actually growled. "You're ungrateful. Talented and ungrateful, which is the worst kind of swimmer to coach."

"Maybe I'm ungrateful." I stood up, collected my things, made zero eye contact. "But you make me not want to swim anymore."

We piled into the bus for the ride back to the school parking lot. I'd taken over the back row like usual, only now I shared the long seat with Indy. Catherine had begrudgingly taken the shorter seat and disappeared into her headphones and the audiobook of the hour.

Indy sat behind me on the dark, cold bus. Their hands moved under my hoodie in the back, massaging. I wasn't wearing my binder, having been too tired to strap it on, and I could feel their fingers on skin that was usually kept away from everyone, even Indy, even in our more riotous explorations of each other. They lowered their face to my shoulder and kissed the back of my neck. I whispered about mouthing off to Coach . . . and coming out to Catherine.

Indy accused me of burying the lede.

"Catherine won't repeat what I said," I murmured. "She believes in collecting but not distributing gossip."

"How do you feel?" Indy asked.

"Better. I wish everyone knew so I wouldn't have to think about this. Wish I could drop a line on social media. Something like, 'Hey, I'm not cis, but leave me the fuck alone about it.' "

Indy was surprised. "Of course you can come out in a post. Put it up and walk away."

I turned to face them, accidentally twisting far enough to lose their hands' tension on my sore muscles. "Taylor swore it was a dick move to come out online."

"The more I hear about Taylor, the more I think she's just a dick move."

"Mom would never forgive me if she found out"—I held up air quotes—" 'the wrong way.' "

"This isn't about her. Or anyone else."

That was easy enough to believe, but there were always exceptions. What about the Chengs or Everett? Surely, I had to tell my brother in a personal way, but I didn't even want to do that. It was bad enough he'd texted me about overhearing Indy call me River, and I'd just . . . never responded.

"I'm done with growing up. Can we be grown now, please?"

Indy kissed me. Their lips were a grounding rod, their body made everything all right. As long as they were beside me, looking at me, I didn't feel dysphoric. I didn't care so much when people misgendered me. As long as they were here, I was here.

Indy turned so I could work on their back for a while. They'd been dumbfounded as to why I wanted them to ride the smelly, dark bus back to the school lot after meets—until I showed them the joy of bus massages. Our collective team exhaustion created this odd bubble of unity, the inverse of training in the pool and goofing off at our sleepovers, and yet just as important. I would miss this part too, and wasn't that strange?

"Tell me. Are you two too queer to attend prom?" Catherine asked, surprising both of us.

I answered *yes* while Indy surprised me by saying, "Depends."

Catherine started coiling up her headphones. We were nearly back at school, and I could already tell that my car was going to be frozen solid in the lot. "Student government is about to make an announcement that I believe you'll find interesting. The hotel we usually invade has a leak in its banquet-room ceiling and will be under renovation for the duration of spring."

"Oh, prom in the gym," I snarked. "That is going to be hard to pass up on."

Catherine didn't say anything, allowing the suspense to build, expression annoyed. "As you can imagine, the gym wasn't a good-enough option, so I made some calls. SeaPlanet has agreed to host at the aquarium. A last huzzah from the marine park of our youth. Prom by shark light. Also, they're evacuating the fish soon, so the dance got moved up a week, right before districts. Josie Fozier is losing her mind with last-minute planning." She was serious. Well, she was Catherine; she was always serious. "Should be a special kind of reunion for you two."

I glanced at Indy, unable to read their thoughts. Sure, we had SeaP memories, but did we want them? Did we need some new, better memory to leave the place behind? Was that how memory even worked? "We'll think about it." I hoped that would be the end of it; it wasn't.

Catherine had that tone; she wasn't venomous but definitely as thorny as a seahorse, perpetually armed. "Unless what happened at last year's prom is too painful to relive."

Indy gave me that look, which meant they weren't going to demand answers, but they were sure as hell hoping for them. I felt foul; the mere mention of prom last year with Taylor was enough to trigger my worst feelings.

The bus stopped in the lot, and we filed out into the ugliness of winter. All the good snow had melted, and what was left on the sidewalks were blackened hunks of ice. The team began to unspool, and I would have happily gone with them, but Kerrig grabbed my shoulder.

"Don't touch me!" I yelled.

Everyone froze. Kerrig's face darkened with what could only be gathering anger.

"And *don't* yell at me. At us. We're tired. Whatever you're mad about can fuck off because I don't deserve this." The words trickled out, coming from deeper than expected. "I don't deserve the way you treat me. Stop it, or I'll talk to the superintendent about your screaming fits. Several of the Littles have videos, so it won't be hard. And while you act like you don't care, we know this is your only way back to the water. And we know how *sad* that is."

Kerrig had turned solid. My nerve was spent as fast as I'd found it, my body shaking. I threw myself toward my car, Indy rushing to get in the passenger door. Indy couldn't drive stick, and I had to get them home before I lost it. Plus, I'd forgotten that I was supposed to give my Little a ride too.

The tall freshman folded up her legs in the back, the three of us simmering in cold. "That was the coolest thing I've ever seen in my whole life," she whispered. Indy barked a short laugh, and I shook my head.

"I think I'm in shock." I shivered in the driver's seat, a stream of curses providing a minor exorcism. The car heated slowly, and the whole time I watched Kerrig pace in the rearview like a furious bear. She wasn't allowed to leave until we'd all pulled away.

Last meet, right . . .

I laughed hollowly. She'd really killed this last year on a team for me. A year that could have been so good with Joss, Catherine, Indy. She'd killed all four years, if I was being honest. "Stay," I said to both of them, regretting the command but still meaning it.

I got out and approached Coach Kerrig with my teeth set.

She saw me coming and swatted at the air as if to swipe me off her tablet screen. "I accept your apology, McIntyre. Get back in your car. We've only got one more competition between the two of us, leave it at that."

"I'm not sorry about what I said. I'm sorry for whatever they did to you."

"They? What are you talking about?"

"Whoever, whatever did *that* to you." She was speechless, which was good. "You're full of hate. I can see it in your eyes and hear it in your voice, and I've lived that way. It's going to kill you. You shouldn't let it."

She sneered and I left, my sting finding its first purposeful mark. I drove to my Little's house, which wasn't close, but I didn't mind. The dark roads and now-toasty air coming from the vents soothed me. We went to Indy's next, and they said nothing, but pulled me out of the car and around the side of the house to a small swing set. They sat on a metal swing, and I sat on the one next to them. The air was bitter in my lungs. The metal creaked with cold. I told Indy an abridged version of what I'd said to Kerrig.

"That was really . . . intrusive of you. Not that I'm judging."

"She started it." I gripped the frozen chains so hard my hands ached. "I keep thinking *I don't deserve this*. I don't deserve this. I keep thinking it, and I don't know, I think I'm starting to believe it, but it doesn't make me feel better. It makes me furious."

"And isn't that the worst legacy of growing up in captivity." Indy took my hand in the cold. They looked distant, worried. "You're right. You don't deserve this, River. You deserve very good things. Come inside, and I'll show you."

Safety is strange when you're not used to it. It settles like snow, makes the whole world quieter.

We were tangled, nearly naked. Ani DiFranco was trying to tell me about righteous love through the speaker.

Indy's head rested on my binder. I wondered whether they could feel my heart through all that scar tissue and spandex. Then I wondered what it would be like to have a chest that I could look at, touch, offer up to them for a pillow. Breathe with. Indy used to show me before-and-after top-surgery pictures of some of their friends before they realized it was too hard for me. Meaning, before I stung them by snapping, "Don't show me things I'm never going to be able to do."

But why couldn't I? Indy would help me through it; I knew they would.

Maybe I was ready to talk about this; Indy had other ideas.

"You were upset before Kerrig." Their voice was mellow but intent. "When Catherine brought up prom last year."

"Yeah, well, it was upsetting." They weren't going to ask what happened, which made me need to tell them. "Taylor shoved me into this drag ensemble, forced me to take pictures with her family, and by the time we made it to the hotel, I couldn't go in. She tried to force me; we fought. Then she tried to drive off angry, and she hit me with her car."

"On purpose?"

"I jumped in front of the car." Indy and I had had millions of conversations so far together, but this subject—this River who had a history of being mildly violent to themself—was new information. "I wasn't hurt. Just some bruises." My voice wasn't good at lying to Indy. There really had only been bruises on the outside. The inside of me was a different story.

Indy sat up, eyes wide. "You wouldn't do that again, would you? If you were upset?"

I panicked. "I wouldn't. I don't hurt myself anymore, I swear." I tried to kiss them, and they turned away. "I swear. I promise. That's all . . . that's not me. Not since I met you. I'm so happy sometimes I'm *glowing* now. You can ask Catherine."

"Just give me a second to process." Indy wasn't telling me something. It'd never felt so large between us. For days they'd had this middle-distance look. My fists tightened over and over, until I was able to somehow convince myself that losing my Lebanese temper right this second would end horribly for all involved.

"Okay, so we go to prom together. Make new memories," I bit out. "The best outfits?"

They took too long to make eye contact. My bound chest pounded.

"Coordinated outfits," they bartered. I agreed, kissing them. Their mouth could melt away the worst feelings, even if it felt a little like I'd lost count on my strokes and was headed fast for the wall.

— 20 —

I WAS STANDING AT MY OWN FUNERAL, otherwise known as the pre-prom photo shoot in my front yard. I'd agreed to go to the dance, outfitted to the nines with my love, but the rest was pure hell.

"This is the dumbest prank you've ever pulled, brother. I'm going to get you back. Oh yes." We posed for Mom's camera, and I squeezed Everett's shoulder so hard he yowled.

Indy cut in, pushing Everett out of the way. They wore a dark purple fitted suit with silver Converses and no shirt. The buttoned suit coat allowed for a long plunge of Indy skin. Mom kept trying to position me so that I hid Indy's chest with my arm, and we had entirely too much fun foiling her attempts. When they took me around the waist and posed looking up into my eyes, their mom and her girlfriend rushed forward with cameras and *awws*.

Mom did not. "She's so . . . bold with that shaved head, don't you think?"

Indy's mom nearly levitated, but they signaled for her to calm down. After that, our moms took defensive stances at either end of the extra-fertilized yard. Our dads—yep, I got to meet Mr. Waits and the two blond emperors who climbed Indy like a tree—held court in the middle, small-talking. They both worked in Downtown Cleveland, but all other similarities disappeared from there.

"You know, all my friends' parents like each other. I swear I saw this going differently," Everett whispered. He was home for the weekend with Karina, attempting a new strategy, which was also our oldest game, the one with no rules and only three words: Make Mom Happy. Thus he'd set up this parental circus photo shoot without telling me. He wasn't wrong; Mom loved this stuff. Though, she wasn't enjoying it either. Not with Karina photographing Indy in the corner of the yard. Indy posed joyfully. Smiling, serious, laughing, spy.

I checked my watch. "Ten more minutes. How the hell are we going to fill ten minutes? If this isn't the saddest group of humans . . ." My brother and I looked out at the parents, all lonely little planets like a disbanded solar system. "We're not going to get that sad one day, are we?"

"No," he said, and frowned. "We are not."

"We have to hold each other accountable."

We shook on it. I put my sunglasses on. "Good."

"Also, don't worry about filling time. I called in reinforcements." He pointed at a Jeep coming down the street. The Chengs arrived with the same hooting excitement they had on game night. They honked into the drive, jumped out with smiles. Freya had a large, professional-looking camera around her neck, and Bea was wearing a blazer. Of all the parents, she was the only one to respect our formal wear with an extra effort on her part. And Hugo hopped out of the Jeep too, barking as he trundled toward the group that now felt like a small party.

"Take a picture of me with Mrs. Cheng." I shoved my phone at my brother and jogged to cross the yard and hug her. Something about seeing her reminded me why anyone would want to do this in the first place. We took pictures endlessly, shuffling the whos and wheres around the yard. The other parents left, until it was just the Chengs.

And Mom, who kept a distance, sitting on the front step.

"Okay," Freya yelled, laughing too hard after nearly falling over Hugo. "Did we get every shot? All the shots? All shots that could ever be conceived of?"

Everyone left yelled *yes*, and I knew we didn't. I hadn't taken a picture with my mom. Not a single one. When I looked back up to the steps, the front door closed behind her.

Mrs. Cheng caught me looking and put a hand on my shoulder. I waved my arms around a few seconds before the words could come out. "What do I do with her? With that?"

"Give her space and time. Took my mother seven years."

"But now she loves me!" Freya hollered, leading the charge back to the cars. "Come, children! You must go dance with the fishes!"

I got into the passenger side of Indy's car, watching Bea take Freya up around the stomach and lift her into a kiss. They'd been together for twelve years. I looked over at Indy. "So, we're going to prom now, huh? Sure about that?"

Indy winked, drove, and I was ready. Prom might still feel crushingly heteronormative, but it could also mean something to us. And I had a good idea how.

Indy parked in the SeaPlanet employee lot, swinging into their favorite spot, the same one they'd been parked in the day I'd run through here half naked and furious.

We got out and looked over each other again. They groaned.

"I still think you're going to get in trouble." My voice cracked.

"With whom?" Indy's smile was openmouthed, eyes bright and rimmed in kohl. "Are you afraid my chest is going to get *you* in trouble?"

"Of course I am." Indy and I had gone far more glamorous than AFAB pantsuits. Girls in tuxes were now about as common in the dinosaur community as those who went full bare midriff. A bold move, sure, but only earth-shattering to *those* parents. No, Indy was serious about dress-up. It was as if we were cosplaying European models. Slick as some kind of spy, but not too serious about it. They untucked my shirt and opened the top buttons down to my binder. Then they messed up my hair, so pleased with their success that while I looked at myself in the car window reflection, their hand almost sunk down my pants with brilliant intention.

A few car lanes over, Gia walked by in a dress that consisted of a necklace-styled halter top and a hip-hugging miniskirt. She winked at me, which was surprising. And could mean a lot of things. Indy stared after her. "That's far more skin than I'm showing."

"Yeah, but we're—"

"Promise me you're not going to say *the gays*."

"Walking targets," I finished. As much as I wanted to believe that my high school could keep their act together with a bunch of sexy enbies streaking through their binary paradise, I knew better. My peers and I were taller and had all our permanent teeth, but we'd been raised by a school who couldn't have a GSA because it "might make people upset." The same community that waved hate flags in Indy's ten-year-old face and looked the other way while Mike Dweiller assaulted us one by one.

"River?" Indy's arms were around my waist, and I came back.

"Scared," I muttered.

"Yeah."

"Mad that I'm scared."

"Yeah."

I looked at their upturned face. Their hair was long enough to be sculpted into an adorable faux-hawk. "The safety math on this is not good. I feel like they might skip the administration and go straight to the cops when they see us. Is this be gay, do crime?"

"Yes. The worst crime of all. We'll be happy."

I kissed them, and then we had to get back in the car all over again. Eventually, we made it to the aquarium doors where nearly two hundred overdressed upperclassmen had bottlenecked, some taking photos with SeaPlanet mascot Keemee in front of a life-sized breaching orca. The aging statue was wearing teal Mardi Gras beads and oversized SeaPlanet sunglasses.

Indy skipped the line and entered the code to a side door, and I saw a new side of SeaPlanet. Behind the carpeted walls of the inner aquarium was more than the backs of the tanks. This was where the marine life was cared for. State-of-the-art equipment gleamed, some wrapped in shipping plastic, labeled with park names. One read ORLANDO. The other SAN DIEGO, and one in the back read ABU DHABI. There was a SeaPlanet in Abu Dhabi? Those poor Antarctic penguins.

I took in every piece of equipment, appreciating it. "They should have let us see this side of SeaPlanet. The conservation and science side."

"Those attractions didn't go over well here." Indy led us around the maze of the lab stations, stopping by a familiar tank. "They do a bit more conservation talk in the Orlando park, and they have a lot of it in the California park."

"Ah, the many perfections of California."

Their face grew serious, only a hint of play. "No making fun of California. We both know you're just jealous." Indy tugged at my collar until it was attractively misaligned. "Anyway, they tried to open up this back area and do science tours and no one came. Ted, who has been here *forever*, said it was embarrassing how little this population cared about helping sea animals in the wild. They replaced the youth science lab with an exhibit of animatronic dinosaurs purchased from the renovated Universal Studios park. Ted said the merchandise sales silenced all the critics."

"So you're friends with Ted? Tall Ted? Who does the terrible hiring interviews?"

"I mean, no one is really *friends* with Ted. We all just sort of learn weird things about the North American parks from him."

"Indigo, he's the guy who named me. Well, he called me River because he was too bored to scroll up and read my name and he remembered that it had something do with water."

"Not Ted."

"Ted! He wanted to start his own TED Talk about being a Ted. Oh, I should hook him up with Everett's roommate, Harvey. They can write a show together. Can you imagine?" We both started laughing. I kept talking, words pouring out like comedy. "I know *a lot* of my life has been warped by this odd place, but imagine finding your name from a person like Ted?"

Indy held the strategic buttons of their suit coat. I tugged them into my arms, our hips kissing. "I love you," I said when they'd nearly come down from the laughter.

"Yeah, you do." Indy dabbed at corner of their eyes.

It wasn't the first time I'd said it, and they'd pulled back. In fact, it was one too many. I didn't look at them, but I held them tight. "If you don't love me, I need to know that. If you don't want to say those words, I need to know that."

"The second one," they said into my shirt. "Did I tell you I graduated from my program? Mom framed the diploma and everything."

"Congratulations. Should we start planning a neighborhood-sized party?" Trying to find room for laughing again was hard. "My brother had a legit lamb roast in the backyard."

"Very funny." Indy was straightening their clothes, and I pretended to do the same. Instead I faced the back of a large tank and found myself nose to bulbous head with Sally the pink octopus, who was actually more red than pink. It felt like she'd been listening, watching. I'd heard that octopuses had souls from enough scientists to know something had spooked them. Or maybe we just assigned a creature a soul when it was smart enough to know it was in a prison.

"Sally's an escape artist. Aren't you, Sally?" Indy said.

"You're friends?"

"We spent a lot of slow hours together. She usually comes out when she sees me."

"Oh." I don't know why, but it was a letdown to know Sally was most likely appearing before Indy like usual, not visiting me in some final, poignant way. "Where's she going?"

Indy looked around the side of the tank. "Looks like San Diego. You okay? I can explain the love thing. It just isn't the easiest talk."

The love thing.

"Let's just . . . go inside."

Indy opened a door into the carpeted inner aquarium wall. We stepped through, and it disappeared behind us when it shut.

A cadet in full uniform stood beside the front side of Sally's tank.

"Hey, Anders," I said. He didn't recognize me, and I wasn't surprised. I hadn't seen him in years, and even though Catherine showed me pictures of him, I doubt she sent him pictures of me. "It's River."

"River?" he asked.

Indy cleared their throat. Of course no one knew that name but Indy. Not even my childhood best friend.

"McIntyre," I tried. "Oh, she probably just calls me the pain in her ass."

He held out a military-inflected hand to shake. "I believe I know of whom you speak."

Catherine strode over to meet us in a glorious pantsuit. "I approve this look, Micks. This is what you could have been like all four years of high school if you hadn't been so shut down all the time."

"Harsh, Catherine." I laughed. "But fair. Nice pleats."

"Anders did them for me."

Anders pinned his hat under one arm, his other elbow offered to Catherine. "We will dance."

The dance floor was set up before the massive column of the shark tank. Already the glowing floor tiles housed dozens of bad dancers, and the DJ's playlist drilled an upbeat tempo. The aquarium of our youth had donned some streamers and balloons for the occasion, but mostly the place looked like it always had. The black carpeted walls felt like a dark womb containing a hundred tanks of glassy-eyed mourners.

We started walking around the curving halls of the aquarium, the little pockets of tanks. When we passed the velvet curtains of the Jellyfish Haven, I leaned in and around the corner. Indy followed, bumping into me. I'd stopped in surprise. All the jellyfish tanks were empty, the black lights glowing through the glass and water, illuminating nothing. "Where did all they go?"

"Alien abduction," Indy said, arms wrapping around my middle from behind. "I feel like we're fighting. I hate feeling like we're fighting."

I held their arms. "It's this place. I can't believe they wanted to have a dance here."

"People get married here *all* the time. You'd be shocked. I hated working special events. That's when people truly enjoyed the Jellyfish Haven, if you know what I'm saying." Indy continued, "Apparently, the aquarium is popular for first dates, and what's more romantic than getting married on the spot of your first date?" I looked at Indy, and they shook their head once. "The shark tank was not our first date. I think that dive tryout was our first date. We can get married in a pool, if you need that kind of symmetry."

"Marriage is far too dinosaur, certainly," I teased, but Indy stared at me with such love.

"I'd marry you. I want to already, and that's an *insane* feeling. It's why I can't start telling you I love you. Once I give in, this is happening. No stopping it."

I worked to comb through the sweeter parts of their speech without falling too hard on the stinging ones. So, they didn't think we were together right now. I could fix that. I could show them how much this was working for both of us. "Let's go see the penguins."

We left, unable to face all that new emptiness. Crossing the floor, I pushed through the shark-tank dancers. Indy pulled me into a spot for a few minutes of fast moves, but they could tell I was too busy looking for sharpshooters to enjoy dancing in this crowd.

The hallway to the Penguin Encounter was cooler, and we passed sets of teenagers who were so far into making out they seemed like extras in a hit teen movie. My drive to do something a bit more romantic than usual waned, even if the Penguin Encounter was the best place to share some specific feelings.

The moving walkway was turned off. I stood at the lip where the ground and floor plates met. Indy took in the enormous shadowbox of penguins. I stopped too. There were three penguins in love with their mirror image in the glass wall, huddling for warmth with themselves. "They look so unhappy when you're not moving."

Indy sat on the handrail, kicking their legs up like that time so long ago. "These fellas are always unhappy. Why did you want to come here?"

"To tell you that the walkway takes one minute and forty-three seconds."

Indy seemed impressed, or worried. "Wow, how do you remember that so specifically?"

"I timed it because something happened on this walkway, and I wanted to know all the details afterward. I never want to forget." They smiled, always listening. I could do this.

"You let me out."

Indy's smile was questioning, and then it drooped.

"Remember when you pulled me out of the shark tank and I was saying—"

"I remember."

"You let me out." Oh, this had sounded a lot more romantic in my head. "When I saw you here during the field trip, I went from not knowing why I was drawn to people like you to full-on queer-o. Staring at you obliterated my questions. Now I can say I'm trans, one of the nonbinary sort, I guess. I can say this because you let me out. You make me feel safe and seen. That's a great reason to love you, but you know it's deeper. I know you love me too, which is why this is starting to mess with me. I don't know where we are. You just told me you'd marry me, but you won't say I love you."

Indy jumped down from the railing and grabbed my lapels. They pressed their face to my neck. "My mom got me a graduation present. The one she promised me eight years ago when I started that ridiculous elite homeschool program. A flight to California. I'm going to go stay with my grandparents until I find a job and place of my own." I tried to pull back, look into their face, but they pressed closer to my chest. I knew they were going away; I'd always known. But we were all leaving come next fall. I was going to be ready by then. We'd find our way. We had time.

Unless Indigo was going a lot sooner.

"When are you leaving?" I asked.

Indy held tighter.

Someone yelled my dead name, and I went cold in the teeth at Taylor's voice. My ex drunkenly ran up to me and Indy, trampling our moment. She had a drunk Beth in tow, and the two of them looked like a passed-out end to their evening was nigh.

"You look amazing." Taylor paused and smiled at me, waiting.

I was too distracted for this. "Yeah, you look like a mermaid, Tay."

"A sexy mermaid," Beth added loudly. "Taytay."

Indy's mind was still caught on what they'd just unloaded on me, and so was mine. We couldn't even look at each other. Our drunken companions misread the awkwardness.

"Are you two together, or aren't you?" Taylor yelled. "All this fake drama. I *knew* you were into her last summer even when you swore you weren't."

"Yeah, I was lying. I've always been into Indigo Waits. As long as I've existed"—*all six months of it*—"I've loved them."

Indy mouthed playful curses. My gods, looking straight at this person lifted every single piece of me, sent me sailing.

How could they leave?

"I'm dating Beth!" Taylor held up their conjoined hands. I didn't react; I'd forgotten that she existed. "We wanted you to know. It's serious."

"All-the-way serious!" Beth hollered, and then quieted to add, "No hard feelings?"

I blinked. "Are you talking to me? No hard feelings. I mean, if you're a girl, you're already doing better than I did with Taylor."

"Of course I'm a girl," Beth said, confused.

Taylor charged right up against me. "I'm going to become an author of lesbian romance, and you're going to be the rejectable hunk in every single book."

"Cool," I said.

"Can I be the bisexual skank?" Indy held up a hand. Taylor wasn't amused. She'd clearly thought that this would be a much worse insult. She tugged her girlfriend away, leaving Indigo and me before an audience of over fifty miserable, forgotten penguins.

"Let's go somewhere else," I begged.

Indy led me out the quiet wing of the Penguin Encounter, back to the aquarium proper. Most everyone was dancing now, arms raving over their heads, hips spinning, and I felt in slow motion as we wove our way to the exit in the great shadow of the shark tank.

Back in Indy's car, they turned on the engine, and we waited for it to warm up. "I'm excited for you," Indy said with such tenderness. "Thank you for telling me. I know how you feel about coming out."

"Yeah." Loud voices shouted very different things inside of my mind. *You came out, and they're happy for you. They love you. But not enough to stay. Or even say it.* "Your dreams of getting out of here are coming true. This is great."

"Oof, that was hard to hear you try to say." They nearly smiled, but my look turned their humor off. "Wait till you hear the worst part. Flight's next week. It's one-way. I don't know when I'll come back." Indy waited, but I didn't possess words. Anxiety pounded through my entire body. "I'm gonna skip districts because I have to pack and line up some things. Also, I wasn't going to dive, so I'd probably only distract you from your events. Especially now."

"Wow. So, this is really over."

"That's exactly what I don't want to happen," Indy said, riled. "Let me explain how I see us." Indy began to talk, but I couldn't hear anything.

Fear took hold of me. I couldn't move. Indy drove me home. Is that why they'd wanted to drive? Because they were going to tell me this, and I'd go catatonic? They always knew too much about me before I did. I unbuckled when they parked, got out, nodded away anything they said with "We'll talk later."

Walking up the driveway, the orca in the tree was singing "It's a Small World," and I couldn't help thinking how the stupid song was wrong. This was a small place in a very large world. San Francisco wasn't even in my purview. I had never seen the ocean, let alone imagined living up against it. And as SeaPlanet had been promising us all along—their mission statement and reason for existence—animals born in captivity couldn't survive in the wild.

— 21 —

IF YOU'VE NEVER BEHELD a punch bowl overflowing with five pounds of pasta, beside a finished basement of thirty teenagers shaving one another's legs, arms, and heads, you're missing out.

The shaving party was generally a wild moment, and the team even cheered when I trudged in an hour late. Catherine's basement had transformed. The couches were moved elsewhere, the rugs were rolled back, revealing an expanse of marble tile. The seniors had created a little island in the middle out of their towels, and I specifically avoided the spotlight feel, setting up in the back corner beside my little fish, Marie. I'd set my mind to a specific task: shave my whole body and not talk to anyone. Should be easy enough. I lasted about two minutes.

From the time it took me to leave my car and set up in the basement, I'd gotten twelve texts from Indy. My little fish watched me hold down the power button until the phone shut all the way off. "Sometimes you've got to pull the plug," I grumbled. "You know? Too much is too much, to borrow my situ's favorite phrase."

"You and Indy are fighting?" Marie had the spooky ability to know everything I was doing all the time. All the Littles did. I wouldn't be surprised if she already knew about Indigo Waits's Great Escape, T-minus five days and a handful of hours.

"Indy's packing instead of coming to districts, so I didn't pick them up. When I pulled in the driveway here, they texted that they were waiting, that they wanted to come." *Stop talking, River.* "I drove halfway to their house before I realized that I don't want to come here with them.

I don't want to feel this way. So I came back and parked on the street screaming into my jacket until Catherine's father came out to check on me. Wow, my voice is a lot lower than normal."

"You and Indy *broke up.*" Marie crawled closer, adjusting her towel. "Are you okay?"

"Not even a little." I started to shave my legs. The water in my bowl turned pink right away, the shave far too close. I'd finished both of my legs when Catherine reached through the cosmic recesses of my brain and flicked me in the forehead.

"Marie filled me in."

I turned toward my little fish without looking at her. "I appreciate it."

Catherine examined destroyed me. Her imperious nature cracked ever so slightly. "There's just one way out of this. We shave your head. This is your moment, Micks."

This was anything but my moment. This was the lowest common denominator of my existence. "Sure. Right."

Catherine turned on a pair of cordless clippers she'd hidden behind her back. She grabbed the front of my hair and held the clippers to it, stopping just before it hit my scalp. The team gathered around us in a flash, yelling, cheering, feeding on one another's energy.

"Say when," Catherine proclaimed.

Across the basement, I watched Indy come down the stairs.

"When."

Catherine buzzed the front. Joss, Gia, and the other seniors pushed in, taking turns hacking at my hair, and I felt like GI Jane and Aslan and Britney Spears, and every other creature who has had to literally shear at their life to get the point across. The energy was feral, and I bet Catherine's parents heard the raucousness and locked the door to their bedroom suite.

For the last stray strands, Indy's hands slid over my head. I had my eyes closed tightly by then, coils of black hair sticking to my face and body. I could have picked Indy's touch out of a million hands. They turned my face toward the fluorescent light and touched up the missed places. I kept my eyes closed. I tried to find all the pieces of sound. The tired, hot motor of the clippers. The screeching Littles. Joss's booming shouts that turned into a choral cheer. Catherine conducting the room as if it were a symphony of personalities she'd tuned herself.

And Indy whispering my name underneath it all, trying to get me to open my eyes.

I came out by crawling through a hole in the wall of bare, smooth legs around me. I shot into the bathroom and locked the door. My reflection punched me straight in the teeth. My head was shaved, sure, but that part was hardly interesting. My gaze was identical to the glassy-eyed mourners in all those cursed tanks at SeaPlanet. How did I get this bad? What would happen when Indigo was gone?

I felt Indy coming from across the basement and unlocked the door a second before they touched the knob. They turned my chin with their thumb, left and right, inspecting this shorn me.

"I look like Everett." My voice crumbled like old plaster. My screaming therapy from earlier had bashed up something in my throat.

"You're handsome." Indy was very worried about me; I didn't want that. "Your eyebrows stand out now."

"Oh." I looked in the mirror again. "Good."

Indy kissed my jaw, pulled my face toward their face. I kissed them back with a sudden drowning need, until several people started hooting and banging outside the door. I nearly put a fist through the bathroom drywall. But I didn't.

"What?" Indy hollered.

Gia giggled. "Catherine says, 'Don't even think about it!' "

Indy looked back at me.

"They think we're making up," I explained. "Makeup sex."

Indy kept trying to get me to look at them. I kept finding a reason not to. "Please. I don't want us to leave each other all messed up like this."

"I know you have to go. I want you to do whatever you have to do for yourself." My chest squeezed, I held myself, briefly out of breath. "I just . . . don't know how to exist without you. No one else even knows my name."

"If I leave, you'll figure it out. I know you will." Indy tried to pull me closer, but I didn't want it. "This is going to be good for both of us even though it feels like the worst." They touched my cheek. "I can't be the only proof that you exist. You know this."

And I did, but it didn't help.

Indy started crying so hard that it ripped me out of my own pain. I comforted them, kissed their head. Their whole body shook, anger mixing with tears. "We're not breaking up," they said. "We aren't together yet. Someday. Not yet. Soon. *Not yet.*"

Indy couldn't stop saying it, and for the first time, I didn't believe them.

I entered my house a hundred years later. I felt even worse than I had after prom, and that couldn't have been physically possible.

Taking off my shoes took a long time. Hanging up my jacket was excruciating. All the while, I heard Mom come toward me through the house. Out of her bathroom, around her bed, down the hall and stairs, to where she frowned at destroyed, shaved me in the dark foyer.

"I knew this would happen. But I'm not going to get mad. Just to keep you on your toes," she said. I wasn't sure how to respond to that, so I didn't.

Mom stopped me by the sleeve of my hoodie, speaking the only Arabic I ever heard her voluntarily use: a string of delicate curses. She turned my body to look my entire head all over, similar to how she used to give me daily assessments. Mom had given them up around the same time I'd taken up with Taylor. Something about having a relationship with a girly girl made her look at me differently, as if my masculine nature helped with the hetero math.

"You look like a boy," she concluded. "But I see no lumps."

I wept.

My mom folded me up in her arms and held me on the bottom of the stairs, soothing me like she had when I was very young, always too prepared for bad news. "What's this new low?"

"I'm a cliché. Got my heart broken."

"Oh, daughter, what have I taught you?" She held me tight. "Love is a loaded weapon."

I got on the bus to districts at 6:00 a.m., bleary and exhausted. I made it through the moment when we finally pulled away, having waited an extra ten minutes for Indy to show, which they did not.

I swam my four events. Coach—who'd made no mention of our fight—introduced me to the recruiter from OU who wanted me to try out for the women's team. I'd gotten an invitation to try out but not an invitation to the team. Coach explained the difference in a surprisingly civil tone. I agreed I'd accept OU. I'd train all summer at home, so I might have the times to walk on the team in the fall. That was the obvious plan in her mind, and I couldn't see any other way.

For half a year, I did every single thing I was supposed to do, exactly the way I was supposed to do it, and whenever I was alone, I cried until I drowned.

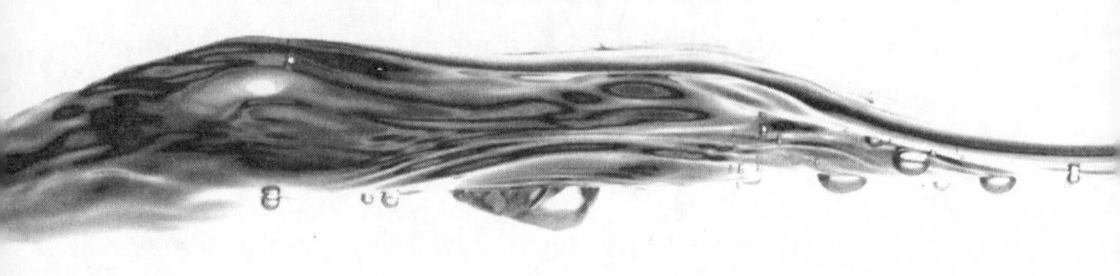

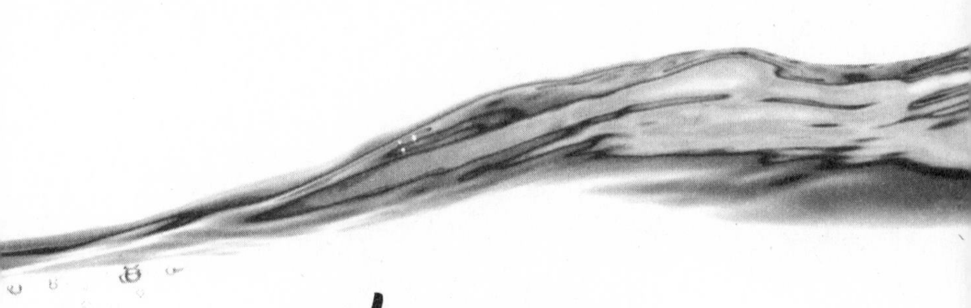

octopuses

Octopuses have three hearts, blue blood, and no bones. Sometimes the female eats the male; other times they breed. Their deaths are part of the mating process, so unbred octopuses in captivity live longer than their wild cousins.

Longer life is better, right? Not really. Senile octopuses become angry and bored and eat their own arms.

I thought the octopus one was going to be sweeter. Sorry, friends.

— 22 —

OHIO UNIVERSITY emerged from the Appalachian hills, its privileged students sprawled across a scenic redbrick campus. Mom enjoyed the roundabout off the highway, sending half of my piled boxes in the back seat into a small crash. I'd been looking forward to moving out for years—and I'd been dreading this day alone with Mom for just about as long.

The air in the overly air-conditioned car permeated the only element of my mom's personality more grating than her negativity: her forced positivity.

"The green is *cute*." Mom craned her head to look out at the downtown stoplight. We'd already been through this intersection twice. Parking in this town was possibly *always* stupid, not just when Halloween took over the streets.

This place looked different in the dog days of summer. Humid and cloistered. A smidge of political blue in an absolute sea of red. Why had I picked this school? Jesus, I'd never made a life choice this slapdash before. We passed the Burrito Buggy, and it felt like bumping into an old sea mine. Was coming here *only* a latent Indy-inspired choice? I managed not to dissolve into a dysphoric reenactment of the *Titanic* but only just.

Mom said my dead name. "It looks like the buildings are pretty new, don't you think?"

I looked, but I saw something different. "It looks like all the buildings are new but made to look old." Great, I'd gotten suckered into a McCollege.

We passed by a series of dorms with hundreds of cars hodgepodged together, and both of us leaned back. "Let's do lunch first," she said, and I agreed.

She drove us back up a hill and down the central redbrick of Court Street. There were more pedestrians than I'd ever seen in a place, and that's the first time I realized I was moving to a town where pretty much everyone would be my age. This was exciting and confusing information, to say the least. I pushed the thought away and helped my mom scout out food. Every single place had a line out the door. Every single one.

We parked at the top of a narrow, cramped garage and wandered through the filled sidewalks, both of us dazed by the amount of people. I smelled something on the wind and wasn't surprised to find my mom's nose already pointed in that direction too.

Between two open, blasting doorways of bars (one playing country, the other *sports!*) was a narrow alley, not even big enough for a car. We followed the smell to a sign sticking out over a door midway down, DAIB'S MEDITERRANEAN CUISINE & MARKET.

"*Mediterranean.*" My mom laughed. I didn't know this laugh; it was delightfully conspiratorial and reminded me of Everett playing D&D. "Clever."

"What's clever?"

"Calling Middle Eastern food 'Mediterranean' to confuse the racists. I had a place like this where I went to college." Her smile tilted, and I knew she was thinking about traumatic things that she'd made sure I would never find out about. "If they'd thought of something clever like this, things might have ended up differently."

Mom didn't talk about college often. Then again, she didn't usually work this hard to be upbeat. She felt like a different person, even more so when we went inside and found a handful of quiet, contemplative patrons beside a few aisles of market goods and a back counter. The insanity of the street outside vanished. Lemon, lamb, hummus. All the smells were right. I would be coming back here.

The older person behind the counter with DAIB stenciled on his shirt looked at us intensely. "Yes?"

My mom ordered swiftly and confidently. Her voice had a daring, lower pitch to it when she was talking to another Arab person. Toward the tail end of the order, he started to bob his head while he was writing it down like he agreed with what she was ordering. About that same time, I realized just how much food she ordered. A feast.

After she paid, he said something to her in Arabic, and she looked at me weirdly before responding. I didn't understand any of it. She'd made sure of that too.

He said something that was more like *sorry* than *thank you for your incredibly large order. It will help us stay in business in a town where nearly everyone is too racist to eat here.*

We sat down at a corner table. "What did he say to you?"

"He asked me if you were a freshman. I said yes."

"That was definitely not the exchange I saw."

"Could you sit up? Straighten your shoulders?" She beckoned for me to rearrange myself, something she hadn't done in years, but oh boy, I remembered the hand signal. "Did you want to put a little concealer on? I have some in my bag. You're probably going to want to clean up in the bathroom before we get to your dorm. Good first impressions don't happen on accident."

I slouched down so far in the seat that my torso disappeared, shoulders at the table's waterline. I was now a man o' war existing entirely of sail. My venomous tentacles could be anywhere. "What did he say to you?"

"He asked me if *my son* was a freshman. I told him he was wrong. He was very sorry. *Why* are you grinning like that?"

"I don't know! I'm hungry!" I glanced over my shoulder at where Daib was rolling grape leaves; yeah, I was coming back here. My limbs reemerged from under the table, human again.

Wow, stress was doing really weird things to me.

Numerous plates came out, and Daib seemed determined to win my mother over for his mistake, aka one of the best moments of my life. She gave him her serious flirting face, and the tension let out. We ate our feast, and I was surprised to find my mom actually eating. Her shoulders might've even come down a bit. Was this because I was getting out of her hair? Or because she was surrounded by things that smelled warmly familiar and forbidden? At least, that's what it all smelled like to me.

"I ordered enough to make sure he remembers you. If he remembers you, he'll like you. Then maybe you can ask him all the questions I don't want to deal with. That being said, if anything happens at this restaurant, you don't come here and fight the idiots doing hate things. That's a promise you're making to me right now."

I had a hunk of kibbie rolling about in my mouth, salty and thick. Suddenly the Syrian bread wrapped around it was tough as jerky. When I finally got it down, I didn't promise; I pushed. "That's what happened to the place you knew in college? Someone went after it, and you got caught up in it?"

"That's one something that happened." She pushed her makeup bag into my hand and pointed at the door to the bathroom. I slid into the closet-sized space that had thankfully not been arbitrarily assigned a gender. I stared at myself in the mirror. No, not myself. I never looked at myself. Man o' wars don't have faces.

I looked at my hands. My dad's hands. Mom and I had both been working so hard to get along for so long. It was exhausting. But I still had another question.

We left Daib's, heading back to the parking garage in silence. I kicked at the question a few times before it found its way out. "Why get me in with Daib back there? Why do that if what you experienced is . . . whatever you experienced?"

"Maybe your brother's behavior after he left for college worried me.

Running off and joining any Arab organization. Those places get scapegoated for things. Blamed, harassed, lit on fire. It's not safe. Is it wrong to want you and Everett to grow up disconnected from that? Free?"

Wow, this was my mom's freedom. Living the high life, white passing in the heartland. I realized we'd been standing next to the unlocked car for several minutes. On either side of the vehicle, unable to open the doors. No one was going anywhere at this rate.

She was looking at me like I broke her heart too much. In return she'd worn me down to nothing a long time ago. I bet she could see that in my face too.

"So, you both feel like I won't let you be Lebanese, is that it?"

Yes, that was exactly it.

But I still had to move into college.

"Nah, we're just discontented youths. Ignore us."

My mom turned the wrong way, accidentally leaving campus until we turned around the block. Siri seemed ready to punch her through the Bluetooth.

We eventually found our way to where I'd be living on South Green and joined the stopped traffic as parents dumped mountains of belongings in strategic piles. White girls with blond hair and short shorts were *everywhere*. They felt like carbon copies of one another. The potential boy specimens were also matching as if they'd all come from the same bros catalogue.

What was more distracting, each student seemed on the hunt. For friends, mates, well-planned mistakes. College was going to be four more years of high school—but like high school on steroids. Even though my mom had been fretting about it for months, I started to worry about *Electra Frances of Columbus*, my assigned roommate whom I knew little about, apart from her feed dedicated to her goth cat, Smithereens.

"Maybe I shouldn't have come here," I said. "Yeah, this is turning into the wrong move."

"You can say that all you want until you make the team. And, *poof,* your mood will change." She turned the air conditioner knob colder even though it was already at its coldest setting. Her forced positivity seemed to boil inside her. Or maybe that was the bottled pessimism. "This was a good choice for you."

"Everyone agreed," I added, not even sarcastically. Even Everett had thought this was a good idea, and he knew a little bit of what I was sitting on. I had to go somewhere, after all. Just not out of state. Come on, who wants those lifelong student loans? At this rate I would graduate only about half a middle-class mortgage in debt.

But where would I live? Go? Do?

"I wish you'd let my hairdresser turn that into a pixie cut." Mom fussed with my overgrown shaved hair. "Pixie cuts are so cute on the right faces."

"But how do I know if I have the right face?" I pulled my hands over my inches of snarled, dark hair. Not that Mom knew anything about it, but my hair was my lasting vigil to Indigo Waits. Wherever they were now. Avoiding Indy the week before they flew away had been necessary. Sliding sideways past their texts and calls for a few weeks was part of surviving, and then I was training all summer. Indy stopped calling, and that was good. I swore it was best for both of us. I muted their feed, and I'm sure they muted mine. The one time we did speak—thanks to too many Jell-O shots at Joss's graduation party—they'd insisted once again that we hadn't broken up because we were never technically together . . . and that made everything worse.

My dorm was still on the other side of this sub-campus neighborhood. (Oh my God, I was moving into an entire Park View peopled by teenagers.) There was even a block party of sorts happening on the green.

My mom squinted at an upside-down person, surrounded by undergrads doing a group counting exercise. "What's this about?"

"It's called a keg stand," I said.

"You're not going to be doing that."

"I already told you. I'm dry for swimming." A girl in a spandex miniskirt that appeared to be a reassigned tube top fell into the hood of the car and then bounced back, laughing with her friends and reassuring us that she was okay. "I have no idea what I'm going to do here."

"I have an idea," Mom said. "Pick a major."

This was the one sticking point of my acceptance to OU. I was listed as undecided, which rubbed just about everyone I told the wrong way. I couldn't tell if they were jealous that I had an opportunity to feel my way through subjects or angry that I wasn't rolling the dice on a random major like the rest of my graduating class. "Mrs. Cheng told me that eighteen-year-olds pick career paths as well as fanny-pack tourists pick restaurants."

"And how many kids does Mrs. Cheng have?"

Whoa. "Cold, Mom."

It stung to think about the Chengs. I hadn't been by for dinner in weeks. They had this pesky of habit of not believing me when I said I was fine, and I didn't enjoy feeling vulnerable. Imagine if I had one of my breakdowns in front of them . . . My family, on the other hand, acted like I'd finally returned to my senses. They needed me to laugh at Dad's jokes, watch movies with Mom. I swam laps until I slept like the dead, and I avoided any talk or mention of anything queer, a time machine to more closeted, quiet days.

I didn't even have Catherine anymore, although I saw a pic this morning of her doing some kind of sunrise meditation at Stonehenge, so I knew she was okay. She'd taken the idea of a brand-new life after high school literally, and even broken up with Anders, though I suspected it was a trial separation—in that Catherine wanted to try out separation.

She seemed to be trying separation with me as well. We hadn't talked in months since she left.

My mom finally parked approximately near my dorm. "Let's look at the room and meet people on your hall, and then we'll bring things up." Mom was so excited to be social. I was hoping for a swift, sudden apocalypse. She shot off for the stairway, and I loaded my arms with a big, heavy box that would hopefully act like a force field to everyone who wanted to talk to me.

I'd picked the wrong box, however. It was so heavy that I had to pause on each landing, and at the second one, another student shot out of their hall with a towel and swim bag hanging from their shoulders. I nearly dropped my box. "Hey," I called out. They paused on the steps. "Pool's open?"

"Open swim is at night." They had a deep voice and that classic swimmer body type. "Can't remember which hours. They even do a swim-in movie night, if you're into that."

"I mean lap swim."

They grinned, approving. "Twice a day. Hours are on the site."

"Thanks."

The swimmer left, and I found some reserve strength for the last landing. I wouldn't be able to get Mom away before lap swim was over for today, but I could be in the pool tomorrow, and submerging myself for even an hour would make so many things more doable.

I found my corner room. Electra must have arrived early that morning because her entire side was set up with an air of burgeoning Type A. My mom sat on my bare mattress, and I could already tell that whatever had transpired between them would make me like Electra Frances: Mom appeared absolutely stumped.

Electra and I waved. Electra was white, Snow White. Down to the murder-red lipstick and black bob. She wore a shiny princess top that must have come straight from Hot Topic.

"Electra has a nickname she'd rather go by," my mom said after an odd minute.

My roommate pointed to the dry-erase board stuck to the front of our door. "My name is Hit It." And that's exactly how it read, HIT IT, SHE/HER.

"*Yesss*," I found myself saying, dropping the box on my own foot. Mom looked alarmed, but it wasn't about my foot.

On the way down to get more boxes, Mom whispered, "I hope she doesn't sleepwalk." We laughed, which helped with the endless process of walking up containers of things and depositing them on the bare mattress. When the last of the small mountain from the trunk and back seat were relocated, Mom didn't come back up to the room. I waited for nearly ten minutes.

Hit It interpreted her absence. "She's not coming back up here. She's terrified of me."

I went down the stairs once more and found Mom in the driver's seat, engine running.

"Are you leaving?" I asked, shocked. "I thought you wanted to get dinner?"

She got out and hugged me, kissed my cheeks thrice. "You want me gone. I can feel it in every sentence between us, and I figure space is the only real thing I can give that you want from me. Thank you for being so good this summer. It meant a lot."

There it was. Me being good meant me being absent. Would it always be that way between us? My mom left, and I watched her drive off. I went up to the room and found that at some point when I was climbing the stairs and hauling things, she'd written my dead name on the dry erase board below Hit It's. No pronouns because my mom wasn't "into that sort of thing."

I erased the name while Hit It watched me, perched on her desk chair like a raven. I wrote, *River, they/them.*

Hit It gusted a sigh of relief. "That makes me feel so much better."

I chuckled because I knew exactly what she meant.

"It is Electra, by the way. I don't know what came over me. I met your mom, and I just had this crushing, overwhelming urge to mess with her. She was horrified by the sight of me."

"I know the feeling."

We chuckled together.

I organized my room. Electra watched every item I unpacked, questioning me about swimming and my hopes of joining the team. I received extra credit for asking about Smithereens by name, and then she revealed the gleanable information from my feed. "So, this Indy broke your heart? You posted a million pictures of them, and then you posted nothing but sad sea creatures with really depressing bios. Do you have a jellyfish thing? I think I should know that going forward."

"I'm from Haley," I said as if that explained everything.

"SeaPlanet townie!" Electra was thrilled. "That makes so much sense. You know the comment bubble where you request the kind of roommate you're hoping for? I wrote, 'No normies.' What'd you write?"

I hadn't thought anyone would read that comment bubble. I turned a little red. "No Madisons."

Electra laughed into a full swoon, puffing up the down comforter around her. A student of Catherine's for so many years, I could tell a lot about Electra from this brief exchange. She'd bug me a lot. She'd need to know things down to the letter. She would never let me get bored, and she would take anyone apart who sneered at me in public.

— 23 —

ON THE DAY OF OPEN TRYOUTS, the rain poured in gray sheets. Electra headed off to work out at Ping—and came straight back ten minutes later because some jerk in an SUV had aimed a puddle at her and driven fast enough to soak her in muddy water.

"This place is overrun with gross cis white dudes." She changed on her side of the room. Electra had an entire array of sequined tops for working out. "I knew this place was Wonder Bread, but the homogeny is downright debilitating. Most of my friends are Black back home. They said, 'Don't go there! You'll get brainwashed by privilege.' "

"I'm a secretly not-entirely-white person." I hoped this would make her feel better, even though in general it amounted to little more than ignorable backstory. "To be honest, I bet there's a lot of us hiding under the stairs around here."

"I wondered when I saw your mom, but I thought she might be *really* into tanning. Iranian?"

"She is *really* into tanning. But she's Arab American, Lebanese, second generation."

"I was way off. Apologies. This is why you don't guess about people's heritage." Electra folded up her legs on her bed. "So we've been here for weeks, and you've been sitting on this rather enormous life detail? What other mysteries lie beneath your artistically ripped flannels?"

I shook my head. "I'm not supposed to talk about it. My mom was in her twenties during 9/11. Something happened to her. Something bad enough for me to know that it happened, but that my mom would rather die than let her kids find out."

"Yeah, but is that weird? Because you *are* kind of white." She paused as if maybe she'd said something wrong. I shrugged; she was right. "But if you ask any of the tools here, they'd yell, 'Arab is *not* white.' And then scream *terrorist* and run around like brain-dead morons."

That seemed harsh and yet probably true. "We're only white when people need us to be. It's more confusing than weird." After all was said and done, I knew I was white, less because of genetics and skin color, more because that was what my parents wanted for their kids by moving away from the Syrian neighborhood where Situ and Jidu lived in New England. I wondered how many more people were like me, something deeply cultural inside that camouflaged under the red and white stripes.

Electra sponged at her muddy shoes. "I can tell you don't want to talk about this because you've got tryouts in an hour, so last question. There is a Middle Eastern food place uptown. Can you take me and help me order the really good things?"

"Daib's? That I can definitely do." I turned back to the array of suits on my ferociously messy bed. The traditional, low-cut-chest, high-cut-hips sporty girl suit was an obvious choice for setting out as a serious competitor, but I'd be wildly uncomfortable and flub my laps. There was also a shorty that was far less thick than the wetsuit I'd trained with last season, but again, that would slow me down. Finally, there was the suit Indy had given me for Christmas from one of their favorite gender-inclusive stores. It was essentially bicycling shorts and a streamlined tank.

"The last one on the right," Electra said. "You're happiest when you come back from laps wearing that one."

"Happy because it makes me think of Indigo Waits the entire time." Not sure that was going to help today, but letting Electra make small decisions was proving to be a daily minor relief. She could see me, and she hardly ever pressed in the wrong direction.

I changed into the suit in a flash and put my basketball shorts and a T-shirt over it. I appreciated that I didn't have to explain why I didn't change in the locker room. "Wish me luck," I said, grabbing my bag.

"You don't need luck. You need confidence!"

I laughed my way down the now-familiar dorm stairwell. The gorgeous fall leaves that had painted the campus like Bob Ross on an orange kick were now falling off the trees in lumps, reminding me of the hours of my youth spent separating the huge wads of leaves at Situ's table. The older I got, the less I knew them, but I suppose, I could still roll a mean grape leaf. Daib had been impressed.

I'd have to thank Electra later for killing my tryout nerves with all this family talk.

The pool wasn't close to my dorm, but it wasn't up any hills. I skipped an umbrella and dashed through the sincere rain, all the way to the back door. I opened it and dripped down the hallway, eyeing the pool and the swimmers already mingling about the deck. They were all tall, an advantage I would kill for in swimming. And they were men, or at least they had been assigned as such. The women's team swimmers must still be in the locker room, being friendly and intimidating to one another in equal measure. Well, I'd be skipping that song and dance.

I headed straight to the deck, dropped my things on a distant bench, and stripped off my outer layer. I dipped my goggles in the lane, my heart thrumming. I saw the coach from across the pool. He'd been watching me while I practiced the last few weeks, but we hadn't been introduced yet.

The guys were palling about, looking back at me, no doubt assessing who I might be. I assumed they'd leave me alone and pulled on a cap over my short hair, surprised when the tallest one of them came over. His lean body was so white it was blinding.

"Hey." I recognized him. "I saw you during move-in. You told me about lap swim."

"Yeah, I've been watching you practice. You're fast."

I shrugged. "I've got lazy legs, but I'm determined to fix that."

He bobbed his head, distracted and nervous, but then so was I. "So, what are you . . . doing here right now? The pool is closed all day for tryouts."

I glanced around. "I'm here to try out."

"Oh, you're early. This is the men's tryout time. The women's is at four."

"I know," I said because I did know. I'd spent literal hours staring at the webpage listing the tryout times. I knew there were two separate sessions, and yet my brain had refused the secondary information. Complete dysphoria zombie. I sat down on the bench and wrapped my goggle strap around my fingers until they turned blue.

He sat beside me. "I'm Kirk. Sophomore. I hate *Star Trek*," he added as if he *really* needed to beat me to the punch.

I surprised myself with a tight laugh. "Nice intro. I'm River."

"You're going to make the team," he said. "Coach already knows about you. You're from Haley, right? The weird Cleveland suburb where killer whales eat people?" Kirk was close enough to the truth. I didn't move, didn't pack up and run. Men's tryouts would start in two minutes. The enormous clock on the wall was glaring at me.

"Kirk, if I was here to try out for the men's team, what would happen to this deck?"

He leaned back and blew out a huge breath. "I gotta tell you . . . we've never had a trans swimmer before. Coach Houser is . . . old-school."

Anger flooded my face with heat. "I spent the last two years training in the lanes with the boys' team. I could beat Joss, and he's swimming second heat for Miami right now. I can't swim with the women."

And I knew why. I wouldn't want to swim anymore if they sent me to the girl lanes. The dysphoria would tear me into tiny sinking pieces. I would give up, walk away. I'd never imagined the implacable wall at the end of my swimming career before. It'd always been a lane that kept going, and now all I could see was Kerrig's scrunched red face and destroyed butterfly dreams. Swimming had been taken from her before she was ready, and now she took it out on everyone the water touched. Thinking about Kerrig was too much. The panic attack destroyed me, and by the time I'd found some way to talk, to remember where I was, I looked up and found the rest of the men's team standing around me. Kirk was filling them in.

A very tall Black swimmer stood out, a firm set to his expression and crossed arms. "So, we get in the lanes. We swim. We don't give Houser a chance to say no."

"That's what I was thinking," Kirk said.

The buzzer sounded through the pool deck. "Warm up!" the coach hollered, his crusty voice echoing in the rafters.

Kirk took me by one arm. "Israel, get the other side." The swimmer who'd spoken, Israel, hauled me upright by my other arm. They led me to the water's edge, a dozen swimmers jumping in and starting their laps with buzzing energy. Kirk did a pike and disappeared beneath the surface.

Israel stared straight into my eyes. "Now you swim. No matter what Houser does."

I put my goggles on, nodded, and we took over the water like a pod of penises.

As it turns out, Houser was so "old-school" he didn't talk to me. Not once. He didn't stop me from racing with the others, and he didn't comment on my difference. Which might sound a little like he was seeing past it, but I could tell he was looking through me instead. My mom had perfected the art long ago. The trick was acting like you couldn't care less.

After tryouts wrapped, the assistant coach came over to where I'd collapsed on the bench. She was young, maybe biracial, with light brown skin and full, natural hair that she kept tucked behind each ear. I knew a lot about her from the way she talked to the other swimmers. She was an assistant coach because she missed the lanes; it was all over her.

She sat beside me and held out a hand to shake. "Ursula Warren. Nice to officially meet you. The rest of them call me Ursula."

"River McIntyre." I was still out of breath, panting while she looked over me.

"What are your pronouns, River?"

"They/them."

"You pushed yourself through warm-down. That'll get you injured."

"I was afraid to go too slowly," I admitted. "When does he post the roster?"

"Next week. You know, you rank in our top three women's heats right now, particularly in free. I'm pretty confident on that even without seeing the other competitors first." She waited, and when I didn't speak, she added, "Kirk is currently speaking up rather passionately on your behalf. As well as the others, but this isn't going to happen. Houser gave me the job of telling you because he's a . . . *specific kind of human*." Ursula stopped herself from adding what she really thought, but I could hear it all the same. Most likely he owned a well-worn, all-red baseball hat like the rest of the old-school humans. "Houser wanted me to tell you that you'll never win a race on the men's team. No matter what. As rude as that is to say, he's right. Your times aren't fast enough to compete on-level with the cis men."

I glanced around the pool deck. "But most of us will never win races at this level. That's not why I swim. There are, what, a dozen spots that will actually matter at any given meet, and the other twenty of us are here to be a team."

She smiled so sadly. "That is exactly what I look for in my swimmers. I do most of the women's coaching, since Houser can't be bothered. Are you sure I can't persuade you to start with me? You could transition, and we could revisit in a year or two? Maybe Houser will retire, or he'll stop producing All-Americans as if he'd created a factory. He's untouchable at this institution, but you didn't hear me say that. I thought last season would have finished him. It didn't." Her words ground out in the back of her teeth. "Think about it?"

It was an awfully nice invitation, and I could not accept it. "I'll go before they come out. I wasn't raised to make a fuss." What a gross and true thing to admit.

Now she seemed genuinely angry. "You *should* make a fuss. You might win."

"Force my way onto *his* team?" It would be Kerrig all over again—except a lot worse. "That sounds like my own personal hell."

I pulled on my basketball shorts and looked out over the pool deck. Over the last few weeks, I'd gotten through boring, basic classes in a student body that didn't have room for people like me by tucking in here, sometimes twice a day. The coach might have turned out to be a problematic asshole, but the facilities were top notch. This pool already felt like a good friend I had to say goodbye to, and these days I PTSD'd hard on goodbyes.

The next week was ephemeral. Each minute took forever, and yet the days dropped in handfuls. My sleep was bad. I hadn't spent a solid week not swimming in years, and I dreamed of Henrietta Churchiness in her coif and shoulder pads. *Depression sneaks up on you when you're not physically active. Did you know God said that?*

God did not say that, I told her. In my dream I had long, bleached-blond hair, and I was so sick inside that I was dying. Haley was dying around me too, teal blood bubbling up through all the sidewalk cracks.

Dream Henrietta wasn't done. *God builds humans to work that way, so from a certain point of view, God did say that.*

So according to you, God built me this way, so this is how I'm supposed to be?

Ew, no, she said.

I thrashed myself awake.

Electra stared at me from her bed. She hadn't asked about tryouts. She probably thought I blew it. After all, OU was Division 1; who did I think I was to try and walk on the team? "You gurgle when you have nightmares. Sounds like you're drowning."

"Well, you speak in tongues."

"Oh, I know. I've recorded it. Someday when I have money, I'm going to hire someone to translate it for me. I have a feeling that I'm writing a great work of fiction in a language no one can yet understand."

I sat up, crossing my arms over my chest. I'd finally stopped sleeping in my binder; it had taken weeks to feel like I could be unbound in front of Electra without pain of conversation on my DDs. I picked up my phone. Indy didn't call or text anymore, not after I'd ignored them for so long. Everett was always busy. He'd graduated a year early to move in with Karina, and now I only occasionally received the look-at-my-new-TV texts. I'd heard nothing from the Chengs after I skipped our goodbye dinner and went to college without a farewell.

And now I was so lonely I was dreaming about my old, terrible therapist.

"Have you ever gone to therapy, E?"

"Have you not met me? I've burned through half a dozen therapists. The right person is the best. The wrong person can ruin your life. I'd washed out of like three offices before I read online that you're supposed to comparison shop for mental health help."

"I definitely had the wrong one in high school."

"The campus has queer-affirming therapists, you know. People who get it." Electra seemed to weigh her next words carefully, which was interesting because she never did that. "There's a whole queer community you haven't tapped into yet. They even have a house. I hear the parties are epic."

I got up and dressed like the Flash. Some things about swimming would be with me forever. "Yeah, I've been to that house. I went to the Halloween party last year."

"Can I come with you if you go again? I hear allies are welcome." Electra pointed her toes toward the ceiling. "I get the biggest crushes on effeminate bisexual man."

"Queer groups aren't really my thing," I admitted. "I get nervous and then I say something offensive." Plus, walking onto that porch meant facing memories that I kept locked in my heart's closet. Halloween was coming up. I'd planned to go home to Haley for the weekend, to escape any possible reminiscing. I hadn't told Electra yet; she'd be pissed.

I went to my classes, saying nothing to everyone. I thought about calling Freya, and I found myself standing outside the hole in the bushes where I'd once crawled through a portal and into Indigo Waits's life. Currently, there were three people crammed in the small space smoking weed. "We have prescriptions!" one of them hollered when they saw me. "Go away!"

It was a weird last straw.

I followed the three hundred links on the OU website until I found my way to open therapy hours at the college's mental health clinic. Climbing the stairs in one of the campus's *actual* old buildings, I started thinking about my grandparents. Situ and Jidu's stairwell smelled exactly like this, and I didn't know if it was because this was some aromatic paint left over from the nineties, or if maybe someone in this building cooked pine nuts too often. The smell got me past my nerves, through the lobby check-in, and into a small room where a person greeted me.

He introduced himself as Varian, he/him. He was a trans person, and somehow it made every single tightly wound piece of me unclench. Varian went through all the entrance questions about growing up, substance abuse, and my general habits. I told him about swim team, and my strict nutrition regimen, which had recently gone right out the window. I told him that that's all I had to focus on. No hopes for the future. No career plans. No other hobbies or passions. I told him about Haley and SeaPlanet and how I'd come out of the wrong closet too fast and then locked myself in a different closet, hitting the snooze button on life until I could leave home.

"Okay, I'm going to set you up for weekly sessions, if you're ready to keep talking with me. The administrative assistant can find the best time between classes."

"Weekly? I must sound pretty bad," I tried to joke. Old habits, and all.

Varian didn't laugh. "You sound adrift, River." I appreciated his candor and the water metaphor. This was already more engaging than anything Henrietta had ever said. "Is there anything we haven't talked about yet? We have fifteen minutes."

My mind was drawn to a strange place. Not the trauma of my closed-minded upbringing or the loss of the love of my life or the body I was still a prisoner inside. All those aches were patient, ingrained. This new one wasn't. "I keep thinking everyone hates me for being trans, and then they . . . don't. And I'm confused."

"Hate you?"

"Cultural homophobia and all." But it was more than that, wasn't it? "Transphobia. Cissexism." I told Varian about tryouts, and how Kirk and the team tried to help me. "If this was a movie, they would have been like 'no trans allowed.' Why do I automatically go there?"

"Hollywood is truly intolerant of queer culture. They blame foreign markets. I wouldn't base anything on the box office." Varian was white and had probably transitioned long ago. He had the best goatee. "River, I have to tell you something that I'm truly sorry no one has told you before. You sound like a perfectly normal person who has grown up in cultural captivity."

I actually laughed. The good kind of laugh. The seen kind. "Oh, I'm not normal."

"Technically there is no normal. No average. No baseline human. That's the real lie." He tried to smile, but I could tell he felt sorry for me. I surprised myself by appreciating the sympathy instead of clawing at it like a wounded animal.

"So, I'm normal, and also normal doesn't exist." I picked at a hole in my jeans. Why did that actually make sense? "When I was younger, I hated queer people to distract from my own queerness. But on some level that didn't make sense, not even then, so I started hating everyone, including myself, and then I looked around and realized that everyone hated everyone. The entire Midwest is a smack of cold fucking jellyfish. Be one of them or be dead to them."

Varian squinted. "I'm from the Midwest. Do I seem like a jellyfish?"

"No."

"And you? You're not a jellyfish, correct?"

"I'm a man o' war." I used to say it with such gusto, but I seemed to have sent my charisma to the West Coast along with my heart.

"Ah, the blue bottle. I've seen them wash up on the beaches in Hawaii. They can kill even after they're dead. Accidentally."

"Of course it's an accident. I hate that I hurt Indy by ignoring them, and my mom by lying to her about who I am for all these years, and the Chengs—who wanted nothing but to support me—but it's what happens when people get close to me. Wow, is this therapy?"

"Therapy is turning what you just said into the understanding that there are actually very few jellyfish. In the Midwest and everywhere else. If you're looking for enemies, you'll see them. If you're looking for enemies, you won't see your allies."

"Insanity." But I believed him, and maybe he knew it. "I have a . . .

friend who helped me figure out I have body dysphoria, mostly about my chest. I need a doctor or something. I need to change it, but I also don't want to talk about it. At all."

"You have come to the right place." He pulled out a one-inch three-ring binder and handed it over. "That's a list of trans-friendly doctors, gynecologists, dentists, you name it. There's information in there about testosterone and gender-affirming surgery. Do me a favor and don't search for things online unless you have to. The internet is where transphobes go to spread hateful information. Yes, you can get your transition covered by insurance. No, it's not impossible. None of it is impossible. Some people only want you to think it is."

I opened the binder randomly to a page on top surgery. The heading read, *Female to Male/Nonbinary (FTMX)*. There were pictures with the faces artfully covered. Breasts turned into chests. Impossible translated to possible as easily as before-and-after photos. I'd never let myself think of a future without binders and endless chest pain. That wasn't the kind of wild hope I could let myself have; I'd even resented Indy for bringing it up only half a year ago. But now, the possibility left me a new kind of breathless.

24

THAT NIGHT, I sat at my desk reading every page of the three-ring binder, even the things that didn't apply to me.

"How's it going?" Electra was dying to look at the info too, but I wasn't ready for the conversations afterward. Today she wore a purple wig and inch-long glittery eyelashes that fluttered when she blinked.

"It's illuminating. It's like a manual on how to be who I already am." I paused. "That's a weird theme to my life. I'm trans, but I don't know what that means. I'm Lebanese, but I have no idea what that means. I'm sort of a man, but again, no ideas."

"And you're a swimmer who doesn't have the means to swim." Well, now Electra was just making me miss Catherine. "I'd feel bad for you except you're hot so you already rule the world."

"True enough. It's been my only card to play, and boy, have I overplayed it." I turned a page and started learning about the different ways I could hormonally or surgically remove shark week from my life. Forever. What was this deep magic?

Electra scooted her desk chair close, bumping into me on purpose. "Hey, I've been waiting for a good time to tell you, but I'm pretty sure I've solved our favorite puzzle. Your major was so obvious I smacked myself in the forehead."

"You've chosen my major for me, have you?" I might've sounded snarky, but I couldn't wait to hear what she had in mind. Living with a creative writing major was a hoot. She was going to say something like geology or dragon training, and I truly didn't know which one.

"I had this fantastic English teacher, Mr. Norton. And he said that my major should be something that I'd do for free, which for me was, like, obvs. Fanfiction equals career."

"The only thing I'd do for free is swim, and as far as I know, that's not a major. I'm not becoming a sad high school swimming coach." I thought of Kerrig and shivered.

She grabbed my laptop and pulled up my feed. She scrolled through the marine life headshots and bios I'd created, trying to remind people that it was good SeaPlanet was closed . . . even if none of the animals were freed in the process. Captivity was wrong. "What do you see here, River? Look close."

"A bored, closeted, traumatized human who can't even post about themself?"

"Come on. We talked about not constantly dragging yourself down. It's not funny."

I apologized; she was right. I was getting better at breaking certain habits while others were still knee-jerk. "I did those bios mostly as a gag."

"But you told me all the biology facts are sound."

"I do my research. It's literally the only thing I was allowed to look up online as a kid without being interrogated about it afterward." I clapped a hand over a laugh before adding, "Although this one time my mom seemed generally concerned about my interest in man-of-wars like maybe I *really* liked them."

"Dude, I might've also wondered that about you."

We laughed and got into a pinching fight. Electra was the weirdest nerd I'd ever met and that was including Everett's friends. She won this pinching round. And we went back to our favorite game. "All right, just say what major you've got in your head. I don't like guessing."

"Biology."

"Took it sophomore year. Hated it." Although that was probably because Taylor had been my lab partner, and she's instigated a lot of creation-versus-evolution arguments that brought out the worst in all of us.

Again, she elbowed me out of the way to pull up the page on biological sciences, which was on the honors track system. "Look at that, you gotta be smart. I'm already ruled out."

She glared at me.

"Sorry. I am smart," I said robotically. "I just don't care."

"You're a smart-*ass*. And you've told me your entrance scores. You test well when you try. If you wanted this, it would be yours."

I sat back, crossed my arms. Electra had navigated to a page full of biological sciences focuses. I read through them aloud. "Cellular and Molecular Biology. Nope. Environmental Biology, interesting . . . but no. Preprofessional Program. *Ack,* what even is that? Human biology." I paused to glare at her.

"It's not that one, keep reading."

"Wildlife and conservation biology." Okay, that *was* interesting. "Marine, freshwater, and environmental biology."

I sat up.

"Right?" She bounced. "And you don't have to decide now, just sign up for some classes. But I think you're going to literally save some of these weird creatures someday."

"I'll think about it."

"You're excited. I can tell you're excited. I haven't even pointed out that it's *also* in the college of arts and sciences, so we could have more classes together."

I waved off her enthusiasm, even though I loved it. Someone knocked, and I knew it had to be Electra's fanboy from one floor down. The guy was persistent, I gave him that. I pulled on my oversized headphones and sank into my research.

A moment later, Electra tapped my shoulder, and I lifted away my left ear-doughnut. "There's an overzealous human male in our hallway here to see you."

"That sounds ominous. What do they look like?"

"Like a neon glow stick. With the kind of blond hair and blue eyes that continue to haunt humanity with racist beauty ideals."

A strange, specific thought pulsed through me. Was Chauncey here? I'd seen him from a distance, going to classes. Did he even remember me? Perhaps Indy had reached out to him. Sent him my way . . .

I opened the door and found Kirk. "Hey!" he said. "I found you. It was kind of hard. You have a different name in the directory."

"I'm a trans person, Kirk. It's called my dead name."

"Groovy." He winced. "I . . . Can I talk with you? Houser posted the roster." A thought stung through me. I'd made the team. There'd been some kind of political upheaval while I was drowning in my dry depression, and I'd made the team after all. "You weren't on the list," he said quickly, interpreting my silence rather well.

So, he was the bearer of bad and obvious news. "I knew I wouldn't be. Ursula already told me." I nearly shut the door.

"The team needs you."

I stared at him for a solid moment and then motioned for him to come in. He looked at Electra with palpable distress, and she enjoyed it and *hissed*. "Be advised, whatever you have to say, Electra is going to hear."

"Here for you, roomie."

"Know you are, E." I sat on my bed and motioned for Kirk to sit at my desk. He glanced over the open page on trans menstruation options, and I stole the binder and closed it. "Talk."

"I'm a journalism major, and I work for the campus paper, *The Post*. I want to write a story about you trying out for the men's team."

Electra actually growled. I could barely believe this guy.

"I'm doing a bad job. Wait. Okay, so Houser is a demon. You got that much at tryouts, right? Only he's so good at pushing his swimmers that the college has stood by him after several huge issues. Did you know that last season, he wouldn't learn Israel's name? He called him 'you.' We reported him, and yeah, they made Houser start saying his name, but he's still a damn racist. And he's still our coach."

"I'm not sure how an article about my tryout is going to help you with that."

"Houser's got a lot of marks against him. This could change things. We talked, all the guys, and we agreed. If you were to go public with who you are and all that—about how he treated you—it might be the last straw. I was going to just write the article, but I had this great class on journalistic integrity. Consent is important."

"Can I hit him?" Electra whispered.

I held up a hand to quiet my tiny dragon of a roommate. Kirk was awkward, for sure, but I didn't hate what he was trying to say. "So, if I go public, Houser could get in enough trouble to get canned, and I would be free to swim on the men's team."

"It's a lot of ifs," he admitted. "But there's a chance. He's a terrible coach. Have you ever had a terrible coach? He makes us all not want to swim."

I stared at the ground. "I'm not out at home. If this article got picked up by any other news, it'd be . . ."

What, exactly?

An incredibly succinct way to come out.

"I highly doubt anyone outside of Athens will notice. The college will totally squash it," Kirk pointed out. "They hate this kind of publicity."

"I do enjoy the poetry of using their immorality against them," Electra added.

"Okay," I said.

"Really?" Kirk whipped out his phone from his pocket. "You sure?"

"No, but you've caught me on a brave day."

"I already wrote the story. I just need a quote from you, and my editor wants written permission that this is cool with you."

Now Electra did stand up to punch Kirk in the shoulder. He took it well and handed over his phone. I scrolled through an article about a trans swimmer from the northeast who'd trained hard to walk on the men's team but got turned away by Coach Houser. My name wasn't on it yet. Electra held her hand out for the phone and read the article too.

"I just want to swim," I said. "Can that be my quote?"

"Ah, aloof jock isn't going to be eye-catching. Can we do some sort of *Rudy* angle? This is all you've ever wanted, and you're really plucky, and Houser totally ruined it for you?"

"You're putting words in their mouth." Electra gave his phone back. "Besides, you need the real River McIntyre. They've got this hot-bad-boy routine." Electra handed over her phone to Kirk, showing him my much older feed, from the half a year I'd been Indy's and felt nigh untouchable. "They got their heart bashed to pieces but look at this possibility. If that's not trans James Dean, I'll eat my best Pokémon card."

As much as I appreciated Electra, I turned red. I hadn't felt like that person in so long. The person who entered a room and mapped the situation. Who made friends easily and conquered dares and dismantled anyone who tried to take them down.

I missed that person, not their evil superpowers, but their poise for sure.

"Be gay, do crime."

"What's that?" he asked.

"That's my quote." I looked at him straight in the face. "It means I don't follow arbitrary rules. And neither does identity."

Kirk's face lit up. "That's . . . fantastic. I could edit the whole article around it. Oh, that's *great.*" He held up a hand for a high five, and I obliged. He stood to leave, jazzed. "More soon! I'll let you know how it goes when my editor reads it. She's probably going to want a picture of you on the pool deck."

Kirk left, and Electra watched him go, her observations all sliding together. "That glow-in-the-dark Popsicle just gave you a high five. I think I like him. This is going to get out, you know. All the way home to Haley."

"I know." I swear I heard Indigo Waits yelling from the length of the country, *Come out anyway you damn want, River.*

Maybe this news would reach all of them.

Electra sat on my bed, her excitement infectious. "Imagine if it works. You'd be a hero. I mean, you already are. That's one of the perks of being trans. You're all so courageous as fuck."

Usually, I hated it when people said that—too hung up on why we needed to be courageous in the first place. Tonight Electra could say it. And she could be right.

— 25 —

A WEEK LATER, in the middle of the night—we had top-of-the-line blackout curtains, who knew what time it was—all the electronics in our room started to hum and dance and light up. Something even tweeted like a bird in Electra's closet.

Electra, ever the monster in the dark o'clock hours, rolled over and howled. "The internet . . . the world . . . something's happening, and it's coming for us!"

I tripped, crossing my trashed side of the room in the dark to snatch my phone. I was surprised to see Catherine's caller-ID lighting up the screen. She wanted to FaceTime? Catherine? Oh, she wanted to FaceTime. That could only mean one thing.

I fell into the hallway, pulling on sneakers and answered. "Hey, Catherine. Or what do your friends say in England?"

" 'Hey, Catherine,' " she deadpanned. God, she really couldn't small talk. "I'm thinking I'm the first to call you and offer my congratulations. It's ten here."

"Here?"

"In Essex, and it's five in Ohio, and why am I detailing international time zones? I've called you with my face." But it wasn't truly Catherine's face. She was power walking, talking into a headphone mic. The camera swung at the length of her arm, showing off mostly her side and the tiniest sliver of her hat. "That's how urgent this is. You know how little of an e-footprint I prefer to leave."

"Sounds like you're missing Anders."

Catherine snorted and then sighed, as if I'd pinpointed something she preferred not to recognize. "I miss you as well. And over the next few hours people are going to start drinking coffee and binging midnight news. And you were midnight news. I'm assuming you know exactly of what I speak."

"So the story crossed the Atlantic?"

"And a few other oceans. There was some trash-fire law passed in some horrid middle state last week that protects bigots who shun trans people from retail establishments and restaurants. No biggie, America isn't Germany in the 1930s or anything. People got rightly furious on the internet, and then they were gift wrapped and delivered that trans James Dean picture of *you. Rebel in a lane.*"

"*The Post* article went viral?"

"I read it reprinted in the *Haley Advocate*. The Oprah bot had retweeted it."

"Shit."

"You've become a rallying cry, McIntyre. I wanted to be the first to offer my congratulations and to say, at least one time, I told you so."

"You told me *what*?"

"I've been yelling, 'HEY, YOU'RE TRANS,' at you for about five years now."

"You have not."

"It was implied," Catherine said. "I was being respectful. I read a book about gender, and it said not to push those who are questioning."

"You know I like it when you push me. How do you think I got into college? Or didn't walk away from Kerrig first week of frosh swim?"

"Subtle, am I? Next time I'll write a five-act musical about it." And I believed she would. "It'll be called, *Secondary Point: Move to California and Win Back Your Soul Mate, Idiot.*" We laughed and fell into an old, established silence. It felt so good to talk. Why had it taken us this long? And how long would it be before we spoke again?

"I haven't spoken to Indy in one hundred and twenty-seven days."

"So fix it."

"Let's catch up soon, Catherine."

Catherine went silent on the other end. Most likely she didn't know how to tell me that if I wasn't in her daily life, I wasn't in the picture. I had always known that about her. We'd had an expiration date just like Indigo and me. "I promise you this. You call me the next time you do something enormous with your life. Tell me about it."

"You'll do it in return?"

"Of course. River, I'm hanging up. Call your mom." Catherine's swinging side disappeared. I took a moment to appreciate having my name come out of my oldest friend's mouth for the first time. She said *River* like I'd always been River. Why hadn't I been able to trust her earlier with all this? Why hadn't I been able to trust anyone but Indy?

Thumbing through all the notifications on my phone, I realized that Catherine might have been the first to reach out, but the news had been going strong since last night. I had emails from my professors, all in support. I had six messages from Kirk, who was crying from the journalistic exposure alone, thanking me and freaking out in equal measure. And there was an invitation to come to the pool office *today* and meet with the OU president and Assistant Coach Warren. *Couch Houser will not be in attendance*, the message assured.

By the time I returned to my room, Electra was awake and abreast of the entire situation. "I think we need pancakes," she said solemnly.

We walked through the misty morning on campus, to Jeff Hall, one of the real old buildings, and ate the starchy discs loosely referred to as pancakes. No one else was in the dining hall, which was weird.

"I'm gonna be honest, Riv, I think this one got away from us."

"You're telling me!" I shouted. "I have to go face the president of the college. Today. And then at some point—also today—I'm going to have a conversation with my mom." Holy shit. I was finally going to have the conversation. After today, it would never hang around my neck again, dragging me under. I was excited and terrified all at once.

We ate more pancakes.

"You think Indy will call?"

I dropped my fork, and it clattered from my plate to my tray to the tabletop and nearly off the edge before I caught it. "Why would Indy call?"

"This is huge. There's no way she didn't see, considering our algorithms. Indy cares about you. She's going to check in." Every once in a while, Electra liked to let on that she followed Indigo Waits's feed, occasionally dropping a knowing pronoun. I tried not to snag on those tiny pieces, but I couldn't help it. So, Indy was she/her right now. I wondered what her hair looked like and what odd collection of clothes she'd put together that had somehow collated into a unique and eye-catching aesthetic. I'd muted her feed so long ago. It hurt far too much to have images of California and her newly bronzed face lighting up my feed.

I looked at the article on my phone for the millionth time. Over 1.8 million views. "Electra, I think I need a better haircut."

"And definitely some tattoos."

There were so many other things to think about today. The team. My mom, Dad, Everett . . . the Chengs. And yet every time I lifted my phone from my pocket, I was looking for a message from Indy. And every time, I didn't find one. Was Electra wrong? Would Indy not see what had transpired in the armpit of a state she'd left behind? Or would she see it and think that I still didn't want to talk with her?

My dad was the first person in my family to check in. I received a text—oh, dads and their formal letter texts. *Dear River, So proud of you. Let me know how it goes with the team. Should I change your name on my phone? I think I need some literature on people like you. Currently flying to Germany, more soon. Love, Dad.*

An hour later, I received a photo text from Freya of Mrs. Cheng holding up the *Haley Advocate* article—and it had been framed because they are *huge* dorks. Most of the articles had been picked up with Kirk's title, "Rebel in the Lane," but the *Advocate*'s headline read, HALEY TEEN BECOMES FIRST TRANS SWIMMER AT OHIO UNIVERSITY. The accompanying text from the Chengs made me tear up. *We love you. Come stay with us for the holidays.* They weren't mad I'd disappeared on them. Of course they weren't. Those two had the uncanny ability to accept me, which was so foreign I still didn't know how to trust it.

Love you too, I texted back, and then because I couldn't not share, I sent them a picture of my new faux hawk. My mom hated haircuts like this. *Trying to get attention*, she'd say. But my mom wasn't here, a point made clearer with each passing hour.

And hey, I looked brilliant this way. I matched me.

Not hearing from Everett or Karina was starting to itch. As a bonus, I got the most obnoxious message from Taylor about how hard it had been for her to find out "in this way." Electra cracked her knuckles when she saw it and did something in retaliation online that I did not want to know about. Electra had her work cut out for her, to be honest. There was so much support pouring in. And then there was hate. Anonymous hate. They rolled over me and fell away; Indy's armor had finally rubbed off. Those people were like Kerrig. Something was so wrong inside their own identity that they had to stab at other people. I honestly pitied them. And I knew how a person could feel that way, and how horrible it is live like that.

Time funneled away until it was four o'clock, and even though I'd heard nothing from my mom or Everett, I slipped away to the pool deck, determined to be alone when I met with the president and Assistant Coach Warren, which was a silly thought because when I arrived at the pool, I could barely get in. There was an entire crowd outside the doors. I expected some of the hate that had filtered through the internet, but it was all very loud, supportive people.

The rest of the men's team was there to greet me too. Kirk and Israel took up their places at my sides just like they'd done at tryouts, and we went in. There were news cameras on the pool deck, and the moment I walked in and saw Ursula and the president, I knew things had gone exactly the way Kirk had hoped. Houser was canned. Ursula wore a polo that had COACH stitched on the front chest pocket. She was holding an OU team jacket, which reminded me far too much of high school, but I knew this was the olive branch.

I was happy, on a team, exhausted.

She hadn't texted.

That evening, I finally found myself alone, outside of my dorm on the bench. There was a heterosexual-appearing couple on the metal bleachers. They were on a first date, maybe. I could tell by their body language, ever-inching toward each other. I watched them kiss from the length of the soccer field, and I found a pretty decent star and wished them well.

Still nothing from Indy.

Still nothing from Everett.

I texted him, *Are you mad that I came out to you this way?*

And I waited.

And when I couldn't wait any longer, I called home. Mom answered after an average amount of rings. "Hi, daughter, having a big day?"

My heart exploded; she knew what she was doing.

I gripped my chest on the bench. "Hi, Mom. How are you?"

"Oh, I have yoga in a few."

She waited for me to press, and I hated her for it. "I'm assuming you read the article?"

"I didn't, but Mrs. Winooski filled me in. That's a rather big lie you're setting out just to get on the team."

A lie? My pain split into anger. "Have you ever met me, by any chance?"

"I know who you are because I gave birth to you. And I'm not talking to you about this *like this*. You're confused and young and looking for attention." She sighed, so practiced, so controlled. "Trying to say something like this is childish. Honestly, Lake, you aren't thinking about my feelings at all."

"Yeah, well, that's not my name, so I guess we're even."

I hung up.

And I roared so loud and deep that the lovebirds scattered. I surprised myself by having zero tears. I was done with her. With our relationship.

I was free.

I sat on that bench until it got very dark. When my phone hummed with a message from Everett, I jumped to my feet. *Where the hell are you? Your roommate is freaking out.*

"What?" I muttered aloud, heading toward the side door of my dorm and running smack into my big brother.

He was here. On campus. To see me. I grabbed on to him like a lifeline, and he laughed. "Oh, you love me so much," he teased. "Look how much you love me."

"You drove here."

"You came out to the entire world today. Literally. Of course I drove here." He waved his phone at me. "And what's this message about being mad at *how* you came out? Anyone who gives you crap about how you do this is an asshole." And because Everett was my brother, and we'd been through all of this together from the very beginning, his shoulders slumped. "Mom?"

"I'm . . . relieved. Like I opened the door on my life and closed the door on her bullshit."

He nodded.

But I didn't want to talk about her today, my first day of actual freedom. I knuckled away the random tears that were trying to spring out. "Taylor tried that crap as well. Have you ever noticed how similar they are?"

"Did I notice you were dating a girl who was just like Mom? No . . . not at all." His sarcasm made me tackle him, throw him in a headlock. "Uncle," he said, and I released him. "Let's go up. Karina is with Electra. You did not tell me your roommate is a walking Tim Burton character."

"She's a pure, eccentric delight. Way overinvested, but I love the support."

I grapple-hugged my brother all over again, and he's never been into close contact, so he joked, "Now you're making it weird, Liver."

"Oh gods, no." I laughed, let him go. "No, no, no. Not liver."

"Shiver? Giver? You've got to forgive me. I'm only just unearthing the potential."

We climbed the stairwell together.

"Hey, me too."

— 26 —

WHAT HAD TAKEN KERRIG four years to make worse, Coach Warren took one week to diagnose. "You're fast but undependably fast. For you, we won't talk about personal best. We're going to average your weekly times and aim to bring that average up."

"Okay." I snapped my goggles on and dove in, already at home in these lanes. I did two lengths underwater without coming up for air, a ritual that Kerrig had had no patience for and one that Warren believed "warmed up my lungs." When I breached the surface, I felt a million times lighter.

Israel was adjusting his goggle strap in the lane next to mine. He was million miles tall in the shallow end, and I tried not to notice how good he looked in the world's tiniest Speedo. "You've got lazy legs," he said. "I did too. Can I show you how I got them involved?"

"Yeah, sure."

"Swim with your hands open at practice." Israel showed me his long hand transformed into a bear claw instead of the mandatory hard scoop. "You'll get so frustrated at how slow you are, your legs will wake up and try to make up the difference."

"Sneaky. I like it." I could tell that the rubber strap on his goggles was defeating him, and I held out a hand. "I've got nimble fingers. Perk of the extra X chromosome." I was starting to dig trans jokes. It felt like the opposite of all those ruthless, cruel sessions in Henrietta's office where I joked to keep from dying inside. Now I joked because some of this was humorous.

He handed his goggles over. "Trying to get them looser about an inch. I usually compete in those, but I'm trying to wear them all the time now. They're giving me a migraine."

I adjusted the strap for him. This time I wouldn't chicken out. I wouldn't act like Israel wasn't fighting a whole battle on this campus that not one white person had to think about, let alone fight. "Sounds like Houser was a raging racist. I'm sorry you had to swim under that."

Israel smiled huge, emanating a stunning sort of comfort. "Thank you for saying that. If one more of them"—he cocked his head toward the rest of the swimmers in the lanes—"told me Houser was *old-school*, I was going to lose it."

I couldn't *not* smile back. "We should meet for real." I held out a hand over the lane line. "River McIntyre, from Haley, Ohio."

He shook it. "Israel Miller, from DC."

"Those guys"—I cocked my head at the swimmers—"also say you're going to be an All-American."

He turned bashful, which was equally stunning, especially since he was dripping from the fruits of his warm-up. "Probably. Have to avoid burnout and injury, which means I should definitely not go to the party at the Rainbow Haven tonight that they're throwing for *you*."

Rainbow Haven. I couldn't help but think of jellyfish, although maybe this place was the antidote. "I'm pretty intimidated that the queer house on campus is throwing me a rager."

His flirting smile was even better than all the other ones put together. "I'm sure it'll be tasteful and sedate. Because this campus is so good at keeping things chill." I laughed. Coach hollered at us to finish warm-up, and we pulled our goggles down in tandem. "Go with me?"

"Okay."

We pushed off the wall in tandem too, disappearing into the water, side by side, until his height and strength and immense talent sent him far beyond me. I did some exaggerated freestyle, each stroke stretching my muscles and tendons. All the while, my mouth kept filling with water because I was smiling so damn hugely. Oh my god, was I interested in someone again? No, not possible. I'd forgotten what it felt like to talk with another human and sort of . . . harmonize.

I started using the bear claw stroke technique, immediately realizing that Israel was a swimming genius. I got so frustrated with my arms that my legs started sawing at the water, and by the end of practice, my abs and thighs burned.

Israel Miller met me at my dorm, which felt slightly dinosaur-y, but as Electra pointed out, nothing involving me could ever be that Dinosauria. I couldn't help but feel hot. Electra had helped me lean in to this trans James Dean look, complete with leather jacket. I'd even gotten a new binder to replace the ones I'd been doubling up on, which, according to Varian's magic folder, could lead to serious health problems like cysts and stress fractures in your ribs.

Two things happened every time I learned something new about being nonbinary trans. One, it explained everything. Two, it made me ache for every lonely trans heart out there in this universe who thought their questions were answerless. How could I reach them? Tell them that we man o' wars are fearsome and gorgeous and as numerous as the ones in the ocean. Which, National Geographic had taught me, were so prevalent that the IUCN hadn't even evaluated their extinction rating. In a time of global crisis when most animals needed us to keep a head count, man-of-wars were accidentally washing up on Venice Beach in the thousands.

"I'm thinking about man o' wars. I must be nervous," I admitted as we walked the loud, dark streets of campus.

"The jellyfish?" Israel asked.

"They're not jellyfish. They're symbiotic colonies of polyps that resemble the eighteenth-century warships at full sail." Well, now I sounded obsessive. "I'm getting a tattoo of one." I pulled up a picture on my phone to show him, and he did me the great courtesy of not being weirded out.

"I could tell you're nervous." Israel had dressed in all black, and he looked ragingly attractive. "That's why I wanted to come with you."

"Queer people intimidate me. Especially the ones who've been out forever. I didn't grow up around that kind of . . . acceptance."

"I went to an all-white private school. I know that feeling far too well. That's probably why I came to OU. I feel sort of white with my Black friends and Black with my white ones. It's hard to explain."

God, maybe all of us were growing up in captivity.

"I'm Irish–Arab American," I said. "Lebanese. I know I don't look it."

"You do look it." He pointed to his nose, and I laughed. I loved my bumpy Arab nose, even if most people thought I'd taken a few too many punches to the face.

We crested Jeff Hill, running into an entire herd of drunken white undergrads wearing matching white T-shirts. They were doing a Court Street Shuffle, which meant trying to have a drink in every bar uptown before they passed out. There were eighteen bars uptown, and the bragging rights of having completed one was highly admired. Perhaps it was the true competitive sport here, definitely more well-attended than any swim meet or football game. This shuffle had been to at least a dozen bars already from the amount of signatures on their shirts.

One of the white shirts stumbled toward me, and I recognized Gia after a long beat. She was blitzed. "Hey! It's me! It's me!"

"It's you!" I agreed. "What are you doing here? Don't you go to OSU?"

One of the shuffle cohort hollered at her, and Gia whipped around to yell, *Shut up, I'm talking to my old friend.* Oh, we were old friends, were we? She swung around and hugged on me. "Ohmygod, I've missed you and the team so much. Why aren't you wearing any eyeliner? The next time I see you, you better be wearing eyeliner. I don't care if you're boy or girl. Eyeliner!"

She stumbled away, and I stared after her.

Wow.

Israel chuckled. "Was that your first run-in with someone from back home?"

I nodded. "I want to tell you that I saw that going differently. But I'm not sure I did."

We laughed together, nearly there. I knew where the Rainbow Haven was by heart; I hadn't passed by it in all my weeks at OU. Instead I went around the block and my lingering, stinging memories of Indigo Waits. Whenever I thought of Indy, my phone grew heavier in my pocket. My silence to her hundreds of messages this summer haunted me, her absence since I'd come out somehow more ghostly than this haunted campus.

The party in my honor was screaming from the sidewalk, a banner over the door reading, TRANS RIGHTS WIN! Someone had written under it in Sharpie, *Fuck you, Houser*, and Israel marveled at it for a moment. I was relieved that this whole process had helped him too, but still irate that the racism alone hadn't been treated with the same seriousness. I could tell Coach Warren was too. My dad was too often blindsided by how racist this country could be, and yet every time he blustered at something on the news, my mother would go in the other room. Not because she didn't care, as I'd always assumed, but because she knew that the racism, like chlorine, was in the water. I imagined she could taste it in every sip. I could.

A thought occurred to me right then that stopped me on the front walk. No matter what had or would transpire between my mother and me, I would feel bad for her forever.

Also, motherfucking *Chauncey* was playing cornhole on the lawn.

I made a mental note to steer clear of him all night on the off chance that he remembered me. Unlike Halloween, people were inside and out, and I was saved from a view of that porch couch where Indy'd slept off dank pumpkin bread by the seventeen people currently sitting on that couch—no joke, I counted, and they were engineering how to add more before the legs gave out. It reminded me of the shenanigans from our swimming sleepovers, and I started to relax.

A riotous cheer went up when I was recognized, and the festivities unrolled around us in a haze of drinking games and celebratory shouts. Israel and I were inseparable, less because we'd come here together and more because when you're two people drinking water out of red Solo cups while everyone else downs PBR, you are bonded for life.

When it was late enough for us to be out of nerves, Israel and I sat shoulder to shoulder on the porch. "So, how much physical transitioning are you going for? If it's okay to ask?"

I surprised myself by appreciating his question. "I don't know. I'm pretty nonbinary, but I am going to have top surgery as soon as humanly possible. I'm still trying to figure out how to get my dad's insurance to cover it, and I won't be able to train for possibly six months. I'm going to try to halve that recovery."

"Ouch." He knew how much that'd set me back. I couldn't help but feel it, and yet it had to happen. Now that I'd started letting myself imagine a life without a permanent bulletproof vest, I had to have it. "Will they let you compete if you're on T?" he asked.

"I don't know. There are conflicting theories. I'm going to pass on hormones right now." I glanced down at my powerful legs and arms, happy with how strong I'd gotten lately. "Most of my body fits at the moment." And that was something else I'd learned from Varian in under two sessions. Not all trans people started out feeling like a different gender trapped in their skin. Some find themself a little at a time, a door inside that unlocks and reveals new doors, and new doors after that, and so on. I longed to tell that last bit to Indy; she would love it. "I'll probably make new decisions later on."

Israel was staring with a sweet, bashful smile. "Can I tell you something real? I like you, but you know the team, Coach, etc. . . ."

"We should probably be casual," I said, going with him on this rising tide. Was there actually a chance I was getting laid tonight? It had been *so long.*

"I like casual," he said. "I like it a lot. Can we make out now?"

I stood up and leaned into his side, his arm went around my waist. I kissed Israel, enjoying the differences in our bodies . . . and all the similarities.

"RIVER MCINTYRE!"

Shit. I pulled away from Israel and turned to face the music, nearly lifting a fist.

Chauncey had given my name many extra drunken syllables. I marveled at how there was something Harley Quinn about him even when he was wearing shorts and a button-down covered in bananas. His long blond hair was pinned up messily in a manbun.

"Hello, Chauncey. I wondered if you'd remember me."

"Hey!" He picked me up in a flying hug. "I don't remember you! Do we know each other? I was just coming over to say you're a damn hero."

I peeled myself out of his long arms. "Last time we talked was Halloween when you were Harley Quinn. Last year. You were with . . ." I couldn't say her name.

He squinted at me. "Oh yeah. You." Who knows what kind of memory he'd retained of Indy's breakup-by-proxy while high as a satellite. Chauncey lit a cigarette and sat beside us, one long leg kicked over the porch railing.

Israel picked up my Solo cup. "Look at that. We need a reason for me to split *and* refills. How convenient."

"Keg's out," Chauncey said. "But there's some hard stuff in the kitchen."

Israel looked at me. "Let's go wild. Soda?"

"Sure."

Israel went inside, and Chauncey actually giggled. "He's an Adonis. And he calls pop *soda*. That's adorable." I didn't say anything, although I agreed.

Chauncey was clearly trashed, and the one-sided drunk conversation was not my favorite. "I do remember you now. I know exactly who *you* are." He pointed at me with the two fingers pinching the cigarette. "You're the one who broke Indigo Waits's heart."

Sounds came out that weren't words. He watched me sputter with mounting interest.

"Indy broke *my* heart," I managed. "It's like what you said a year ago. She was always on her way out."

"Did I say that about him? Harsh."

"She's in San Francisco now."

"Nah, he's up in the redwoods. Been camping for weeks."

It felt like we were dueling pronouns. I didn't like it. As far as I knew, Electra had the most recent intel, but then maybe Indy still needed to edit their queerness online, for some awful reason. Maybe Chauncey still talked to Indy. And now I was jealous of him all over again, and it burned like a shock treatment of chlorine.

Not to mention, he was enjoying himself, grinning like a cartoon feline. "Let me guess. You muted his feed and have no idea what's up. I get it. I've been there with Indy." Chauncey looked sexy while he was smoking, and he knew it. He poised the cigarette in his mouth and pulled up Indy's feed, launching his phone at my lap. I caught it, turning the screen over. "Tell me that's not one brokenhearted Indigo Waits."

Indy's feed was a string of poignant images. No matter how beautiful the view of the ocean or the bay or the ancient trees behind them, their smile wasn't on. His smile. On some, his comment turned the image sad. And it was worse than all that because he'd posted lyrics from our favorite songs. Further back, a few months, there were pictures of our bodies twined up without any identifying marks. Only I knew it was us. And where I'd been posting endless pictures of tangled man o' wars, he'd been reminiscing on tender details. Calling out to me.

I stopped scrolling on a picture of his old Converses, one turned upside down to show off teal paint caught in the treads. My voice was rough. "How can you possibly tell someone's lonely by a picture of their shoes?"

Chauncey peered over my shoulder at the screen. "Those're sad fucking shoes. What'd I tell you? Indy was *the* heartbreaker of northeast Ohio, and you broke him." He slow-clapped, dropping ash on his shorts in the process so that he had to whack at his own dick or risk setting it on fire.

My throat made another sound, emotions bubbling up from the bottom of my soul. I shoved Chauncey's phone back at him, and Israel returned with our cups. Chauncey scooted over on the railing, giving us a little space. I didn't know how I could pick up kissing Israel again with Cheshire Cat Chauncey watching and my head spinning with sad photos of Indy.

Luckily, or perhaps most unluckily of all, a glorious-looking person in platform shoes, ruby lipstick, and a curvy plaid dress started hollering for everyone's attention. My heart immediately turned into a kick drum. *Please don't talk about me. Please . . . fucking . . . don't . . .*

"Greetings, folx of shining creativity and endless beauty! If you *don't know*—and shame on you if so—I am the reigning empress of Rainbow Haven, King Aisling." I couldn't tell if I was supposed to laugh. I couldn't tell what was a joke; they were all fluent in a language I could barely speak conversationally.

Chauncey hooted and danced on the porch ledge, and Aisling waved him off. "Down, court jester! Where was I? Yes, the patented microaggression drinking game. In which we dismantle words leveled at us with booze and communal laughter."

"Oh, this is actually really fun." Israel grabbed my hand and pulled us in to join, shoulder to shoulder with the rest of the out and loud campus queers. The circle on the porch was dozens of people large, ever shifting to let in more folks. Almost everyone was loose-bodied and glassy-eyed from drinking, and my body thrummed with sudden fear.

"What am I supposed to do?" I asked in a low voice, my breath frantic, sticky. "Rules?"

"Easy. If someone says a microaggression you've heard before, you drink. When it gets to you, say one that's been eating at you." Israel smiled kindly. "It's fun, I swear. And bizarrely empowering."

King Aisling handed a glittering scepter to the person on their left. "Get us going, Gert."

Gert took the scepter, held it high. The porch grew quiet in anticipation. Gert cleared their throat. "Are you sisters?"

Curses shot out, people relating sharply, and I still didn't understand. *Are you sisters?* Strangers used to ask that to Taylor and me because we were too familiar. Too close. Those strangers always had that demanding don't-be-queers look in their eye. Taylor liked to punish them and kiss me as an answer. I always felt like we were about to be shot.

I lifted my drink and took a tentative sip.

Israel squeezed my shoulder. Christ, I could not feel empowered by this. I was never going to be like the rest of them. My eyes teared up, and I noticed someone directly across the circle who had also drank begrudgingly. We made eye contact, and they saluted with their cup.

The scepter passed to the next person, who shouted, "Hey, my cat is totally gay too!" The laughter rolled up. Israel snorted into his drink and took a big swallow.

Chauncey was next, and I found myself overly curious about what people leveled against someone as conventionally beautiful as him. "Bi and pan people don't *have* to be gay," he bit out more seriously than I'd expected. "They choose it!"

The porch erupted in angry toasting and swearing, and surprisingly, I felt pretty good when I lifted the cup to drink in communion with the rest of them. My mom had told me that one, as if she'd cracked some important secret of my identity. So had my cousin. And Gia.

The next person rang out, "How do you know you're queer if you've never had sex?" The laughter rolled over the porch like the fake tide pools at SeaPlanet, a loud rush. I stopped being afraid for a second and just listened to what they were saying.

"You don't seem queer."

I drank.

"My [insert random relative] is gay too."

I drank.

"I can't learn new pronouns. I'm too old."

I drank.

"But you can get married now, so stop complaining."

I drank.

"I met you by this name, so changing it is going to be really hard for me."

I drank.

"*Queer* is a bad word to *my* generation."

I drank to the bottom of my cup on that one.

By the time we'd gotten to "Just don't tell Grandma," I was truly thankful that I wasn't drinking alcohol because I would have been absolutely tanked.

When the scepter got to Israel, I was feeling so damn seen that I was excited to hear whatever he was going to say. He paused long enough for people to quiet and lean in. "I bet you just love *Queer Eye*."

Everyone hollered, and I swore everyone drank.

Israel held out the scepter to me, and my mind went blank. There was nothing there. I was as empty as the pillar tanks in the Jellyfish

Haven the last time I saw them. The porch got quiet as if I were stalling on purpose, and then the crowd hustled with nervous energy.

"You can pass!" Aisling sang out. "No judgment for passing!"

But I didn't want to pass, I wanted to be as courageous as the rest of them.

I gripped the rod of cheap metal tighter. I stared at the rainbow crystals on the scepter. And I thought one single nail of a word.

"Daughter."

"What was that?" someone shouted.

"Daughter!" I shouted, and the porch erupted in unity.

Someone screamed, "Hey, ladies!" and then gendered labels were firing off into the air like we'd all turned into a bunch of queer cowboys trying to shoot down the stars.

"Young man!"

"Girls!"

"Son!"

"Hi, *boys and girls*!"

Beside me, Israel growled, "Queen."

And everyone's drink was empty after that, and it felt like something else was empty too, something that I had never, ever let the drain out of before. Israel slung an arm around my shoulders, and I surprised myself by laughing so hard that my abs ached.

Was I having a good time? I was. How weird.

And what a terrible way to tempt fate.

Israel headed to the bathroom, and Chauncey scooted right back over as if he'd had a brand-new evil thought.

"What if we just say hi?" He hit a button on his phone, and the night fractured around me. Broken glass seemed to fall from inside my brain as the FaceTime call picked up.

Indy had answered.

"If you're drunk dialing me *again*, Chauncey, I'm going to post imperfect pictures of you on the internet, which I retained all this time for this very situation."

"You'll forgive me when you see who I'm with, Gogo." He snuggled closer, threw his arm around my shoulder, and shoved my face into the screen. If I wasn't so busy trying to breathe, I would have tossed him over the railing.

Indy and I made eye contact for a few seconds. He looked exhausted, disheveled, and handsome, his brown eyes deep. Indy was making a low sound that seemed to come from some unfathomable depth. I expected anger. Anger would make sense. Instead Indy turned from the camera, talking but refusing to look at me. "River, hi. I'm just back from camping. I saw your news. It's fantastic."

I couldn't look away from him. It was, by far, the worst voice I'd ever heard come out of Indy. I was hurting him. My presence on his screen was *hurting* him.

I had no words.

All three of us fell silent, and Indy laughed that I-can't-believe-this laugh, and hollered, "Stop torturing River, Chauncey. And lose my number, you foul instigator!"

Indy hung up.

The thing about drunk people is that they don't really know what they're doing. And that's usually why they got drunk to begin with. To have an excuse to do anything. I looked around, and I was surrounded. A bunch of people who were aching to be reckless and stupid, as long as it wouldn't matter tomorrow. I couldn't be one of them, and I didn't want to. I'd wasted enough days of my life with my soul shut down, my heart hitting snooze.

I walked out to the front lawn, where Israel was playing cornhole. "Need some air and a walk. We'll do this again?"

"You all right?" he asked.

"Yeah, that guy . . . We had an ex in common."

"Bad ex?"

"Bad ex." I left Israel and took the long way home. I walked the quiet, dark path by the library toward the bushes where Indy had once been hiding, asking for me. I crawled in and sat down. I thought about calling the Chengs, rehashing what had happened, but I knew what they'd say. They'd been disappointed in the way I shut Indy out. Everett and Karina were too. And Catherine had nearly written a dissertation on it. I could see the title now, *The BS You're in with Indigo Waits: A Treatise on Adolescent Stupidity.*

I thought of every person I knew and loved, but none of them could answer the question that hauled through me like a tsunami. Indy's teasing voice came up instead, escaping from wherever I'd buried my memories. *Someday you're just going to ask me and start living.*

I called Indy. No faces this time, just my lips to his ear.

"Hey, River." He answered as if he'd fully recovered from the shock of Chauncey's call, even though it couldn't have been more than a half hour ago. "I know what you're going to say, and you don't have to. I get it."

I couldn't speak. His voice was like coming home and finding all the furniture packed up and gone. This was where I lived, and yet it also wasn't mine anymore.

"Honestly, I'm back from two weeks in the wilderness without a shower, and I need to scrub off at least two layers of skin and dirt." He paused, softened. "I really am happy about your news. I always knew you'd take off without me around to distract you."

But that wasn't what happened at all; how could he think that?

"Indy, I'm at your bush."

"Are *you* drunk too? I deserve to know if you're not going to remember this in the morning."

"Sober," I said. "Have to stay sober for training." I pinched my leg so hard that I woke up a little more. "I'm at the bush, the one you climbed in at Halloween. When I came and got you." Now it was Indy's turn to be too quiet. "I'm sorry. I miss you. So much. I need to tell you I—"

"I'm seeing someone. We . . . I moved in with her. My girlfriend."

Well, that one hurt. "That's . . ." *Must not sting.* "Commitment."

I hit myself in the forehead a little too hard.

He laughed sadly. "Yeah, things are different now. I wish I could explain. Ohio was . . . smothering me. I couldn't breathe. I tried to tell you, but you couldn't hear me." Indy sniffed on the line, and I wiped at tears that fell and fell from my eyes, and at the very least, I now knew we hurt the same amount and that had to mean we still felt some of the same things.

"I'm sorry too," Indy said. "We definitely broke up. I can feel it now *so* obviously. I'm sorry I tried to convince you that it wasn't . . . what it was. I was trying to save us both some of this hurt, which, wow, *really* didn't work."

We both laughed a little.

My question rolled up and through me. It leveled everything on its way out, clearing the breath from my lungs, washing away my reserve. "Can we still be friends?"

Indy's answer was immediate, its own tsunami of relief. *"Please."*

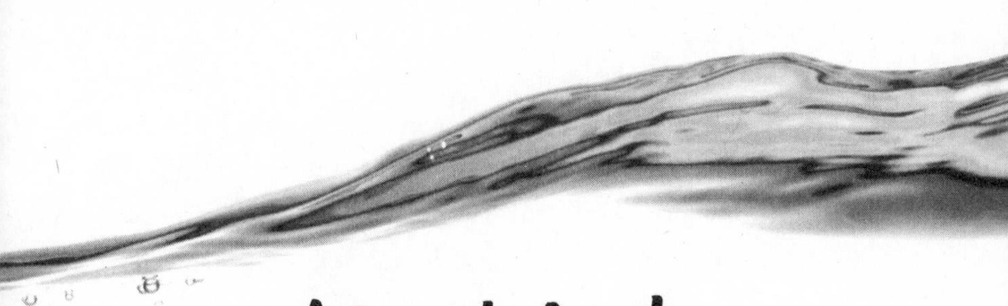

blackfish

Killer whales are dolphins. They live in generational families and have different cultures based on specific hunting behaviors and genetic distinctions, just like humans. They are polyamorous, extremely maternal, and go through menopause.

Orcas are also one of three animal species on this planet to have a spindle cell, apes and humans being the other two. A spindle cell allows the orca to feel deep emotions. They can fall in love and die from depression.

And they know joy.

— 27 —

“AS SOON AS POSSIBLE.” I’d said that twice now; I needed to calm down. Leaning on the chest-high counter between us, I added, “Thank you so much,” in the kindest, deepest voice I could muster.

The surgeon’s office was extra cold, and I was nearly humming with nerves. I’d hit some traffic on my way to Cleveland from OU and had been the last of the group of FTMX top-surgery patients to arrive at the consultation, which was followed by my one-on-one with the surgeon. I’d been the only person in the group to come without a friend, family member, paramour, what have you. That was probably why I’d gotten the extra questions. Had to be.

“Have you had a COVID vaccine yet?” the receptionist asked, adjusting her mask with kittens on it.

“A few weeks ago.” I got my vaccine card out of my wallet and handed it over the counter. It felt like I’d been here twice as long as everyone else. The waiting area was empty, and the clock reported that we were fifteen minutes past closing. The surgeon was even getting her jacket out of the closet from the slice I could see of the employee room behind reception.

But none of that mattered because I was getting a date.

“We’re mostly scheduling in early September,” she said.

I had a minor heart attack. “That’s too close to swim season. I swim for OU and I’ve got to be done with recovery before the season picks up in October. It’s my last year on the team.”

"We could put you on our cancellation list? Something might come up this summer."

"When I called a few weeks ago, someone—I think it was you—said you were scheduling in July."

She exhaled, puffing out her mask. "Yes, but there's only so many spots for this type of surgery at the medical center, and it's just been so popular lately. It's like your whole generation came out of the pandemic with different genders."

I put on my best smile, which was useless behind the mask. "I can assure you that none of us are signing up for the pain and expense of major surgery because it's the cool thing to do." My voice purred these days. God bless testosterone.

Her face pinked around her kitten mask. "I'm sorry. That sounded insensitive on my part." It *was* insensitive, but I let her keep her half apology. I managed not to point out that many people in many generations were coming out of isolation newly done playing gender games by rules no one agreed to in the first place. Who knew that being alone with your body might encourage a person to make choices based on one's needs and not other people's identity-box shortcuts.

Hey, that was growth, me holding back from dismantling a cis person for their limitless microaggressions; Indy would be so proud when I texted them later.

She clicked her keyboard like a mildly irate flight attendant. "So, there *is* a cancellation for May thirtieth. That's three weeks from now."

"That's great," I jumped in fast. "I can make that work."

"Hun, your shirt is having a little trouble there." I glanced down and found that I'd somehow gotten two entire buttonholes misaligned when I got redressed after meeting the surgeon. She turned to her computer, and I unbuttoned my shirt and rebuttoned it all over again. "To make that date work, we need to rush this insurance paperwork and to do that we need the psychiatrist's letter. Can you get that to me by Monday? I should be able to get the green light from Blue Cross within that window *if* I have letter in hand on Monday. By noon."

"The psychiatrist wrote it," I reassured her. "He just wants proof that I saw a counselor for gender issues in high school, which I did. I'm just having a hard time tracking that person down." Who knew that years of calling my terrible first therapist *Henrietta Churchiness* would come back to bite me so very hard in the ass? I didn't know her real name, Dad couldn't remember it, and neither could anyone else, apart from my mother, who wasn't speaking to me. "I will have the letter in your hand by Monday at noon," I vowed.

"Do you need an appointment card?" she asked.

"No." I was grinning like a fool under my mask. "Wait, yeah, I think I'll have it framed."

She handed over the card, and I took it reverently. I walked out of the lobby, down the hallway to the elevators. I pressed the down arrow, but what were six floors when I felt this invincible? I danced out the door of the Northeast Ohio Clinic, across the parking lot, and into my car, where the rest of my life nearly fell into my lap when I shut the door too enthusiastically.

Everything from my junior year at the Rainbow Haven was currently in my trunk, back seat, front seat, and a solid percentage of the ceiling space. It was more than my room, honestly. Everett and Karina had used their holidays with our parents to rescue things from my old bedroom. I wasn't going into the house these days, which sounded dramatic but it was more like me and home . . . we were taking a break.

And now I was carrying my house on my back like a damn turtle. At least I had my old car. Dad had sworn it was mine, and he wouldn't hear anything else about it. Everett did his best not to imply that my parents were fighting about me, but he didn't quite sell it.

Coincidentally, I'd had the best three years of my life, pandemic included. My teammates were everything, I loved studying marine life biology, my coach was an actual coach, therapy and transition were making my life easier left and right. Not to mention I had a splendid hookup situation with Israel, a raging retro crush on Indigo Waits, and now . . . drum roll, please?

A date for top surgery.

I stared at the card lovingly. But where would I put it? My car-life was about to come crashing down around me, and still I'd promised to make certain things happen. In one weekend, I had to find that old therapist, get her to confirm our sessions so that my psychiatrist would forward the letter to the administrative assistant, who would then persuade Blue Cross Blue Shield of Ohio not to be transphobes in time for me to *keep* this date.

I would make it happen. I'd moved larger mountains before.

I *roared*, accidentally startling the sanity out of the person placing a heavy bag into the car beside mine. She shouted, nearly dropping everything. I jumped out to help her and recognized the white, kind-faced, small-boned surgeon, Dr. Louise Jackson. She had a sweet mom vibe about her, and her skin was beyond flawless.

"I'm so sorry I scared you. I am so excited, to have a date. I was celebrating."

Dr. Jackson clutched her chest. "Well, I was exhausted and worried about the drive home, but now I'm pumped full of adrenaline, thank you. It's River, right?"

I said yeah, but my heart yelled *nooo* because Dr. Jackson looked into the chaos of my car. She shut her door and sort of planted her feet. Her stare fell on me, and I answered her question before she could ask it. "I don't live in my car. I'm moving back home from college . . . right now."

"You told me you're going to your brother's house for recovery, yes?" she asked. I nodded. "How old is he?"

"Mentally or physically?" My joke didn't land. "Twenty-three. He lives with his girlfriend."

"And you have a bed there, and food, and *serious* help so that you don't fall or injure yourself? Can your brother and his girlfriend handle body fluids? You're going to need someone to empty your drains twice a day. The first few days you might not be able to do anything for yourself. Or keep track of your pain medication."

Now this was turning into a repeat of the inquisition I'd gotten in the exam room.

"Everett and Karina are the best. Summa cum laude, from Miami U. Both of them," I promised. "Everett's coming with me to the surgery. You can meet him then."

Dr. Jackson finally seemed satisfied. "For me, the hard part takes two hours. The hard part for you is two months. Two months is a long time to stay anywhere that's not home."

Jeez, Louise, not everyone is privileged enough to have a home.

"I heard recovery was more like two weeks."

"Two weeks of complete immobility. Two months of fragility. Six months before you should be raising your arms over your head or your scars will stretch."

"I can do it." The truth was that if she told me the procedure came with the unintended side effect of a shark fin sprouting out of my back, I would have agreed. I needed to do this.

I gave her my most earnest smile, and we went our separate ways. She drove off, and I stared at the little card on my steering wheel. I took a picture of it and sent it to Indy, Israel, and Electra. I'd tell the Chengs and Everett in person, and I already had this idea to call Catherine the night before. She did say to reach out when I did something huge . . . and this was *everything*.

I drove southeast to Haley without the GPS. The highways were ingrained in my brain in a way I didn't know how to process. After forgetting so much for so long, this place was going to stay with me forever no matter what, and hey, maybe it was time to make peace with that.

A half hour south of Cleveland, I passed the enormous teal billboard for SeaPlanet of Ohio. Someone had red spray-painted over it in all caps, CLOSED. I followed the exits decorated with octopuses, dolphins, and the penguin mascot Keemee, a surprising tightness in my chest at each one. The first two summers it was closed, SeaPlanet had remained mostly intact, as if they were hoping to pull a rabbit and save the park. When that hadn't happened, the place was gutted one attraction at a time, the pandemic slowing the demolition.

But that didn't mean Haleyites weren't still working there.

It was getting dark when I pulled down the drive, under the stripped bars that once held the main signage, and parked at the first security tower. I checked my phone and found many huzzahs from Israel. I winked a smiley face at him. Electra had sent about seventeen gifs that conveyed an entire range of extreme emotion. Nothing from Indy yet.

I honked and got out. "Ever Rat McTire?"

Everett came out of the booth with a worn sci-fi paperback in his hands. At least they didn't make my brother dress in those Confederate gray uniforms. He was working in a black polo that read SECURITY in white stitching. His long hair was in a bun at the back of his neck. We performed the manly back-slapping hug we'd perfected as kids when our parents needed us to visually make up, and then he clicked on his flash-light and looked into my car. "Well, that doesn't look safe. Where are we going to put all this stuff?"

"The Chengs said I could use one side of their garage."

Everett exhaled audibly, and I got the weirdest little poke like maybe he wasn't that excited about me living with him. Or maybe that was the firm talking to I'd gotten from the surgeon still wearing off. "How'd it go?" he asked.

"May thirtieth," I said, proudly.

"Liver, you said July!"

"They were scheduling in September, but they had this tiny cancellation window. I still might not make it happen. I have to track down my old therapist first. As in, *this* weekend."

Everett sat on the bench outside the guard tower, just another honors grad working night security at an abandoned marine life amusement park. "Okay, don't hate me."

"I don't love that start."

"I'm going to propose to Karina." He dug out the old, cliché fuzzy box and held it out to me. I inspected the cute sapphire. "She doesn't believe in diamonds."

"Intriguing." I handed the ring back. "This is nice. Of course I'm happy you're going to propose. What's the part where you knife me?"

"I'm doing it on the road trip we've been planning, with all the money we saved graduating early. We're going to drive across the US, up the West Coast, and then back through Montana. We leave next week."

Oh, okay. Now I saw where this was turning into bad news. "How long does that take?"

"A month, at least. Everything's all booked. The campsites, all of it," he said. I sat beside him on the bench. The little card in my pocket was worthless. The circus acts I'd gone through to make this appointment by the skin of my teeth in my dumpster of a car was all worthless. "Oh God, you're devastated! I told you not to book without talking to me."

"I'll be fine."

"Can you stay with the Chengs? They housed you over the holidays."

"Freya's seven months pregnant. I'm not about to ask if they'll wait on me hand and foot for weeks after major surgery." I must have said something more intensely than I had before, because Everett grew concerned.

"What did the surgeon say?"

"Apparently, I have to have the most intense type of top surgery. She actually used the words 'square foot of scar tissue.' She's worried about my ability to train. She suggested an entire season off, which isn't happening." I tried not to punish him with my sudden, blinding dysphoria. Booking in September meant waiting another four months instead of three weeks. It meant being on the bench for my last season on the team. Not to mention it'd mean spending another summer suffocating inside my binder. I couldn't breathe.

Varian had warned me about this. The closer I got to surgery, the more desperate I became. It was one enormous Pandora's box of *this must happen now*.

"Okay, I'll call back Monday and reschedule." I cleared my throat. "Good news is, I have extra time to locate the worst therapist in the Midwest."

Everett stood up, always jerky in his mannerisms when he was feeling things. "Should we take a walk down the spookiest lane of memories in possibly the entire world? You should see how they gutted this place." I wasn't in the mood. I shook my head, and my pants buzzed with a text. "Karina's home at the apartment if you want to head over there and unpack."

I checked my phone, sitting up. Any text from Indy made me sit up, but this one far more than usual. "*Read.*" I held out the screen to my brother. "Is Indy messing with me?"

"That'd be a tactless way to mess with you."

Indy had texted, *News that good should be celebrated in person. Where are you?*

"When's the last time you two were in the same state?" he asked.

Twenty-seven months.

"Some time."

"And they're home for the summer or a visit or something?"

"No. Well, Indy hasn't said anything about that, at least."

"If you don't know where they're living this summer, you must not talk often."

"We do, every week, but we rarely talk about our lives. It's complicated. Indy's got longtime Leia. And with training, I only have time for casual—"

"Do me a favor and don't finish that sentence," my brother begged. "Karina heard from some *Chauncey* on her feed that you are accomplished in the ways of the undergrad Lothario."

I pointed at him. "No slut shaming. If you spent most of your life squeezed in the wrong gender, you might also come out of it hungry to make up for lost time." He yielded, shrugged. "Plus someone's got to have all the sex you aren't having."

"There it is. And you're welcome to it." He pointed at my phone. "Tell Indy where you are. No, wait! I have a great idea. Don't say anything yet." Everett beckoned me to follow him around the back of the tower gate and used his flashlight to illuminate a paved path. A shortcut I'd never known about connected the main drive to the west part of the park where the dome of the long-abandoned orca stadium was still standing tall.

"Should we be here?" I asked. "Are there other security guards?"

"I'm not the one who has gotten kicked out twice," he joked. "But, no, I'm the only guard. I'm to scare away drinking and sexing youth and call the cops and hide in my booth for anything else. I'm really glad I got that college degree for this." But I knew he was joking; he had been applying to fellowships overseas before the pandemic, and now he had to wait it out.

In front of the stadium, the breaching, life-sized orca statue that had once adorned my prom was back where it had been in the old days, bolted in the middle of the walkway, parting ghostly crowds in my mind. I turned and faced the rest of the park for the first time. The dark scrubbed out most of the loss, but even the silhouette was deeply changed. Some of the buildings were still standing while others were gone as if by a clean, exacting alien abduction.

I turned back to the orca. His name had been Keely. For some reason SeaPlanet gave all the animals nearly identical names. He'd been a living breathing mammal that had had the bad luck to be born in captivity, separated from his loving mom and shipped here when he was too young, cursed to swim in an orca-sized hot tub and jump whenever he heard the trainer's whistle.

"Weird that Keely's back, isn't it?" I asked. "Kind of ominous."

"He hasn't been gone too long," Everett said. "When did they stop doing orca shows?"

It was strange to me that Everett and I had both grown up here, and yet we knew such different things about this place. Then again, he hadn't obsessed over the weirdness of the park like I had, always drawn in by the animals and their utter lack of choice.

"They stopped in 2015; I was eleven. Before that every time we came to the orca show, when the blackfish would beach itself on that platform at the front of the stadium"—I paused, my education kicking in—"in nature, that move is for hunting baby seals on pebbly beaches."

"Creepy."

"Yeah, well, they'd sit some kid astride the orca with victory arms. Grand finale. Mom wanted me on that killer whale's back even though I nearly pissed my pants at the idea of it. She used to grab my wrist and hold my arm up. She'd point to my head and holler. Thing is, I never once told her that I did not want to do it, and she never once asked if I wanted to, and I think this is how it's always going to be between us."

"She'd talk to you," he said. "If you walked over there right now and asked her about that therapist, she'd give you the name. She told Dad as much." Interesting. Dad had not told *me* as much. Most likely because he didn't want me to get pulled into her manipulative schemes.

I looked back to the orca stadium, more interested in the dark history of the captive blackfish than my family life. "A drunk guy jumped in Keely's tank one night, got eaten, and within days he was shipped to Florida, gone forever. Or at least that's the urban legend."

Both of us spooked at the same moment, turning to glare at the gaping maw of the orca stadium gate that had been closed for so long. Someone had kicked it in. The NEW ATTRACTION COMING SOON! sign was hanging by one peg.

I wanted to go in there. I'd wanted to go in there for so long, the same way someone might long to see the rusting bars of Alcatraz.

"Is it weird that I think I'd do the same thing in the whale's place?" my brother asked, breaking my bleak reverie.

"They're dolphins. Not whales. It's been pure cock-ups for orcas from label to life."

"Hey, there's that marine biology degree kicking in." Everett climbed on the orca statue's back. "Come on! You get on too!"

"Did you just miss my impassioned speech about respecting wildlife? Besides, you look amazing. Don't move." I sent a picture of Everett on the orca, responding to Indy's *Where are you?* with *You'll never guess. C'mere.*

"Did you do it?" Everett was still astride the orca statue. "Are they coming?"

Indy's next message came fast, *Give me twenty.*

"What is happening?" I shouted. Zero cool. I was down to absolute zero cool.

Everett swatted at me. "Go find a fresh shirt that doesn't smell like you've been driving in a fast-food truck all day."

"Thank you, brother. Great advice." I streaked up the old secret path in the dark. My Indy was coming, and my mind shifted and charged. The card was forgotten in my pocket, along with my brother's ill-timed vacation, the worst therapist in Ohio, and my killer whale of a mom.

I changed in a flash by the tower gate, and the whole time my brother chirped at me like a heckler at a standup show.

"Are you going to hug straight off?" Everett pondered dangerously. His big brain had gotten me into too much trouble in the past. "No one wants to be the side of the equation who goes in for the hug only to face-plant on the wall of no reciprocation."

I paced beside my car. "We'll hug."

But would we?

"What if they . . . she . . . What are Indy's pronouns right now?"

"They change a lot," I said. "Daily. I'm starting to think that the change is more important to Indy than the words. I vary them in my head." I took out my keys. "Ev, is the employee lot still standing?"

"Yes. Overgrown but still there."

"When Indy pulls up, have them meet me over there."

"But then I don't get to watch the big reunion!"

"Exactly!" I drove off, around the main gate. After the length of a block, the drive split. To the right, all the guests would park in basically Egypt and take a small shuttle to the entrance. I went left, down a cracked road to the little spot where, nestled by trees, so much of my life had caught the wind and twisted. I parked and crossed the knee-high weeds to the picnic table where I'd gotten caught making out with Taylor by the person I'd been dreaming about for over a year.

It was a hundred lifetimes ago. And also yesterday.

I sat on the splintered wood and tried not to remember scurrying in my pearl-diver's suit between the lanes. My locked car. Indy's open door. And then all the sudden, I was seeing Indy and me kissing fiercely in our prom outfits—the very last time we were together without California between us.

In the end, SeaPlanet had a lot of marks against it, but it had also been an island of note in landlocked meaninglessness. I would always be able to close my eyes and hear cheers echoing through Haley each summer night, feel the sting of the splash zones, for-profit, fluorescent zoology at its best. And yet, I could have been working at Target or wandering a strip mall during these years. Instead, I'd made a second home at SeaPlanet. Season passes were a steal the way we used them. Go every day for the taffy. Dare each other up the pirate-ship cargo nets, encounter the penguins' air-conditioning, and commune with the other marine life who were so far from the ocean it might as well not exist.

— 28 —

INDIGO WAITS PULLED UP in the very same car, although now it hummed and groaned like an old walrus. Indy parked next to where I had and didn't get out right away. My heart pounded so hard beneath my binder it was downright painful. I could see just a little bit of her. A few inches of handsome hair. Was that a plain white tank top? Nothing about my Indy was ever plain.

They got out and looked around, and I waited for them to find me.

I'd thought a bit of distance between us when we saw each other again would give me some time to work out the logistics of this reunion, but it had the simultaneous effect of dragging out the walk we made to meet each other.

Indy stopped about twenty feet from me, and I stopped too. They looked like they'd come straight from the mountains in hiking boots and worn cargo shorts. I wondered if they ever wore a bra anymore, let alone a binder, their skin so bronzed.

"Are we going to hug?" I blurted because this was killing me, and I'd never been a playboy with Indy. Never the trans James Dean, but an affectionate fool. The realest me.

Indy's response was to run, launching themself into a full-body hug that wrapped their legs around my waist and their arms about my shoulders. "I missed you," Indy chanted in my ear. Over and over. "I missed you, I missed you."

"Me too," I managed. They were smaller than the last time I held them. Lean but still acutely strong. They didn't let go, and I didn't want them to. I tried to sit us on that old picnic table, but it *whined* under our weight with the promise of collapse, and we parted to stand up. Indy was pushing away tears. I hadn't expected that. I was the one who loved them too much.

This felt different.

Indy was different. I was different.

They looked around at the crumbling amusement park. "This place is effed up."

"Since when do you say 'effed'?"

"I've been camping with my little brothers all week. Trying not to turn them into sailors before their time."

"You've been in Ohio all week?"

"A few weeks." Indy looked mildly guilty. "I didn't tell you because you had classes, and I didn't want to interrupt your life and . . . Mom sold the house. She's moving in with the absurdly stable girlfriend of her dreams. Mom flew me back to help pack and say goodbye to the place. It's been bittersweet."

"When are you going back to San Francisco?"

"Tomorrow. I'm taking my car—and all my stuff—home. Assuming the old bucket makes it." There was that word again. *Home.* Such a sneaking bomb that kept detonating over my day. Indy had made a home in California with Leia; I didn't have one. I tucked that dark feeling down deep, determined not to let jealousy ruin this evening.

"All my stuff is in my car too," I joked. "Looks like I live in there. Hey, we nearly missed each other. All over again." Why did those words stab so much?

"Leia and I are over."

I froze. My whole body turned to water. Was I supposed to say I was sorry? There was no possible way that would come out sounding sincere.

"I'm moving into my grandparents' carriage house in Pacific Heights. I'll have to go back to volunteering at the shelter kitchen every night to stomach the privilege of that sentence."

Perhaps I looked horrified. Who knew how I looked; I was spilling everywhere. "Are you okay?"

"Yeah, well, it's amazing my first legit U-Haul lasted as long as it did."

My phone buzzed, and I read a text from Everett. *How about some mood lighting?* The footlights that lined the many crisscrossing paths of the park all turned on at once. What was a murky, bleak park became lined with illuminated walkways.

"River, what are we doing here?" Indy asked, dazed.

"Well, I am hoping to get a tour." There was my flirting voice. Nice of you to join us finally, Christ. "What are your pronouns?"

"All of them," Indy said. That was new. "The same pronoun all the time makes me claustrophobic. I've come to new ground with being agender, which felt great until I finally stumbled across a queer subject my mom does not understand. Maybe you can give me advice."

"You don't want my advice. I don't even have a home anymore." I winced. Oh yeah, I forgot that when Indy was around, I didn't have a filter. I had cutting honesty and raging emotions and entire tides of hope and hormones to get swept away on.

"Do you . . . want to talk about it?"

"Not at all. My pronouns are they/them." Indy could hear the pause in my voice, and so I added, "He/him is also on my mind, but I'm waiting until after surgery to use it."

"You don't have to wait."

"I know." And I did. "But what I want right now is that Indy tour I always heard about." I motioned to the lit pathways. One route led out of the employee lot, but from this vantage, it split into so many roads we could take, one to every corner of the park.

Indy tugged my hand, sending my nerves into a frenzy. I followed as they took us to the front gate. Here everything had been graffitied and kicked in. Not a single pane of glass remaining. I stared at one wall bearing the words *Mike Dweiller is a predator.*

"I didn't do that," I said. "I swear."

Indy cleared their throat, turned on a tour-guide smile, and started walking backward. "Welcome to SeaPlanet, the Midwest's *only* marine life interactive family amusement park." Oh, she was going for it, my love. "Founded in 1972, the park covers over two hundred acres of recovered swampland that was deemed uninhabitable for the developers of the town of Haley, which we're currently standing in." I raised my hand; Indy pointed at me. "I believe the Gentleman Jack—who is definitely too attractive for their own good and going to interrupt me this entire tour—has a question?"

"How did people not know they were in Haley? That couldn't have been part of the tour."

"They were barely aware that they were in Ohio. Mostly the international tourists were the only ones to sign up for the historic walking tour." Indy motioned for me to zip it and went back into the monologue. "There are over three thousand different kinds of animals and marine life here at SeaPlanet, almost all of which were saved from endangered areas and disrupted ecosystems, or were born in captivity and cannot survive in the wild."

I raised my hand again. "So, instead of putting a shit ton of money into finding ways to reintegrate the animals into their natural environments, they dumped cash into enormous tanks and, what, turned the refugees into circus acts?"

Indy didn't bat an eye. "I see we have an animal lover on our tour today. What a blessing for all of us. Here at SeaPlanet we're determined to help better the quality of life for every single marine animal on this big, beautiful water planet. Those within our care *and* those thriving in the wild. That's why sixty percent of all our proceeds, after the expense to care and feed the animals, goes back to helping oceanographic conservation."

Huh? "Was that true?"

"It was. But SeaPlanet wasn't profitable for years before it shut down, so I think it's safe to say they haven't plucked a single piece of plastic out of the Pacific since the nineties." We kept walking, Indy kept talking, and even though this had started as a joke, I found I was entranced.

I stopped in one vacant spot and looked around. "No one else would remember, but this is where I beat up Mike Dweiller."

Indy's tour-guide persona disappeared. "I never told you that I saw you. Saw the whole thing. That's how I knew you were in my car. I followed you."

"You did?"

"You didn't beat him up. You shoved him around. You embarrassed and screamed at him, but he wasn't injured at all. Let your conscience go free, River."

"I don't have a guilty conscience about Mike Dweiller," I tried to joke.

Indy's smile was sad. "You used to have a guilty conscience about everything."

"Well, I'm getting better."

Indy's eye caught on something on the ground. "Do you see writing?" We engaged our phone flashlights, illuminating the pavement. A few dozen people had spray-painted on this exact spot. All in different colors and different handwritings. All the same words.

Mike Dweiller is a predator.

I stared and stared. Indy put an arm around my waist and squeezed.

We stopped next in front of the aquarium, the doors chained and padlocked. The Penguin Encounter jutted off to the side. "There might be a side way in," they said.

"I don't want to go in there. That feels too much like returning to dark places."

This time I tugged Indy's hand, leading us toward the pearl-diving pool. The "Japanese House" had been leveled, leaving a clear spot that looked out across the small lake that the entire park had been built beside. I took a picture for Mrs. Cheng, but it came out as a few smudges of light glinting off water.

"Everett says there are talks about turning this place into a water park. Swim where killer whales swam. How goth." I stooped and picked up a broken piece of teal cement and held it out to them. "For your rock collection. Something to remember this place by."

They pocketed it and winked at me. My throat was so dry.

"So, you're driving to California tomorrow all alone in a car that had its glory days around the same time as Maroon Five. I don't love this plan, Indigo."

"Leia was supposed to fly out and drive with me, but the weirdest thing happened when I came back here. I didn't miss her. At all. She didn't miss me either."

"I could drive with you." *Too bold? Who cares.* "I have nowhere to go and nothing to do for approximately four months."

Indy looked so confused. "How could you say that? You're having top surgery!"

I sat on the curb. The truth about the corner I'd painted myself into was almost too embarrassing to admit. "I have to . . . reschedule. There's some insurance snags, and Everett's got to tour the US as a platform to propose to Karina."

"Insurance snags." Indy had that lightning-rod intensity in their voice. "Explain." I did, including the trap of my mom's icy détente. Halfway through, Indy started texting someone, commanding, "Tell me everything you remember about that therapist."

"She was Christian, although she tried to hide it. Her office was on

Pleasant Street in Kent, but it's a hair salon now. She hated me, I tortured her. How did you ever put up with me? I was such a miserable ass when I lived here."

Indy didn't look up from her phone. "That's far too simplistic for what you were back then. You were a man o' war. Gorgeous, intense, and occasionally, you'd sting."

I wanted to hold Indy's hand. I ached to weave our fingers. So many people could see me these days, but Indy *knew* me. If there was no more Leia, was there a chance for us again? No, couldn't be. Indy was still bound to a coast I only had vivid, longing dreams about.

"If Everett and Karina are going away, does that mean you're taking care of their apartment?" they asked.

"I guess so. We haven't gotten that far in the discussion."

"So I'll stay. I'll take care of you after your surgery. We can hole up in their place."

Whoa. "It's not two weeks of recovery like I thought. More like two months, according to my overly protective surgeon."

"So I'll spend the summer with you. If you want."

I chuckled; Indy looked confused. "You can't do that. You have a life to get back to."

"I'm in between jobs, and the carriage house isn't going anywhere." She shrugged. I stared at her a lot longer than I had when she first pulled up. Indy's phone buzzed, and she held the screen out to me, showing off a picture of Henrietta Churchiness in all her buttoned-up, coiffed glory. "Is that her?"

"How did you—"

"Mom's girlfriend is a counselor too. They have a whole database." Indy clicked a link and read the description. "Karen Grocer, LMHC. Now practices out of Grand Rapids, Michigan. Office opens at nine a.m. on Monday morning. If you send the contact info to your psychiatrist, the two offices can talk to each other directly, and you should be all set."

I got up. I started to walk away. Away from Indy's ability to straighten my life out with a calculated flick. To offer me things that were beyond dreams. I wanted to cry. I wouldn't let Indy stay here and take care of me, of course, and now I was angry they'd offered. I had to fix myself—that had been the plan for years. I would fix myself and *then* go to them.

"Are you . . . mad?" Indy called out, panic in his voice. "Now you're being an ass!"

I kept walking, calling over my shoulder, "There's something I have to do."

The dilapidated orca stadium was on the other side of the park. I walked swiftly, standing on the threshold of the half-broken gate. Indy padded up beside me, looking in.

"You know I never saw an orca show. Funnily enough, my parents wouldn't let me come here. They thought this place was a bit evil. By the time I was hired, this stadium was shut up."

I walked in, reaching back for Indy's hand, finding their fingers waiting for mine.

The blackness wouldn't relent. I knew the stadium seating by memory, the rows and rows of cement blocks that could house a thousand people easily. The yellow *splash zones* down front. The nosebleed seats so high they gave you vertigo. In the dark, they looked like lines of graves. But I wasn't here to face the ghosts of empty spectators.

I kept walking until I knew I might be in trouble. Here was the platform where the orcas beached themselves, dorsal fins flopped over, entropized, tail held shakily high while they waited for a pat and a snack. Anything to be treated as if they had feelings.

A motion-detecting sensor flipped, blinding us in a spotlight. We shielded our eyes for a solid minute before they adjusted.

"Oh. Wow." Indy's voice shook. We were indeed standing on the precipice before the huge, deep tank. The bottom was full of leaves and muddy water, but the stage behind it had a timeless quality. All those years sealed up had preserved the old logo for SeaPlanet with the tandem cresting orcas, before they rebranded with smiling penguins. I looked up at the red ball, still dangling from the cavernous domed ceiling on a long wire.

Indy stared up at it too. "What was that for?"

"The orcas used to jump thirty feet in the air to tap it with their nose. The audience loved it. You know they have more emotions than humans do."

I wept.

By the time Everett made it over, drawn by the sensor on the security light, he found me collapsed in Indy's arms as if nothing had ever changed between us. I was a mess; they were my rock. But that wasn't entirely true, was it?

"River? You okay?" Everett asked.

"Yeah." I stood up, surprised that I was actually okay. I kept a firm hold on Indy's hand. "In the words of my therapist, I'm just accepting all of this as part of me." Varian would be proud; he'd spent the last few years walking me around the idea of acceptance. Around and around it. *Accept others for being gender abusive and pro-captivity? Accept a culture that ruins animals and people alike in the name of capitalism? Impossible. Wrong. I couldn't.*

I'd felt that way only yesterday in session. But today was different.

All of this was a part of me, and it wasn't a reason to give up the war against hate, it was the reason to fight a lot harder for joy.

Indy and I got into our respective vehicles, leaving SeaPlanet for the last time. I was thankful that neither of us had room for the other person in our packed cars. We had to travel separately, and that meant something, didn't it?

We had to go our separate ways.

As soon as we parked somewhere, I was going to have to explain that I was still too in love with them to be friends. And to have them care for me? Make my gender-affirming surgery possible only for them to jet away again to a liberal haven? I imagined queers bloomed on the streets in San Francisco, holding hands and kissing in public. Indy had assured me it was hardly a paradise, but I knew it was still beyond my new and shaky understanding of acceptance. And the truth was, I'd never survive a second loss of Indigo Waits.

Indy headed to their old house, and I followed, watching them turn into their neighborhood. I went left instead and took a spin into Park View. My parents' house came from pure muscle memory. I could have driven it with my eyes closed, but for the first time, I didn't pull into the driveway. I idled on the side of the road.

The place seemed too dark and small. No lights. A McRanch left over from the sixties. I couldn't hear the orca in the tree, and maybe it had fallen down or finally killed its battery, but it was always going to be there, taunting me about this small world, with its singular moon and deified sun, its dividing mountains and wide oceans.

I parked and got out, crossing my parents' barbarically fertilized lawn. It even looked deeply green in the dark. The front stoop was ready for me. I sat down, imagining all the years I'd been stuck here, wondering when she'd let me be. If she'd ever let me out. It had been so impossibly hard to learn the truth: My freedom wasn't up to her.

I pulled the little appointment card out of my pocket along with a pen and wrote a few words on the back. When the door opened behind me, I jumped, stood up.

My mom was standing in the dark foyer. The moon lit up her face unevenly. The pandemic had taken years from her, and yet, maybe, in some way I wouldn't assume to understand, it had been good for her too.

I held out the card; she didn't take it. "It's only three words."

She sighed. "I love you too, but—"

"It's not those words."

She looked stumped. "If you've come to apologize, I don't want—"

"It's not that either."

I walked away.

I drove to Indy's house for the last time, determined to explain my somewhat extreme reaction to their kind and life-changing offer. Indy was sitting on the front stoop, possibly crying from the droop in their shoulders. I got out, crossed the distance between us, and folded her up in my arms. She held on to me like a lifeline.

When it started to rain, we went inside. The house that had always felt bursting with inclusiveness and affirmation—so much more than the Rainbow Haven could ever brag—was completely empty. Indy wound their way down the hall in their own state of muscle memory, kicking off their shoes where the boot tray used to be, entering their room. I followed.

"We've got the whole house. Mom is at her girlfriend's."

Everything was gone. The bed, the couch, every book, and rock. Everything but the dozens of crisscrossing light strings and a camping bedroll. "Mom promised these could be the last to go. I can't bear to take them down." Indy plugged them in, and the room glowed as fiercely as it used to.

I took Indy's hand. I kissed their calloused knuckles. "You can't stop your whole life to take care of me for months. I won't let you." Indy started to speak, and I shook my head. "Hear me out. Last time we were in this position, I lied to myself. I said it didn't matter if you were leaving someday because the day at hand was too amazing to turn down. Then you left, and my misery undid me. I can't do it again." I kissed their wrist. Twice.

Indy was somber, pleading. "Please let me do something."

"You already did. I'll keep the date, if I can. I'll ask the Chengs if they can take care of me. I'll have to do something extreme to make it up to them, but I'll figure it out." I kissed their thumb, and the rest of their fingers, none of it was enough. None of it could be, unless it was the rest of our lives. "I'm never going to love anyone more than you."

Their shoulders slumped. "Am I supposed to feel like I win, but also can't have you, River? Or do we both lose because our timing doesn't line up perfectly?"

"You know what I mean. You always know. We can see each other when no one else can. And that's the most romantic thing I've ever heard of." There was a heartbeat of distance between us. The lights glowed red and orange around us, yellow, green, and purple on their skin, blue water in their eyes. I didn't need rings or dates or tours around this cursed country. I needed us, even existentially. "Will you marry me?"

"Yes."

"Not now," I added in a rush. "When we're on the other side of surgery, recovery, physical therapy, training . . . one more swim season, graduation . . . Then I'll come to you. To California, I promise. There's an internship at the aquarium for rehabilitating marine life and actually rereleasing them. I think I'm pretty good candidate, and—"

"I said yes. Kiss me before I die."

By the light of a few thousand indoor stars, I kissed Indy. Her lips were soft, but firmer than I remembered. The other mouths I'd known over the last two years washed away, leaving only two: the Indy I knew and this new person.

At first, we kissed as we always had, sweet with raw attentiveness. An earnestness of clasping hands and wanting sounds. I saw us in my mind's eye as we were in high school, swaddled deep in the safest, most beautiful closet of a room, in this fishbowl of a town. Kissing Indigo Waits meant remembering why I loved Indigo Waits—the world needed me to be aware of all the pulling tides, but she put the wind in my sail. I opened my eyes, gasping as if I'd come up from the bottom of the pool. I buckled over, holding my chest.

"River?" Indy gave me space, and then rubbed my back. "You okay?"

"Big one," I said, shaking all of it free.

"Did kissing me make you go dysphoria zombie?" They were alarmed.

Honestly, so was I.

"Yes, but it was important. I just . . . felt all this guilt leave me. I don't care what they think about me. Or say. I don't care if they whisper about my surgery or if my mom ends up in a hundred tiny embarrassing conversations at the grocery store."

"That sounds good." Even Indy's voice was different, slower. Kinder.

"Very good." I looked at them from eyebrow to kneecap. They were new to me, and I was to them. Indy slid their palms up my arms, marveling. "You can thank Israel for the muscles. He's into weight training."

Indy wiggled with jealousy, playfully so. Their hands trailed my chest, wrapped around my shoulders, and I lifted them close so they could feel just how different my body was now.

Indy laughed with a deep purr, hands tracing the lines of my harness beneath my jeans, their thigh pressing into my manhood. "And is this also, 'thank you, Israel'?"

"Nah." My voice cracked cutely. "That's all me. Though he did show me how to use it."

Indy made a starving sound, their hands finding all the new pieces of me with new energy. When we started kissing again, all the teenage kinks had been worked out. We made love all ways, and no offense to the boy I used to be, but if *intention* is the true difference, we intended at an entirely new level. Indy was loud and verbal, and said that they *loved me, loved me, loved me* while we were shaking together, our bodies whole.

Afterward, they put a hand on my heart. Without my binder, it was easy to find, and while parts of my chest still mocked me, they weren't so bad now that their days were numbered. "I've never been naked before," I admitted.

"Never, never?"

"You know what I mean." I felt freed. It would be over soon. So soon. Not just my surgery but all of this powerlessness. After so long being pent up, I swore I could smell the ocean, the water calling. "Hey, we're older now. Remember when I really needed that?"

Indy kissed my fingertips. "How could I forget."

I chuckled. "Mrs. Cheng told me that being young is one wild night. It's fun until it gets old, and then you sleep it off like a tequila hangover."

Indy laughed, such a rich joyful sound. "Hey, will you do something for me?"

"Anything."

"Let me stay until your surgery. Afterward, I'll leave you in the trusting hands of the Chengs. I can't be waiting on a text while it's happening. I need to be there."

I lifted Indy's hand off my chest, kissed his palm. "We already line up more than we think. I need you there too. And I need you to distract me for three weeks." I sat up and placed kisses on her stomach.

"Three weeks?" Indy laughed again, their muscles pressing against my lips. "Easy."

— 29 —

ON MAY 30, I learned that good memories can also be slippery. Time moved sideways, and I did my best to hang on. Instead of traveling to the hospital with Everett as I'd planned, I was crammed in the back of Mrs. Cheng's car with Indy.

My phone lit up with comments on my last *before* picture. From Joss, Gia, Kirk, Indy's mom, even good old Harvey left me a comment—and Mrs. Winooski offered prayers. There were texts too. From Dad, Everett, Karina, Catherine, Israel, Electra, and Coach Warren.

Indy looked over at the endlessly dinging screen. "Lot of people care about you."

"That's still so weirdly hard to accept."

Indy snuggled into my shoulder. "I know."

Freya looked back from the passenger seat. "You two are my favorite."

And then time skipped and jumped, and I was getting prepped for surgery. The room was too cold, and they warmed my arm to place an IV. The anesthesiologist told dad jokes. The nurses used my pronouns. I couldn't stop smiling. Joy dripped off me in embarrassing streams.

Dr. Jackson came in and met Indy with a skeptical gaze. "I do my best not to assume genders in this business, but this doesn't appear to be the big brother you promised."

"This is my Indy," I said, "and my parents are in the waiting room."

She smiled with such relief, and so did I. Dr. Jackson marked my chest with a black pen. "You're going to walk differently. This was a lot of weight to carry, but you already know that."

"It's just drag, like in swimming," I said. "I've tricked myself into living with it for so long. Bet I'm pretty streamline without it."

And then I was under, submerged in a dark medical sea, cradled through the worst. A blink of midnight, and then the brightest lights in the world and so many voices saying my name. My chest was on fire and bound tight, and I had lines streaming out of me, a blue bottle at ease.

"They can drop their tentacles down over a hundred feet." My voice was calloused, the drugs moving my thoughts in a whirlpool. "Or pull them up within inches of their body."

A nurse's voice cut in sharply. "Honey, what are you saying? Are you okay?"

"River's waxing poetic about man o' wars," Indy said from beside me. I think they were even holding my hand. "That's really normal for them."

"All rivers lead to the sea," I said.

Indy kissed my cheek. "Yeah, they do."

The day I got my drains out—which felt unholy, by the way—Indy finally left for California.

Also, something else happened.

I left the surgeon's practice, downright hissing from the lingering feel of tubes being hauled out of my skin. I walked with a hunch, holding my chest together with both hands. I'd never felt so much like a man o' war with all those rubber hoses and plastic bladders hanging off me. Measuring and emptying them had become my all-encompassing thought over the last five days. It was hard to celebrate, especially considering my eighteen inches of gnarly stitches.

As a bonus the painkillers often lent the illusion that I was turning polyp. Indy had too much fun making me describe it, curled on the couch together. We were headed toward a future, a shared horizon. I told her I swore I saw us years from now on a line of sand, helping beached man o' wars into the outgoing tide. Indy laughed and called me trans Holden Caulfield.

Vicodin makes you feel like plastic, dream in Disney hues, and think nonlinearly.

Drainless, I got into Mrs. Cheng's car. She barely waited until I was buckled and pulled out. "In a hurry?"

"Freya texted. Indy's waiting to leave. They want to see you."

"She's going to miss her plane!" I held my chest while we accelerated up the ramp and onto I-80. One of my successes the past few weeks was to persuade Indy to sell their old car and not drive from the conservative heart of it all, through the liberal dead zone, and then over the mountains in a rust trap by themself. "They should have left a half hour ago."

"Why do you think I'm taking the highway back?" Mrs. Cheng said.

"But it costs fifty cents." I held myself together when we hit a pothole.

"Queer-o, you're worth fifty cents to me."

"And how much will you pay when I pop some stitches?"

Mrs. Cheng pulled around a semi with the skill of stunt car driver. "You're only fragile in your head. You'll get over it someday. Freya and I have faith. That's why we invested in you as a test child. We passed the test. You turned out pretty perfect."

I laughed hard enough to need to hold myself even tighter. It seemed there would be no end to the you're-our-kid-now jokes. And, if I was to believe them, I'd inspired them to try their hands with one from scratch. I was getting a new sibling.

Mrs. Cheng pulled around an SUV driven by a swearing CrossFit mom. The speed was in the name of Indy's flight, but it was also to get back to preggo Freya, who'd picked up an interest in light construction.

All told, the living room was missing a wall, we'd be lucky if Freya made it to thirty-five weeks, I felt cut in half, Indy didn't want to leave, Hugo was on seven kinds of old-dog medication, and Mrs. Cheng was holding the whole gang together as if we were her last, unruly troop of pearl divers.

And I laughed so much at all of it that I kept bruising my chest.

We passed by a sign that read, SEAPLANET/HALEY 5 MILES.

When would they print a new one? Or would they blank out SeaPlanet, so that it read NOTHING/HALEY? A smiling, wooden Keemee waved at me from a billboard. "Do you ever miss SeaPlanet? Even though we know it was wrong?"

Mrs. Cheng put on her sunglasses. "You know those penguins weren't in love with themselves in the mirror, right? They were sad. Depressed penguins. Narcissistic penguins seemed less problematic to the general public, and so the general public spread the rumor. And Sally the famous pink octopus? She wasn't pink, was she? She was red, and you know what color octopus turn when they're mad? Red. Poor Sally has been angry for years."

For some reason I thought of my mom. "What are you doing, Mrs. Cheng?"

"Distracting us. I see you trying to forgive SeaPlanet. Immortalize your youth and its sins. I won't let you." She thought. "Toddlers took bites out of the starfish on a weekly basis, and yes, the dolphins sexually aggressed everything they came in contact with. And Keely? Well, he ate a guy's junk."

"What?! I thought he ate *the guy*?"

"No, just the junk, which is so much more of an F-you to SeaP in particular and humanity in general. He wasn't even a drunk guy, but a security guard who fancied himself a midnight companion to the killer whale. Took a swim, and Keely took a nibble. I don't tend to feel that bad for him because he had a Confederate flag on his truck."

"Do you feel like SeaPlanet was playing god?"

Mrs. Cheng sighed, slowing down closer to the speed limit. "I think SeaPlanet is proof that humans don't know what they're doing until it's done."

"Then why did you work there for so long?"

She glanced at me like I was nuts. "To help the animals."

"The oysters?"

"The girls shoved in those suits, made to perform for tips. I couldn't stop SeaP from putting humans in a tank, but I could look after them. Someone needed to look out for them." My memories flared. Mrs. Cheng standing on the fake wood of the fake Japanese House, holding out a real dive vest. Helping me into it. Patching my hand. Asking no questions.

Wow.

"But then, why stay here now? Your job isn't here anymore. You two could go anywhere. You could raise my sibling in a place that won't demand them to be something they're not."

"You mean move to Vermont or California with my queer family?" she joked, looked around the highway. "We stay because this is home. I was adopted from China by a white family in the eighties when infant girls were a little too easy to come by. I love my family, this state, and I reclaim pieces of my culture wherever I can. Even Cheng is a name I gave myself."

"Because it's your name."

"You help me believe that." She pinched my leg so hard I yelped. "You're so soft for being so tough. Think that's what I like best about you."

"But you stay here because it's your home, by default," I insisted. "You could leave."

"We stay because we made it home. Home doesn't happen. You build it. You buy a house, marry a gorgeous redhead, get her pregnant, and then she knocks out the living room wall when you run to Target for eggs. That's home, queer-o. If it isn't messy, it isn't alive."

Mrs. Cheng took the exit for Haley with its marine life cutouts still stuck upright beside the off-ramp. Last weekend would have been opening day for SeaPlanet, but there would be no fireworks or random, echoing cheers across Haley.

This place would have to become something else.

"I saw my mom a few weeks ago." She didn't say anything, letting me talk. "I gave her a message. Varian, my therapist, has been helping me practice what I would say to her. I've been too angry to get anything out, but I just had this moment when we were at the empty, sad park, and I finally knew what to tell her."

Mrs. Cheng waited, and then bit out, "And?"

"I am happy."

She stole a look at me, smiling. "Yes, you are."

We pulled into the Chengs' drive, and Indy shot out to meet me. Freya came around from the back swinging pruning shears and wearing bulging overalls. I climbed out slowly, feeling like I might split in half any moment.

Indy held me by the shoulders, gaze on my chest. "I need to see you shirtless."

"Right now?" I asked.

Indy guided me from behind, toward the front door. "I'm already going to have to run to make my flight. Inside. Strip."

I glanced back at the Chengs for help. Bea said, "What? It's a great offer."

Freya added, "Let Indigo see what they're going to miss."

Indy helped me through the front door and guided me into the blue bathroom. All of the bathrooms in this house had a color scheme. This one was robin's-egg blue from wall to tile. I glanced at myself in the mirror. "Is it just me or do I look sallow from the pain meds?"

"Let me help you get that off." Indy plucked the buttons open skillfully as a harpist. They were getting awfully good at that. And now I'd be thinking about them every time I unbuttoned for . . . ever. They slid my arms out of the shirt, and I couldn't pretend I didn't love the way Indy got excited about me, celebrated *this*. I felt too embarrassed. Like any minute my mom would swing by and say something horrible, her negativity a whining ghost in my brain these days.

"River?" Indy kissed me. "Am I pushing?"

"No." I peeled open the Velcro front of the frilly medical binder that I planned to burn as soon as possible. Indy didn't say anything while I looked at myself.

I was so much less of a man o' war without my tubes and bulbs.

At first, we were shy of each other, my body and my self. At first, all I could see were the details. The angry, stitched nipples and rounded pecs. The marker lines from the plastic surgeon would wear off with time, and the stitches would spit out of my body for months. Those sharp, shooting pains of severed nerves backfiring could last years, and I wasn't supposed to raise my arms over my head for six months. I already missed the water far too much.

At first, I was every little separate piece.

And then I was me.

I'd never seen *me* before. This would take some getting used to.

Indy held me from behind, gentle arms around my waist, their chin on my shoulder. "I'd miss a million flights for this."

I kissed them, more seriously than I'd been able to all week. There were tears on our lips, wetting the kiss, and then they left, and I dove into the last lap of my life without Indigo Waits.

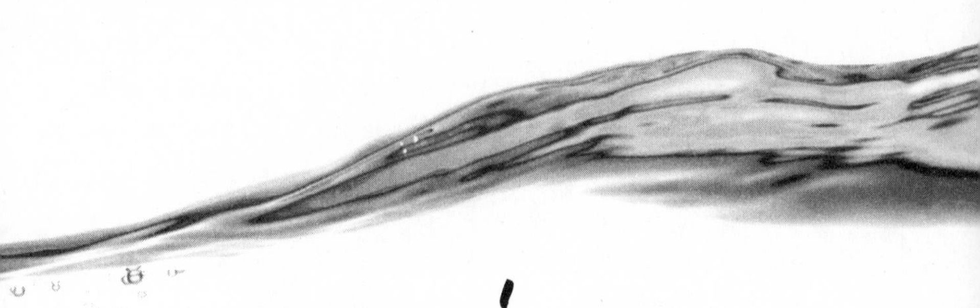

man o' war

By nature, man o' wars are gorgeous masculine fellows. They're also known as blue bottles because of their jeweled, translucent sail. They reproduce however they want with whomever they want. Sometimes they do it all by themselves. They can submerge to avoid predators or capture large marine life with their retractable tentacles.

By nurture, they are too often socialized female to the point of venomousness. Captivity will kill them, as they're meant to exist upon a natural tide, not bound to antiquated, commercial gender roles.

Approach with affirmation. And love.

— 30 —

I CIRCLED THE POOL DECK. The diving blocks were high and steep, but they'd always be jerks. The water was crystal teal, and the Olympic length seemed to stretch on forever.

The surface was smooth as glass, and I went about the business of greeting this new pool. I dipped my goggles in. Tested the temperature, the taste. I examined the flags above and the striped markings on the ends of the lane lines. There were hundreds of spectators, maybe thousands, but I'd finally learned how to shut out the intimidation of their noise. How to bring this all back to water and air, and the line that gravity kept between them.

Senior-year swim at OU had been so different from the others. Israel and Kirk were gone, both managed to become All-Americans. I had a whole batch of baby swimmers to look after, including the two little trans swimmers who'd read about me and followed me here. Indy said it was good to have ducklings, that it meant you were a pretty damn good duck.

The announcer called for the first race, my race, the last of my career. I found my block. The backup timer for my lane was a woman who looked like every mom I'd grown up with, too easily scandalized by difference. At first, she must've thought I'd been assigned male. And then she took in the scars on my chest and her eyes bulged. I winked, stripped off the shorts that covered my racing briefs, and tossed them to one of my teammates.

My cap came down over my ears, my goggles darkening my sight.

"Swimmers on the block," the meet referee called into their head mic, rippling quiet through the pool. I climbed up, leaning back on my heels so as not to pitch forward too soon. Somewhere in the audience, Karina and Everett were here to cheer me on, along with my dad and mom, who turned up to things, even if they kept their distance. The Chengs were here with little Harper, who was probably bouncing on Bea's knee and adding their own delighted screams to the audience's shouts. I'd never met a louder baby in my life, so this was the perfect place for them. Freya had been given strict instructions to film everything for Indy.

Now that I had distance from the closet, I realized there were endless ways of being there for me. Everett and Karina just knew where I was coming from, no questions asked. The Chengs had some wild ideas for all I could be and do after college, and my birth parents had done the brunt of the labor to keep me on this planet. That couldn't mean nothing, and it never, ever should have felt like everything. And far from Ohio in this large world full of small places, Indigo Waits was calling me home, and I was on my way, married to their tide.

But my thoughts wouldn't go to Indy right now. Or flying out to see them tomorrow.

"Swimmers, take your mark."

I cleared my mind the way Coach Warren had taught me. Nothing but the water and the lane. My toes found the gritty edge, my body crouched and loaded like a compressed spring. The tone sounded through the enormous pool hall, and I shot into the air.

The water was as still as a mirror. I broke it with my body.

Hands, head, heart.

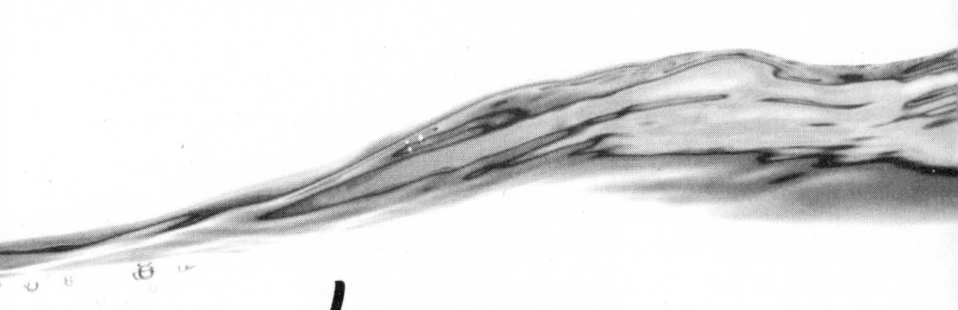

humans

Humans are less complex than their marine life fellows. They could be more complex, but their ability to create systems holds them back. They too often become obsessed with categorization, divorcing those who will not adhere to the arbitrary rules of societal captivity.

For example, several of you aren't even reading this because you're too busy wondering how many epilogues I can pull off. Surely not *another* one . . . Honestly, it's too easy to find negative things to say about humans, but I prefer hope and joy.

Humans are in progress, so let's not transition from one tank to another.

Let's evolve.

2030

SAN FRANCISCO, CALIFORNIA

"*RIVER.*" Indy's sleepy growl reaches me through a dream. "One of our babies needs you."

I don't move because I'm dozing, and apparently when you hit the age of thirty, sleep becomes more important than most other needs. My wrist is humming, over and over, my smart watch letting me know that someone is calling with an emergency. I sit up, cracking everywhere. Indy's body curls around my waist as if they can't let me go, or need my warmth, or both.

San Francisco's spring has a surprising bite in the early morning. The fog comes off the sea, bringing the cool of deep water with it, and we always forget to close the apartment windows. The ocean breeze means too much to both of us, even now.

I'm finally awake enough to look at my watch and figure out who needs me. Indy and I have a habit of adopting young queer-os who flock to the city to escape the captivity they come from, like the Chengs did for me once upon a time—but oh my gods, were we *this* dramatic?

"Is it Chase? Jaycee?" Indy asks, face nuzzled into my hip. "What time is it? Wait, I bet it's Iris. She's the early riser."

"Quarter to six. And it's the aquarium." Which means I need to move fast. I get dressed, and Indy sludges out of bed. "You can sleep, love."

"You know I don't like to miss this."

"But you have a double at the library today."

Indy waves me off and stumbles into some clothes. I get my gear, load up our bikes, and we head downhill to Ocean Beach. My old swim-team goggles jangle around my neck as I ride, a towel thrown over my shoulders.

It's easy to find them. Half a dozen too-early morning joggers are guarding this length of beach from dogs and shooing away the excited birds. High tide brought in an entire fleet of blue bottles, and they're lying in the sand, all crumpled up on themselves. Some are already gone, but there's hope for the rest.

A jogger, who is most likely into weightlifting competitions by neck girth alone, comes straight at me while I hustle across the flat beach with my pack. Indy is close behind. "You're the conservationist the aquarium sent? The jellyfish expert? There are jellyfish *everywhere*!"

"They're not jellyfish. Each one is a symbiotic colony of polyps."

A second jogger comes over. "I told him these were Portuguese man-of-wars. They're deadly! I googled it."

"Not exactly." I unload my supplies on the sand. "And if you call them blue bottles, they're far less intimidating."

"I think we should call the news," the second jogger says. "Shouldn't this be on the news?"

"We can save them or make them media famous. We can't do both." I hand out long rubber gloves to the small group of people who have stopped. I've learned from experience that anyone who stops wants to help. And the rest, well, they just keep jogging. "Time is paramount. In less than a half hour, they'll all be dried out and the birds will be feasting, and too many poor dogs and kids are going to learn that they can sting long after they're dead."

"How bad is the sting?" the muscly jogger asks.

"Very bad. But River has a technique to make sure that doesn't happen. Do exactly as he does, and you'll be fine." Indy takes a bin and runs to fill it with water.

"Hey." I glance up at the pause in muscly jogger's voice. He points to the cedar tree tattoo on my shoulder. "You Lebanese? Me too. All right, what do I need to do?"

We've come at the exact right moment. The tide is turning, and what brought the fleet in is ready to take it back out. I put on rubber gloves that roll past my elbow and find the nearest blue bottle. They're small, young. I demonstrate to my crew of volunteers how to scoop up the sand beneath their tentacles and gas-filled body, placing them in the plastic bin Indy's returned with. The blue bottle slips beneath the surface as everyone watches.

"Is that one dead?" the Lebanese jogger asks.

"No, they submerge when they're threatened. When they're scared." I take the bin out, beyond the low, tugging breakers, and let the little one go, carefully swimming to a safe distance when they're released. I watch for an extra moment as they refill their body, breaking the surface with their sail, returning to life, all blue and purple, pink and teal and turquoise.

Back on shore, Indy has the volunteers scooping up blue bottles, and the beach is covered in bins full of saved life. I'm the only one who re-releases them, skilled at slipping sideways past a wave that might send a tentacle my way. I get stung once this time and swear so loudly Indy calls out from the beach, even though I'm okay.

I kind of love it when I get stung. Karma, and all.

The Lebanese volunteer is now fully Team Blue Bottle and yells that we should all go out to breakfast. He kisses my cheeks thrice, Indy's too; that's how easy it is to feel home together.

When the last surviving sea creature is floating back out into the bay, the surface is still early morning white, the sun burning up the mist.

I place my goggles over my eyes and dive into the blue, submerged to escape all those tentacles.

Ocean Beach is shallow, but I know how to lie on the bottom of water at any depth. I let all the air out of my lungs. The fleet of blue bottles going home is so peaceful, it's worth all the breathlessness in the world.

ACKNOWLEDGMENTS

This is a work of fiction. That being said, thank you . . . to my hometown SeaWorld for the memories and metaphors. To my lanemates for the anecdotes. To my agents, Sarah and Jim, and earliest readers, Kristen, Alex, Ann. To my Lebanese family for understanding that they are not the family in this book. To my found family: I thought I'd have to find you, but you all found me. Whew, what a relief.

Endless gratefulness to the trans-affirming surgeons and doctors who healed my body and saved my butt while writing this book. And to my kind-souled therapist who walked me around and around acceptance, around and around, until it felt like home.

To Amy, my hero and big sib, who kept me upright through the hardest parts.

To my kiddo, who gifts the unbridled gender joy of Gen Z every day and started correcting people when they misgendered me at the age of five.

To Andrew, I wrote this book like I was speaking it aloud to you. You listened to every single word—even the incoherent screams. My gratitude is a sea.

And to my August: you might've read this book and found your name, but I met you and discovered my life. Our joy is my favorite revolution.

FOR TRANS, QUEER, AND QUESTIONING FOLK:

You're perfect. You've done enough adjusting for others. They can come to you.

You have the right to reject anyone for not affirming you. Even your family. Space is not unhealthy; boundaries and safety are important.

Allow for fluidity in your sense of self. You don't have to perform anyone's expectations or interpretations of an identity label. Your identity belongs to you.

Let other queer and trans people be different. Policing other people's identities is a sucky way to live, isn't it? (And don't feed the TERFs; their misery is their own reward.)

Love yourself. You deserve it. And post as many selfies as you want. It's okay if your joy and pride makes other people uncomfortable. That's their problem.

Speaking of, hey dinosaurs, resources on the next page . . .

FOR DINOSAURS

LGBTQ+ youth are not at-risk. LGBTQ+ youth who experience identity trauma (re: the closet) are at-risk. Acknowledge the *real* problem or you won't make a damn difference.

Three step plan for not putting kids in closets:

1. Ask them about their gender/sexuality.
2. Believe them.
3. Keep talking. It's a conversation, not a diagnosis.

It's okay if you do not understand the difference between gender, assigned sex, and sexual orientation. Blurring these lines has been the prized weapon of sexism, cissexism, and homophobia for centuries. The patriarchy and capitalism need you to tell other people who they are . . . so don't.

Gen Z often embraces this PANTS metaphor:

- Assigned sex is about what's *in* your pants. Categories include female, intersex spectrum, male.
- Gender is *how* you feel about what's in your pants. Categories include transgender, nonbinary spectrum, cisgender, agender, two-spirit, man o' war, etc.
- Sexual orientation is about *who* you want in your pants and/or *how often*. Categories include homo, pan, demi, bi, and hetero sexualities, as well as hyper, ace spectrum, and allo sexualities.

Consider this a starting point but know that identity is often fluid and labels can be limiting. This is *not* all-encompassing or foolproof, and you should learn more and read widely across culture and race.

On pronouns:

Always use a person's current pronoun(s) *without commentary*. Do not refer to the past with old pronouns or dead names. If you screw up, say *I'm sorry* and reissue the sentence correctly. Do not center your embarrassment and excuses.

Most people who struggle with misgendering are trying to make an exception for a nonbinary/trans person. Instead, you should aim to become aware of unconscious gendering. It takes practice. Try going a week without using pronouns for anyone. Try referring to strangers by descriptions instead of assumptive language. (For example: "That woman needs . . ." becomes "That person in the purple hat needs . . .")

On safety:

Do not out people with anecdotal overshares; this country is on fire. Also, you do not have the right to understand how other people identify or pressure them to come out. Your understanding should never be prioritized in your relationships with queer and trans folk. And hey, if you don't assume/closet people, we won't have to awkwardly tell you that you're wrong and you've hurt us.

A moment to thank you for reading this through. Many won't. I wish you luck on your journey to being more open, understanding, and healthy toward yourself and all the gloriously different, beautiful humans around you.

Finally, you don't have to be what you've been assigned to be, and I'm deeply sorry if no one told you that before. You're not too old to live as yourself. And if you're starting to figure out some stuff, turn back one page, and welcome home to our glowing, vibrant, joyful community.